# THE COWGIRL'S LITTLE SECRET

BY
SILVER JAMES

MILLS & BOON

Published in Great Britain 2015
by Mills & Boon, an imprint of Harlequin (UK) Limited,
Eton House, 18-24 Paradise Road, Richmond, Surrey, TW9 1SR

© 2015 Silver James

ISBN: 978-0-263-25258-3

51-0415

Harlequin (UK) Limited's policy is to use papers that are natural, renewable and recyclable products and made from wood grown in sustainable forests. The logging and manufacturing processes conform to the legal environmental regulations of the country of origin.

Printed and bound in Spain
by CPI, Barcelona

**Co... ... ... ... ...ty**
**damn sure was his son more firmly**
**...n his lap.**

...Is he mine?" He was pleased his voice remained calm and
...ounded reasonable. Inside he was a seething cauldron of
...ger.

...e stopped squirming, as if he sensed something
...momentous about to happen. His eyes jittered between his
...n and Cord.

..." Jolie looked away. "Cord...you don't understand."

...o. I guess I don't. Since you didn't give me a chance. Or
...plain. But you didn't answer my question. He is mine,
...'t he?"

...ger swirled, cramping his gut. His eyes stayed fixed on
...olie, and even though they burned, he didn't blink. How
...uld she do this to him? Did she hate him that damned
...ch?

...hen he'd caught her crying over him in the hospital, he'd
...ped for a second chance, but she'd obviously wiped the
...te clean and eradicated him completely. His heart turned
...granite when he realized what Jolie had done—and had
...ne deliberately. If he said a word, his face would crack,
...ttering just like his heart was doing. But he had to know.

...Were you ever going to tell me?"

* * *

**The Cowgirl's Little Secret**
is part of the Red Dirt Royalty series:
...hese Oklahoma millionaires work hard and play harder.

**Silver James** likes walks on the wild side, and coffee. Okay. She *loves* coffee. Warning: her muse, Iffy, runs with scissors. A cowgirl at heart, she's also been an army officer's wife and mum and has worked in the legal field, fire service and law enforcement. Now retired from the real world, she lives in Oklahoma and spends her days writing with the assistance of her two Newfoundland dogs, the cat who rules them all and the myriad characters living in her imagination. She loves interacting with readers on her blog, Twitter and Facebook. Find her at www.silverjames.com.

To my family and friends for not laughing when
I talk out loud to the characters living in my head.
To my readers, who bring joy and enthusiasm into my
world and keep me at the keyboard day in and day out.
To the fantastic Harlequin folks who give great edits,
support and covers. All y'all are the best!

# One

Cordell Barron was always in control—of his life, Barron Oil and Gas Exploration, everything that made up his world. Except for now. At the moment, Cord's world was crashing down around his ears and his life seemed to be spinning out of control.

He stared at his hands, curled so tightly around the steering wheel that his knuckles were white. *Jolie is home. Stay away from her.* The words, spoken just over a month ago by her father, were seared into Cord's memory. Like the woman.

Jolene Davis. Juliet to his Romeo—right down to their feuding families. Cord had walked away from her, not once but twice, if their hookup for "old time's sake" five years ago counted. Technically, she'd walked away the second time—before he could. Turnabout was fair play and all that crap. That was what he'd told himself at the time. He hadn't wanted to admit how much it hurt—waking up hungover to find her gone, the sheets still smelling of her sweet mimosa scent. Even now, all these years later, he hated spring when the mimosa trees bloomed.

Jerking his thoughts back to the present, he stared out the windshield of his crew-cab pickup. His fingers drummed a nervous tattoo on the console. He should call his brother Cash. Technically, they were half brothers, but Cord was head of Barron Security. He could find out everything about Jolie in an hour. Her phone number. Where she lived. Worked. Boyfriend's name. His heart thudded at the thought she might have one—or worse, a husband. He pounded the heel of his fist on the console, making his phone jump onto the passenger seat. Cord had no right to dictate anything about Jolie's life, but the thought of her in another man's arms, accepting his kisses, sharing his bed…

What was wrong with him? He was supposedly the easygoing Barron, the good ole boy comedian. He didn't get angry. He didn't slam his fist into inanimate objects—especially when it would hurt like hell. Except when Jolie was around. He was always off balance where she was concerned, like a pinball game with lights flashing and bells clanging as a huge TILT strobed in front of his eyes. Yeah, that definitely summed up their relationship. They'd been headed for a big, fat game over from the moment he first laid eyes on her.

The tune of "Take This Job and Shove It" rang out from his phone, sending him scrambling to retrieve it. He unclenched his fist and answered with a terse "What?"

"Hey, cuz, catch you at a bad time?"

Cord clamped down on his emotions, shifting into business mode to talk to his cousin Cooper Tate, operations manager of BarEx, the Barrons' energy company. "Funny, Coop."

"Just as I suspected, we lost the drill bit down the hole." Annoyance and something akin to chagrin colored Cooper's voice. "The crew has to fish it out. You gonna get outta the truck and come up or what?"

Glaring through the windshield at the group of men standing around on the floor of the drilling rig, Cord replied, "Or what, smart-ass?"

"Will you just get your butt up here? We need to talk."

A wicked dust devil of red dirt kicked up and spun across the bare expanse of the well site. Rather than cooling the air, the wind seared everything in its path like a blast from a furnace. The block and tackle attached to the crown of the derrick creaked and swung in a desultory arc, and a length of drilling pipe gripped in the hoist tongs swayed with a gust.

Inured to the hot August weather, Cord shoved his phone into the hip pocket of his jeans, snagged his hard hat from the passenger seat and climbed out of the white truck bearing the BarEx emblem on its doors. The metal steps leading from the ground to the drilling floor rang beneath Cord's boots. Heat waves shimmering around him, Cord gripped the steel handrail during a quick flash of vertigo. His hand felt scorched as he released the rail and climbed again.

On the rig floor, Cooper introduced him to the tool pusher. "Cord, Tom Bradley, best damn rig manager we have."

Cord shook hands with the older man, who then turned to spit tobacco juice before saying, "Damn rig sure seems to be jinxed, boss. Y'all think there's somethin' to the problems we've been having?"

Taking off his hard hat for a moment to brush fingers through his hair, Cooper finally spoke. "I… Maybe. Too many injuries. Too many delays. We should be down to oil sand by now but we aren't even close. Seems as if something happens every other day."

His cousin took a long, controlled breath. Coop was rock solid, and if he was nervous about the situation, then something was definitely wrong. Cord waited for the other man to continue.

"Remember how much trouble we had acquiring the rights to drill this one?"

"Yeah." Cord didn't like where Cooper was probably headed.

"We had a helluva bidding war with Davis Petroleum." Coop inhaled again. "Do you think they might be behind our troubles?"

His gut cramped. Coop had gone right where Cord suspected. J. Rand Davis was a rabid competitor. The man had a habit of interfering in Barron family business. Not to mention he was Jolie's father.

"No," Cord replied after some consideration. "I don't think so. Ah, hell, Cooper. I have no frickin' idea if the man would stoop that low or not." He swallowed the flood of saliva in his mouth and jerked his cousin a few steps away. Lowering his voice, he said, "Jolie's back."

Not everyone in the family knew about the fiasco that had been Cord and Jolie in college. That drunken night when, as a senior at the University of Oklahoma, Cord had run into her at a fraternity party and the bright-eyed freshman, well on her way to a massive hangover, had fallen into his lap, kissed him and cussed him out for never asking her out in high school. Learning she'd wanted him like he'd wanted her had felt like a kick in the gut from a twelve-hundred-pound Brahman bull.

But Cooper was Cord's age, a fraternity brother and friend. He'd covered for them when Cord couldn't stay away from the daughter of his father's biggest rival. And Coop had been the one to act as designated driver the night Cord had broken up with Jolie because his father, Cyrus Barron, had dictated that his second son walk away from the one girl he'd ever loved. Coward that he was, Cord had done as his father decreed and then proceeded to get and stay drunk for a week.

"Ah, hell, cuz. That sucks."

And didn't that just sum it up in a nutshell. "Yeah. It does."

Coop turned back to the tool pusher. Tuning out the continuing discussion, Cord studied the rig with a practiced eye. The workers stood around in groups, hands shoved into jeans' pockets, hard hats pushed back on their heads, clothes covered in drilling mud and grease while they waited for orders. The derrick hand was camped out on the monkey board—the platform at the top of the derrick. His job at the moment was to trip pipe—adding or subtracting lengths during the drilling process. Cord recognized the guy and waved, getting a yell in response.

"Yo, big boss! Let's get the damn bit fished out so we can get back to work."

The man had a point. More talk wouldn't get the rig back to drilling for oil. Cord turned to the knot of men still arguing outside the doghouse.

"Billy's right. We have to get that bit out before we can do anything."

At Cord's order, the crew snapped to work. The heavy, burned-oil smell of diesel mixed with the chemical tang of drilling mud. Cord grinned. He felt alive out here on the rig. These guys were real. Hard men in a hard industry. He'd started as a roughneck, back in college, learning the business literally from the ground up. If things had been different, he could have happily worked the oil patch and not missed the Barron lifestyle.

Maybe.

He returned to the mind space he alternately avoided and spent way too much time in lately—thoughts of Jolie. Back when they were younger, he'd been short of options. Stay with her and fight to work in his chosen profession or say goodbye and have his career guaranteed and filled with perks. His father had threatened that Cord would never work in the oil business if he disobeyed him. And as kids, the Barron boys knew their old man didn't make empty threats. No rival company would hire him, according to his father, and he'd believed it. In hindsight, things might have been different, but he'd been too immature and spoiled at the time to test his father's decree.

With the workers settling into a well-rehearsed routine, Cord turned to enter the doghouse. A panicked shout halted him in his tracks.

He spun around and swore time warped into slow motion.

A chain snapped from the stand of pipe just above the

drilling hole. One end whipped out, catching one of the roughnecks across his chest. The man fell to the deck as his coworkers ducked. A section of pipe swung wildly from the tongs at the top of the derrick. Up on the monkey board, Billy scrambled to control the block and tackle. Men scattered amid the grinding clash of steel on iron and the wet smack of metal meeting flesh.

Cord tracked the arcs of both the chain and the falling pipe. Cooper stood squarely in the path of both. Acting completely on instinct, Cord lunged toward his cousin. Shoulder lowered like a linebacker, he caught Coop in the middle of the back, toppling the other man off the edge of the drilling floor. Arms flailing, Cooper hit the dirt twenty feet below. Cord had no time for regrets or to worry about how bad Cooper was hurt. The loose pipe crashed into his back, driving him to his knees, where the end of the flailing chain clipped him around the top of his rib cage. As his head smacked the steel flooring, he had time for one thought before succumbing to darkness.

*Damn. This is gonna hurt when I wake up.*

Jolie Davis stared at the empty whiteboard filling an entire wall of the intake section of University Hospital's Trauma One. She was bored out of her skull. And she was pulling a double shift.

When she moved back to Oklahoma City, she'd planned to get out of the ER, but then University had offered her a big salary and a humongous sign-on bonus. She'd jumped at the opportunity to prove to her dad she could take care of herself. And CJ. It was bad enough her father had bought her a house and hired a nanny. He'd take over her entire life if she didn't fight him every inch of the way. That was his modus operandi. The man was a type A personality and she was his only child, which made CJ his only grandson. To say J. Rand Davis was a little overprotective was like calling the Grand Canyon a ditch.

Midweek was a slow time for the ER. Usually. But this was Oklahoma. A late-season thunderstorm could blow up and wreak havoc. Or there could be a big wreck on one of the major interstates crisscrossing the Oklahoma City metroplex. Tinker Air Force Base and Will Rogers World Airport meant airplanes. Lots of them. They could… Not that she really wished ill on anyone, but when things were slow, she had way too much time to think.

Every time the front doors slithered open, she could see the monolithic Barron Tower arrowing up into the hot blue Oklahoma sky. Cord's office was there. No. She would *not* think about him. That part of her life was over. She was better off without him.

The thought squeezed her chest as tight as Scarlett O'Hara's corset. Jolie remembered to inhale when white dots sparkled in her vision. Thoughts of Cord always did this to her. Everyone told her to live her life. How sad was it she only wanted to live that life with him? Despite everything. Because of everything. But there was a zero percent chance of that happening. The imaginary corset cinched even tighter as guilt washed over her. He'd never forgive her for what she'd done.

Jolie rolled her head from shoulder to shoulder, and then stretched. Maybe she'd go wash the empty whiteboard. Again. Whirling the desk chair around, her legs collided with a smiling man. Dr. Perry, attending surgeon on duty and head of Trauma One. She squeaked, her heart pounding. "Dang! Don't sneak up on me like that."

Absently rubbing his knee where she'd banged the chair into him, Dr. Perry chuckled. "I didn't think I was. I'm headed to the cafeteria. Want me to bring you something back? You know what it's like in the ER. We eat when we—" The doctor tilted his head as if listening to something she couldn't hear.

Sirens. So much for a quiet afternoon. She did her best to hide her elation at being busy.

After a couple hours, things had settled back down. A med tech had his hip propped on Jolie's desk and was teasing her while she sipped the mocha frappuccino he'd brought to bribe her to go out with him.

"Do you like kids?" She knew how to nip his interest in the bud.

"They're cute in the petting zoo."

Jolie rolled her eyes. "I'm not talking about baby goats."

"Neither am I." His eyes twinkled, though he managed to keep a straight face. The theme song from *Pirates of the Caribbean* filled the air and he dug his cell phone out of his scrubs. With a wave and a wink, he disappeared around the corner.

Leaning back in her chair, Jolie exhaled. So far, they'd dealt with a suspect bitten by a police dog, a teenage girl who'd twisted her ankle during a fast-pitch softball game and a guy who'd tried to amputate his thumb with a chain saw. The cops had flirted with her, the softball player's parents had been upset the girl might miss the rest of the tournament and Chain Saw Guy's wife had yelled at him for being stupid. Jolie sort of had to agree with that assessment.

Just then, the statewide emergency network radio squawked. Dr. Perry appeared out of nowhere and snagged the microphone before she could. He acknowledged the call and put it on loudspeaker without missing a beat. Jolie took triage notes while he questioned the EMT on the other end.

An accident on a drilling rig. Three patients. The most critical would be arriving by the MedFlight helicopter currently being dispatched. Jolie activated a second chopper to bring in the second patient, a man who'd fallen twenty feet.

Trauma One looked like an anthill that had been kicked. Scurrying people appeared from nowhere, everyone intent on preparing the ER. Jolie kept track of the trauma clock— the indefinable golden hour providing the best odds for full recovery.

The electronic exit doors whooshed open and closed but

she heard it—the *whap-whap-whap* of helicopter blades. The radio crackled. She breathed—and it seemed as if Trauma One breathed with her as the pilot's voice ghosted from the speaker.

"MedFlight One to base."

She cleared her throat before keying the microphone. "This is base. Go ahead, Med One." Jolie wrote on the whiteboard as the flight nurse gave her the rundown on the patient's life-threatening injuries while the chopper landed.

"Roger that, Med One."

Medical personnel scrambled to the helipad, returning quickly with the first victim. As Jolie fell into step beside the gurney, she glanced over and saw the patient's face. Then faltered and tripped. One of the interns bumped into her, but kept her from going down with a steadying hand under her elbow. She murmured apologies and trotted to catch up.

This wasn't happening. That was *not* Cordell Barron on that gurney. *Oh, God, it couldn't be.*

# Two

Instinct kept her making notes as her conscious brain froze. One word kept screaming through her mind. *No. No, no, no, no, no* turned into a litany. This was so wrong. Things weren't supposed to end this way.

The flight nurse passed Cord's driver's license to her and Jolie accepted it with numb fingers. "Patient's ID says his name is Cordell Barron. Thirty-three years old. Wonder if he's one of *the* Barrons?"

Jolie nodded mutely. Oh, yeah. Cord was definitely one of them. Her fingers shook as she tried to type in information on the computer pad.

The gurney was wheeled into the trauma bay but she stopped at the edge of the curtain. She had to call his next of kin. It was her job. That would be his father. Cyrus Barron. The man who'd ruined her life. She couldn't do it, couldn't speak to that man for her life. Or Cord's.

The steady beeping of the monitors switched to a sharp alarm. He was crashing. Jolie forgot everything but saving the life of the only man she'd ever loved. Reflexes honed by five years working trauma kicked in. She passed off the pad to another nurse, pulled on latex gloves and waded into the mix.

Thirty nerve-wracking minutes later, Dr. Perry and the trauma surgical team finally stabilized Cord and whisked him off to the operating room. Jolie watched the elevator doors close behind the gurney before she turned back to the ER bay where they'd worked so feverishly to save his life. Her knees wobbled, and she had to lean against the wall to stay upright. Her night wasn't over yet. Cooper Tate was still being worked on by the orthopedic team, his compound fractures serious though not life threatening. He'd be following Cord into surgery shortly.

Trauma One looked as if a tornado had torn through it. Jolie went through the robotic motions of cleaning up and resetting the bay for the third patient coming in by ambulance from the well site. She should be back at the admitting desk filling out the paperwork on Cord and Cooper. Should be notifying their families. The clothes Cord had been wearing, along with his personal effects, had been shoved into a plastic bin for safekeeping. She tucked the tub under her arm and shuffled back to the intake desk as the janitorial staff moved in to mop and sanitize.

Sinking into her chair, Jolie felt as if she'd just run a marathon—her arms and legs were leaden, her brain still in shock. Shivering uncontrollably, she wrapped her arms across her chest and hung on, breathing deeply until the worst of the reaction passed. There wasn't time to collapse. Not yet. She had to make notifications. No matter what. It was her job as admitting nurse. She couldn't pass it off—no matter how much she wanted to do so. Bad enough she'd all but abandoned her post to work on Cord.

The bin with Cord's belongings sat at her feet. She bent over and dug through the ripped and bloody clothes. She flipped open his wallet. Credit cards. A couple of receipts. No list of contact phone numbers. Jolie tucked the wallet and his driver's license into a plastic baggy. She did not stare at his photo. She didn't sigh over those sculpted cheekbones and that strong jaw, the golden-brown eyes. She didn't rub her thumb across the plastic pretending it was his face and she could feel his skin. Well, just once. Or twice.

Something dinged. Startled, Jolie dropped the ID and grabbed her cell phone. Its face remained dark. The strains of something country and western played from deep in the bin. She found Cord's phone in the hip pocket of his jeans. The caller ID read Cash.

Knowing she should answer, Jolie let it roll to voice mail. Cash didn't like her. Truth be told, none of Cord's brothers liked her. Well, except maybe for Chance. While he might not *like* her, he didn't hate her like the rest of the family. Chance and Cooper. They'd been the only ones to ever give her the time of day when she'd dated Cord.

Cord's phone was password protected. Of course it was, because nothing could be easy tonight. She stared off into the distance, thinking. She tried his birth date. Nope. On a whim, she tried her own. That had been his default password for everything when they dated in college. When the screen opened, she almost dropped the phone. Jolie scrolled through his contact list, making note of pertinent numbers for the hospital's records. She had to stop dithering and make at least one call. Chance's number was at the top of the list. She dialed it on her desk phone but remembered Chance was on his honeymoon, so she hung up.

Jolie remembered the big dust up from early in the summer as she had been moving home. Seemed as if Cyrus Barron was still screwing up his sons' lives—Chance's this time. The woman he'd fallen for had led an old-fashioned cattle drive from her ranch to the stockyards to get her steers to market so she could pay off the mortgage lien Cyrus held on the place. She knew how Mr. Barron reacted to his sons thinking for themselves. He wouldn't like it one little bit, especially if Chance went against his father's dictates, siding with a woman Cyrus had declared an enemy. Jolie had heard all about that day because her dad had been waiting on Cassie Morgan to arrive so he could buy the herd. Yeah, her dad liked screwing with the Barron family.

Worrying her bottom lip with her teeth, Jolie stared at the phone numbers on her list. Chance and Cord were close, with Cooper their third musketeer. As soon as Chance heard the news, he'd be on the next plane home anyway—honeymoon or not. Decision made, Jolie used Cord's phone to call.

After six rings, she was afraid her call would roll over to voice mail. Chance picked up on the eighth ring.

"Dude, this better be important." His voice held a teasing growl.

Using her most professional voice, Jolie said, "This is University Hospital Trauma One calling. Mr. Chance Barron?"

"What the— How? What the hell's going on?"

"I'm sorry to inform you, sir, but your brother Cord was critically injured. An accident on an oil rig."

"Is he… How bad?"

"He's—" Her voice cracked and she had to swallow around the constriction in her throat. "He's in surgery, Cha—Mr. Barron."

She almost blew it, calling him by his first name. After giving him all the information she had, she heard Chance's barely polite goodbye before he hung up on her. Jolie huddled her shoulders, shaking again. What if Cord died?

The 11:00 p.m. shift change arrived. Jolie was dead on her feet and emotionally drained. She'd finished her double shift in automatic mode. Standing in the humid air outside the ER, she stared in the direction of the parking garage. She should go home, take a long bubble bath and put everything behind her. But she couldn't.

Cord Barron had almost died today. Her stomach cramped so hard she had to bend over from the waist. Jolie choked back a whimper. She wanted to hate him. Had tried to hate him. She'd been the one wanting to kill him—with air quotes around that sentiment. *Kill 'im dead.* Every day since he'd walked out without a word. No goodbye. No explanation. Nothing. Until she had seen him sitting at the bar in Hannigan's that long ago St. Paddy's Day. She'd recognized the hungry look in his eyes and the bulge in his jeans. And something had snapped. She'd wanted to hurt him as badly as he'd hurt her.

Oh, yeah. She'd really taught him a lesson that night—spending the night and then slipping out of the penthouse hotel room at dawn. Only she was the one with the constant reminder. Every time she looked into her son's eyes and he smiled, Cord was right there all over again.

Rubbing her temples, she breathed deeply to hold back nausea. Jolie didn't head to the parking garage. She pivoted on her heel and headed back inside the hospital. Marching to the elevator, she berated herself for her weakness with each step until it became a mantra.

*This is a bad idea. A really bad idea.*

Cord was out of surgery, but she had to see for herself. She needed to make sure his injuries weren't as life threatening as they'd looked when he'd stopped breathing in the ER.

Pushing through the double doors of the ICU ward, Jolie passed her hand under the automatic dispenser for hand sanitizer from force of habit. The hushed whoosh and thump of respiratory machines were a soft counterpoint to the electronic beeps of heart monitors. Bright lights kept shadows confined to corners. Life and death battled here, with medical personnel on the front lines.

She glanced at the board to locate Cord's room number. Determined to just stick her head in to assess his condition and leave, Jolie parted the curtains of his cubicle. He looked drawn and pale amid the snaking mass of wires and tubes. She glanced at the monitor, judged his heart rate, respirations and blood pressure.

A touch on her shoulder caused Jolie to clap her hand over her mouth to contain a startled scream. The charge nurse offered a crooked smile.

"What brings you up here, Jolie?"

Jolie nodded toward the bed. "He's a…" A what? Friend?

Lover? Ex? More? Definitely less at this point in time. "I know him." That was a generic-enough response. "I was in the ER when he was brought in. I just wanted to check on him before I head home."

The nurse studied her for a long silent minute, and then her expression softened with something akin to understanding. "Sure, hon. Take your time."

When the nurse stepped away and ducked into another room, Jolie logged into the computer station outside Cord's room and checked his chart. Things were serious but he was no longer at death's door.

She should go home, but the thought of the empty house waiting for her didn't appeal. CJ was staying with his grandfather and Mrs. Corcoran, the nanny, was off visiting her sister. Without giving her motives too much thought, she pulled up an uncomfortable-looking chair and sank gratefully into it. She'd never get this opportunity again—the chance to study Cord, to hold his hand, to pretend what might have been. Jolie curled her fingers around his and simply devoured him with her gaze.

Dark hair hung over the bandage circling his head. He still wore it shaggy, though one side had been shaved for the stitches needed to close the gash on his head. More bandages covered his abdomen, and a wound vac clicked with each draining suck. Though his eyes were closed, she knew they were the color of burned honey. His face was sculpted into stark planes. A dark shadow covered his cheeks and chin. Though bristly now, the stubble would be soft by morning. The fingers of her free hand curled and flexed with the effort not to stroke him.

Cord's bare chest—what she could see of it—and his shoulders had the raw look of a man who worked for a living. He'd always been buff. In high school, it was sports and summers working on the Crown B Ranch. In college, he worked the oil patch, getting a hands-on education supplemented by his classroom studies.

A wide yawn cracked her jaw. She glanced at the wall clock, surprised it was almost 2:00 a.m. She started to pull her hand away, but Cord's fingers tightened on hers and his eyelids fluttered. Thrilled, her heart and lungs performed *Riverdance*, but she didn't want to examine his reaction too closely, choosing to pretend it heralded a change for the better in his condition. Not something else. As if he knew it was her.

"Don't go."

His voice rasped across her nerves and Jolie could no longer hide from her feelings. His grip tightened around her fingers, and his respirations and heart rate kicked off alarms on the monitor.

"Please."

Tears burned behind her eyelids. "Okay."

Her whispered assurance eased him, evidenced by the way the monitor sounds evened out. One corner of his mouth quirked into a faint semblance of the cocky grin she'd once loved so much.

"Okay." Darkness dragged him under again.

The sweet summer scent of mimosa filled Cord with a sense of rightness. Jolie. Jolie always smelled like mimosa. He cracked one eye open, ignoring the obnoxious sounds of his hospital room and the pain. He inhaled again but that sweet aroma was overwhelmed by the stench of antiseptic and alcohol, of sickness and death. Walls painted institutional gray surrounded him but he found his balance. Jolie. Here? He was too groggy to wonder about the how or why of it.

Slumped over, her head resting on the bed, Jolie held his hand. She puffed air softly in her sleep as a sunbeam kissed her cheek. He hadn't dreamed her. She *was* here. Touching him. He ached to touch her chestnut hair but knew any movement would do two things: hurt like hell and startle her into letting go. Instead, he remained content to simply be with her. He'd wanted her and here she was. Sleeping in a position guaranteeing a trip to a chiropractor, holding his hand and making those cute breathing noises he still dreamed about.

Five years ago, during their brief and disastrous reunion, despite the fact both of them had had far too much to drink, he'd made love to her and she'd fallen asleep in his arms. He craved the feeling again like an addict falling out of a twelve-step program. He could admit, at least to himself, that he'd loved her since high school. Not that it did him— or her—any good. Jolie was a Davis, her father a rival of his. And Cyrus Barron always made damn sure Cord and his brothers played by his rules. He hated his old man.

A commotion out in the ward ratcheted the noise level up a notch. Speak of the devil himself. Cord slitted his eyelids. Maybe his father would go away if he thought he was still unconscious.

"What the hell is she doing here?" Cyrus Barron bellowed as he entered the room, and would have lunged for the bed if not for Cash restraining him.

Jolie jerked awake, her heart pounding from the adrenaline rush. Glancing around in an attempt to focus her sleep-fuzzy mind, she remembered. She'd fallen asleep at Cord's bedside.

The supervising nurse followed Mr. Barron and Cash into the small room. "Keep your voice down, sir, or I'll ask you to leave."

Cyrus, red in the face and looking ready for battle, opened his mouth to launch into what promised to be a scathing retort. Cash cut him off.

"Enough, Dad. Cord's still unconscious. We don't want to disturb him."

Lowering his voice, Cyrus issued orders. "Get her out of here. That woman is not to be anywhere near my son. Especially not with her head on his damn bed!"

Jolie bristled, but the nurse replied before she could. "Ms. Davis is doing her job, Mr. Barron. If you interfere with her or any of my personnel, I will have you not only removed right this instant but banned from this hospital." She fisted her hands on her hips. "I don't care who you are. This is my department and you will follow my rules. Or else."

Jolie rolled her lips between her teeth and bit down to hide a grin. No one but no one ever talked to Cyrus Barron that way. The man was completely flummoxed and left speechless for a moment.

"What is your name?" he demanded.

"Meg Dabney, RN." The nurse arched a brow. "I'm the day-shift supervisor." Giving Cyrus her back, she stared at Jolie. "Do you have the patient's vitals, Jolie?"

Meg was giving her an out—thank goodness. Jolie stood up and quickly assessed the monitor numbers, while twisting her hand to make it look as if she'd been taking Cord's pulse manually. She read off the statistics while the older woman made notes on her electronic pad. Jolie came close to freaking out when something tickled her palm: Cord's index finger. She peered at him and noticed his eyelids flickering. Faker! He was conscious and enjoying the show. Relief warred with irritation. This was so like the blasted man.

Dropping his hand, Jolie backed away from the bed. Head down, refusing to make eye contact with Cyrus, she slipped around Meg. The brush of a hand on her bare arm startled her and she glanced up. Cash inclined his head in a slight nod and offered a sympathetic smile, which surprised the dickens out of her. Cash hated her. Didn't he?

Before she could get away, more Barrons crowded in. Chance and a woman she recognized from the society pages as his new bride, Cassidy. Chase, the Mr. Vegas playboy brother, and even Clay, who must have come all the way from DC. All five Barron brothers in the same small space were enough to put a girl into libido overload, as evidenced by the envious looks from the other nurses.

She escaped, but not for long. Chance caught up to her in three strides.

"Jolie?"

She shoved her hands into the pockets of her rumpled scrubs and wished she'd had time to brush her teeth. With her head still down, she glanced at him from the corner of her eyes. "Hi, Chance. Uh…congratulations on your marriage. You got here quickly."

"Thanks. The joys of having a fleet of private jets on standby. Are you okay?"

That brought her head up and she met his concerned gaze. "Why wouldn't I be?"

As Cord's brother studied her, she tilted her chin and pasted a blank expression on her face.

"How is he, really?"

She'd bet this was not the real question on the tip of his tongue, but Chance had a reputation as one of the best courtroom attorneys in the state. She lifted one shoulder in a negligent shrug. "Far better than he has a right to be."

Chance's eyes narrowed and a frown tugged at the corners of his mouth. Realizing how that sounded, Jolie hastened to explain.

"He almost died, Chance. And probably should have." A shiver skittered through her. "He coded in the ER last night, but he's strong. And stubborn." And far too aware of her presence this morning, damn him. "The doctors are worried about the liver tear and the spinal injury."

"What about the trauma to his head?"

She choked on an involuntary giggle. "As thick as his skull is?" She sobered and exhaled. "He'll recover fully from the concussion. The scar will be hidden once his hair grows back out."

Disconcerted by Chance's continued scrutiny, she turned away. "I have to go."

He gripped her shoulder gently, halting her in her tracks. "Thank you, Jolie. Thank you for being here for him, for not leaving him alone. And for calling me."

She twisted her head around to stare at him. While not as big a playboy as Chase, Chance had been a player and rather shallow, except where his brothers were concerned. The Barron boys were nothing if not absolutely loyal to each other. She glanced toward the blonde, who stood in the doorway of Cord's room watching them. Cassidy Morgan had changed Chance Barron for the better.

Jolie glanced back into the cubicle where Cord was still faking unconsciousness. Too bad he appeared to be the same old Cord.

# Three

Jolie tiptoed past the ICU waiting room. Even after a week and at five in the morning, at least one Barron family member was camped out there. She shouldn't be here. Had no right to slip into his room to check his chart, to stare at him, to miss him so much she couldn't breathe sometimes.

Cordell Barron was the man she loved to hate. And hated to love. But love him she did, God help her. She remembered the first time she'd seen him as vividly as if it had happened yesterday. Her first day of high school. Standing at the top of the stairs, she'd glimpsed the guys all the freshmen girls were talking about. The Barron brothers. Cord. Chance. And their cousins, Cooper and Boone Tate.

Rooted to the spot, she'd gazed down at him. He'd looked up and snagged her with his gaze. That maddening smile of his had slid across his face and broadened until dimples appeared to bracket his full lips. Love at first sight. But then Boone had said something and Cord's expression had sharpened before they'd all turned and walked away. She should have seen the truth even then. That was only the first time he'd walked away from her.

As she parted the curtains of his room, the sight of him kicked her in the chest just like that first time. Unshed tears prickled the back of her nose and her throat burned. Her fingers itched to comb his thick hair off his forehead before tangling in the dark silk of it. Why did she come every morning? This was torture. Things hadn't changed. His father still hated her, still pulled all the strings. And it wasn't just herself she had to worry about now. There was CJ, too.

"You just gonna stand there or are you gonna come in and say hello?" Cord's raspy voice raised goose bumps on her arms.

"I didn't mean to wake you."

"C'mere."

"No. I mean...I have to go. My shift starts soon."

"Jolie. Please."

Oh, God, how could she ignore the pleading in those beautiful burned-honey eyes of his? Dragging her feet, she approached the bed and stood at its foot. His gaze raked over her, hot and hungry, and...yes, there was the hurt she expected to see. Well, good. Now they were even.

"Thank you."

She blinked as her jaw dropped a little. Those were not the words she'd expected to fall out of his mouth. "F-for what?"

"For being in the ER. For calling Chance. For staying with me."

"You remember?"

"Yeah. I'm sorry my old man is such an asshat." He offered a crooked grin that indented only one cheek with a dimple as he held out the hand not plugged full of needles and tubes. "C'mere, Jolie."

Her fingers curled and her hand started to reach for him of its own accord. She smoothed her palm against her scrub pants and forced her fingers to grab the cotton instead of his warm flesh. "I can't, Cord. You know that. I have to go." She turned to leave but his voice stopped her, the plaintive tone twisting her heart.

"Jolie?"

She listened to him inhale and her shoulders slumped. He sounded so...defeated. Glancing over her shoulder, she forced her feet to remain planted. Everything in her wanted to run to him, to wrap him in her arms. The pain—physical and emotional—on his face almost undid her.

"I…I can't, Cord. We can't." She fled, dashing tears from her eyes as she pushed through the ICU doors only to smack into a very solid chest. Strong arms gripped her biceps, holding her up.

"Jolie? You okay?"

Chance. Just her luck.

The timbre of his voice changed. "Jolie? Is it Cord? Is he okay? Did something happen?"

*Oh, yeah. Something happened.* She'd fallen in love with a man she couldn't have, she'd seduced him to get back at him, and then she'd kept a big ole honkin' secret from him. One that would make him hate her. Breathing deeply to steady her nerves, she blinked away the tears.

"He's awake, Chance. You can talk to him. I have to go. I'm on shift in a few minutes." She tried to step around him but he didn't release her.

"He still loves you, Jolie."

Her heart ripped just a little more. "No, he doesn't. If he loved me, he would have never broken my…broken up with me."

She jerked free and stalked away. She kept her head up and shoulders stiff even though she wanted to hunch over to contain the pain ripping her apart.

Jolie didn't come back. Cord was disappointed. And pissed. Was she just teasing him again? Anger washed over him like a big ocean wave, filling him with enough bitterness to choke him. One week rolled over into two weeks, and then the third one dragged by with no sign of her. Fine. He was stupid to think they might have a chance, that she'd visited because she still cared.

He fidgeted, waiting for the doctor to arrive. After a month in the hospital, rumor had it he might be discharged today. He was more than ready to get out. To get away from any reminder of Jolie. She was just a few floors away, down in Trauma One. He'd caught a glimpse of her once, as a physical therapist had wheeled him past the cafeteria. She'd taken one look at him in the wheelchair, blanched, turned and all but ran away.

Yeah. He knew the feeling. He hated the freaking chair. Hated that his legs still didn't work quite right, that his head felt like a watermelon splattered on hot pavement whenever he looked into a bright light, that he was crippled. Cord wanted to go home, where he no longer had to see pity on the faces surrounding him.

Chance and Cassie arrived, followed closely by the doctor and his entourage of medical students. Ah, the joys of University being a teaching hospital. *Not.*

Seeing his state of undress, his sister-in-law immediately split, offering to grab coffee from the waiting room. Cord would be damned glad when he could wear clothes again so his dangly bits didn't offend anyone.

He put up with the poking, prodding, comments and advice. The doctor used a stylus to record stuff on a touch screen tablet, frowning as he filled in blanks. Cord's heart sank. He was going to be stuck here even longer.

"Meg will bring all the paperwork and go over your therapy plan, Mr. Barron." The doctor glanced at Chance. "You've arranged for a home health aide?"

"Wait," Cord interrupted. "Does this mean I'm getting out of here?"

"That's what it means, Mr. Barron."

"Hot damn. Chance, you better have brought me a pair of pants!"

It took three hours to get out of there. Three freaking hours to clear up all the paperwork, but Cord was finally free. Sort of. He was still stuck in the wheelchair. But he wore real clothes—jeans, boots, a T-shirt that hung a little loose on him. He'd lost weight and muscle tone in the hospital, despite the burgers, fries and pizza his brothers had sneaked in and all the physical therapy exercises. But he could go home now. Get away from the hospital, where he wondered every day if he might catch a glimpse of Jolie, wanting her to come back to see him, needing it as much as a man needed water in the desert. That was how he felt. Parched. He wanted to drink her in, knew he could drown in her presence.

Chance insisted on pushing the wheelchair while Cassie carried the bags of medical supplies, paraphernalia and other stuff he'd accumulated. They rode the elevator down to the first floor in silence. Cassie waited with him while Chance went to get his truck. Once he was settled in the front passenger seat and they were underway, Chance glanced at him.

His brother cleared his throat before saying, "I thought we'd take you to the ranch."

As much as he wanted to go home to his condo and hide from the whole world, Chance's suggestion made sense. They had staff at the home place, the Crown B Ranch. Miz Beth and Big John, the caretakers who'd been with the boys for as long as they could remember. And according to the doctor, a home health aide. Cord hated being an invalid. But he'd have the place to himself. The old man, when he was in town, kept an apartment in Barron Towers. His brothers all had their own places. Only staff and Kaden Waite, the ranch manager, would be around.

"Yeah, fine. Whatever." He swallowed the snarl and added, "But I'm starved. I want a steak before we head out there."

"Cattlemen's?"

At his nod, Chance changed lanes and made a left turn to head back toward Stockyards City and the famous steak house.

Chance found a space in the parking lot behind the historic building housing Cattlemen's Cafe. After some frustrated manipulation, Cord settled into the wheelchair. Cassie insisted Chance push and Cord grimaced.

"I can push myself. I'm not helpless."

"Of course you aren't." Cassie hastened to soothe him. "But this is your chance to make Chance your minion."

Cord still wasn't happy, but the way Cassie phrased it took the sting out of the fact that he was stuck. Not for long, though. He fully planned to be rid of the freaking wheelchair as soon as possible, if not before.

They had missed the lunch rush and were too early for the dinner crowd, so they were seated immediately.

While Cord and Chance went for the large filet, Cassie opted for prime rib. Their salads were quickly followed by their entrées, and they dug in like starving people, which Cord was. Beef, for him, was its own food group.

Their meal finished, Cassie maneuvered Cord's wheelchair through the narrow aisles between seating areas while Chance stepped ahead to handle the door. The entrance to the restaurant consisted of two sets of heavy glass double doors, their handles shaped like the horns of a longhorn steer. They'd just passed through the inner doors only to stop when the exterior doors were opened by a woman wearing scrubs, holding a little boy's hand.

Jolie.

Cord watched her eyes widen to deer-in-headlights proportions as her gaze darted between him and the child beside her.

Nobody moved until Cassie elbowed Chance and whispered, "I didn't know Cord had been married."

Her voice broke the spell and both Cord and Chance stared at her.

"He hasn't."

"I haven't."

The men answered all but simultaneously.

"Why would you think he had, Cass?" Chance muttered the question.

The kid tugged at Jolie's hand. "Ow, Mommy, leggo. You're squeezin' me too hard."

Cord stared at Jolie then the boy. Mommy? She had a son? His heart shriveled like mud under a hot August sun. She'd found someone else and married him. Had his child. He relaxed his fists and smoothed damp palms along his thighs, hoping to hide his agitation. And sitting in this damned wheelchair sure didn't help his ego.

Cassie hissed, "If that little boy isn't a Barron, then I'm deaf and blind."

All the color drained from Jolie's face. Her gaze jerked to the child beside her before returning to meet Cord's stare. She swallowed convulsively and guilt radiated from her. Cord couldn't speak for a minute as Cassie's words sank in.

"Jolie?" Her name rasped across his tongue, which felt like sandpaper.

"Cord." She blinked several times and her grip on the boy's hand tightened even more.

People knotted up behind them, wanting out. Cord pushed the chair forward, and Jolie had no place to go but backward onto the sidewalk. Chance and Cassie followed a step behind.

Brown eyes as curious as a chipmunk's stared at Cord. This time, he was the one who swallowed convulsively. "What's going on, Jolie?"

"Who're you?" The boy's lips pursed and his brows knitted together.

Tilting his head so he could watch both Jolie and the boy, Cord replied, "I'm Cord Barron. Who're you?"

"I'm CJ. Do you know my mommy?"

"I thought I did." Cord was pretty sure his voice dripped icicles. Cassie was right. Everything about the kid screamed Barron. His aggressive stance, his expression. Looking at CJ was like seeing a picture of himself as a kid.

"Cord…I…I can explain."

Jolie looked terrified as he pushed the wheelchair toward her, only to be brought up short by his brother's hand on his shoulder.

"Easy, Cord. Let me handle this."

Chance was using his lawyer voice. Rather than shaking off his hand, Cord inhaled deeply. It wouldn't do to lose his temper. Not here in the middle of the sidewalk. Was it possible CJ was his? He knew nothing about kids, or how to judge their ages, but the boy couldn't be more than four, five at the oldest. He stopped breathing for a minute. St. Patrick's Day. Five years ago. The Bricktown Street Party. Hannigan's Pub. He felt the color drain from his face and now he surged forward, jerking away from his brother.

"Why didn't you tell me?"

Jolie backed up several steps, dragging the boy with her. CJ pulled free and charged. His little fists hammered Cord's thighs as Cord jerked the chair to a stop to avoid running over the kid.

"You leave my mommy alone."

Cord picked him up, hiding the twinge of pain in his ribs, and placed him in his lap, one arm corralling the kid's legs so he couldn't kick. Oh, yeah. CJ was all Barron. He had no doubt.

"Cord? Please…"

He glanced around CJ to stare at Jolie. She had her hand raised, reaching toward her son, her eyes pleading with him. Folding the kid in his arms, he settled the child he was pretty damn sure was his son more firmly on his lap. "Is he mine?" He was pleased his voice remained calm and sounded reasonable. Inside he was a seething cauldron of anger.

CJ stopped squirming, as if he sensed something momentous about to happen. His eyes jittered between his mom and Cord.

"I…" Jolie looked away. "Cord… You don't understand."

"No. I guess I don't. Since you didn't give me a chance.

Or explain. But you didn't answer my question. He is mine, isn't he?"

Anger cramped his gut, but his touch remained gentle as he held the boy in his lap. His eyes stayed fixed on Jolie, and even though they burned, he didn't blink. How could she do this to him? Did she hate him that damned much? When he'd caught her crying over him in the ICU, he'd hoped for a second chance, but she'd obviously wiped the slate clean and eradicated him completely. His heart turned to granite when he realized what Jolie had done—and had done deliberately. If he said a word, his face would crack, shattering just like his heart was doing. But he had to know.

"Were you ever going to tell me?"

Jolie flushed and her chin rose to a stubborn angle. The anger in her green eyes flashed like emeralds lit by firelight. "No, Cord. No, I wasn't."

# Four

"Let go of my son, Cord." Jolie reached for CJ, but the boy shook her off, curling in closer to Cord's shoulder.

CJ ignored his mother and cupped his hands on Cord's cheeks. The boy pulled his head around to draw his attention.

"Do you have a little boy?"

Where the dickens had that question come from? Cord studied CJ's face, noting the similarities.

"Yeah, it seems like maybe I do."

"Oh." The kid's expression shuttered as he tucked his chin against his chest. He squirmed a little, as if to get away.

With a touch of his index finger, Cord got him to look up. None of this was CJ's fault. But he had to know. *Was* there another man in Jolie's life?

"Do you have a dad?"

"No." The boy lifted his shoulders up around his ears and shot his mother a guilty look as he whispered, "I kinda wish I did."

The kid's voice did something to Cord's chest. He remembered wishing the same thing, but his old man was always too busy. At the same time, relief washed over him. There didn't seem to be a father figure in the boy's life.

"Dads are important." He offered CJ a hesitant smile.

"Cord…" Again Chance's voice, brimming with unspoken legal advice, intruded. "We need to step back from the emotions here, talk about this someplace else."

"Like your office?"

"Or home." Chance sounded diplomatic.

Cord focused on CJ. "Have you ever met your dad?"

The kid shook his head, a little smile beginning to tweak the corner of his mouth. Then he glanced around at the serious faces of the adults, and his budding smile wilted when he fixed his attention on Jolie. "Mommy? Are you cryin'?" He squirmed to get off Cord's lap.

"Don't do this, Cord. Please. Not like this."

Cord swallowed around the fist-size lump in his throat and ignored the tears shining on Jolie's cheeks and the plea in her voice. Her anger had leached out, leaving only sadness. "There's something you should know, CJ. I'm your—"

"Cord, no!" Jolie's anger was back, and it prickled his skin like dozens of needle pricks.

"Dammit, Jolie—"

"Uh-oh. You aren't s'posed to say that word."

Cord absently rubbed CJ's back as he controlled his own anger. "Yeah. I know, bubba. I'll have to start a swear jar for when I forget and say words like that in front of you."

"A swear jar?"

"Yup. Whenever you or I say a bad word, we'll have to put money in the jar. To remind us not to say them."

CJ cut his eyes to his mom and lowered his voice to a loud whisper. "Am I gonna see you again?"

"We have to go, CJ."

Jolie stood rooted about four feet away, as if afraid to approach. Probably a good idea. Not that Cord would physically harm her. He didn't hit women. But damn if he didn't want to hurt her as badly as she'd hurt him. She'd eviscerated him, spilling his heart and guts right there on the sidewalk for everyone to see.

"No."

She blinked at his cold command and opened her mouth to argue.

"I'm his father. CJ's coming with us."

CJ whipped his head around to stare, his brow crinkled. He mouthed the word *father* but Cord mostly ignored the boy, his gaze fixed on Jolie.

"The hell you say." She bore down on him now, a tiger mama ready to rip his head off.

"Bad mommy. You aren't s'posed to say those words, either!" CJ chortled and clapped his hands, oblivious to the tension among the adults. "She has to put money in the swear jar, too, right?" He blinked, long dark lashes shadowing brown eyes so reminiscent of Cord's own. Looking shy, he gazed up. "Right? Uh…" He patted Cord's cheek again to get his attention. "Are you my daddy?"

Cord felt the word deep in his chest as CJ uttered it and something shifted—something both fierce and tender.

"Absolutely, pardner." He glared at Jolie, daring her to continue the fight.

She wasn't about to back down. "C'mon, CJ."

"But, Mommy," he whined, digging in his heels by wrapping his legs around one of Cord's legs and pulling against her grip. "I want strawberry shortcake."

"Not today. We're going home."

"You're not going anywhere, Jolie. Not until this is settled."

Her gaze whipped to meet Cord's, and then skittered away from the seething anger in his expression.

"Cord, let them go. Cassie can drop me at the office and take you home. I'll get a writ of *habeas corpus* drawn up along with a request for a paternity test and file them this afternoon."

"You wouldn't dare!" Jolie barely managed to utter her outraged words.

Chance's mouth thinned into a disapproving grimace. "Damn straight I would." He ruffled CJ's hair after Cassie glared and elbowed him. "And I'll put my dollar in the swear jar, too, bubba."

"Everyone should step back a little and take a deep

breath," Cassie urged. "And Chance is right. We need to take this someplace more private." Her hands lifted in a fluttery gesture to indicate the curious stares from people passing by.

Cord didn't care if they were being filmed for a segment on the ten o'clock news, but his sister-in-law had a point. "Yeah, good idea, Cass."

Chance glanced at Cassie. "Darlin', would you get them to pack up a strawberry shortcake to go?" He winked at CJ as Cass ducked back inside the restaurant. "Are you sure we can't move this to my office?"

Jolie bowed up like a half-broke mustang, and Cord worked to school his expression. She always did run toward hot tempered.

"And give you Barrons home court advantage? I don't think so. I'll tell ya what. Let's go to my dad's office. We can talk there." She folded her arms just under her breasts, plumping them under the misshapen scrubs she wore.

Cord sucked in a breath. This woman had always had power over him. From the first moment he'd laid eyes on her standing at the top of the stairs in high school.

"I don't care where the he—" He glanced down at CJ and bit off the word. "The *heck* we go. I want this settled, and settled now."

"Now? After all these years you're in an all-fired hurry to settle it now?"

"Since I just learned I had a son less than ten minutes ago, yeah, Jolie. I'm in a big hurry to settle it now."

Jolie jammed her fists against her hips. Cord had to remember to breathe. Her cheeks were flushed and her green eyes sparked. The best sex they'd had was makeup sex after their fights. There'd been many. He'd forgotten that. The passage of time had smoothed over those memories so only the good ones stood out. But man, those particular bad times were so *good*!

Gesturing down the street toward the bank on the next

corner, Chance suggested adjourning to the conference room there. Cord had to stifle a laugh. His brother was being such a sneaky lawyer; the bank belonged to Barron Enterprises. Not exactly neutral territory. He could live with that. He needed every advantage, especially since he felt as if his world had tilted on its axis. At Jolie's nod, Chance pulled out his cell and made a call.

Cassie appeared with a foam box and winked at CJ. "So what's the plan?"

"We're going to the bank to use the conference room." Chance gripped the handles of Cord's wheelchair and started pushing.

Giggling, CJ squirmed so he was sitting facing forward. "Make it go fast?"

"No," all four adults answered simultaneously.

Once they were inside the bank, Cassie disappeared into the break room with CJ in tow. When Jolie followed, ready to argue, Cassie showed some of her own temper.

"Good grief. The kid is going to eat his strawberry short-cake in here. Do you seriously want him listening to the two of you slinging mud at each other? Really?"

There was a reason Cord loved his sister-in-law. She didn't take crap from anyone. Not his brothers, not Chance and definitely not his father. As he watched, some of the starch wilted out of Jolie, especially when Cass reached over to touch her arm.

"Look, Jolie, I get why you're nervous. I promise I'm just going to sit with him. We'll both be here when y'all get through talking. Okay?"

Jolie blinked several times, inhaled deeply and relaxed. "Okay."

And that was that. Jolie pivoted and marched toward the conference room door, where Chance and Cord were waiting. She brushed past them and a wisp of sweet mimosa scent followed in her wake. Cord had to shift in the chair to ease the fullness pressing against his zipper. He inhaled shallowly, but her scent still perfumed the air. He needed his head clear to deal with this situation.

On one level, he was so angry he wanted to punch something. But on another, the twisty, bendy parts of his psyche were plotting ways to use the fact they had a son together to his advantage. He wanted Jolie. He always had. Now he had leverage.

"I need some space." Cord stared at Chance.

"That's not a good idea."

"Get out, Chance. I want to talk to Jolie. Alone."

His brother wasn't very happy, as evidenced by the tense set of his shoulders and grim expression, but Chance did as he asked and vacated the conference room. Once they were alone and he was positive Chance didn't linger at the door to eavesdrop, Cord studied Jolie. She looked nervous. Defensive. And, oh, yeah, there was a healthy dose of guilt, too. That was good.

"What do you want, Cord?"

"I think it's pretty obvious."

"Well, it's not."

"I want to work things out. Between us. And I want something else, Jolie. Space."

Jolie watched Cord closely, waiting for the rest of his demands, but air escaped from her lungs in a soft whoosh of relief regardless. She could handle space between them. "Okay. Yeah. I guess that's a good thing."

When she'd first run into Cord at the restaurant, Jolie had never been so angry in her life. Despite moving back to Oklahoma City, despite harboring some romantic notion that Cord might have changed and that they might grab a second chance, she knew it to be the pipe dream of a naive girl. She no longer had stars in her eyes. She was a mother. And a darned good one. She'd brought CJ into this world all by herself and she'd taken care of him. All. By. Herself.

She didn't need Cord Barron. And she didn't want him to have a place in CJ's life.

Then she felt fear. Seeing her son sitting there in Cord's lap had panicked her. The Barrons were just as powerful as her father. Why had she been stupid enough to come home? It was inevitable that this would happen, and she'd been an idiot to believe otherwise.

But now it looked as if Cord was willing to give her some breathing room.

"I don't think you understand." Something hard glinted in Cord's eyes, a flash as bright and inevitable as lightning in a summer thunderstorm. "I want time, Jolie. Time with CJ. And the space to get to know him on my terms."

Was it possible to sweat icicles? To be so hot and cold at the same time? Jolie stared at him, the word *no* already forming on her lips.

"Do you really want to drag him through the court system?"

She sputtered and had to breathe through the surge of anger. "You'd do that to him?"

"To see my son? To spend time with him? To be acknowledged as his father? Damn straight I would. You've already cheated me out of so much, Jolie. You don't want to deny me this."

She forced her fingers to loosen from the fists they'd formed without her knowledge as she considered Cord's threat. The planes of his face looked as if they'd been carved from the alabaster stone that formed amid the red dirt of Western Oklahoma.

"I want to get to know my son. To make up for the parts of his life you stole from me."

Her eyes burned with a hot flush of tears, but she blinked them away. Straightening her shoulders, she pasted on her best poker face. "No."

Cord did nothing except raise one eyebrow as if to say, "Really, Jolie? You truly want to do this?" He wore the mask well but he looked so pale, so…wounded. He'd almost died from his injuries, but now she knew without a doubt that she'd ripped out his heart. Just as he'd ripped out hers.

# Five

Cord didn't argue with Jolie. He rolled to the door, opened it and maneuvered his wheelchair out. Chance was leaning against the wall nearby but straightened immediately.

"What's the plan?"

Cord lifted his chin to indicate Jolie was right behind him and Chance offered an almost imperceptible nod. They'd talk later, and Cord would lay out his plan then. His brother knew him well and didn't press for an answer to his question.

Jolie huffed to a stop behind him, unable to squeeze around the chair without bumping into him. He stifled the smile threatening to reveal his thoughts. She'd thrown down the gauntlet, and he'd picked it up without hesitation.

Giggles drew his attention as his sister-in-law and CJ appeared at the end of the hall. The boy stomped toward them, stopping in front of Chance.

Rearing his head back, hands fisted on his hips, CJ stared up. "Who're you?"

"My name is Chance. I'm your—" He glanced at Cord before shifting his gaze to Jolie. "Your dad and I are brothers."

"What's that mean, Mommy?"

Jolie's eyes narrowed and her lips pursed. "I don't want to talk about this right now."

"But, Mommy—"

"He's your uncle, CJ. Okay?"

"Okay. Do I have more?"

"You do." Cord replied before Jolie could. "Besides Chance, there's Clay, Cash and Chase."

"Are they all grown-ups?"

"Yup."

CJ sighed and offered puppy-dog eyes. "Are there any other kids?"

Jolie choked, and Cord wondered if he'd have to perform the Heimlich maneuver, but then remembered he couldn't stand up to administer it. Instead, he grinned at the boy but watched Jolie's face. "Just you, CJ, but maybe your mom and I could work on that for you. Maybe a little sister." Oh, yeah, that got a rise out of her. He glanced back at his son.

His son—and wasn't that a kick in the pants—screwed up his face as if he'd just taken a swig of lemon juice. "No girls. Girls are yucky." CJ had the good graces to glance up at his mother and then over at Cassie. "Well…some girls are okay. Like Mommy and Miss Cassie."

Jolie's face turned red, and had they been in the cartoons, steam would be hissing from her ears. He'd forgotten how much fun it was to push her buttons.

Without pausing for breath or giving his mother a chance to respond, CJ launched into his next subject. "Miss Cassie has horses. Do you have horses…uh…?" At a loss for what to call him, CJ's voice trailed off.

"I do have horses, bubba. And you can ride them whenever you want." He reached for the boy and tugged him a little closer. "Not sure what to call me, right?" Big eyed, CJ nodded. "Well, *Dad* works. Or *Daddy*. Whatever you'd like."

"*Daddy*. I like that."

Jolie made a strangled noise and reached for CJ, but Cord ignored her. "I like that too, bubba."

"We have to go, CJ." Jolie was about to snap, judging by her tone of voice and expression.

"No. I wanna stay with Daddy."

Shoving the wheelchair out of her way, she took CJ's arm. "No. Not today." She glared at Cord, her expression promising retribution with a big dose of "not now, not ever."

Cord figured he had to be the most perverse man who ever lived, because fighting with Jolie had been something he missed. A lot. Forget the makeup sex that came after. There was something…exhilarating about seeing her color rise, her fists tighten and her stubborn chin jut toward him as her eyes flashed like broken glass under a hot summer sun.

"No. Not today," he agreed easily. "Tomorrow." He smiled at her but caught Chance rolling his eyes. His brother was extremely familiar with his expression and the tone of voice.

"Cord." She clenched CJ's hand.

"Jolie."

"We're leaving."

"I'm not stopping you, Jolie. But I will see CJ tomorrow. I'll send Chance to pick him up, bring him out to the ranch."

"No."

Cord shrugged as if her resistance meant nothing. It stung, but that didn't matter. Not in the long run. "You know what the alternative is."

"You're bluffing."

A rolling gasp of laughter escaped from his chest and exploded out of his mouth. "Then, you don't know me at all, Jolene. Have him ready by nine. If he's not, Chance's next stop will be the courthouse."

"Which it'll also be if the two of you aren't home, Jolene." Chance just had to butt in, but Cord had known he would and had counted on it.

He tuned out Jolie's blustering and smiled at CJ. "Wish I wasn't in this chair, bubba, but I'll still show you some of our horses, and if you want to ride, our foreman, Kaden, will help you." He tousled the boy's hair. "Okay?"

"Okay!" CJ launched into his arms and Cord had to blink

back the sting of tears. Barrons didn't cry, but damned if he didn't want to. He had a son. And he had the woman he loved, even though she didn't realize she was his. Yet.

Jolie seethed and just barely managed to contain her anger. She wanted to beat her fists against the steering wheel but CJ was strapped into his car seat behind her and could see her face in the rearview mirror.

How dare Cordell Barron swoop into her life and steal her son away? There was no way on God's green earth she would let the Barrons sink their claws into CJ. She needed to call her dad. He had a whole firm of high-priced lawyers at his beck and call. They could file an injunction or something. Make sure Cord wasn't allowed anywhere near her or CJ.

She suddenly went cold, as if a bucket of rainwater had been dumped over her head. Was her reaction about CJ? Or her? Not long ago, she'd fantasized about rekindling a relationship with Cord. Some fantasy! The reality of the man—the truth of what it would mean to share her son with him—hit her square in the heart. She couldn't do it. But the alternative meant hurting CJ. She'd have to figure out some way to deal with the situation without getting her heart—or her son's—broken.

She glanced in the rearview mirror and recognized the stubborn tilt of her son's chin. It was about the only thing he'd inherited from her. "How about we stop and buy a movie on the way home?"

"No."

Yes, her son's temperament hit a little too close to home. "But you want to see that new—"

"No. I'm mad at you, Mommy."

"Fine." Oh, great. Now she was getting snippy with a four-year-old.

"Fine," he snipped back.

When they got home, dinner and bath time were a battle. CJ refused to watch TV with her, holing up in his room instead. When she went in to offer a bedtime story, he crawled into bed, turned his back and ignored her.

Out of sorts, she sprawled on the overstuffed couch in the area her Realtor called a media room. Some inane romantic comedy laugh tracked its way across the giant TV screen affixed to the wall. The thing had come with the house and there were times she enjoyed it. Tonight, not so much. Pushing off the couch, Jolie paced around the room, her thoughts as chaotic as the storm clouds gathering outside. Deep down, she knew she didn't have a legal leg to stand on. She couldn't prove Cord meant to harm CJ. She couldn't ding him for lack of child support because he hadn't known he was a father.

Her earlier conversation with her father as she was preparing dinner had been short, to the point and disappointing. And now she was mad at him because he seemed to be taking Cord's side. Then again, he'd always gotten biblical with her.

"You reap what you sow," he'd told her on numerous occasions, quickly followed up with his belief that she was wrong for not telling Cord about CJ. Tonight, he'd told her he'd hire an attorney to represent her in the paternity suit they were both sure Cord would file.

Could she really do that to CJ? Drag him through the newspapers, because they darn sure would glom onto the story—the legitimate press *and* the tabloids. Possible headlines flashed across her thoughts and none of them were pretty.

"Argh!" She wanted to hit something. Or throw something against the wall—something that would crash and break into a million pieces. She had no choice. She needed an attorney so the Barrons couldn't run roughshod over her, but she would have to let Cord see her son. *Her* son. Not his. She'd dealt with the three months of morning sickness. She'd brought CJ into the world with no help from the Barrons. She'd dealt with his colic, teething, earaches and everything else. All by herself.

*And whose fault is that?* No matter what she did, she couldn't muffle the sound of her conscience.

"Okay!" She yelled the admission. "My fault. It's all my freaking fault! Are you happy now?"

No, she wasn't happy at all. But she had to face the consequences. She had to allow Cord to spend time with CJ. She blinked and a wry smile crinkled her cheeks. Cord was a Barron. Barrons never stuck with anything that even hinted at personal responsibility. They got bored too easily. And hated having to make an effort. They expected to snap their fingers and everybody would line up to do their bidding. Well, Cord had a lot to learn about being a father. Especially since his own father was such a lousy example.

Jolie did a short happy dance. That was the ticket. Cord would get bored with being a father, and once he had his fill, he'd ignore CJ. Her heart contracted, knowing CJ would more than likely get hurt. But better he discovered now what a jerk his father was than later, when he'd have a harder time getting over it. She shoved those uncomfortable feelings away. She never wanted to hurt CJ, but ever since Cordell Barron entered the picture, hurt was inevitable. For both of them.

She trudged to her room, doing her best to ignore her feelings about—and for—Cord. The man drove her to distraction. He always had. All he had to do was smile, and her knees went all wobbly while her heart raced and goose bumps prickled her skin. And when he touched her? Her pulse—and other places—throbbed with the thought. She needed a cold shower stat, and headed to the master bath.

Jolie had dated postbreakup with Cord, in an I'll-show-him way, and most often with disastrous results. Nursing school had convinced her she didn't have time for men. And then CJ. Men didn't want a woman with the baggage of another man's child. Not just *another man*. Cord. She balled her fists on the granite vanity top and stared at her reflection.

"Get over him, girl!"

Her brain could list all the reasons why she should tell him to take a flying leap, but her body was up in arms and rebelling. She *wanted* him in that hot, skin-to-skin seductive way a woman wants the man who inflames her inside and out. And darn if her heart wasn't standing there on the edge of the cliff ready to take the leap with her girlie bits.

She crawled into bed, hit the remote control and found a program guaranteed to bore her into sleep. Her dreams, however, were far from boring. Tangles of arms and legs, deep kisses until her lips were swollen and she couldn't catch her breath. Flushed, she pushed off the linen duvet coverlet and flopped onto her back, arms wide. The ceiling fan washed a desultory breeze over her that did nothing to dissipate the heat. The digital clock on her bedside table blinked an accusatory three-thirty in her direction.

The TV droned in the background, casting flickering shadows around the room. For a brief moment, Jolie wondered what Cord was doing. Focusing on the program, she thrust thoughts of the man out of her mind—at least until her brain processed what she was seeing on the screen. She'd gone to sleep to a documentary and awakened to a man and woman writhing in ecstatic, no-holds-barred, down-and-dirty sex on a dining room table.

"Really?" She didn't know whether to laugh, cry or get out the vibrator. She didn't believe in signs, but if ever there might be one, this would be her luck. Giving up on any chance of sleep, she shoved out of bed and padded into the bathroom.

Cord twisted his hips, first right then left. He followed up with some of the other exercises his physical therapist insisted he do. Sometimes his insides still felt like scrambled eggs, though at the moment, it was his thoughts that more closely resembled food. Spaghetti. A big ole knot of it, twisted and tangled.

"I have a son." He tested the words by saying them aloud. "I'm a father." That one didn't settle, as well. He wasn't a father. Thanks to Jolie. She'd made sure he missed out on those all-important early years with CJ. CJ. He wondered what the initials stood for. Surely she hadn't named the boy after him. He made a mental note to ask CJ when he saw him.

Tomorrow. Cord glanced at the clock. Today, he amended. He'd have the day to spend with his son. He glared at the insectile shadow looming against the far wall of his childhood bedroom. He hated that wheelchair with a passion bordering on rabid. He would be rid of it as soon as possible.

Despite the sweat beading on his forehead, he redoubled his efforts, lifting his legs, holding them elevated until his abdominal muscles screamed and he couldn't breathe. Lowering them to the bed, he panted until the pain passed.

As he rested, his thoughts turned to Jolie. A different kind of pain washed over him, one that was both physical and emotional. His body hardened as he remembered all too well the feel of her curves, the sound of her soft, panting breaths as they made love. There'd been girls before her and women after, but none of them ever stirred him like Jolie. Now that she was back, he seriously doubted there'd ever be another. But at the same time, she'd done the unthinkable. Had she gotten pregnant on purpose? He got mad just thinking about it.

His anger simmered just beneath the surface. He had every right to be furious with her, but he hadn't exactly been a knight in shining armor where she was concerned. He'd acquiesced to his father's demand that he break it off without a backward look. Well, maybe a few glances and a very heavy heart, but he'd been a coward. He could own up to the label now, especially in light of what his younger brother had done.

Up to his old tricks, Cyrus had declared Cassie Morgan's father an enemy, and when the man had died, Cyrus had turned all that venom on Cassie. The old man was determined to steal Cassie's inheritance right out from under her—and would have if not for Chance.

Cord curled his head up, bringing knees and elbows together in a modified sit up. Cyrus had underestimated Chance—and the depth of feelings he had for the pretty little cowgirl. Chance had stood up to their father and never even looked back. If Cord were honest, he'd admit his small part in the epic cattle drive and the ensuing drama at the stockyards had been liberating. Especially in light of his own gutless action when Cyrus had given him the ultimatum regarding Jolie.

As he worked through the rest of the exercises prescribed by the therapist, he daydreamed. What would his life be like if he'd told his old man to shove it? He pictured him and Jolie in a little house with a bunch of kids, him working in the oil patch. He'd be a great dad, playing with the kids, teaching them how to play football and baseball— even the girls. And the nights spent with Jolie in his arms? Oh, yeah. Now, there was a dream he could grab hold of.

Except.

Reality shoved its way into his reverie. Jolie wouldn't have been happy in a little house. And as a lowly roughneck, he wouldn't have been able to afford the lifestyle she was used to. She'd always wanted to go to nursing school. Her father would have helped, but Cord was self-aware enough to know he would have resented every penny J. Rand Davis gave them.

The sweat on his body chilled, and he grabbed a towel to wipe his face. His little brother was damned lucky. Cord shook his head. No, not lucky. Determined. And willing to stand up to their old man. Because of Cassie.

Chance and Cassie. They had a great thing going. His brother worshipped the ground his wife walked on. She'd tempered Chance. He smiled easier, laughed more often. Cord wanted that with a woman. He wanted that with Jolie. He always had. And he'd get it. One way or another. Because that was what Barrons did.

# <u>Six</u>

Cord waited in the doorway of the barn, watching the shiny Mercedes SUV sweep up the drive. Behind him, CJ giggled as he helped the ranch manager, Kaden Waite, feed the horses. He figured it was Jolie in the vehicle, come to pick up their son. His heart contracted and then expanded at the thought. *Their son.* He'd known about CJ—whose full name was Cordell Joseph, though according to CJ, he was only called that when he was in trouble—for less than a day, but already the kid owned him heart and soul. He'd do anything for this child. Hell, he'd do anything for Jolie. All he had to do was convince her they belonged together. The three of them. One happy family.

He lost sight of the SUV as it parked in the circle drive in front of the sprawling stacked-stone-and-log ranch house. Moments later, his cell phone dinged with a text from Miz Beth, the Barron family's longtime cook and substitute mother figure.

U HAV CMPANY

The woman hated to text, but she didn't like calling one of the boys in front of people, either.

Cord texted back, asking if it was Jolie.

u nED to ComE NOW

Miz Beth's message was plain, despite her typos. "CJ, we need to head to the house."

"But I'm not finished helpin' Mr. Kaden, Daddy."

Cord's breath caught in his chest when he heard that word on CJ's lips. "He can finish up, bubba. Someone's up at the big house waitin' for us."

"Who?" CJ dragged his feet but approached.

"Not sure, but Miz Beth says we need to get up there pronto."

Kaden had followed CJ out of the barn. "I'll bring the UTV around, Cord."

The other man ducked back inside and returned moments later driving a two-seat utility vehicle with a bed on the back big enough to hold the wheelchair. After a bit of maneuvering, and more help from Kaden than he wanted to admit he needed, Cord, CJ and the chair were bouncing along the gravel road back to the main house. He stopped at the back, where Miz Beth's husband, Big John, met them.

A few minutes later, he rolled through the house while CJ darted ahead.

"Grandy!"

Grandy? Who was here? Expecting Jolie, Cord worked to school his expression as he turned the corner to find J. Rand Davis standing in the entry hall. Miz Beth stood her ground, chin jutted, hands on hips, blocking Rand from coming any farther into the house. The older man's eyes flicked in Cord's direction.

"Cordell."

"Mr. Davis."

"Grandy, Grandy. Guess what I did!" CJ all but leaped into his grandfather's arms, demanding his attention.

Without taking his eyes off Cord, Rand said, "No clue, CJ. What did you do?"

"I fed horses! And got to sit on one while Mr. Kaden led him around the corral."

Rand ruffled the boy's hair affectionately. "Sounds like you had a fine time today, CJ. Ready to go home?"

"Aww, do I hav'ta, Grandy?"

Cord realized Rand was waiting for him to say something. He cleared his throat. "Since your grandfather drove all the way out here to get you, bubba, yeah, time to go home." Before CJ could launch into an argument, he continued, "But tell ya what. I'll call your mom and see about maybe you coming out and spending the weekend, okay?"

"Like a sleepover?"

"Yeah, like a sleepover."

"Cool."

Rand glanced at the housekeeper, noted her apron with a tilt of his head and sniffed the air, which was filled with scents of apple and cinnamon. "Are those apple fritters I smell?"

"They surely are." The woman, always astute, glanced between Cord and Rand before holding out her hand. "CJ, honey, why don't you come with me to the kitchen. I have some fritters and milk for you to eat before you head home."

The boy squirmed loose from his grandfather and happily joined her. Once they were out of sight and hearing, Rand said, "We need to talk, Cordell."

Jolie paced her kitchen. At one end of her path, she checked the time on the chrome-and-neon clock on the wall. After pivoting and marching back to the far side of the room, she checked her watch. When the phone rang, she all but jumped out of her skin. She snagged the receiver and answered with a worried "Hello?"

"Jolie, it's Cord."

As if she wouldn't recognize his voice. Pleasure warred with panic. "Is CJ okay?"

"He's fine. Your father picked him up about twenty minutes ago. He mentioned something about hamburgers before bringing him home."

"I swear my dad spoils that boy rotten."

Cord chuckled, and the sound melted her bones. "It's easy to do. He's an awesome kid." Silence stretched as she tried to figure out what to say. Luckily, Cord beat her to it. "Ah…thanks."

His gratitude perplexed her. "For what?"

"For letting CJ come to the ranch. For giving me a chance."

She bit back the retort on the tip of her tongue. Something about his voice tugged at her heart. He sounded uncertain. "You're welcome, Cord."

"Can we talk, Jolie?"

Yes, it *was* uncertainty she caught in his voice, and the idea that Cordell Barron might be uncertain about anything rocked her back on her heels. She expected him to be demanding. Arrogant. Confident. All the things he'd always been around her. But uncertain? He'd been so sure of himself in high school. College. Even the night of their hookup. He'd been positive she'd stay the night, that they'd fall back into their relationship. She steeled her emotions even as her skin tingled in remembrance of that night.

"What do you want to talk about, Cord?"

"Our son."

No hesitation on his part. *Our* son. Those words seared her soul like the hot Oklahoma wind.

"I really want to be CJ's dad. I want to spend time with him. Do things and get to know him. Make up for lost time, you know?"

Now he was tugging on her guilty conscience, so she said nothing but a noncommittal "Mmm."

"Can we do this without getting the lawyers involved?"

Still she didn't answer, marshaling her chaotic thoughts. She didn't want to share CJ. She didn't. Especially not with the Barrons. The Barrons… Okay, *Cyrus* Barron was the problem. That horrid old man was nothing but poison when it came to his own sons. She sighed inwardly because Cord was right. CJ was his son, too.

"We have a son together, Jolie. Can't we be friends, at least?"

"I don't know, Cord. I'm not sure that's a good idea." Jolie wanted to bite her tongue. Why did she continue to antagonize him? Cord sincerely wanted to get to know CJ. Even so, she was reluctant to trust him. In addition to the fact he once broke her heart, and could do so again if she wasn't careful, she couldn't get past his last name and the fact that Cyrus would have access to CJ. Yet Cord appeared, at the moment, to be acting reasonable about things. Mostly. Okay, definitely. She was the one being a witchy woman, her broken heart notwithstanding. She had every reason to be cautious. Right? Right.

"You're thinking too hard, sunshine."

*Sunshine.* Her tummy did a cartwheel and she sank down on the nearest bar stool. "You haven't called me that in…forever."

"I haven't talked to you in forever. Not really. You never stuck around my hospital room long enough."

He'd reached out to her as he'd lain racked with pain in that bed, and while part of her turned all warm and fuzzy with the memory, the hurt and heartbroken girl she'd buried all those years ago wouldn't let go of her anger.

"You're still thinking too hard." Cord's voice was thick and husky with emotion, and for the first time, she wondered if their breakup had hurt him, too. That was a place she wasn't ready to explore.

"I know. I have a lot to think about."

An uncomfortable silence reared its head again, and the tension made Jolie fidget. She had so many questions she wanted to ask, but wasn't sure she wanted the answers.

"I should let you go. Tell CJ I love him and sweet dreams when you put him to bed tonight. And…tell him I'll ask you another time about spending the weekend with me." Breath hissed softly from between her lips and Cord inhaled. The moment was as intimate as a kiss. "G'night, sunshine."

The broken connection hummed in her ear before she could respond. Jolie dashed at her eyes, irritated that tears threatened to spill over and drown her cheeks. If she ever succumbed to tears, she'd never stop.

Cord put down the phone and pushed himself up on the bed. God, but she still turned him on. Just her voice had the ability to twist him into a hot mess of nerves and made him want things he'd walked away from, and probably couldn't have again. Like her. In his bed. In his life. But the yearning just made him more resolute. He would make them a family.

He swung his legs over and steadied himself on the edge of the mattress. Today with CJ had been a breath of fresh air, but he'd overdone things physically. Eyeing the wheelchair with something akin to hatred, he braced one hand on the sturdy wooden footboard of his bed and eased into a standing position.

So far, so good. He had fifteen steps to the bathroom. Three of those were close to the footboard. After that, he was on his own in uncharted territory. He hadn't taken a step since the accident without a physical therapist and safety equipment holding him. He hadn't even tried a walker yet, but talking to Jolie, listening to her breathe into the phone did more than just make him aware of how sexy she was. It made him want to get well, to be the man who had once took her to bed and left her panting and moaning his name against his shoulder.

His talk with Rand Davis had also left him off balance—and wondering what Jolie's father was up to. Not to mention leaving Cord questioning everything that had happened between him and Jolie for the past ten years.

Leaning heavily on the footboard, he shuffled toward his bathroom. He paused and stared at the door across the open floor. So near yet so far. But he was sick and tired of being an invalid. If he was going to be a real dad to CJ, if he had any chance of winning Jolie back, he had to suck it up.

Agonizing minutes later, sweating like a racehorse after the Kentucky Derby, he leaned on the cool granite counter and stared at his reflection in the mirror. He'd lost weight and muscle tone, and the gray pallor did not blend well with his fading tan. Time to rectify things. From now on, he was standing on his own two feet. Well, with the help of a walker, but not for long. Nope, not for long at all.

An hour later, he entered the kitchen, standing on his own two feet, though pushing the wheeled walker the therapist had sent over. Miz Beth sniffled and waved him to the broad breakfast bar while she hustled up a plate and silverware. Big John moved the walker back out of the way as Cord settled into one of the tall chairs fronting the bar. A few minutes later, Kaden sauntered in and washed up at the kitchen sink.

The three men shuffled food into their mouths with no time for polite conversation between bites. But after dinner, when Miz Beth served warm apple fritters and coffee, Cord broached a new subject with the ranch manager.

"What do you know about therapeutic riding, Kaden?"

The other man shrugged. "Read some stuff. Saw it when I was up at Oklahoma State gettin' my degree." Kaden turned to face him, a thoughtful expression knitting his brow and pursing his lips. "You thinkin' about getting back in the saddle, boss man?"

Cord barely refrained from rolling his eyes. He and his brothers had known almost from the moment Kaden had been hired that he was a Barron, despite his last name being the same as his mother's—Waite. The Chickasaw half of his heritage explained his tanned skin and black hair, but his eyes—like all the offspring of Cyrus Barron—gave him away. To Cord's knowledge, Kaden never mentioned his father, and definitely never acknowledged he might be

Cyrus Barron's son. Raised by a mother who'd never married, Kaden kept his own counsel and ran the ranch's cattle and horse operations like a man with twice his experience.

"Yeah, I am. Maybe teach CJ to ride at the same time."

Cord caught Kaden's flickering glance before the man answered, "We can do that." Kaden took a long drag on the coffee in his cup and swallowed before facing Cord. "You sure seem to be acceptin' of this situation, Cord."

"He's my son, Kaden. I'm not going to turn my back on him." *Or his mother.*

Taking another swallow, Kaden stood up. "Mighty fine dinner, Miz Beth. Thank you." He tipped an invisible hat to Big John before clapping a gentle hand on Cord's shoulder. "That's what makes you different, Cordell Barron. It surely does."

# Seven

More nervous than a sinner sitting in the front pew, Cord waited on the porch of the main house. Jolie had agreed to let CJ stay the weekend at the ranch. He'd had almost two weeks to get used to having a son. While he was excited to see CJ, it was the anticipation of seeing Jolie and putting his plan into action that had his nerves twanging. Dinner first, with Jolie staying to eat, and then maybe the three of them watching a movie. To ease any nerves the boy might have about sleeping in a new place. That was Cord's excuse. It all sounded plausible to him. Surely Jolie was nervous, too, about leaving her son with virtual strangers.

John and Miz Beth had set up the patio for grilling burgers, all within easy walking distance so Cord wouldn't have to rely on the walker. He'd already mostly abandoned it, but for longer distances. In addition to burgers and hot dogs ready to be slapped on the grill, there was Miz Beth's famous potato salad. Sweet tea—Jolie's favorite—and fruit punch. A tub of homemade ice cream in the freezer. All that was lacking in his perfect scenario was Jolie and CJ.

He'd loved Jolie with an unreasonable fervor when they were younger. And he'd been a dreamer. The old man had put a stop to that. Cord shook off that train of thought. He couldn't go back and change the past. All he could do was work toward the future he wanted. Thoughts of his father filled his chest with cold dread. Thankfully, he was down in Houston looking at an oil refinery to buy. Cord should be there with him, as CEO of BarEx, and would have been but for his accident.

But it was good his father was away. So far, it seemed as if no one had spilled the beans about CJ. That wouldn't last, and when Cyrus found out, hell would certainly break loose. With luck, Cord's plan would work and he'd have Jolie and CJ back before the old man could do a thing to stop him.

The cool night wind prickled the hair on his arms. It was just the wind—or so he told himself. Not a premonition about his father.

Cord went back to his strategy for tonight. Maybe he'd opt for s'mores around the patio's fire pit instead of a movie. His chest tightened, along with his groin, at the thought of snuggling with Jolie on the big lounger. Every night, he slipped into sleep with her eyes and beautiful body foremost in his thoughts. He dreamed of touching her skin and always woke up hard and hungry. And not just since his accident.

Tires crunching on gravel pulled him out of his reverie. He ducked back into the shadows to watch the woman he still loved and their son arrive. As Jolie's crossover SUV swung into the big circle, he ducked through the front door. Wouldn't do to let her see his anxiety. He almost laughed out loud. Anxious? Hell, he was terrified he'd screw this up. And if he did? There'd be no second chance.

When the car rolled to a smooth stop before the wide front steps, he opened the door and strode forward, a mask of confidence plastered on his face. He'd worked his ass off for two weeks to lose the chair and the walker. He couldn't go far, but by damn he could get to the porch and down the steps. Luckily, he hadn't taken the first riser when CJ barreled into him.

"Dad! Dad! Mom! Mom! Lookie. See!" The boy whirled toward his mom, his face alight with happiness. "Daddy's walkin'!"

"I can see that." Jolie quirked an eyebrow as if she didn't believe her eyes. "Don't you think it's a little soon?"

"Nope. The therapist told me to go at my own speed."

"Daddy, Daddy, Dad." CJ tugged at his pants' leg to get his attention. "Can we play ball now? Mom won't play."

That was Cord's cue to quirk his brow. "Really? Huh." He knew damn well Jolie had been an all-state softball player who threw harder than many of the guys in their high school.

Jolie rolled her eyes as she popped the rear hatch and dragged out a backpack, a little wheeled suitcase and a very large floppy dog. She carried everything to the top of the steps and handed the stuffed animal to CJ and the backpack to Cord. "I haven't had time."

"Do you have time now?"

Jolie narrowed her gaze. "To play ball?"

"No, to stay for dinner."

She opened her mouth to decline but CJ jumped in to rescue him. "Please, Mommy?" He bobbed his head in an emphatic nod. "What're we havin'? Is Miss Beth cookin'?"

"Nope, bubba. Me. I have the grill fired up for some burgers and hot dogs." He adopted CJ's winsome expression and turned it on Jolie. "Please? Miz Beth did make homemade ice cream, and if it gets any cooler, I thought maybe we could roast marshmallows and make s'mores. You used to love s'mores." He was not above wheedling shamelessly.

"Please, Mommy. You fix my stuff just right. You can show Daddy. Right, Daddy?" CJ transferred his tugs from Cord's jeans to his hand.

"Right, CJ."

"Don't you think for a minute I don't know what you're up to, Cordell Barron."

CJ giggled, and both adults looked at him. "Are you in trouble?"

Laughing, Cord hefted the backpack up on his shoulder

so he could ruffle the boy's hair without letting go of his hand. "I'm pretty much always in trouble with your mom, bubba." He glanced at Jolie but she wouldn't meet his gaze. "So how 'bout it, Mom? Will you stay for dinner?"

"I have to go."

"So you have plans?" Cord worked to keep his poker face in place. "Stay for dinner, Jolie. Help CJ get settled in, 'kay?"

She narrowed her eyes, and he fully expected her to start shaking her "mother finger" at him. Miz Beth always did when she knew he'd been up to something nefarious.

"Please, Mommy? Pretty please with gummy worms and whipped cream on top?"

Laughing, Jolie put one hand on her hip in mock dismay. "You're the one who likes gummy worms, CJ."

"Yeah, your mom's weakness is white chocolate."

A flicker of surprise crossed her expression and Cord wondered why. He remembered everything about her.

"Nothing's going to happen, Cord." Yet he saw the moment she capitulated.

He did his best to look innocent before turning toward the front entrance. CJ trotted along, still holding his hand. When the two of them reached the massive wooden door, they both turned to check on Jolie. She still stood rooted to the spot where they'd left her.

"S'mores, Mom." CJ had his best look of entreaty firmly in place.

Cord grinned and winked. "Yeah, Mom. S'mores. I even have white chocolate for yours."

Jolie threw up her hands, grabbed the handle of the suitcase and dragged it along with her. She laughed when Cord and CJ high-fived and did her best to nip the warm feelings budding inside her. She'd wanted this her whole life—this teasing closeness that families had. Well, families other than her own. An only child, she'd envied her friends their siblings, including Cord with all his brothers and cousins. One big rowdy family. Like musketeers. She'd wanted to be a musketeer.

Leaving CJ's paraphernalia tucked into an alcove in the entry hall, Cord ushered them through the house toward the back patio. Jolie dragged her feet, turning in the occasional circle to see everything. She'd never been inside. There were soaring ceilings with open beams, a stacked stone fireplace, oversize leather couches and chairs, thick rugs on the heart of pine floor. Native American and Western art adorned the walls.

They passed a formal dining room with a deer-antler chandelier and she got a peek at the gourmet kitchen before Cord opened the French doors leading to the flagstone patio. There was an outdoor kitchen nicer than most people had in their homes out there.

Cord played the perfect host. He'd thought of everything. Drinks—red fruit punch for CJ, sweet tea with a fresh slice of orange for her. A tray with fixings for their burgers. Chili and cheese.

And then there was the man himself, presiding over the grill while CJ played with one of the ranch dogs and she lounged near the fire pit crackling with piñon wood. How many times had she dreamed of just such a scenario back when she was young and dumb? More times than she wanted to admit.

A beautiful heated pool was built into the edge of the patio. Steam rose as the temperature continued to cool, and the lulling sound of a man-made waterfall murmured in the background. Beyond the pool, a beautifully landscaped yard stretched toward the working part of the ranch— barns, corrals and cottages where the ranch hands lived. It was a revelation, and she understood now why all the Barron brothers loved the place. The mansion in Nichols Hills had been their residence during the school year. The ranch was their home. Christmas. Birthdays. Summer vacations.

Jolie had attended parties at the Nichols Hills house.

She'd never been invited to the ranch. Until now. She didn't want to wonder why, didn't want the insecurity, anger and hurt from that long-ago time to rear its ugly head. Tonight they could be friends. They could share her son... She sighed and rethought that. Their son. Being honest, she was terrified Cord would somehow steal CJ away, turn him against her the way Cyrus Barron had turned Cord. And she wasn't ready to share CJ's affection, even as she watched him run to Cord and throw his arms around his dad's thighs and babble excitedly.

She didn't want to see the honest emotion on Cord's face as he listened patiently, as his hand rested on CJ's head, fingers mussing hair the exact same color as his. She didn't have to see their eyes to know they were two peas in a pod. Barron DNA didn't fall far from the tree.

"Mom!"

She blinked from her reverie to realize that CJ had called her several times and now stood in front of her, hands on his hips. "What, baby?"

"I'm not a baby. Daddy says food's ready. I need you to fix my hot dog, 'cept I wanna try some chili and some cheese and lots and lots of mustard."

Jolie glanced at Cord. Chili was his condiment of choice. He ate it on his hamburgers. Hot dogs. Eggs. He'd probably put it on ice cream if the ice cream wouldn't melt. She pushed off the lounger and walked over to the counter next to the built-in grill. With CJ telling her exactly how much of everything he wanted, she fixed his plate and installed him at the wrought iron table, cloth napkin firmly tied around his neck. When she returned to start putting together her own meal, Cord handed a plate to her. Hamburger with sliced Parmesan cheese, Romaine lettuce and Caesar dressing.

He remembered. How did he do that? And did he realize she hadn't eaten a burger dressed this way since they'd broken up? Her throat closed and burned as she blinked back unwanted tears. This was the man she remembered—the sweet one who spoiled her. But she really needed to remember the bastard who'd ripped out her heart and then stomped on it, grinding it beneath the heels of his expensive Western boots.

"Mom!" CJ stood up in his chair, waving his arms at her. "C'mon, Mom. I'm hungry."

"Go sit down, sunshine. I'll refill your tea and be right there."

With a warm hand on the small of her back, Cord urged her toward the table. Did he know? Could he feel the blood rushing through her veins so fast it pounded in her ears? She hoped not. She needed every advantage to keep him at arm's length.

Dinner was a blur, so much so she didn't even fuss at CJ for blowing bubbles—egged on by Cord—through the straw in his fruit punch. He ate everything on his plate and asked for seconds. This time his father fixed his hot dog. Perfectly, just as he'd done with her burger. Ice cream followed, and then CJ headed out into the yard dotted with lights to play tag and fetch with the dog, a huge, shaggy beast of indiscriminate heritage.

"You realize he's going to want a dog now, right?"

"What?" She glanced over as Cord settled onto the giant lounger next to her. His burned-honey eyes glowed warm and tempting in the incandescent shine from the landscape lights.

"He's going to bug you for a dog."

She chuckled. "And? He's been doing that practically from the time he could talk. Why do you think I had to drag Ducky out here?"

Cord got that sexy amused expression that used to melt her panties. "Ah, would that be the shapeless lump of fake fur napping in the entry?"

"Yup."

"Ducky?"

"He's a big *Marmaduke* fan but couldn't pronounce the name. He finally shortened it to Ducky."

"A kid after my own heart."

Jolie rolled her eyes. "Don't tell me you still watch cartoons..."

Cord laughed and every muscle in her body wanted to sing with joy as the sound washed over her. "I could be perfectly happy with only one channel on TV, so long as it was the Cartoon Network."

She let out a snorting giggle—but then wondered what he wore to watch toons in. Did he still wear those fitted cotton boxers—the ones that cupped his butt and hugged his thighs the way she wanted to do? She licked her bottom lip before catching it between her teeth. When she glanced up, she almost recoiled from the look of stark hunger on Cord's face.

Pulling back, Cord rolled to an unsteady stand. After a moment, he regained his balance and turned to tend the fire before calling to CJ.

"Hey, bubba, 'bout time for s'mores, yeah?"

The boy whooped and ran toward them. When he slid to a stop, Cord steadied him away from the fire pit. "Why don't you come inside with me? You can wash your hands and then you can help me bring out the stuff."

"Okeydoke."

Left alone, Jolie inhaled deeply. Several times. She smoothed her hair back from her face with shaking hands. That had been way too close for comfort. She'd wanted to throw herself into Cord's arms, kiss him, be kissed by him. All the feelings she'd suppressed for so many years bubbled up and were within a hairbreadth of boiling out. That wouldn't do. Wouldn't do at all.

By the time Cord and CJ returned, she'd reined in her emotions, stilled her trembling hands and smoothed her expression to hide the turmoil—as much from herself as from Cord. She could not—*would* not—walk down this path again. Her heart wouldn't survive if he turned on her again. Their history taught her to be a realist, and reality dictated Cord would do exactly what Cyrus Barron demanded. Always.

# Eight

Cord left CJ arguing with Miz Beth and Big John about whether Dusty, the ranch dog, could come into the house to sleep on the boy's bed. He refused to make a bet on who'd win that one. Instead, he walked Jolie out to her car, albeit with a great deal of reluctance. Her arm brushed against his and heat flashed through him. He heard her breath hitch and wondered if their casual contact had the same effect on her. He hoped so.

He held her elbow as they descended from the porch, and while he wanted to drag his feet, it was Jolie who slowed as they walked around her car to the driver's door. He reached around her to open it but didn't get the chance when she leaned up against the vehicle. Chuckling, he stepped back from her so as not to crowd.

"Something funny?"

He offered a crooked grin and was gratified when her eyes lit up and focused on his mouth. "Does this feel as awkward to you as it does to me?"

"Awkward?"

"Yeah. Like first-date awkward. You know. Should I kiss her? Do I have bad breath? What happens if we both tilt our heads the same way and we bump noses, or…" He paused to sigh dramatically. "What if we bump teeth?"

Jolie's laugh was rich and deep and sincere—exactly the effect he was hoping for. "Do guys really worry about all that?"

Cord nodded solemnly. "Absolutely. And let's not even talk about boners."

That elicited a peal of laughter. "Seriously?"

"Oh, hell, yeah. Talk about awkward! When you're sixteen, an erection is pretty much a given whenever you're around a pretty girl. Trying to kiss and hide your arousal takes far more coordination than most teenage boys can manage."

Her eyes danced with devilish lights. "What about grown-up men?"

"Wait. Isn't that an oxymoron?"

She lightly slapped his arm before her fingers trailed across his chest only to finally drop back to her side. "Are you telling me men never grow up?"

"Yup. 'Fraid so. When it comes to pretty women, men are perpetual sixteen-year-olds."

"Horrors."

Cord realized his fingers had curled into his palms in an effort to keep from touching Jolie. This teasing banter was familiar, natural, the way they used to be. As he watched, he saw her shiver. The wind carried a real chill now, and her short sleeves did little to keep her protected from its cold fingers. Without thinking, he reached for her and ran his hands up and down her goose-bumped arms to create some friction heat.

Jolie leaned into him, and he forced his feet to remain planted on the driveway. Every sinew in his body strained to step closer, to press against the length of her body and hold her close. Just when he thought he'd lose the battle, she did the unthinkable. She stepped to him, her arms circling his waist. He gathered her close and buried his nose in her soft hair, inhaling the scent of mimosa and warm spring days. His heart thudded, and he could feel hers softly echo even through the flannel shirt he wore. Cord was afraid to speak, afraid of breaking the tentative connection humming between them. He felt her smile against his chest.

"Awkward," she mumbled, and chuckled, even as she pressed closer to his arousal.

He laughed. "Aah…perpetually sixteen. What can I say?" He sobered a moment later and whispered into her hair, "Thank you."

"For what?"

"For tonight. For dinner. For letting CJ stay the weekend." There was so much more he wanted to tell her, to thank her for. Mainly for carrying his child—when it would have been so easy not to—for raising him to be the funny, bright, amazing kid who was at that very moment convincing Miz Beth to let a shaggy, flea-infested ranch mongrel not only into her spotless house, but into bed with him. But Cord couldn't put all those feelings into words. Not yet.

When Jolie leaned back and raised her face, she stared at him for a long time, her eyes searching his expression. The moment she closed her eyes, he knew. She was waiting for his kiss. Brushing his lips across hers, he tightened his arms, and then let her go. Her eyelids popped open and she regarded him with puzzlement. Cord smoothed his thumb along the ridge of her cheekbone before catching a stray strand of hair and tucking it behind her ear.

*I missed you. I want you. I need you.* The words tumbled in his mind. He searched for his anger, his sense of betrayal, but her nearness overwhelmed those emotions. He never did have any sense of preservation where Jolie was concerned. If he truly was the son his old man wanted, he'd be plotting revenge simply because that was what Barrons did. But he couldn't—not the way Cyrus would. He wanted Jolie. He wanted his son. And he'd have them even if he had to play a little dirty to get them.

He wouldn't voice those hidden feelings out loud. Jolie would run for the hills if he did. It was too soon. He knew that, and if his plan had any hope of working, he had to keep those thoughts to himself.

"What?" The word feathered across his skin as Jolie exhaled.

"Hmm?" He was suddenly lost in her gaze.

"What are you thinking?"

He blinked and straightened, focusing on the here and now. A laugh escaped before he could swallow it. "Yeah, no. I'm not going there."

"What are you afraid of?"

Cord hid the cringe twisting his muscles. This conversation reminded him far too much of the games he played with his brothers. It always started with that question and quickly devolved into "I dare you" followed by "I double dare you." Those challenges never ended well. One or more brothers ended up at the ER and the rest whipped and grounded for life.

What *was* he afraid of? Simple answer—never seeing Jolie and CJ again. Of being stupid and messing things up—again—so that she left. Of spending the rest of his life without her, alone.

"More than you realize, sunshine." He pulled her closer and rested his forehead against hers. "More than you could know."

Her arms slipped back around his waist and she hooked her thumbs in his belt loops. "I wish you'd talk to me."

"I wish I could."

His honesty startled her into growing still, though her curiosity wouldn't let things stay that way. "You know, Cord, it's pretty easy. You just open your mouth and words come out."

"Easy for you to say." His wry chuckle disguised the tremor threatening his voice.

Jolie sighed and dropped her hands in preparation of pulling away from him. He tightened the arm around her waist and kissed her forehead before stepping back. "I would like to talk, Jolie. We sort of got off on the wrong foot."

The huff of angry air she blew out was just as expressive as her frustrated sigh moments ago. "Look, I know you want me to apologize—"

He held up his hands, cutting her off. "No. It's too late for that." Even in the dark, under the reddish glow of mercury vapor security lights, he could see her color rise. He backed up and half turned away as he tunneled fingers through his unruly hair. "Don't, Jolie."

Cord actually heard her jaw snap shut. Jamming his hands into his hip pockets, he stared up at the moon. Out here, away from city lights, the Oklahoma sky was a swathe of black satin dotted with diamonds while the giant pearl of a moon hung from a chain of clouds. Resisting the urge to sigh as loudly as she had, he watched her from the corner of his eye.

"This isn't easy for either of us. Yes, I'm still mad. And hurt. But you got hurt, too." He held up a hand to stay her arguments. "Just listen, okay? You're the one who wanted me to talk."

Closing her mouth, Jolie crossed her arms, lifting and plumping her breasts. When his gaze zeroed in on her chest, she growled at him and he laughed.

"Permanently sixteen, remember? If you stand there emphasizing them, I'm gonna look, babe. I'm a man. We like looking at pretty women. That's how we roll." He sobered and offered a conciliatory smile. "What's done is done, Jolie. All we can do now is move forward, right?"

She nodded with one quick downward jerk of her stubborn chin. It wasn't much to work with, but better than nothing, so he continued, "Now that I know about CJ, I want to be in his life. I want to be his father." He ruffled one hand through his hair again. "I had a piss-poor example, so I damn sure want to do a better job. We need to talk—maybe not tonight, but soon. About…things. About custody and support and stuff."

Cord didn't like the way her back stiffened when she asked, "Stuff?"

"Yeah, Jolie. Stuff. I want us to be friends. Or at least friendly." Oh, he wanted a whole helluva lot more than that, but he wasn't ready to play all his cards yet. "CJ needs two parents. And he deserves two parents who aren't at each other's throats all the time." He breathed a little easier when she visibly relaxed and appeared to consider what he said.

"CJ and I have gotten along just fine without you." She sounded defensive.

He swallowed the angry retort forming on the tip of his tongue. Instead, he watched her, the silent weight of his thoughts leaking into his gaze until she looked away, no longer defiant. She dropped her arms and fumbled behind her for the door handle.

"Why did you come back?"

Jolie froze. "What do you mean?"

"Just what I asked. What made you leave Houston, come back here?"

She scuffed her toe against the cobblestone driveway and refused to look at him. She mumbled something he couldn't quite make out so he nudged her again. "Jolie? Why?"

"I was homesick, okay?" She shifted from foot to foot and looked distinctly uncomfortable.

Cord grabbed her hand and tugged gently. "If we're going to talk tonight, we might as well be comfortable. Come back inside. You can kiss CJ good-night and we'll go out on the patio, talk out there in private."

"I need to go."

"Are you working tomorrow?"

"No."

"Have a hot date?"

"No!"

"Then what are *you* afraid of?" Oh, he'd very neatly turned the tables on her. Jolie flattened her lips into a grimace. "Certainly not you. Fine. Of course, if CJ complains and wants to come home with me, you have no one to blame but yourself."

He walked her back up the front steps, his palm a warm brand on the small of her back. Jolie prayed he didn't feel the shiver dancing through her. How was it possible he could still make her knees wobble? Even when she was furious with him, her heart thudded not from the fury but from lust. She craved him, no ifs, ands or buts.

Holding the front door, he let her precede him into the entry hall before leading the way up the stairs to the private part of the house—the bedrooms. Some of the doors were open—though there were no lights on inside—and she did her best not to gawk. She couldn't help but wonder which room Cord currently occupied. That way led to disaster. Her nights were already fraught with memories—the two of them in bed, on a blanket at the lake, in his apartment in college, in hotel rooms.

She was so engrossed in her thoughts, she ran into Cord's broad back when he stopped. She stumbled and he quickly whirled to grab and steady her.

"Shh." He held his finger to his lips. Cord nodded toward the open door of a bedroom.

Jolie peeked inside. A night-light cast a soft glow over the room. CJ, snuggly in his flannel pajamas, was sound asleep. One arm was thrown over the back of the shaggy mutt occupying the bed next to her son. She had to clap a hand over her mouth to stifle a giggle. Tiptoeing over, she swept her hair back so she could bend to place a kiss on CJ's cheek. Before she could, the dog licked her arm and she couldn't catch the laugh.

"Mommy?" CJ's eyes fluttered, and she smoothed the hair off his forehead.

"G'night, sweetheart. Mommy loves you," she said, kissing him.

"Night, Mommy. G'night, Daddy."

"G'night, bubba. Sweet dreams."

Cord stood beside her, ruffling the dog's fur with one hand and cupping the back of CJ's head with the other. She sucked in a breath as her heart seemed to freeze. How many times had she dreamed of this moment—of the two of them standing beside CJ's bed wishing him good-night? The dreams didn't even come close to the reality. Emotion swamped her and she turned away before Cord saw the tears glittering in her eyes. She stumbled out to the hallway and leaned against the wall, breathing heavily and dashing the back of her hand against her cheeks.

"Jolie? Honey, what's wrong?"

Before she knew what was happening, Cord pulled her into his arms and her cheek found its favorite resting spot against his shoulder. "Nothing," she murmured.

"Mmm-kay."

He obviously didn't believe her but didn't press for an answer. Instead, he tucked her under his arm and moved her down the stairs and into the great room. He guided her outside to the patio and settled her on the double lounger before disappearing back inside the house. Cord returned a few minutes later with a glass mug topped with whipped cream. Irish coffee. Damn the man. His memory was far too perfect. She accepted his offering and cupped it in her hands while he poked flames back to life in the fire pit.

Cord joined her on the lounger without asking. She didn't argue. Part of her needed his nearness much more than the part wanting him far, far away. He held a longneck beer bottle and offered her a toast.

"To what?"

"To…our son."

How could she resist that? She clinked her mug against the bottle, then took a sip. Her Irish coffee was as perfect as if she'd made it herself. Jolie didn't want to bring up the past, but the present was still too nerve-racking and the future was something she refused to contemplate. Being a coward, she lay against the nest of pillows at her back, watching flames dance along the fragrant piñon wood in the fire pit and sipping her drink.

Despite her best efforts to stop it, a tear perched on the ends of her lashes. This was what she'd dreamed of—evenings like this with Cord, the two of them sharing comfortable silences while their little one slept just inside. She'd wanted what all her friends wanted. A man who loved her, whom she loved. A man who wanted to spend a lifetime making her happy. But she'd fallen in love with Cordell Barron, the one man she could never have.

Cord relieved her of the cup and slipped his arm beneath her shoulders, snuggling her closer to his side. "Don't cry, baby. Your tears break my heart."

And that did it. With a sob, she opened the floodgates. All those tears she'd held back for so many years burst through her emotional shields. Cord held her, touching her with gentle hands, dropping soft kisses on her hair, forehead and cheek. She'd be embarrassed when her outburst subsided, but for now she absorbed his warmth, his kindness, and accepted the fact he cared.

Jolie's sobs eventually turned to hiccups. Cord patted her back as if he wasn't sure what exactly to do. She lifted her head. When he shifted, she caught the flicker of a wince before he turned away. Despite the way he'd been moving all night, she'd bet his injuries still bothered him.

Cord offered her a smile. "Need my shirttail?"

She hiccupped again, around a little laugh, and he interrupted her before she could apologize. "Don't, sunshine."

"What? Don't blow my nose on your shirt?"

Cord laughed. "Yeah, it's okay to blow your nose on my shirt." He pressed a kiss to her forehead, and then shifted his position again. When she looked up at him, he offered a murmured, "Ah…awkward," in response.

Jolie brushed her cheek moving against his shirt. What

was she doing? He leaned and twisted, trying to see her face. She pressed her lips together, but the smile spread despite her best efforts. He glared at her. "I refuse to apologize for getting turned on around you, Jolie. I pretty much stay that way if you're anywhere within fifty feet of me." He chuckled. "Okay, to be honest, you don't even have to be in the same room. All I have to do is think about you."

She tilted her face, unsure she believed him, wanting to see his expression. She didn't speak at first, just searched his face in solemn concentration. "You really mean that, don't you?"

"Yeah. I've… Ah, hell, Jolie." He pushed away and sat up. "I'm gonna be honest here."

The debate raging inside Cord was obvious to her. Did she really want him to answer her question? She felt as if she was standing on the edge of a precipice and if she took one more step she'd fall.

*No, no, no! Bad Cord. Don't do this. It's a* really *bad idea. You'll ruin things. Again.* His brain wouldn't shut up so he imagined a gag. When Jolie's hand touched his shoulder, the voice in his head shut up.

"I think about you all the time, Jolie. Always have." The soft intake of her breath made him pause. Silence loomed between them until he added, "You had every right to hate me. Hell, I hated myself. Still do. I was a fool, Jolie."

"You broke my heart." Her whispered words escaped before she could stop them. He looked as if she'd ripped him into jagged pieces like a glass shattering on concrete.

"I know." He inhaled a ragged breath and combed tense fingers through his hair. "But you got your revenge. You broke mine."

# Nine

Jolie balled up her fist, ready to slug Cord. How dare he make this all about him? He'd left her, shredded her heart and her self-esteem. Walked off laughing at her for being the foolish girl she was. She thought back over the things he'd revealed tonight—whether he meant to or not.

Like air hissing out of a tiny hole in a balloon, her anger leaked away.

She sat up and folded her legs tailor-style. Rubbing eyes still swollen from her crying jag, she really hoped she had no more tears left. Things were headed into unmapped emotional territory tonight. Her own feelings were hot and raw, and she desperately wanted to put off this inevitable conversation. But she'd been waiting a lot of years.

"Why, Cord?"

His shoulders hunched as he scrubbed at his face with the heels of his hands. "Short answer? My old man. He hates J. Rand. Hell, Cyrus hates just about everyone he's ever come in contact with."

His explanation felt too much like an excuse, and Jolie wasn't going to let him get by with it. "What's the long answer?"

Cord pushed off the lounger and paced toward the pool. He stood at the edge, hands shoved into his hip pockets. Jolie shivered, cool night air invading the space he'd vacated. She grabbed the chenille wrap draped nearby and tossed it around her shoulders.

"Jolie, all I ever wanted was you. That day in high school, standing there joking with Chance, Cooper and Boone? I looked up. Saw you. And damn if my world didn't come to a screeching halt." He glanced over his shoulder, saw what she'd done and moved to put another log in the fire pit. He poked until the log caught. "Then Boone told me who you were." One shoulder lifted in an apologetic shrug. "Your father's name was pretty much a nightly cussword at the Barron family dinner table. I was seventeen and our old man ruled the roost with an iron fist."

Jolie considered what she knew of Cyrus Barron but didn't speak.

"You were…beautiful. And I wanted you like I've never wanted anything in my life."

"Then why did you date so many girls?"

"I couldn't have you." He shrugged both shoulders. "That simple and that complicated. No one else compared to you. I know. I think I dated every girl in the school before I graduated. And then I started over in college. But you weren't there where I could see you every day. Where I could—" He snapped his mouth shut.

"Where you could what, Cord?" Her voice sounded soft to her own ears but somehow he heard her.

"We used to have a mimosa tree in the backyard of the house in Nichols Hills. I'd sit under that thing in the spring." He half turned away from her and stared out across the ranch. "I took a chain saw to it in college."

"I…I don't understand."

"Mimosa, Jolie. You smell like mimosa."

She barely resisted the urge to sniff her skin as the implications became apparent. "But we were dating. We were together all the time. And it was good between us. I need to know, Cord. Why did you break up with me?"

"Why did you fall into my lap at that frat party to begin with?"

"I asked you first."

"I've been answering your questions, Jolie. I think it's time you answered some of mine. Why?"

Jolie tugged the wrap tighter and considered what to say. "Easy answer? I was drunk and I had a crush on you. Had since that day in high school."

"And the hard answer?"

"Forbidden fruit." A half smile tugged the corner of her mouth. "While not a nightly topic, your family made it into conversations at my house, too." She laughed, but the sound was dry and brittle. "You know, if you'd *been* the Cord Barron everyone told me you were, I think that one night would have been the end of it. If you'd taken me to bed and said goodbye in the morning, that would have gotten you out of my system. But, oh, no. You couldn't do that. You had to be all noble and stuff. You took me back to the sorority house. You held my hair while I puked my guts up. You tucked me into bed, kissed me on the forehead and left." Tears sprang up behind her closed eyelids. "Damn you, Cord. Why couldn't you have been a jerk?"

The cushion beside her dipped, and before she could protest, Cord's arms wrapped her in their strength. He lay down and pulled her with him, cuddling her so that her head rested on his shoulder. She sniffled, but determined to continue, she added, "You made me fall in love with you and then you just…left. 'It's over,' you said. No explanation. Those two words and then you walked out the door."

"I spent the next week dead drunk." His voice grated the words.

"Why, Cord?"

"I told you, my old man. He…ah, hell, Jolie. He found out. About us. I still don't know how."

Something twisted deep inside her as Cord's words confirmed her suspicions. She curled her fingers into the placket of his shirt. "Tell me."

"He called me into his office. Made me stand there while he canted back in that big ole leather desk chair of his, hands folded across his ribs. There was a cigar burning in the ashtray and he wouldn't look at me." He gulped a couple of breaths. "When he finally looked at me…I… Dammit, Jolie, I wished he'd gotten out of his chair and decked me. It would have hurt a whole lot less than the look he gave me."

Her eyes burned and she closed them, hoping to hide the moisture threatening to spill. *No more tears*, she commanded her heart.

"I'd disappointed him, he told me. Worst son ever. All the typical BS he trots out. Every last one of us has had that manure thrown our way. But this time…this time was different. I can't say why, but it was."

Jolie rubbed her cheek against his chest, partly to smear away the tears but partly to see his expression. Cord's eyes were open, but he was staring at some spot in the redwood-planked roof above them. One hand rubbed back and forth along the curve of her hip, but she didn't think Cord was even aware of the caress. His face looked drawn and tense.

"He took me down a couple of floors, showed me the office for the CEO of BarEx. Then he said, 'Your name should be on that door, but it won't be now. You see her again, I'll strip you of your name, of your inheritance, of everything you ever dreamed of.'" Cord's voice broke on the word *dreamed*.

She stretched so she could place a gentle kiss on the point of his chin.

"I figured I could work to finish school. In the oil patch. And then go to work for just about anybody. But, oh, no. He had it all figured out. Promised I'd never work for any oil company. If I couldn't work, I couldn't have my dream."

Cord kissed the top of her head and settled her just a little bit closer with a gentle squeeze of his arm. His hand covered hers on his chest and pried her fingers from his shirt so he could lace his fingers through them. "I wanted to marry you and have a family. But I couldn't do that without a job. Or so I thought. I was young and dumb and a coward."

She opened her mouth to say that her dad would have hired him, but the words didn't come out. She thought about it. They'd been sneaking around and she had never lied to her father—until Cord. At the time, there'd been a downturn in the oil and gas business. Prices were down, the government was tightening regulations, leases were hard to come by. There would have been no way her father would hire the son of his biggest rival.

"So I ran. The night I broke up with you, Cooper drove me to the nearest liquor store and I spent about five hundred bucks. I skipped classes for a week. Coop and Chance took turns babysitting. They made sure I didn't do something stupid."

"I hated you."

"Yeah, I figured." He inhaled, held it and then exhaled slowly. "I sort of hated myself."

Neither of them spoke, and the night thickened around them. A log in the fire pit popped. Off in the distance, a mockingbird trilled a lonely warble. He spread the chenille throw out so it covered both of them.

"If you start snoring, I'm leaving."

"I don't snore, Jolie, but you do."

"Do not!" She thumped his chest with their entwined fists for emphasis.

"And you make these little mewling noises. Like a kitten." He continued to tease her.

"Liar."

"Truth."

"How would you remember that?"

"I remember everything, Jolie." His voice held no hint of teasing.

"Like what?"

"Like the way you look when you wake up. All doe eyed with your hair mussed. Like that giggle-snort thing you do when something hits your funny bone. Like the way you watch me, your eyelids half lowered, when I'm getting ready to kiss you."

"Do not."

"I'll prove it."

He pressed up from the lounge back, cradling her across his chest. She wanted to wipe the smirk off his face until he bent his head. Darn if he wasn't right—her lids drooped and she watched him from beneath her lashes. His lips touched hers and her eyes closed all on their own. She didn't fight. Her body was way past the fight-or-flight point. It was all about the shut-up-and-kiss now.

Jolie parted her lips, inviting Cord to deepen the kiss. He did. His fingers threaded in her hair and he angled her head so he could assault her mouth with heat and need. His. Hers. It no longer mattered. Her tongue danced with his, eliciting a soft groan from him. His arousal was impossible to ignore as she shifted her hips. Her core tightened, throbbing with the thought of having Cord buried there. She wanted him now as much as she ever had.

Her breasts ached, and she wished that he'd touch her there, that he'd run his thumbs over their peaks. She arched and rubbed against his chest, and thank goodness, Cord spoke her body language fluently. The hand in her hair dropped to press between her shoulder blades while his other hand cupped a breast. Air hissed from her lungs in a satisfied sigh. Her thighs tensed and she pressed her knees together as her center throbbed with need.

Then he broke the kiss. And set her away from him.

"What the—?"

"I'm sorry." Cord swung his legs off the lounger and his fists curled up on his thighs.

"Sorry? I don't understand you, Cord. What are you sorry for now?"

"For…this." He refused to look at her. "I didn't mean to…seduce you."

"Seduce? Me? Seriously?" Her burst of laughter came out more like a snort. "I think it was mutual, dude."

"No."

"I beg your pardon? I seem to remember kissing you just as hard as you were kissing me." She added, "Among other things," in an undertone.

"This isn't right, Jolie."

"What?" Totally confused, she couldn't decide if she was angry, amused or embarrassed.

"I want you. God knows I've always wanted you. But not like this."

"Uh...what does that mean?" She leaned forward and to the side so she could see part of his face. What was he up to? Was this some game he was playing?

"I just think jumping into—" With one hand, he made a vague waving gesture between them. "I want to take it slow. Do it right this time." Now he turned to face her, and the stark need on his face felt like a punch to her stomach.

"So what now?" Her voice quavered, and she prayed Cord didn't pick up on it.

"Not sure, sunshine." He cupped her cheek and leaned in to brush a gentle kiss across her lips. "I need to learn how to be a father. To CJ. We need to be friends. Not just—" He did that vague wave again.

Jolie studied his face. So many emotions congregated there she couldn't read them all.

"What do you want?"

Cord looked away, stood and put distance between them as he stared out over the pool. "Time with CJ. Well, more time with CJ. And maybe time together. As a...well, the three of us. As...friends."

He wouldn't look her in the eye, and she was positive he was planning something. "I don't trust you, Cord."

A flash of anger consumed his expression for a moment before he controlled it. "That goes both ways, Jolie."

His voice chipped at her walls like a sharp chisel. She

opened her mouth to retort, and then snapped her jaw shut. Yeah, okay. He had every right not to trust her. She'd kept the biggest secret of their lives from him.

"You're right. I'm sorry." She drew her knees up to her chest and hugged them. "This is like doing the two-step through a minefield."

"You got that right." He stepped closer, but stopped just out of her reach. "Look, can we agree that we each hurt the other? Deeply. I really do want to move forward, Jolie. I can't undo the past. I screwed up, okay? I know that. But all the apologies in the world won't change a damned thing. Here's what I want. I want the chance to make it right. To fix things."

That was the very core of Cord. He was a fixer. The classic middle child. He negotiated. Smoothed over hurt feelings. Compromised. She'd loved that about him, once upon a time. She'd watched him protect the twins and Chance from their father, but she'd also watched him surrender to Cyrus's demands. She didn't want to admit that he hadn't really changed all that much. Not in the fundamental things—an odd combination of protector and defeatist.

Though she wasn't sure she was ready to trust him, she admitted he still had way too much boyish charm to be healthy, and he oozed his way through her defenses no matter what she did to thwart him. The fact her panties were damp testified to that.

"You're insidious."

His bark of laughter echoed through the covered patio. "Don't forget incorrigible."

"You're definitely that, too. You just won't stop, and then you slime your way back into my life."

"Well, that certainly paints me in an attractive light."

"And you know what else? You're right. Sleeping with you would be a horrible idea."

He looked amused now.

"Horrible, huh?" He glanced at her chest. She knew her traitorous nipples were peaked and obvious.

Folding her arms across her chest in self-defense, she nodded emphatically. "Yes. Horrible. I momentarily lost my mind. I swear you're like one of those rainforest frogs with the poison skin. You kiss me and I lose all sense."

"I figure that's a good thing, sunshine."

Her previous thoughts returned, swamping her with misgiving. "Don't, Cord. I'm…I'm not ready for this."

"Not ready for what?" He looked cautious now.

She waved her hand between them. "This. Us. You in CJ's life. I don't trust your father, Cord. I don't trust that you'll—"

"That I'll what, Jolie?"

Now he looked angry, but she wasn't ready to reveal her thoughts, to tell him that she didn't trust him to choose her and CJ this time. She scrambled off the lounger and headed toward the door. "I'm going home."

His laughter surrounded her, so rich and warm it tasted like s'mores on her tongue, and she wavered for a moment.

"Are you sure I can't convince you to stay for the sleepover?"

"I am *not* sleeping with you, Cordell Barron. Not tonight. Not ever."

# Ten

Cord reread the report. Despite any conspiracy theories to the contrary, the stuff happening on the drilling rig—including his and Cooper's injuries—appeared to be just unrelated accidents. Despite this information from Cash's investigator, Cord wasn't completely convinced. He couldn't forget how J. Rand had warned him away from Jolie at first, even though they'd declared a truce of sorts in the talk they'd had later at the ranch. And while Jolie's father wasn't nearly as cutthroat as his own, Cord couldn't completely shake the idea that the problems his company was facing were tied in somehow with Jolie's return.

He set the folder aside and stared at the drilling run reports on his desk. Though Cooper wasn't fully back on the job yet, Cord had been back in the office for about a week. But the view from his office window lured him away from work more often than not. The medical complex on the hill across town held too many memories. Bad—the pain of recovery and rehabilitation. And good—the serenity of waking up to find Jolie hovering at his bedside.

His phone buzzed and his assistant's voice informed him that Cyrus was on the line and insistent. With a grimace, he stabbed the blinking light.

"I'm busy."

"So am I. Did you really think you could hide it from me?"

Cord did *not* want to have this conversation. "Hide what?"

"Your bastard."

Anger and adrenaline surged through him, making him reckless. "You mean my *son*?"

"Not until you file the paperwork, Cordell. Do it. Now. Or I will."

The old man hung up before Cord could retort. His day had just turned into a big whole heaping pile of dog crap.

Business. He had to focus on BarEx. His private life was screwed at the moment even though he'd managed to work out a schedule of sorts with Jolie, giving him time with CJ—but not time with her. He was still kicking himself for calling a halt to their lovemaking that night. And now his old man knew about CJ. "You are all kinds of a fool, son," he muttered.

"So what else is new?"

He whipped around, surprised he hadn't heard the door open. "Damn, Chance. Give me a heart attack next time."

His brother laughed and dropped into a guest chair, legs stretched toward Cord's desk, booted feet crossed at the ankle as he made himself at home. "Glad to see you back."

"And that's reason enough to sneak up on me?"

"Nope. I'm here at Cassie's behest."

"And?"

"She's thinking about Thanksgiving."

"Thanksgiving." Cord repeated the word, his thoughts still on the conversation he'd just had with Cyrus—a conversation he wasn't ready to share with Chance.

"Yeah. I know. It's September and state fair time but she's already planning for the holidays."

The Great State Fair of Oklahoma. All sorts of possibilities ran through his head. Cord grinned and mentally rubbed his hands together. Perfect. He'd call Jolie, invite her and CJ. He'd run out of time. He had to convince Jolie they belonged together.

"Earth to Cord."

"Wha—? Oh. Tell Cassie whatever."

"I see the wheels turning, bro. What are you up to?"

"Nothing to do with Cassie, I assure you."

Chance rolled his eyes and laughed. "Yeah, I figured that. Let's firm up Thanksgiving, and then you can fill me in on whatever nefarious plan you're cooking up. Cassie wants to do a big family dinner at the ranch."

"Yours or ours?"

"The Crown B. We'll be lucky if our house is ready by Christmas."

Chance and Cassie were building a new home on the Crazy M, the ranch she'd inherited and saved from the old man's machinations. "Why the hell would Cassie want to do it at the B?"

"I keep asking her that and she just rolls her eyes." Chance shrugged. "I think it has to do with the fact that we consider the ranch home. Cass is all about family and home now."

"What about her and the old man?"

Chance leaned his head back and laughed. "My wife is fearless, and I quote, 'Let that sorry old bastard do his worst. I'm not afraid of him. The ranch is your family's home and that's what Thanksgiving is all about.'"

"Well, all righty, then. Cass scares me sometimes, bro."

"Yeah, you and me both. But I don't foresee any problems unless she and Miz Beth fight over the kitchen."

"Does the old man know about this crazy plan of hers?"

"Yeah, about that? I don't think so. Cass isn't worried. And frankly? Watching my wife tear into our father is worth the price of admission." Chance's gaze shifted so he was no longer looking directly at Cord.

He waited, knowing there was more to come. "What?"

Chance's smile disappeared. "She wants to invite CJ. And Jolie."

"Ah. That could be a problem if it's a *real* family event. If the old man is around—" Cord snapped his jaw shut and inhaled several times. "That would *not* be a good idea."

His hand dropped on top of the file and he drummed his fingers on it as he stared at his brother. "Have you seen the notes from the investigation Cash ran on the accident?"

"Changing the subject, big bro?"

Cord lifted one shoulder in a negligent shrug. He wasn't quite ready to get personal yet. He needed to work, focus on what he did best—find oil and natural gas, tap it and get it to a Barron refinery. "Business, Chance."

"I got a copy of the report. What about the tool pusher? Is he sloppy?"

"I don't buy it. Cooper has complete faith in the man. And Cash's guy couldn't find any signs of sabotage."

"I hear a *but* in there, Cord."

"Just seems a bit coincidental. J. Rand warns me away from Jolie, and then the well on the lease we outbid him on suddenly develops problems? I don't believe in coincidences."

"What's the pusher's safety record?"

Cord tapped the folder again. "Impeccable." He swiveled in his chair and stared at the hospital complex on the hill. He heard Chance shift in his chair and the sounds of rustling paper. "Thanksgiving isn't the only reason you came. What's up?"

"Did you look over the proposal on the Houston refinery?"

He swiveled back around and resisted the urge to roll his eyes. "Yes. And the old man seems to have covered all the bases despite my lack of input." Something in his brother's expression made him lean closer. "What? There's something in the deal you don't like?"

"Cyrus wants to set up a shell corporation for the refinery."

"For tax purposes?"

"Ostensibly."

"I hear a *but* in there, too, bro."

"He wants the shell separate from the family trust."

Cord considered the implications, and then rubbed his forehead to smooth away the furrows that thinking created. "He wants control of it. Just him."

"That's my thought." Chance shifted uncomfortably. "You're still CEO, Cord. The sale doesn't go through without your signature, despite what the old man says."

Cord ran his fingers through his hair, glad it was finally growing out from where it had been cut in the hospital. "We need the refinery, Chance. I'll go through the file, make some calls. Anything else?"

Chance pushed to his feet and turned toward the door. He hesitated and glanced over his shoulder. "Maybe the problems are a little closer to home, Cord. The old man is still pissed that I outsmarted him on the family trust."

Or it was a way to control Cord. Again. Chance left, shutting the door behind him, leaving Cord with far too much to think about.

Jolie slipped her cell phone into her pocket as Liza, the on-duty flight nurse, pulled up a chair and got comfortable by propping her feet on Jolie's desk. "You look as if you just bit into a lemon. Man trouble?"

Trying her best not to sigh, Jolie shook her head. "No. Yes... Sort of."

Her friend laughed. "Well, which is it?"

"It's Cord." As if that explained everything. To Jolie, it did.

"Honey, he's good-looking, employed, rich and he dotes on your kid. I don't see this as trouble."

"You'd be surprised," Jolie muttered darkly. "He just called asking to take CJ and me to the state fair."

"Wait. The dude is a Barron. He could fly you to freaking Paris for dinner and he wants to take you to the state freaking fair? Hon, you *do* have man trouble!"

Liza's expression was so comical, Jolie had to laugh.

"No, he called to see if he could take CJ, and then included me in the invitation."

"Wait. Asking you was an afterthought? What's wrong with the guy?"

"Liza, you do realize that Cord is CJ's father, right? We...have a history."

The nurse's boots hit the floor with a thud as she came straight up in her chair. "Wait, what? Cordell Barron is your baby daddy? Holy cannoli, woman! That is some history."

"I don't exactly tell everyone."

"I'm not everyone. I'm like your new best friend. I should know these things. But more important, at least to me, is there more like him at home? 'Oh, wait, why, yes, Liza, my new best friend in the whole wide world, there *are* three more Barrons at home and I'd love to fix you up on a double date.'"

Jolie snorted and the swig of coffee she'd just taken exited her nose. Coughing and laughing, she mopped up the mess while she caught her breath. When she could speak again, she shook a finger at Liza. "Trust me. You do not want to be anywhere near the Barron brothers."

"Trust me, yes, I do! Rich, handsome and single. What's not to love?" Liza winked and nudged Jolie's chair with her foot. "So talk to me, woman."

"There's not much to talk about. Cord and I used to date. Then we didn't. Then we sort of had a drive-by date and... nine months later, CJ popped out." She refused to look directly at Liza, preferring to straighten a desk already so neat it would make an OCD sufferer proud.

Liza gave her the stink eye and Jolie could picture the wheels turning in the other woman's head. She knew the moment Liza figured it out. "Oh. Em. Gee, Jolie. He didn't know. Damn, girl. Why would you not tell him?"

Jolie wished the heat flooding her cheeks would go away. Liza had her pegged dead to rights. "That's a really long story—one far too reminiscent of Romeo and Juliet to make me comfortable. Plus, there was that whole we'd-broken-up thing. And it was just a one-night stand. The thing is, he knows now and wants to make up for lost time."

"Again, this is a problem *why*?" Liza stared so long and hard, Jolie had to look away first. "You still care about him. Honey, this isn't a problem. Why not go out with him? See if the sparks are still there."

"Sparks? It's more like a forest fire." Jolie ripped the alligator clip from her hair and combed her fingers through the tangled mass before twisting it back up and reattaching the clip. "The man drives me crazy."

"So go with him and CJ to the fair. Drive *him* crazy for a change."

Liza's suggestion made sense, but for one thing. He'd asked to take CJ, and then included her as an afterthought. Besides, her ego still stung that he'd stopped short of making love to her when she'd all but thrown herself at him.

"I'll see." Not much of an answer, but it was the only one she currently had.

Cord stared at his son as CJ danced impatiently in front of him. The kid had insisted on going on every ride he was tall enough for, and dragged Cord along because he didn't want to ride alone. He'd held out hope that Jolie would change her mind at the last minute and come with them but she'd insisted he and CJ needed bonding time—just the two of them.

Cord had finally steered CJ away from the midway, but then the kid grazed his way down the food row. Deep-fried cupcakes. Deep-fried watermelon. Funnel cakes. Hot dogs—deep-fried with chili. Cotton candy. Fresh-squeezed lemonade. A suicide snow cone.

"Dang, bubba. Where are you puttin' it all?"

"Uh-oh. Is dang a swear jar word?"

"Nope. *Dang* is safe. But seriously, CJ. Haven't you had enough to eat?"

"Nuh-uh. One more, Daddy. 'Kay?" CJ tugged him down the row of food-vendor trailers. He stopped in front of a place advertising deep-fried strawberry shortcakes. "Please, Dad? I want one. I promise I won't eat anything else. Please? Please, please, please."

Hiding his grimace, Cord stepped to the window and ordered. When the food arrived, he walked CJ over to a picnic table and made the boy sit before putting the treat and a handful of napkins in front of him.

"Want a bite, Daddy?"

"Ah…no." Cord did his best not to look askance at the glob on CJ's spoon. He liked deep-fried food as much as the next red-blooded American male but some things were just *not* meant to be dipped in batter and fried.

CJ inhaled his dessert, declared he was thirsty and pouted briefly when Cord insisted he drink a bottle of water.

By the time CJ was done, the midway was shutting down. The little boy was dead on his feet as they walked toward the parking lot. Halfway there, Cord picked him up and carried him. Despite walking all over the fair, Cord felt remarkably fit.

CJ was all but asleep by the time they reached Cord's sleek little sports car. He buckled his son into his car seat, and a few minutes later, they were headed across town to Cord's condo in Bricktown.

He was happy to be home again. Once his physical therapist had cleared him and he'd started back to work, the commute from the ranch was a pain—not to mention he wanted his own space. Of course, he'd worked his butt off in PT to get out of the damn wheelchair and then to get rid of the walker.

Waking up when Cord unbuckled him, CJ groaned. "I want Mommy," he whined. "My tummy hurts."

Cord picked up the boy in a reverse piggyback across

his chest. "I'll call her as soon as we get upstairs, bubba. Just hang in—"

Something hot and wet splattered down Cord's back. He barely set CJ down before the next wave of vomiting hit. He went to grab his cell phone, but stopped when he realized the thing was in his hip pocket—the pocket covered with deep-fried something.

Thankfully, he had a private entrance on the ground floor. He got CJ inside, undressed him and laid him down on the couch with an ice pack, a wet washcloth and a plastic bucket.

Stripping out of his clothes with the utmost care, Cord donned a pair of rubber gloves he found in the supply closet and fished the important stuff out of his pockets. Luckily, his phone didn't seem any worse for the wear. He dialed Jolie's number just as CJ called for him. He got back to the living room barely in time to hold the bucket.

"Cord?" Jolie's voice echoed from the other end of the line.

He wiped CJ's mouth and snagged his phone. "Jolie? Thank God. Can you come over?"

"What's—?"

"Is that Mommy? I want Mommy." CJ raised his voice. "Mommy? My tummy hurts and I upchucked."

"Cord, what in the world is going on?"

"We're at my condo. Can you come? I'd come to you but... Hold on."

After he dealt with another round of sickness, he grabbed the phone again. "CJ's—"

"I can hear, Cord. I'm on my way."

By the time the doorbell rang fifteen minutes later, CJ had been able to hold down a few sips of ginger ale and was dozing on the couch. Cord realized he was wearing nothing but his socks and boxers only after he opened the door to Jolie's arched eyebrow.

"Let me guess, you haven't done laundry and you had nothing else to wear."

"Well…" Cord scratched his chest. "Actually, I threw the clothes we were wearing in the washer but I haven't started the cycle yet. I've been a little busy."

"I can imagine." Jolie stared at his chest—was that a look of hunger in her eyes? At his suggestive chuckle, she dragged her gaze back to his face. "How is he?"

"Better, I think. He had some ginger ale and is asleep."

"See, you can handle it. Not sure why I'm here."

"Because he wanted you?" There was no rancor in his voice. He remembered being sick as a kid and wanting his mom—his real one or Helen, the second Mrs. Barron. Too bad neither of them had survived to see the Barron boys grow up.

He offered what he hoped was a winning smile. "C'mon in. I'll go grab some jeans."

Cord insisted Jolie precede him. No sense letting her see just how much she affected him—which was all too evident by the activity in his boxers.

He grabbed a clean pair of jeans from the dryer, started the washer and headed back to the living room.

"Can I get you something to—?"

"Rule number one, Cord."

He stopped dead in his tracks as she held up one finger. Remaining silent, he simply arched a brow.

"Little boys do not need to eat everything in sight."

"Yeah, I sorta figured that out."

"Rule number two." She added a second finger. "Little boys will beg to eat everything in sight. Refer back to rule number one." The way she enunciated the last three words made Cord want to laugh.

He worked on his expression so he could appear chagrined rather than amused. Hoping boyish charm would help, he said, "I'm sorry, Jolie. This is all sort of new to me, y'know?"

Her face clouded up and he once again held up his hands, palm out, in hopes of placating her. "Whoa, sunshine. I was simply stating a fact, not casting blame. Okay?"

Jolie huffed out a breath that ruffled her bangs and nodded. "Okay."

He tried another dose of charm by way of a crooked grin as he pressed his suit. "And you know, we could have avoided this whole situation if you'd just come with us."

She glared at him but he caught the twinkle in her eye. "Oh, so this is *my* fault?"

"Why don't I get you something to drink while we figure out who's at fault?"

Jolie followed him into the kitchen. "Don't think for one minute that your charm will get you out of this one, Cord Barron." She narrowed her gaze and all but shook her finger at him.

"Ah, so you admit I'm charming." He flashed another grin and waggled his brows at her before ducking behind the refrigerator door. Cord bit back his laughter at her exasperated huff. He emerged with a pitcher of tea and fixed her a tall glass with ice from the freezer door. As he watched her take a sip, the tightness in his chest eased—and the tightness farther south ramped up a little. He'd gotten the sweetness in the tea right, judging by the look on her face, but seeing her swallow put all sorts of thoughts in his head, thoughts he throttled given their son slept on the couch in the next room.

He offered her a chair at the kitchen table, sitting once she'd settled. "I'm sorry, sunshine. I told you I need to learn to be a dad. Those self-help books don't help at all."

She choked back a quick laugh, but her gaze softened as she regarded him. Progress. "I should have warned you but there's no better teacher than experience."

Unable to resist the urge, he touched the back of her hand, and then ran his fingertip up her arm. Goose bumps.

Yeah, he liked that he could still affect her like that. "Thanks for coming when I called."

"You're welcome. I suppose I should get him home."

"Do you have to go?"

She gazed at him and he didn't flinch. There'd been too much secrecy between them. He wanted everything out in the open. Ever since their talk at the ranch, when he'd barely stopped from making love to her, he'd been wearing down her defenses. He wanted her in the worst way, but he wanted to do it right this time. He wanted to build a real relationship—one based on trust and friendship as well as the heat they generated. Chemistry made for great sex, but it took more to make a relationship. And he wanted a relationship with Jolie, one beyond the fact she was the mother of his child. The time for hesitation was over.

"Go out with me, Jolie."

"What?"

"Go out with me. A date. Dinner."

"I don't think that's a good idea."

"I think it's an excellent idea. I'm not ashamed of CJ, Jolie. Or you."

"What about your father?"

"Let me worry about Cyrus. Frankly, I'm more worried about yours."

"Dad?" Confusion filtered into her expression. "Why would you worry about Dad?"

"He warned me away from you. Last summer."

"It obviously didn't work."

"Nope. It sure didn't. So? Dinner?"

# Eleven

Mrs. Corcoran, the nanny, answered the door, and Cord did his best not to fidget under her intense gaze. A week had passed since the state fair fiasco, but from the way the woman glared, Jolie had told her all about it. As she continued to stare, he brushed past her and surreptitiously checked his fly to make sure it was zipped.

"Daddy!" CJ flew at him, and Cord braced for his son's leap into his arms. His ribs only pulled a little.

"Hey, bubba!"

"Mommy'll be down in a minute. She's gettin' pretty. Where you gonna take her? How come I can't go? When will you—?"

"Whoa, CJ. One question at a time. I'm taking your mom out to dinner at a really fancy restaurant. You can't go because this is a grown-up date and you don't like escargot."

"Easy car go? What's that?"

"*Escargot* is the French word for snails."

"Eww. You're gonna eat snails?"

"Nope. Not me, but your mom likes the little suckers."

"I do like them." Jolie had crept up behind them, and she gave CJ a teasing pinch on his side, making the little boy giggle as he arched away from her.

"Wow. You look…beautiful."

"Gee, thanks, Cord. Don't sound so surprised."

He couldn't tell from Jolie's wry expression if she was upset, which would be weird because she did look beautiful. Something about her tone of voice finally clicked the lightbulb on. "Oh. Oh! No, no. I didn't mean it like that. I'm not surprised, I'm… Wow." He winked at CJ. "Bubba, you have the most beautiful mom in the entire world and I'm the lucky man who gets to take her out to dinner tonight." He set the boy down and turned to Mrs. Corcoran. "We won't be out too late."

"CJ and I will be just fine. Go have a good time."

The restaurant atop the Founders Tower had been known by many different names during its years of operation. Like the famous Space Needle in Seattle, the outer rim of the restaurant slowly spun around the central tower, offering up the full vista of Oklahoma City. The center held the reception area, elevators, bar, dance floor and kitchens.

As they headed to the top floor, people in the crowded elevator remained silent. Canned music filtered through a tinny speaker as everyone stared straight ahead. Jolie hated elevators, not that she was claustrophobic or anything. She leaned closer to Cord, and when he took her hand, she cut her eyes to gauge his expression. He, too, was staring straight ahead, but the dimple on his right cheek was peeking out at her.

His profile—heck, his whole face—never failed to make her heart skip a beat. All the Barron boys had been blessed, and they each bore the distinctive stamp of their DNA, as evidenced by Cassie Barron's immediately recognizing CJ as being one of the clan. They were handsome, but Cord had something more. Laugh lines feathered around golden-brown eyes that glinted with mischief. Sculpted cheekbones, jaw and nose. The man could pose for a Greek statue.

While his features would make any girl look twice, it had always been his personality that kept Jolie's interest. He was funny, wise and ornery—often at the same time.

He squeezed her hand and pulled it up to his mouth.

After placing a soft kiss on the back of her hand, he glanced down and winked.

If she didn't stay on guard, Cord could steamroll right over her emotions. *And what's wrong with that?* She wanted to swat the annoying inner voice whispering in her ear every time the subject of Cord came up.

The elevator doors slid open and the passengers surged forward. Cord held back until the crowd cleared out, and then escorted Jolie off. The maître d's gaze landed on them almost immediately.

"Mr. Barron. Good evening, sir. Right this way. Your table is ready."

Those waiting to be seated parted like the Red Sea, but as the crowd closed back in behind her, Jolie heard the whispers start. While some of those murmurs were from diners upset that she and Cord were seated immediately, others were about Cord. Stories on the Barrons often appeared in the media.

The maître d' paused on the edge of the dance floor, waiting as tables slowly passed by. A moment later, their table arrived, and he cautioned them to be careful as they stepped onto the revolving section.

Once they were seated, Cord ordered champagne before opening his menu and commenting, "They've completely renovated the restaurant and updated the mechanics so this part rotates again."

"I remember coming here with Dad when I was a little girl."

They reminisced over memories of their childhoods and how many near misses they'd had in meeting before that fateful day in high school. Jolie fought to smother her laughter as Cord inhaled his steak. She managed to get through her lobster without wearing it. The table they shared was narrow, and every time she shifted in her very comfortable chair, her foot or leg or knee grazed Cord's. He pretended to ignore the contact just as she did—*pretend* being the operative word. Each touch revved up her heart rate and reminded her of the feel of his body pressed against hers.

She'd look up at odd moments to catch him watching her, something hot and sexy in his gaze, as if she was every bit as delicious as that steak as he was savoring. Jolie would get fascinated by his mouth, his lips, and she really wanted to taste them.

"Are you finished, Jolie?"

She jerked her gaze to his eyes—the ones twinkling even as his mouth curved up in that irritating grin of his. The waiter stood patiently, holding Cord's plate.

"Oh. Yes. I am. Thank you."

The man whisked her plate away and handed both sets of dishes off to a hovering busboy. "Will you be enjoying dessert tonight?"

Jolie knew what she'd like to have for dessert, and by the way Cord was looking at her, he was imagining her covered in chocolate and whipped cream. Just to tease him, she ordered cheesecake.

While they waited for dessert, Cord stood, took her hand and walked her onto the dance floor. A small combo was playing live music, and he took her into his arms for a slow dance. His cologne, something brisk and citrusy, caused her to inhale deeply. The music changed, and without missing a beat, Cord led her in a passable samba.

"I didn't know you could dance."

"Mmm. There's a lot of things you don't know about me. Personally, I'd rather be doing a two-step at Toby Keith's, but this'll do for now." His lips brushed across her forehead a moment before he stopped dancing and escorted her back to their table for dessert.

As she spooned the rich caramel cheesecake into her mouth, Jolie couldn't decide which was more decadent— the creamy treat or the man sitting across from her watching through hooded lids as she took each bite.

She resisted scraping the plate to get the last bit before she finished the ice wine Cord had ordered with dessert. He looked as if he wanted to lick her the same way she'd been licking her spoon. Blushing, she watched him from the relative safety of a tilted glance.

"So what's next on the menu?" she asked.

His dimple played peekaboo with the upturned corner of his mouth, and Jolie suddenly realized why heroines in romance novels swooned.

"What if I said *you*?"

She wanted to fan her face. And other places, warmer and damper. For a brief instant, Jolie considered knocking a glass of ice water into her lap. With her luck, steam would rise and Cord would know exactly what she was thinking. She knew better than to answer. Any reply would come out a squeak.

His gaze heated and focused on her mouth. Raking her teeth across her bottom lip, she was gratified to see his irises dilate. He was as turned on as she was. But this was their first official, grown-up date. Falling into bed with him—no matter how badly she wanted to do just that— would set a dangerous precedent for the rest of their relationship. However things worked out between them.

"C'mon." He pushed back from the table, stood and held out his hand to her.

Placing her hand in his was a leap of faith on her part. He pulled her to her feet, tucked her hand into the crook of his elbow and guided her across the dance floor toward the exit. He said nothing in the elevator, nothing as they waited for the valet to return with Cord's car. He remained silent as he handed her into the passenger seat and settled behind the wheel. Then they were off. Problem was she had no clue where they were headed and Cord still wasn't talking.

He passed the exit that would take her home, which made sense once she thought it over. CJ was at home. And Mrs. Corcoran. She didn't want an audience. When he headed into the heart of Bricktown, she pressed her knees together. His condo. Except he passed the street where it was located. A few minutes later, he pulled up in front of the newest club in the downtown entertainment district.

A valet opened her door and she slid out, a question on her lips as Cord came around the back of the car to meet her.

"I hope you don't mind mixing a little business with our pleasure."

Jolie quirked a brow. "I'm not sure I understand."

"Live band. Chase asked me to give them a look."

"Oh. Is he still in Vegas?"

"No. He's in Nashville at the moment. He's expanding, taking Barron Entertainment into the music business. Chance is tone-deaf and only listens to country music. Cash is out of town. That means I drew the short straw."

Before she could question him further, two muscular men waved them past the waiting line and opened the front doors. A wave of sound crashed over her as she entered. She would have turned around and run if Cord's hand hadn't landed on the small of her back, urging her forward.

He found an empty table with tall stools near the bar. A harried waitress paused long enough for Cord to whisper in her ear. The next thing he did surprised Jolie. He handed her a set of earplugs. She stared at the orange lumps in the palm of his hand, and then glanced up. He grinned and winked as he fitted a second set into his own ears with his other hand.

After she'd stuffed the spongy plugs in, the noise level dropped to almost acceptable levels. The waitress returned with a scotch on the rocks for Cord and a frozen margarita, extra salt, for Jolie. The man never forgot a thing. She needed to remember that.

The musicians provided a driving beat and Cord offered her a dance. When they returned to the table, a group of rowdy men had taken up residence at the next table. The two facing her looked her up and down, their interest obvious.

"Will you look at that? That is one hot-damn bitchin' woman, fellas."

The other two turned to look. One grabbed his crotch and rubbed. "I'd sure like to nail me some of that."

Despite the loud music and earplugs, their obnoxious comments filtered across her consciousness. Cord stiffened beside her. He hadn't missed the lewd suggestions, either. All four men were obviously inebriated. And Cord wasn't 100 percent recovered from his injuries, despite his assurances to the contrary. Four against one weren't good odds on his best day. She put her hand on his arm as he stood up.

"Let it go. They're drunk jerks."

He ignored her and she sighed. Testosterone drained a man's brain of all common sense. Cord kissed her cheek, but it felt too much like a pat on the head for comfort. *Here*, he seemed to say with the gesture. *Big bad caveman will take care of his little woman.*

She couldn't hear what he said to the men, but the biggest guy in the group jumped up, knocking his stool over. In the blink of an eye, he was swinging on Cord, who ducked under the blow and came up with a fist to the guy's gut. The other three jumped into the fray. Fists and elbows flew—the four jerks landing blows on each other as often as they managed to punch Cord. By the time the muscular bouncers arrived, Cord had gotten more than a few licks in, to good effect. Two of the men were on the floor unconscious and Cord was holding his own with the other two. The bouncers separated the men, and with the help of a couple of additional security types, all of them were bundled off to the back of the club.

Jolie followed, not quite sure what else to do. The bouncer standing watch wouldn't let her into the secured area, so she waited in the hallway as the police arrived. She paced and fidgeted as the fire department and then EMTs appeared. Had Cord been hurt? Panicked, she pushed past the man standing guard at the door. He had his arm around her waist attempting to subdue her when Cord's voice cut through the hubbub in the office.

"You will take your hands off her now."

The guy dropped her as if she had girl cooties. "Cord? Are you okay? What's going on?"

One of the cops turned to give her an appraising once-over. Cord growled, and that was when she realized he was in handcuffs. "Wha-what's going on? You aren't arresting him, are you? That's not fair. They jumped him."

"We're taking them all in, ma'am."

"Jolie, my keys are in my pocket, along with my phone. I'm sorry, sunshine. Call Chance and then drive yourself home."

The police allowed her to get his keys and cell and then hustled the men—all cuffed—out the back door of the club. The club's chief of security touched her shoulder. "Miss Davis? I'll escort you out front and have Mr. Barron's car brought around for you."

As she waited for the car, she called Chance, filled him in and asked where to meet him. Ten minutes later, she was parked in front of the county jail building. Chance wouldn't be there for at least thirty minutes. She called Mrs. Corcoran, told the woman she'd be late and settled in to wait.

A tap on the window brought her up out of an uneasy doze with a start. Sharp pain lanced through her neck and her pulse was racing. Chance and Cord stood next to the car. Chance looked amused. Cord looked as if he'd gone nine rounds with a heavyweight boxer.

She climbed out of the car, Cord's injuries her immediate concern. "I need to take you to the ER."

"Sunshine, I'm fine."

Jolie glanced at Chance, who nodded. "EMTs checked him over. Nothing needs stitching, no broken bones. He just needs ibuprofen and ice."

She blew out a breath, and while she really wanted to chew Cord a new one, she was relieved he wasn't seriously hurt. Still, she wanted to check for herself—not that she didn't trust the EMTs, but… "Get in. I'll drive you home."

Cord was dozing, head braced against the passenger window, when Jolie pulled into her driveway. She'd driven to her home instinctively. Thinking discretion was the better part of having to explain her evening, Jolie left Cord sleeping in the car while she made sure CJ and his nanny were both asleep.

Getting Cord out of the car and inside her house was another matter. He was stiff and sore, and no matter where she touched him, he winced. Without conscious thought on her part, he ended up sprawled across her king-size bed. Her bedroom was on the first floor, the guest room on the second. That was the excuse her libido kept giving her conscience.

Grabbing as many frozen gel packs as she had in her freezer, Jolie returned to her room.

"Hey." Why did she feel so shy?

"I'm sorry."

Cord's apology stopped her midstep. "Sorry?"

"Yeah. Not exactly the way I wanted this date to end." He patted the bed beside him. "Come keep me company while you slap those cold puppies on me." He moved to scoot over to make room and winced. "Damn. I hurt everywhere."

She positioned the cold packs on his injuries before ducking into her bathroom to rummage for pain meds and a glass of water. After he swallowed the pills, she settled on the edge of the bed.

"You always were a white knight, Cord, but trust me when I say tonight wasn't worth you getting the crap beat out of you just because those jerks were mouthy." She worried when he closed his eyes and blanched. His brow furrowed in pain. "I wish there was something more I could do."

One corner of his mouth quirked, pulling at the split in his lip. "Oww." He didn't open his eyes as he added, "You could kiss it and make it better."

# Twelve

Cord peeked through one eye to see what Jolie's response would be. She rolled her eyes and snorted. Not what he was hoping for, but better than a slap.

"I don't think there's one spot on your entire body that isn't beat-up. I don't want to hurt you."

He opened both eyes and studied her expression. "Sunshine, there's no way you could hurt me." Not physically anyway. She'd already pretty much laid his heart bare, but the more time he spent with her, and with CJ, the quicker that pain receded from memory.

With a sassy smirk, she dropped a kiss just above his swollen eye. "Does this hurt?"

"A little. Maybe kiss me here?" He pointed to the corner of his mouth. She leaned in and carefully placed a kiss there. Fighting the urge to turn his head and take her kiss full on the mouth, he waited until she straightened. Next, he pointed to a spot on the side of his throat. "Doesn't hurt here."

She again bent and nuzzled him. Oh, damn, but that felt good. Little spasms of electricity danced all the way to his groin, and things stirred down there in response.

"Uh...how 'bout here?" He managed to unbutton his shirt and pointed to his chest.

Jolie trailed her fingers through the dark hair sprouting there and made a funny noise in the back of her throat. Oh, yeah. He liked the sound of that. Before he could encourage her any more, CJ's voice echoed from a monitor on the nightstand beside them.

"Mommy?"

Jolie pushed to her feet. "I'll be right back."

Cord took advantage of her absence. Rolling off the bed, he kicked off his boots and headed to the bathroom. He washed his face and hands, assessing his injuries in the mirror. He looked like something the cat dragged in, ate and spat out as a hairball. And felt worse. Stripping out of his ripped dress shirt, he padded back to the bedroom.

Jolie stood in the doorway, staring. He arched a brow.

"Is there any part of you that's not black-and-blue?"

He glanced at the floor and chuckled. "The soles of my feet?"

"You're nuts, Cord. You know that, right?"

Yes, he knew. He was nuts about her. Nuts for ever walking away. And maybe he was nuts for trying to convince her to let him back into her life.

"I don't know how you do it." The words tumbled out before he could think about them.

"How I do what?"

"Be a mom." When she bristled, he held up a hand to keep the peace. "A single mom. I mean, I know you have help. But damn, honey. It's hard work."

Jolie took half a step back, almost as if she'd taken a blow. This conversation wasn't going the way he'd played it out in his head.

"Wow. I don't think I ever expected to hear something like that from you."

He walked closer, but she looked so nervous he stopped at the foot of the bed. "Why didn't you tell me? I would have married you, you know."

And damn if that wasn't what he meant to say, too. He needed to get his brain in gear and find a muzzle, ASAP.

She flushed and crossed her arms over her chest. After

several tries, she choked out, "I didn't want you because of your misplaced sense of duty."

"I don't think that's it." Her eyes narrowed, but this time his brain was agile enough to keep his foot out of his mouth. "It's because I'd already left you once, right? You didn't want to take the chance I'd do it again." He swallowed his anger and tunneled his fingers through his hair. "I don't want to fight, sunshine. I screwed up. Royally. I know that. I'm sorry."

Her expression softened. "I'm sorry, too, Cord."

He inhaled several times while he marshaled his thoughts, and an idea that had niggled at him for some time finally solidified. "Don't you get it?"

Jolie's face scrunched up into that inscrutable expression indicating she didn't. "Obviously not."

Convinced he was on to something, he blurted out, "If you'd told me, it would have been our way out. Hell, if I'd been smart enough to think it through, I'd have gotten you pregnant in college."

Her mouth opened and closed a few times, and he had to fight the urge to grab her and kiss her until she connected the dots.

"Honey, we would have gotten married. You being pregnant? That would be the one reason the old man couldn't stop us from being together."

"What?" Her voice rose in a screech and her face flushed, the pink coming all the way up her chest and neck to stain her cheeks. "Of all the stupid, idiotic…insane things to say to me, Cord Barron."

He offered the grin that always made her eyes go soft, and they did, right on schedule. "Think about it. A story about Cyrus Barron having an illegitimate grandson hitting the media? He'd be screaming defamation and slander. My old man wouldn't have liked it, but he wouldn't have fought us."

Of course, the rumor of his father having a few children born on the wrong side of the blanket had never fazed the sorry SOB—not that any of his legitimate sons could officially prove they had half siblings out there—Kaden Waite's family resemblance notwithstanding. They'd never broached the subject with Kaden, but none of his brothers would object if he wanted to have a DNA test done.

Jolie took a step toward him. Then another. Suddenly, she was running. Cord braced himself, but she stopped right in front of him. She was so close, and he wanted her in his arms. Wrapping them around her, Cord toppled backward onto the bed, bringing her with him. He just managed to hide his grimace as pain lanced through his entire body.

Cupping his face in her palms, Jolie attempted to keep her weight off him. Her face hovered inches from his and he did his best not to look at her cross-eyed.

"Oh, you beautiful, impossible man."

Was she complaining or was that somehow a compliment? She kissed him, so he took it as a good thing.

"I never wanted to leave you, Jolie. I was stupid. And a coward and—"

"Shut up, Cord." She kissed him again, gentler this time as she remembered his injuries. "Make love to me."

One part of his brain wondered how he would manage that with her on top and in charge—and him beat all to hell. Then another part perked right up and muttered something about letting Jolie be in charge. Not to be left out, his heart spoke up, making sure to be heard when he spoke out loud.

"Always, Jolie. I always want to make love to you."

She reared back, staring down at him with a little V forming between her brows. "That's how you feel? It wasn't just sex?"

"Caring about you. Wanting you. I have since the moment I looked up and saw you at the top of those stairs."

As her eyes went all gooey, his libido fist pumped. He'd found the perfect thing to say. His conscience twinged a little, but he mentally told it to shut up. He *had* loved her from that moment on—at least as much as he understood love. He'd wanted her, and once their relationship started in college, she'd made him feel things he hadn't felt before. Wasn't that love? He was stupid for letting her get away—something he fully planned to rectify from this moment forward.

Jolie reached to turn off the bedside lamp, and he stopped her with a gentle hand on her arm. "I want to see you, Jolie, want to watch you when you come."

"I... I'm not that wide-eyed girl anymore, Cord."

She blushed. The girl who had all but seduced him in the party room of his fraternity house had gotten shy? "Jolie?"

The pink flushing her skin turned crimson. She started to climb off him. "This is a dumb—"

He wrapped an arm around her, keeping her in place. "No, sunshine. You aren't that girl. You're so much more. You're a beautiful woman. You're the mother of my—"

She jerked away again. He let her go, and then sat up on the edge of the bed. "Jolie, come here." She complied. Reluctantly. He stood and turned her around with gentle hands on her shoulders. Unzipping her dress, he brushed it off her shoulders, letting it slide down her body to puddle at her feet. He walked around her, pausing to kiss her before he looked his fill.

Her breasts were plumper than he remembered, her hips wider. She'd blossomed from a slim girl into lush womanhood. He inhaled sharply, the front of his slacks tenting. "Damn but you're beautiful, baby."

Jolie shook her head, refusing to look at him. He grabbed her hand and pressed it to his erection. "If you don't believe my words, believe this. I may be beat to hell and back, but I want you. So. Damn. Much."

She jerked her hand back and he let it go. Her arms folded across her abdomen, but he pulled them away and sank to his knees, kissing her tummy.

"Don't." The word came out strangled.

"Why not, Jolie? What are you afraid of? What don't you want me to see?"

Her hands fluttered across her skin, and then he saw the fine feathering of white lines. Stretch marks. From her pregnancy. He kissed a trail along one of the lines. "These are beautiful."

"Yeah, and you're crazy."

"Been called that before, but they are, Jolie. You're beautiful." His palm cupped the rounded pooch of her tummy. "My son was here. Growing. Damn, woman, there's nothing sexier than that."

"Your *son*? I suppose if I'd had a little girl, that wouldn't be sexy at all."

She spit the words, but he deflected them with a smile as he rose. "A baby girl. Now, there's a thought to give a man a heart attack." His eyes twinkled as he nuzzled his way across her breasts to kiss the soft skin under her chin. "I don't think there would have been enough shotguns in the world to keep the boys at bay if we'd had a daughter."

He cupped her cheeks and kissed her, his tongue teasing the seam of her lips until her jaw relaxed and he could taste her mouth. Margarita and chocolate. Those were two tastes that shouldn't work together, but in her mouth? Perfect. He broke the kiss, resting his forehead against hers. "I'm going to make love to you, Jolie. It won't be as good or as thorough as I'd wanted for our first time back together—"

"Are we?"

Cord raised his head to look at her. "Are we what?"

"Back together."

His thoughts ran full out on the hamster wheel of his man brain. He knew, instinctively, this was a crossroads. He'd either screw up royally or he'd win this woman back. "That depends on you, I guess."

That intriguing V formed between her brows again, and he kissed it. "I don't want to make assumptions, Jolie. I want us to be friends at the very least. I want to be CJ's dad, not just his sperm donor. I want it to be you and me. Us. We. A couple. But what I want doesn't matter much if you don't want the same thing. What do you want, sunshine? Because from where I'm standin', the ball's in your court."

Aw, hell. Tears spilled from her eyes, turning her long lashes spiky. He'd screwed up. Again. Then she threw her arms around him and rode him down to the bed. "I was right. You are an impossible man. Impossible and perfect and…and…"

Cord kissed her in self-defense. His palm curled around a breast and he smiled as her nipple tightened. He managed to get her bra unhooked and off. Panties slid off easily, and then he had her naked and glorious, and if it was possible, he was even harder.

Jolie helped him out of his trousers and boxers and made him stand there at the side of the bed wearing nothing but his socks. He didn't care. Before she was ready to stop looking, Cord climbed onto the bed and stalked her, socks and all. Still laughing, she scooted up until her back was braced against the pile of pillows shoved against her headboard.

"I'll show you funny," he mock growled at her. Pinning her wrists, he kissed down her side until she squirmed and giggled breathlessly. His Jolie was still ticklish. *His.* Man, he liked the sound of that. He teased her breast, swiping his tongue across the nipple before fastening his lips around it and sucking. She arched into him. She'd always responded so perfectly to his touch. Trailing a hand down her side, he palmed her tummy, and then dipped lower. She gasped and widened her thighs as he cupped her. She was hot and ready for him.

He wasn't drunk this time—unlike that long-ago St. Patrick's Day—and he released her breast to gaze up at her. "Birth control?" He had a condom in his wallet, but hell if he knew where his wallet had ended up.

"Pill. We're good."

"Sunshine, we're much better than good." He settled between her thighs and it felt as if he'd come home. He kissed her fluttering eyelids as he sank deep into her moist center. Stroking in and out of her, he forgot about his injuries. He forgot about anger and hurt and everything but how good it was to have Jolie surrounding him.

He tucked a hand under her hips and urged her to wrap her legs around his waist. She hesitated until the new angle guided him over the one spot guaranteed to roll her eyes back in her head. She gasped and met him stroke for stroke, urging him to push into her faster and deeper.

Cord braced himself on one arm and watched Jolie's face. Her emotions played across it like a movie, and he was positive she felt their connection as acutely as he did. His hips pumped and she rose to meet him, her breath hitching whenever he withdrew.

She whispered something, a one-syllable word that he realized was his name. "Cord." This time she said it louder. "Oh, Cord. Yes…please. Cord…"

And then he was breathing as hard as she was. Lights sparkled in his peripheral vision as his whole body tightened. Jolie's body clenched him, and then he couldn't see anything at all as they exploded together.

Later—much, much later—he managed to get them under the covers, the light turned off and Jolie gathered to his side. He kissed her temple and tangled his hand in her hair as she nestled her head on his shoulder. As she drowsed, memories swamped him. Sex had always been amazing. It was the emotional stuff that twisted them up. Had he ever loved her or was it just sex, just a way to get back at his father?

She murmured something in her sleep and he kissed her forehead. He'd never considered himself to be a tender man, but damn if this woman and the little boy upstairs made him wonder if he could be.

# Thirteen

"Mommy? Mommy? Mom!"

Someone groaned in Jolie's ear. Cord. CJ! She bolted up in bed, scrambling to keep the sheet pulled up over her naked chest. The little boy bounced at the foot of the bed with barely contained excitement. She glanced at Cord. He'd pulled a pillow over his head, but continued to groan.

"Stop, CJ."

"Mommy, Daddy's here. Right here." He bounced again and would have fallen on Cord if she hadn't let go of the sheet long enough to grab her son before he landed on his father.

"CJ. Enough. Yes. But be careful. Your dad got hurt."

The boy quieted immediately, eyes wide as he stared at Cord. "You gots a boo-boo?"

"I got a couple of boo-boos, bubba." Cord emerged from beneath the pillow.

"No, Daddy. You didn't gets boo-boos. You gots big owies." CJ crept forward on his hands and knees and very gently poked Cord's face.

"Yeah, you should see the other guys," Cord muttered under his breath.

Jolie bit her lips to keep from giggling. "CJ, you need to go watch TV or something until we get up."

"I'm hungry, Mommy. Can I have pancakes?"

"CJ, go watch TV until your mom and I are ready. Then I'll take you both out for breakfast, and yes, you can have pancakes. But—" Cord held up his index finger "—no pancakes if you come back in here. We'll come out when we're ready."

Her little boy's brow furrowed, and his mouth scrunched up as he considered the implications. Jolie recognized the look and the tactic. She settled back to see how Cord would deal with the subtle blackmail. "Chocolate-chip pancakes?"

"Blueberry."

"With whipped cream?"

"No syrup, then."

"Hmm." CJ crossed his arms and tapped his chin with a finger.

Jolie pulled the sheet up to her nose and coughed away a laugh.

"Can I have little piggies?"

Cord glanced at her for translation. "Link sausage."

"Ah." He appeared to consider the question. "Yes. Blueberry pancakes, whipped cream and little piggies."

"Okay." CJ bounced off the bed. "But hurry, okay? I'm really, really hungry."

Before either of them could respond, the boy raced from the room.

"Shut the door, CJ," Cord called after him. "And no slamming." Seconds later the door slowly swung shut and latched. "Remind me to lock the door next time."

That did it. She lost it, laughing so hard she could barely breathe. When she could talk without giggling, she admitted his performance had impressed her.

"Hey, I was a kid once. I know how boys think. Plus, I'm a better negotiator. I have more practice." He waggled his brows and reached for her. Snagging her wrist, he pulled her back to his side and tucked her in close. "Now, where were we?"

"We were sleeping."

"True, but now that we're awake…" He nudged her chin up so he could capture her mouth with his. He didn't just kiss her. His lips latched on to hers, moving across them, sucking and nibbling. Heat pooled between her legs, making her squirm against him.

Cord brushed his hand down her side, cupping her hip while he deepened the kiss, and then continued down until he'd reached her knee. He hooked his fingers and pulled so that her leg was half sprawled across his groin. She smiled into his kiss. He was very happy to see her this morning.

She broke the kiss. "I need to brush my teeth."

"Too late for that. I've already kissed you, dragon breath. I'm immune now."

She laughed again, but clapped her hand over her mouth. What in the world had gotten into her? Oh, yeah, Cord. That elicited a snorting giggle. Despite the fact they'd been caught in flagrante delicto, Jolie felt freer than she had in… She couldn't remember that far back. Cord was in bed with her, the morning after, hard and wanting her. He hadn't batted an eye when CJ stormed in and woke them. And he wasn't too worried about getting caught making love to her again. She should get up, go lock the door, but she was so…comfortable.

He brushed her hair back over her shoulder and cocked his head. "What?"

Smiling, she stretched to kiss him. "I'm happy. That's all."

"No, sunshine. That's everything. At least to me."

He pulled her over on top of him so she was straddling him. He barely winced as she pushed against his shoulders and straightened. "Raise up, baby," he murmured.

She rocked up on her knees. He fitted his erection at her entrance and she slowly sank down. Breath hissed from his lungs, followed by a quick inhale as she rocked up again. Setting a slow, easy rhythm, Jolie decided she liked being in charge.

"I see what you're thinking up there, pretty girl. Don't get cocky."

She laughed, arching her back and rolling her hips forward. Cord groaned, and she increased the tempo. His large, slightly calloused hands rested on her thighs, and he squeezed gently before moving to grip her hips. The beginnings of her orgasm stirred in her center, and she lost the rhythm for a moment. Cord took over, thrusting up into her, his hands holding her right where he—and she—wanted her.

"Do you know how gorgeous you are?"

Her skin heated and she tucked her chin, once again faltering in her rhythm. Cord cupped her cheek, and then curled his fingers behind her neck to tug her gently down for a kiss. "Don't, sweetheart. You are beautiful. Even more now than when we were kids."

Her protest was swallowed by his kiss. Last night had been hot and heavy and needy. This morning was sweet, forming a connection between them that she'd missed more than she could believe. She didn't want to think about what might have been. She didn't want to remember what had been. She simply wanted here and now, the man she'd never stopped loving filling her.

"Ah, Jolie. What you do to my heart, sunshine."

She stilled, everything slowing—heart, lungs, brain. Noise faded to silence as though her ears had been stuffed with cotton balls. Her vision narrowed to focus on the man lying beneath her and what he'd said, what it might mean. He'd never been one for romantic words. Then he offered that quirky grin and his dimple peeked out. The world rushed back in with a whoosh and she inhaled like a drowning woman coming up for the third time.

"Oh, Cord." Her eyes misted as she lowered herself to kiss him again before tucking her face into his shoulder.

Jolie lay still on top of him. Cord didn't want to move, but he was throbbing inside her. Whatever he'd done, it had been something so right he needed to make notes. And bottle it. So he could do it again. Especially when he made her mad. Then he realized her breaths were coming in little hiccuping sobs. Crap. That couldn't be good. Could it?

He patted her back awkwardly. "Shh, baby. It's okay. I'll fix whatever it is. Don't cry."

"You're impossible," she sniffled.

Well, so much for the moment. He'd screwed up again, obviously. Before he could ask what he'd done wrong, she turned her head and nuzzled down his jawline, careful of his bruises. Her inner muscles squeezed him and he gasped. The reaction wasn't very manly, but the feel of her surrounding him made it hard to breathe.

Rolling his hips, he stroked up gently. She met him with a roll of her own. This he could do. He could finish their lovemaking. Make her feel how much he loved being inside her. With great care, he shifted their positions so she was lying beneath him and he now had more control. Her eyes remained closed but her lips were parted and her tongue and teeth worked her bottom lip. He lowered his head to nip at its plump temptation.

Sweet and slow quickly turned to needy and fast. They came together, and he was so spent his arms shook as he braced above her. Hating to break the connection, he also didn't want to face-plant on her chest or squash her. He leveraged to her side and sank into the mattress.

He lost track of time as he cuddled Jolie to his side. Each time he touched her, each time they made love, it just got better and better. Her presence did wicked things to his body, but it also eased his soul. Cord just managed to swallow the snort that thought prompted. If he spent much more time around this amazing woman, his brothers and cousins would demand he surrender his man card. At this particular moment in time, he would have burned that sucker himself. He didn't want to be anywhere but here.

The shuffle of feet and heavy breathing caught his attention. He glanced toward the door and saw a shadow moving back and forth in the crack under the door. CJ. Who clearly wanted their attention.

"Jolie?"

"Mmm?"

"We need to get up, sunshine. CJ's waiting."

"Mmm."

"Why don't you grab the first shower."

"Mmm?" Her forehead crinkled, and he kissed the V between her brows. He liked it when she made that face and his lips smoothed the wrinkles away.

"Shower. You take longer to get ready so you go first."

"Oh. Right."

Cord didn't mention that he had ulterior motives—such as watching her walk to the bathroom, only to follow a few moments later so he could watch her through the fogged glass shower door. Oh, yeah. He would have to take care of the woody he now sported, but he'd wait for his own shower. If he got in with her now, their son would likely starve to death. His stomach rumbled. Cord would, too, if that noise was any indication.

The shower door slid open and Jolie's face appeared. "Are you watching me?" She sounded outraged, but he knew she wasn't.

"Damn straight I am."

"Pervert."

"Guilty as charged."

Her gaze traveled down his body, stopping at his groin. Something twinkled in her eyes, and Cord couldn't decide if it was lust or humor. "So why don't you join me?" she purred.

He laughed and palmed himself. "Trust me, I'd love to, but then CJ and I both would starve to death."

"Party pooper."

"Somebody has to be the responsible adult."

Jolie giggle-snorted and slapped her hand over her

mouth to diffuse the sound. He widened his stance and crossed his arms over his chest. "I rest my case."

"Oh, okay." She muttered something under her breath that he couldn't decipher before she added, "But you're gonna get yours one of these days."

"I certainly hope so. And I hope that you're the one giving it to me because, honey? I promise I'm gonna be giving it to you."

Before he could react, a sopping sea sponge flew across the room and nailed him right on his pride and joy with a wet splat. Jolie's deadly aim had not diminished with the passage of time. "Careful, woman," he roared.

Stalking toward the shower, full of comical indignation, he plotted his revenge. Jolie cringed in the corner of the stall, which was more than large enough to accommodate two. She'd armed herself with a loofah. Cord plastered a smirk full of male superiority on his face, leaned in and grabbed the handle used to adjust water temperature. He cranked that baby to full cold, slammed the door shut and held it.

"Cord!" Jolie sputtered. "Dang it." She jerked the door handle on her side, and then beat on the glass with the palm of her hand. "Cord, please! It's freezing."

"Of course it is."

"Let me out, Cord. Before I turn into an icicle."

Relenting, he grabbed a towel that had been on the warming rack, opened the door and gathered her into his arms. Wrapping her in the towel, he offered to pat her dry. She impolitely refused.

"Get your shower," she grumped.

Laughing, he leaned in to readjust the temperature. "Sore loser."

"You bet I am. And you'd best remember that." She arched a brow and did her best to scowl at him.

Cord stepped into the shower, but looked at her right before sliding the door closed. "I remember everything about you, Jolie."

# Fourteen

Dating Jolie was akin to walking a tightrope. Balancing her needs, CJ's needs and what Cord wanted was a real stretch. Two weeks of swallowing what he wanted in favor of what would win Jolie over. Two weeks of dodging his family, except where business was concerned. The hell of it was, he didn't know if he was making any headway with her. He deserved brownie points for tonight regardless.

They were at the bar of Starr's, waiting for their table. Jolie was doing Jell-O shots, which came under the heading of A Very Bad Idea. The fact that Cord was matching Jolie shot for shot with tequila qualified him as a finalist for Dumbass of the Year.

When he'd picked her up after work, she'd been in an odd mood—quiet and withdrawn. So here they sat. He needed to shovel some food into her. Preferably food with lots of carbs to absorb the alcohol.

"Drinking game."

A puzzled expression furrowed his forehead as Cord attempted to follow her non sequitur. "Drinking game?"

"Yesh. Let's play." She tossed off another shot and shook her finger in his direction. "Things you wish you hadn't done."

This couldn't end well, especially with her already starting to slur her words. "Jolie, you need to eat something."

That got an eyebrow waggle from her before she flagged

down the bartender for another shot. When he returned with a fresh drink, she downed it.

"I'll start." She had to stop and inhale deeply before continuing, "Going to nursing school."

Cord didn't expect that to be the first thing out of her mouth. Before he could ask her why, she banged her glass to get the bartender's attention. "Your turn."

*Leaving you.* But instead of saying that out loud, he offered a wry smile. "Suggesting we get a drink first instead of going straight in to dinner."

"Oh, pooh. Doesn't count. This ish serioush." She gulped another shot, wiped her lips with the back of her hand and stared at the top of the polished bar. She didn't look up, but Cord watched color drain from her face as she said, "I killed a kid."

And there was the source of her rush to intoxication. "Jolie—"

"Don't *Jolie* me. A little girl died in the ER today. We couldn't save her." Her voice lost the drunken slur in the force of her emotion. "If I hadn't gone to nursing school, I wouldn't have been there. I wouldn't have been responsible."

"You aren't responsible—"

"*I* couldn't save her, Cord." Tears leaked down her cheeks, and he wanted to take her into his arms, protect her from the hurt in her heart.

"C'mon, sunshine. Let's go home." He tossed money on the bar and urged her to stand.

"Not telling you about CJ." Diamond-glazed eyes stared up at him as her voice firmed again. "That's my biggest regret."

"Mine's walking away from you." There. He'd said the words. Truth at last, but she didn't even glance at him.

He kept her tucked under his arm and moving, pausing only briefly to cancel their reservations. Neither of them spoke on the drive to her house, and whenever he glanced over, her eyes remained closed. He got her to the front door and rang the bell rather than dig through her suitcase of a purse to find her keys.

Mrs. Corcoran didn't say a word as he guided Jolie inside, his arm around her waist. When he tried to get her to walk toward her bedroom and she stumbled, he gave up and simply swept her into his arms to carry her. The older woman followed and wordlessly shooed him out after he'd placed Jolie on the bed. The woman was still tsk-tsking when she joined him in the kitchen ten minutes later.

"Good thing CJ is already in bed and asleep. He shouldn't see his mama like that." She glowered at Cord as if Jolie's condition was all his fault.

"She had a rough day. They lost a little girl in the ER."

That news knocked the wind out of Mrs. Corcoran's sails. "Bless her heart. She takes what happens at work so hard. Poor thing."

Her glower returned, and Cord raised his hands in surrender. "She doesn't have to work, ma'am. I'd support her and CJ, or her father would, but she works because she wants to."

"That may well be, but that little lady needs someone to take care of her."

"Absolutely."

Once again, he'd left her speechless—for a few minutes, at least. "So what're you gonna do?"

"My best, Mrs. Corcoran. I'm going to do my best to convince her that the three of us can be a family."

Jolie stared at the rack of Halloween costumes. Where had time gone? How could Halloween be a week away? She and Cord were dating—sort of. And he hadn't mentioned her drunken confession—thankfully, though he'd dumped her and run, rescheduling their dinner for the next night. Still, she would have been mortified if he'd thrown her admission in her face. Instead, he pushed for more in their relationship.

In general, though, she didn't allow Cord to spend the night; they used his place as a stopover for sex before he took her home. With the arrival of cooler weather, he grumbled about getting out of a warm bed. She knew he wanted more from her. He wanted a commitment—one she wasn't ready to give. She hadn't forgiven him for breaking up with her, and wasn't sure she ever wanted to.

Her focus had to be CJ, what was good for her son. She had such mixed feelings about Cord—and his family. CJ was no longer the shy little boy clinging to her hand when she dropped him off at preschool. As much as she hated to admit it, Cord's influence had something to do with that. Okay, he had a lot to do with it.

They did *guy* things together—Cord and CJ. They'd gone fishing. He'd taught CJ to ride, and her son was turning into a cowboy fanatic. He refused to wear anything but Western boots—just like his dad's. Jeans were de rigueur. They both had black felt Stetsons, creased and shaped identically. Cord had a picture of them dressed up—same hats, shirts, belt buckles, jeans and boots. They were two peas in a pod, and he displayed the framed photo on his desk for everyone to see. He was so dang proud of being a dad.

Cord got to be the good guy, the parent who gave treats and fun times. She was the parent stuck with the responsibility. She administered time-outs and bedtimes, and said no. Whenever CJ returned from one of their outings, it was "Daddy this" and "Daddy that" and "Daddy and me." Her son had no room in his thoughts for her. She was losing him as Cord seduced CJ away with promises and presents.

She didn't want Cord in her life. Did she? Oh, the sex between them was as hot as it had always been. But sex wasn't enough. She'd thought they had something back in college. Something real and permanent. Boy howdy, had she been wrong about that. And her easy seduction of him on that fateful St. Patrick's Day was proof. The man's brains all resided below his fancy Western belt buckle. And no matter how good he looked in those butt-hugging jeans he favored, no matter how sweet he was to her son, Cord was still Cord *Barron*. The Barrons were…Barrons. Egotistical. Overbearing. Thinking they were entitled to anything they wanted. No matter how much Cord professed to have changed, had he? And what about Cyrus Barron? He was bound to find out about CJ sooner than later. What then? What would Cord do? But more important, how could she let CJ be around the hateful old man who was his grandfather simply because they shared DNA?

Jolie couldn't figure out why—or when—her thoughts had turned so negative where Cord was concerned. Being honest, she could admit that since he'd dumped her at home, left to Mrs. Corcoran's tender mercies after getting drunk, she tended to snarl whenever thoughts of him cropped up. She didn't discuss her feelings with him. He said he knew her. He should know what was bothering her. And besides, it was just like a man to cut and run. Especially this one. He had the history for it. Things got tough? Cord Barron disappeared. Except he hadn't yet. He wanted to officially acknowledge CJ, make things legal. She panicked at the idea. She didn't want to hand over that kind of control to him.

Noise filtered back into her consciousness, and she shook away the negative thoughts. Halloween was coming and CJ needed a costume. Jolie flicked through the nearly empty rack and pulled out an Iron Man suit and held it up. CJ shook his head, arms folded stubbornly across his chest. What happened to September? There was no way Halloween should be right around the corner. Oh, wait… Cord. He'd filled her time—even when he gave her time off from CJ. In fact, Cord had volunteered to escort CJ and some of his friends when they went trick-or-treating, but she wanted to go, too. She checked the size on the Spider-Man costume.

"No, Mommy. I don't wanna be a superhero."

"Fine. Then what do you want to be?"

"I told you. I wanna be a cowboy. Like Daddy." He shoved his hands in his pockets and slid her a sly glance from the corner of his eyes.

She didn't like that look at all. "What?"

"Nothin'."

"CJ?" She used her this-is-your-only-warning voice when she said his name.

"If I go as a cowboy, Daddy might bring a horse."

Jolie did not want to ask. She inhaled, but then screwed her eyes shut and exhaled, knowing she'd regret it. She had to ask anyway. "A real horse?"

"Uh-huh." CJ's eyes crinkled from his ear-to-ear grin. "How cool is that, Mommy? I told all my friends. We're all gonna be cowboys!"

Oh, boy. She didn't know whether to kill Cord or leave him to the mercy of his son's disappointment. Making outlandish promises always had consequences, and the sooner Cord figured that out, the better. He'd worked really hard at spending time with CJ and managing to act like a father—at least the times he wasn't trying to win her over. If she didn't stay on top of things, Cord would spoil their son rotten without a second thought. He needed to learn not to do that because she wasn't going to clean up his messes whenever he brought CJ home. She would *not* be painted as the bad guy because she made and enforced the rules. As much as she didn't want to, she had to sit down with Cord and spell out the ground rules.

If she was honest with herself, she needed to spell out the rules to herself, as well. She didn't mean to fall into his easy trap. He was always there, wanting to see CJ...to see *her*. It was easy to be with him as if time hadn't passed, as if he hadn't broken her heart, as if she hadn't broken his. How did one get over that? She didn't think there was enough superglue in the whole world to mend her heart.

Despite Cord's sweetness and apparent concern—now. She swallowed her frustration. He'd always been sweet, but she couldn't trust him to stay.

Her cell phone buzzed with the chorus from Kelly Clarkson's "Since U Been Gone." *Speak of the devil.* She swiped her finger across the face of the phone, her lip curling far enough to wrinkle her nose as she answered, "What do you want?"

Warm laughter filled her ear before Cord's voice followed. "I think you miss me, sunshine."

"Don't flatter yourself. What the heck did you promise CJ about Halloween?"

Silence. She couldn't even hear him breathe. He finally replied, his tone cautious. "Halloween?"

"You're coming to take him trick-or-treating, yes?"

"Yes." Cord drew out the word, making it sound like two syllables.

"He wants to be a cowboy."

"And?" Again, two syllables.

"Are you bringing him a horse?" Silence again. She was ready to light into him when she heard a deep inhalation.

"Not exactly?"

"Don't answer a question with a question, Cord. What *did* you say?"

"Ah…didn't you just answer a—"

"Shut up, Cord." Her exasperation leaked out. Why did she have to be the only adult? "Just explain, okay?"

"Okay. I told CJ that we could have a Halloween party at the ranch. We'd do a hayride and the kids could ride horses in the corral."

"Without asking me?" She made sure her voice sounded frigid. How dare he do this! The man kept insinuating himself into her son's life. Despite all his sweet words and *good* intentions, she wondered at his real motivations. Deep down, she realized, she didn't entirely trust Cord.

"Uh…not exactly? I told him that we'd talk to you. And

that if there wasn't enough time to do it for Halloween, then we'd do it for his birthday."

A band tightened around Jolie's chest, cutting off any air she might be able to suck into her lungs. His birthday? Cord was making plans for CJ's birthday and hadn't bothered to ask her? "You're presuming a helluva lot."

"Bad Mommy. That's a dollar in the swear jar."

She'd forgotten CJ was standing there listening to her. "I can't talk now. We'll discuss this later."

"By which you mean that you'll dictate terms to me and expect me to fall in line. That's not going to work anymore, Jolie. I've been patient, but now I want things official. I want to be CJ's father legally. I'll pick you up for dinner tonight. We'll go somewhere quiet where we can talk this through."

Dead air. He'd hung up on her. Before she could hang up on him. She grabbed CJ's hand without a word and turned toward the exit.

"I don't wanna go. Mommy." He braced his feet and pulled back against her grip.

People stared, some stopping and turning to watch. Jolie closed her eyes and breathed deeply to center herself. When had she become such a raging shrew? Easy answer—the moment Cord had walked back into her life. Even if he'd been strapped to a gurney and almost dead at the time. She knelt down and curled her fingers over CJ's shoulders. "Look, Mommy is very angry at your father right now. I shouldn't take it out on you, but do me a favor, okay? Just c'mon. No fighting. No whining."

His bottom lip quivered and Jolie wanted to bang her head against the nearest wall. Instead, she rose and held out her hand. CJ took it and she led him from the store. She had to get a grip on herself and control of the situation with Cord. She'd allowed him far too much leeway in her son's life. And now he wanted it legal? He'd take complete control because that was what Barrons did. CJ was *her* son.

Except…CJ was Cord's, too. Guilt raised its head like some stupid Whac-a-mole. No matter how many times she clobbered the feeling with a sledgehammer, it just reappeared to suck out all her resolve.

Emotion roiled inside her—a flash flood hitting a dam with a pounding rush. The water level kept rising, and one of two things was going to happen. Her emotions would spill over the top and slowly relieve some of the pressure or she'd drown in them. She couldn't afford for either event to happen. She could not lose control. Not of CJ, which she would if Cord continued to press his parental rights. Not of her heart if the man continued to assault her with his easy smiles and sexy ways. Her life teetered on the edge of a precipice. Part of her wanted to snort at the analogy but she couldn't. That was the way she felt.

She had to make a stand. Sooner, not later.

# Fifteen

As soon as she entered the restaurant, Jolie knew this was a stupid move on her part. She'd refused to let Cord pick her up, insisting she'd drive herself and meet him there. The stupid part was letting him pick the restaurant—his compromise to her unyielding "no" and for stalling this meeting until after Halloween. He'd shown up to take her to dinner the night before Halloween but she'd dodged a confrontation by taking an extra shift at work.

Then Cord had arrived Halloween evening to take the kids trick-or-treating, and according to Mrs. Corcoran, he'd come with a compromise—a handmade stick horse for CJ to "ride." She'd volunteered for extra duty at the ER with Operation X-ray as an excuse to avoid Cord. As community outreach, Trauma One offered to X-ray Halloween candy for hidden dangers. She had plausible deniability, since that volunteer time was important. She wasn't afraid to face him. Not at all.

The host led her on a winding trail through tables filled with couples. This was so not a family restaurant. The thought of CJ eating here sent cold chills through her. This was a date place—for men out to impress their ladies, for parents to get away from the kids to remember they could still be in love. Low lights, soft music, a place steeped in romance.

Pristine white cloths draped the tables. Crystal and silver gleamed in flickering candlelight. Delicate but aromatic flowers flowed from sparkling vases on each table. Cord was already there, sitting at a table in a secluded corner. He stood as soon as he saw her. He appeared stoic. Dang, but the man had some kind of poker face. She'd always hated that about him—all the Barron brothers, in fact. Dealing with them had taught her, though. She continued to work on her own demeanor.

Something flickered in his eyes as she neared. She did her best to ignore it, but little frissons of awareness skittered across her skin. Even wary, she wanted him. She always had. Candlelight danced across his face. It pasted shadows where none should be. And it added light to places that should have been dark.

Cord nodded to the host and the man veered away, leaving her on her own to face him. He gracefully held her chair, scooting it beneath her thighs as she sat. He bent while doing so and brushed his cheek across her hair.

"You're beautiful."

The words whispered across her consciousness, leaving goose bumps on her psyche. *No. No, no, no, no.* She stiffened her spine and raised her chin. She would not succumb to Mr. Cowboy Sexy, even if he did look good enough for dessert. As he settled back into his chair, she studied him. She could see the candle flame in the depths of his burned-honey eyes. He wore his hair shorter now, a result of part of it being shaved in the hospital, but it was growing out. A dark comma accented his forehead while shadows defined the planes of his face.

No one would doubt Cord and his brothers were related. Somehow, though, he'd ended up with slightly softer features. He was still rugged, with the dark black hair and golden-brown eyes of his siblings. They were all handsome as sin and just as irresistible to the female population. Cord was more relaxed than the others, except maybe Chase. Chase was a horse of a totally different color, living only for wine, women and song. She pitied any woman insane enough to get involved with him. Heck, she was insane to be sitting here with Cord, and he was the nice brother. What did that tell the world about the Barrons?

"A penny for your thoughts."

His husky voice vibrated over her skin and she tensed up. She needed to be on her guard, not sitting here day-dreaming about how sexy this man was. He was not above using that—or any other advantage he might gain—against her. They had things to settle here and now. She could not lose sight of that.

"I'm not sure you want to know."

"That's where you'd be wrong, Jolie. I want to know everything about you."

"According to you, you already do."

The corner of his mouth quirked in that devil-may-care grin that once melted her heart. Over and over and over again. Not anymore. She arched a brow in response and he laughed. Reaching across the table, his big hand enveloped hers. She fought the urge to turn hers palm up and twine her fingers with his. Not even the waiter's appearance provided enough of a diversion for her to pull away.

Arrogant as always, Cord ordered for both of them. The fact that he picked the entrée she would have chosen only served to make her angrier, and reinforce the idea he did know her far better than he should.

His expression smoothed out into that blank poker face the Barrons were infamous for. "You're the one who said you wanted to talk to me back before Halloween—and you've avoided me for over a week now. I want to talk about Thanksgiving. Every time I bring up the subject, you shut me down."

Or she diverted him. He'd been talking about Thanks-giving for almost a month. Luckily, the man was easy. A few kisses and caresses and they were off to bed for some fantastic sex. Cord couldn't think beyond the sexy bits. Jolie knew getting intimate was a bad idea but she couldn't seem to help herself. He was still the only man who made her toes curl with a kiss. But he wanted more than sex. He'd been clear about that from the moment he'd discovered CJ was his. He'd wanted joint custody but she didn't. CJ was hers and had been for his whole life. The idea of giving up any control at all terrified her.

Cord squeezed her hand, pulling her attention from the serious intent in his eyes to the way he held her hand—with strength and gentleness. Too bad he hadn't handled her heart the same way.

"This is not the time or the place, Cord."

"Wrong. This *is* the time and place because we're both here."

"I can get up and leave anytime I want."

"Yes. You can." He released her hand, leaned back in his chair and stared at her. Temper glinted in his eyes now. "Are you going to run forever?"

Her nostrils flared and her eyes narrowed. "Wow. You just had to go there, didn't you?" She leaned forward, forearms braced on the table. "I'm not the one who ran."

Cord smirked. It was that or reach across the table and shake her until her teeth rattled. He'd never laid a hand on a woman in anger and he wasn't about to start now. "Pot, kettle, sweetheart." He watched her throat work as she swallowed. Hard. He'd hit the mark with that one. "We both ran. I've admitted I was stupid. You, on the other hand—"

"What about me?" She interrupted him, her green eyes flashing despite the low lights in the restaurant. Oh, yeah. She was pissed now.

"You hid my son from me." The thought still rankled. He'd tried in the past few months to understand her motivations, to forgive her. Getting to know CJ and spending time with Jolie had helped a long way toward that. Until now. Cord didn't understand why she was being so stubborn—why she was shoving him away and blocking his right to acknowledge his son.

"So what? You didn't deserve him."

She flung the words like a shotgun blast, and they blew a hole in his heart. "You didn't exactly give me a chance, did you?" He choked back his hurt and anger, keeping his voice soft, with no inflection. What the hell had gotten into her? "He *is* my son, Jolie. I have the results from the paternity test."

Her mouth dropped open as her eyes rounded in shock. "You went behind my back? You ran a test on him without my permission?"

"I knew from the moment I saw him he was mine. The DNA test is for the lawyers. To cover the legal bases."

"Lawyers?" She spit the word out like a bitter pill—or maybe he was the only one who felt that way. He didn't want to go to court, but Jolie was very quickly leaving him little choice in the matter. Cyrus, as soon as he had found out, made threats to do things his way. Chance would keep things on an even keel—and civil. Cyrus wouldn't.

The sommelier arrived and served their wine with no fanfare. He'd obviously picked up on their mood. Their waiter slid in right behind him, efficiently depositing their salads and moving away without a word.

Cord sipped his wine, watching her over the rim of the crystal flute. She sat so rigid her muscles were almost spasming. Her hands were hidden in her lap, but he'd lay odds they were clasped tightly together. He wanted to gather her into his arms, kissing her until she let go, until she admitted he was right. He wanted her, dammit. And CJ. They could be a family. He was positive of it. He just needed Jolie to understand. And to agree. He reached into his jacket pocket and fingered the velvet box hidden there. He'd hoped to convince her they could be a family, and he'd taken to carrying the ring as a good luck charm. And if he were honest, he'd admit he was considering proposing tonight, if things went his way.

All he had to do was chip away at her anger. He'd already breached her defenses where making love was concerned. She desired him as much as he wanted her. He had her body. Now he wanted her heart, and he'd solemnly promised himself he'd take far better care of that treasure than he had the first time. Once Jolie agreed to marriage, they were a done deal—one Cyrus had no control over.

He swallowed his anger with the next sip of wine and allowed a fleeting smile to show as she attacked her salad, stabbing innocent greens with a fork. Cord was positive she was picturing that fork buried over and over in his chest. Setting his wine aside, he picked up his fork and ate calmly, a counterpoint to her frenzy she wouldn't appreciate. That was all part of his plan. He had to keep her off balance to get what he wanted. Her. CJ. A life and family together.

"Can we talk about Thanksgiving, Jolie? Why don't you and CJ come out to the ranch? Cassie and Miz Beth are pulling out all the stops so we can have a real family get-together. If you're worried about my old man, don't be. As soon as Cassie started organizing a family dinner, he made plans to fly to Vegas. He'll be at the Crown Casino for the long weekend."

He offered what he hoped was a disarming grin. "Heck, Clay is coming into town for it. He's bringing his speech-writer to work on campaign stuff, but he'll be there. Cassie even managed to lure Chase back to town, assuming he doesn't back out at the last minute." He watched her but couldn't decide her mood.

Jolie paused in her chewing to offer him another glare before returning her gaze to her plate. He leaned over the table and lowered his voice to a conspiratorial undertone. "Don't tell anyone, but I think Cyrus is actually afraid of Cassie." He bit back laughter when she glanced up, startled. He winked and continued, "I know the rest of us are. As for Cyrus, Cash thinks he has a showgirl on speed dial, and with Chase back here for Thanksgiving, the old man will have free rein."

A busboy appeared and whisked their used plates and utensils away while refilling water glasses. Moments later, the waiter arrived and served their entrées. The man waited stoically while he and Jolie sampled a taste and nodded their satisfaction. Cord bit back a sigh. He would have taken her to Cattlemen's for dinner, but this was her sort of restaurant, and honestly, he wanted to impress her. Just because he preferred jeans and boots didn't mean he couldn't dress up. Like all the Barrons, he could move in what he called the silk-panty social circles. The Barrons commanded incredible wealth. J. Rand Davis did, too. Hell, the man had written a check for half a million dollars to Cord's sister-in-law, drawn on his personal account. Cord was still chapped that J. Rand had warned him away from Jolie that day.

He didn't like where his thoughts were headed, so he reined them in and concentrated on the problem at hand. Jolie continued to eat, ignoring him again. He was tired of playing that game. "What happened to you?"

Her head snapped up and she glared at him. Her "laser death stare" was probably lethal to anyone but him. He thought the look was adorable, but he hid his smile.

"What happened to me? I have no idea what you're talking about."

"I think you do." He leaned forward again and this time dropped his voice to a husky whisper. "What happened to the cowgirl who used to ride bareback and take her horse swimming in the lake? Where's the girl who sat in the bleachers cheering me on at the rodeo?"

Her face paled, but she held his gaze. "You, Cord. That's what happened to me. You walked in, told me you were done and walked out. That girl no longer exists."

Jolie's words sliced his heart as she'd meant them to. He bit back the retort forming on his tongue, breathing through the emotional pain as he continued to watch her. As he knew she would, she dropped her gaze. Neither of them truly had the high moral ground in this thing between them. "That's too bad. She was special."

He reached for the wine bottle and refilled their glasses. Jolie gulped hers, looking for liquid courage. He sipped again, needing to keep his wits about him. He'd worked too hard to nurture the tiny sprouts of feelings she'd developed for him to ruin it by snapping back at her. He'd already done damage tonight with his sharp retorts, which became obvious when he watched her eyes skitter back and forth as she looked anywhere but him. He softened his voice to add, "She still is."

"What are you doing, Cord?"

"Trying to talk to you. About CJ. About us."

"I don't want to talk."

He took another sip of wine, watching her, assessing her mood. "Why didn't you tell me?"

"We've been over this."

"Yes. And you still haven't been honest with me."

Jolie closed her eyes and her shoulders drooped. Cord almost felt sorry for her. He definitely wanted to take her in his arms, hold and kiss her, to tell her how he felt, that everything would be all right, over and over again until she believed him. Instead, he waited—outwardly calm but coiled like a tight spring on the inside.

"It was a one-night stand, Cord. That's all. Payback. I didn't have feelings for you anymore."

"Liar." He smiled when he said the word.

"I didn't," she protested. "And then, bam. Two months later, I find out I'm pregnant. I know how you think. How all of you think. I'm not stupid."

"I never thought you were." His forehead furrowed in consternation. "But I'm confused. What are you talking about?"

"You. Your brothers. How many paternity suits have been brought against you?"

He blinked in surprise. "Me? None. Clay's cleaner than a

bottle of bleach. Chance was too careful. Same with Cash."
His lips curled into a wry smirk. "Chase, however, has
probably made the headlines more than he should. But,
sunshine, that has nothing to do with us. With you and me."

"Don't *sunshine* me." Jolie huffed out a breath that ruffled her bangs. "Still."

"Still what?"

"Just…still. You didn't love me. I didn't want to trap you
into a relationship that you'd end up hating me for. Besides,
you wouldn't have listened."

His smile disappeared, and he leaned close enough to
cup her cheek in his palm. "Do you believe that? That I
didn't love you?" Had he never told her? He couldn't, for
his life, remember if he had or not. Had she ever said the
words to him? To his embarrassment, he couldn't remember that, either. He'd just assumed she knew how he felt. "I
did. I do." He shoved his other hand back into his pocket,
closing his fingers around the box, but he could already
feel the moment slipping away. Until he was fairly certain
she'd say yes, Cord was not going to ask her to marry him.

"You're just saying that."

"No, sunshine, I'm not. I do love you. I love CJ, too. I
want the world to know he's my son—that we made something special together."

She tilted her head away from his hand, so he dropped it
to the table and leaned back. "You need to stay away, Cord."

"That's not going to happen. CJ is mine. No matter what
I have to do, I'm going to make sure of that."

"What do you mean?"

"Exactly what I've been saying all along. I want to be a
part of CJ's life. And yours. I want to take care of you both."

"We don't need you to take care of us." Her eyes narrowed in speculation and worry. "Make sure of what? What
have you done?" Her face flushed and her hands once again
twisted in her lap.

Jolie believed she was always in control of her emotions.

Cord knew better. He'd swallowed her screams as she came apart in his arms when they'd made love. He'd absorbed her tears and anger. He'd made her laugh and had laughed with her. She was his everything, no matter what she said.

"Nothing." His gaze never left her face. "Yet. Chance drafted some paperwork. CJ is my son. I want to petition the court to issue an amended birth certificate." He covered her hands with his and she tensed. "You know I want to be his father legally, Jolie. It's for his protection."

She jerked away and scooted her chair back. He tunneled his fingers through his hair. "The accident made me think, sunshine. About the future. About my life. I didn't know CJ even existed, but I do now. I could have died. I want to make sure our son is provided for."

Jolie hissed like a cat dunked in a bucket of cold water. "I have more than enough assets to take care of CJ. And Dad set up a trust when he was born."

"He's still my son, Jolie. I want us to be a family."

"No." She looked around in a panic. "I'm not ready for this, Cord."

Cord concentrated on remaining calm. "Please don't fight me, Jolie. I don't want to go to court. For CJ's sake."

"If you really cared about CJ, you'd drop this. You can hang around with him. That's fine. But you aren't his father. No matter how many papers you file. You never will be."

"Never? That's not a threat you want to make."

# Sixteen

Cord watched Cassie and Miz Beth maneuver around each other in the kitchen. Big John sprawled on one of the oversize stools pulled up to the breakfast bar, begging for tastes with big puppy-dog eyes. The women laughed and teased him as they sailed by, intent on chores only they could accomplish. Cash and Chase played pool in the game room, volleying good-natured, if loud, bets with each stroke of the pool cue. Chance and CJ were flipping through TV channels waiting for the football games to start.

The only Barron brother missing was Clay. He was in the house, but holed up in the study with his speechwriter, Georgie. Politics were afoot and Cord suspected his US Senator brother was looking into a run at the presidency. This was a working vacation for Clay. Georgie had no family as far as Cord knew, so she'd been welcomed into the impromptu family group for Thanksgiving.

He had only one regret. Jolie had refused to come. The fight they'd had three weeks ago still stank up the atmosphere. He hadn't meant to push things, but he was tired of waiting. He wanted her to agree that he had a legal—and emotional—right to CJ. And her. He wanted to marry her, wanted them to be a family. He glanced around again. She'd fit right in with Miz Beth and Cassie. His brothers would come to love her, too.

He'd cajoled, Jolie had haggled and finally they had compromised. He'd proved Cyrus would not make an appearance and she'd reluctantly relented, allowing CJ to come for Thanksgiving. He'd asked her to come again when he'd picked up CJ that morning. She'd refused, tight-lipped and still angry, muttering about his father's shortcomings. She was right. Cyrus wasn't prone to family occasions. He'd left that up to the mothers who'd provided his sons. After Helen, the second Mrs. Barron's death, each wife du jour got younger and younger, and they usually wanted to travel to exotic places rather than deal with a pack of rowdy boys. Miz Beth and Big John had organized the holidays. Birthday parties. Thanksgiving with all the trimmings. Christmas. They'd provided chocolate bunnies and Easter egg hunts, Fourth of July watermelons and Halloween trick-or-treating.

Feeling melancholy, Cord wandered into the great room and sank into one of the massive leather chairs. Sprawling his legs out, he pasted a smile on his face as CJ started jabbering about football teams and who he wanted to win. Chance caught Cord's eye above the boy's head and winked. He grinned at his brother, surprised by the feelings of contentment stealing over him. They hadn't gathered as a family since Chance's wedding. They'd paused in their busy lives to celebrate, and then scattered almost as soon as the reception ended. Cord's near-death experience didn't count because his brothers had visited in shifts. Today was different—laid-back, Clay's work notwithstanding.

The ranch house had evolved through the years, and it now rivaled the house they'd occupied in Nichols Hills when it came to size and amenities. The mansion had never felt like home. This place did. Pictures of all of them as kids lined the rough-hewn fireplace mantel. Colorful Southwest-patterned rugs and blankets added cheer to the great room. The homey scents of roasting turkey, pumpkin pie and baking rolls perfumed the air. Cord wanted this feeling. Wanted this sense of family with his heart and soul. All he needed to do was win Jolie back.

Before he could focus on what he should do to ensure his success, Cassie called them to the table. CJ happily dashed through the house to get "Uncle Clay and the pretty lady." When they were seated, more feelings of family swamped Cord. The massive oak table had come down through the family. Scarred, sanded and refinished countless times through the generations, it was one of the few stable things in their lives. Miz Beth sat at the end nearest the kitchen. Georgie, Clay's assistant, sat on Miz Beth's right, Clay beside her, then Cord and CJ. Big John sat at the other end. On his right down the opposite side sat Cassie, Chance, Chase and Cash. There was room for even more chairs.

Big John said grace, and then food was passed around the table, the Barron brothers fighting over drumsticks, white meat, olives and rolls. CJ had pitted black olives stuck on all the fingers of his left hand and was eating them one by one. No one told him that was rude. This was Thanksgiving.

Dinner ended with pumpkin, pecan, rhubarb, apple and chocolate meringue pies, and CJ winning the wishbone break with Cash—a family tradition for the two youngest Barron males. CJ chortled and bounced on his toes beside the table.

"I win. I win, Uncle Cash. What do I win?"

Rolling his eyes, Cash pushed back from the table and stood. "Ask your father." He turned on his heel and strode away, angry for a reason Cord couldn't fathom. CJ's exuberance captured his attention.

"Daddy, Daddy, what do I win?"

"You get a wish, CJ. And since you won, your wish is supposed to come true."

Cassie slipped her hand into Chance's, smiling at the little boy as she asked, "What do you wish for, CJ?"

A look that Cord almost thought sly slid across his son's face before he spoke. "I want a dog. An' a horse. And Mommy and Daddy."

Cord grabbed CJ and hugged him tightly. "Good wish, bubba."

An hour later, dishes were done and the football game was playing on the massive plasma-screen television. CJ was all but asleep on the floor in front of the TV. Cassie and Georgie visited quietly in a small sitting area off the great room. Big John snored in his chair and Miz Beth had disappeared with a picnic basket. Cord suspected she'd headed to Kaden's house. He'd been surprised the foreman wasn't present. Miz Beth would only say that he'd been invited, but had declined. His brothers had disappeared, but Cord didn't care.

Full and happy, he sprawled in the chair, legs propped on the matching ottoman. His eyes drifted shut as the commentators droned on the TV. Family. His might be dysfunctional, but he truly believed they were finally getting their lives in order and their loyalties on track. Then his phone dinged. A text message.

Cord sat up and rubbed his eyes. The women were visiting in the kitchen while Big John and CJ napped through the football game on TV. He checked the message.

COME TO OLD MANS CONF RM 4 MEETING

Cash had sent it. Cord heaved out of the chair and headed toward the hallway that led deeper into the private areas of the house. The room next to the study had been set up as a conference room. Chance sat on the near side of the table. Looking more like twins than ever, Chase and Cash sat opposite him. Clay sat at one end, and the old man himself occupied the chair at the head. What the hell was Cyrus doing back? Cord's first thought centered on Jolie, and he was glad she hadn't come. His second took a moment to catch up. This wasn't a meeting. This was a Barron family intervention.

When had his father arrived? And why hadn't Chance

warned him? Too late now. He stared at each of his brothers.
Chase and Clay had the good graces not to meet his gaze.
Cash smirked and arched a brow. Chance offered a slight
nod—the only sign of solidarity he'd get in this group. Now
knowing how Chance had felt last spring when they'd all
ganged up on him over Cassie, Cord braced his shoulder
against the doorjamb.

"Took you long enough." His father's glare went nuclear
when Cord simply lifted a shoulder in acknowledgment.
"Sit down." Cyrus gritted out the order.

"Thanks, but I'm comfortable right here." Oh, yeah. He
had the height advantage standing up and wasn't about to
relinquish it.

Cyrus grimaced and turned his baleful stare on Clay,
who had to swivel uncomfortably around in his chair to
speak directly to Cord. The glance was his older brother's
cue to deliver the coup de grâce. Cord waited, more curious than worried.

Clay cleared his throat, unusual for the brother raised
to be first and foremost in the public eye. "Cord, please
come in and sit down."

"I can't stay long, Clay. I have to get CJ home. Spit out
whatever words the old man is putting in your mouth so
we can all get back to our lives."

Cash snorted and leaned back in his chair, the picture of
negligent disdain. "I'll spit it out. You need to sign the papers Chance drew up to get your son away from that bi—"

No one had a chance to intercept him as Cord came
over the top of the conference table, sliding across the polished surface to land on his feet in front of Cash's chair. He
knocked Cash backward and twisted his fist in his brother's
pristine shirtfront. "You watch your mouth, little brother.
Jolie is the mother of my child. You will speak of her with
respect."

The room had gone dead silent. Cash had a couple of
inches and about twenty pounds on him, and Cord still

wasn't back to 100 percent from the accident, but he was so filled with righteous anger that he was positive he could take the other man. He might be mad at Jolie, but no one in his family had the right to say anything about her.

Cash's smirk widened, but he lowered his eyes in a brief display of submission. Cord loosened his grip, straightened and with a deliberate stride, returned to the doorway. "That goes for the rest of you. CJ is *my* son. I'm dealing with this situation." At least he hoped he could without things escalating further. Due to Jolie's continued stubbornness on the matter, he wasn't too sure.

His gaze zeroed in on his father. "I'm not a stupid frat boy anymore, old man. You keep that in mind. What I do with Jolie and *our* son is none of your business." He pinned each of his brothers with the same glare. "That goes for the rest of you, as well. We clear?"

Nobody moved. Chase continued to stare at his hands lying clasped in his lap. Cash glared back. Clay briefly met his gaze before looking away. Chance's eyes twinkled, though his expression gave nothing away. This was all the satisfaction Cord would get from his brothers, but he hammered the point home with his father. "I mean it, Cyrus. I know you. I know what you did to Chance and Cassie. I'm warning you here and now. Don't mess with Jolie and CJ. Don't mess with me."

His old man slowly clapped his hands in derisive applause. "You always were a disappointment, boy. I've given you time and enough rope to tie up this deal, but you've always been weak. That boy is a Barron. He belongs with his family. Get it done. Or else." He glanced at Clay. "My study, now." Pivoting, Cyrus headed to the connecting door. Clay exhaled a heavy breath, rose and followed their father. The door closed behind him, the sharp sound like a period ending the conversation.

Cord turned to duck out the door, ignoring the twins, but he offered Chance a brief tuck of his chin in acknowledgment of Chance's support. He needed to grab CJ and get the hell away. Sometimes it really sucked to be a Barron. He didn't believe for a New York minute that his father would back down. Cyrus wanted control—of his companies, his sons and now his grandson, and the old man wasn't squeamish when it came to playing dirty.

Halfway along the hall, a closed door caught his attention. The back stairs to the playroom. The hairs on his neck prickled. He hadn't been up there since…he couldn't remember when. He wanted to go up, look around, but hesitated. Surely Clay would keep their father occupied for a while. He'd have time to satisfy his curiosity before taking CJ back to Jolie. He opened the door and slipped through. The bare-wood stairs were dusty. Considering Miz Beth's almost obsessive need to clean, the neglect surprised him. The steps stopped at a wide landing with a door. A right turn led to a long hallway that curved back toward the bedrooms.

The thick wooden door looked just as he remembered it—odd colors of flaking paint, wrought iron hinges and door handle, grooves embedded in the wood. He traced his fingers over the scratches and spelled out each of their names, carved meticulously with a pocket knife. He still had a scar on his hand from the exercise. He pressed the handle and pushed. The door swung open on rusty hinges. He stepped inside and flicked the light switch. Nothing happened. Unerringly, he crossed the floor to the nearest window.

Cord flicked the blinds and watched dust motes dance in the late-afternoon sunlight. He hadn't stepped inside this room in years. Part nursery, part playroom, it contained the detritus of five boys growing up. Clay's bookcase full of biographies and histories. Chance's hard-plastic palomino spring horse, its metal frame rusty. Mud-stained equipment bags full of leather gloves and baseball bats belonging to Cash and Chase. A deep set of shelves under one of the room's windows that held games and a whole motor pool of toy trucks and cars. He smiled and hoped CJ liked trucks as much as he had. He'd bet money half of his collection was still buried out in the yard somewhere.

Picking through boxes, he relived memories from childhood. Not all of them were good, which added a layer of melancholy to his search. He glanced around and realized there was something up here he wanted to look at. He found what he'd been searching for over in the corner. The Barron family cradle, the wood carved and shaped by the hands of his great-great-grandfather. Five generations of Barron babies had slept in that cradle. He rubbed dust off with his hand, fingering the spindles turned on a hand lathe. Five generations. But not the sixth. Not his son.

Jolie had robbed him of that by stealing his son away, by running from him without a word. He'd missed almost five years of his son's life. And her pregnancy. A profound sadness settled on his shoulders. Every time he tried to talk to her about it, she threw up walls.

*You wouldn't have listened.*

She'd flung the words at him as if they shielded her from responsibility. He damn well was listening now, wasn't he? *She* was the one turning deaf ears to him. Fine. He was a Barron and so was CJ. Cordell Joseph Barron, even if the damn birth certificate listed Davis as his last name.

Tunneling his fingers through his hair, he worked to calm down as he tried to figure out why they continued to fight over this. He still had every intention of asking her to marry him. Even now, the velvet box resided in the pocket of his leather jacket currently hanging downstairs. He wanted official acknowledgment that CJ was his son. He thought he'd made a simple request. *CJ is my son. I want to petition the court to issue an amended birth certificate.* The kid had his own room at the ranch as well as one at Cord's condo in Oklahoma City. Jolie admitted CJ was his. What was the big deal? But she'd freaked out. Big-time. What was she afraid of?

Cord toyed with his cell phone. He wanted to talk to Jolie. No, he *needed* to talk to her. He'd been patient. He'd courted her, given her space and done everything he knew how to reassure her. Christmas was just around the corner. He wanted his family together for the holidays. Jolie and CJ were his family. The best Christmas present in the world would be his name on CJ's birth certificate and his engagement ring on Jolie's left hand. What was wrong with that?

Evidently everything, judging by Jolie's reaction. He hadn't even gotten to the proposal yet. She didn't trust him. She'd tossed that little gem into his lap, too. Well, trust was a two-way street, and he realized he didn't quite trust her, either. She'd kept their son a secret from him. Anger swelled, deep and raging as bile rose in his throat. He swallowed it down.

"Getting mad isn't the answer," he muttered. He'd get even. That was what Barrons did, right? He had the results from the paternity test. CJ was his. Chance had the papers ready to file. The devil on his shoulder tempted him to give Chance the go-ahead to file suit. Which would be the worst thing he could do. Inhaling the dust and mustiness in the air, he huffed out a breath. He needed to forgive and forget. And so did Jolie. It would be the only way they could move forward.

A scuffing noise had him whirling. Cash stood in the doorway, a smirk on his face, thumbs hooked in his jeans' pockets, his expression nonchalant.

"I didn't figure you for a nostalgic fool, Cord."

His youngest brother resembled their father more and more every day, a thought that worried him. "What are you doing here, Cash?"

"I live here, too."

Cord just managed to stop the eye roll. "None of us live

here anymore. You and Chase have made a point of stay-ing away, in fact."

"Some of us have jobs that keep us on the road."

"You didn't answer my question. Are you spying on me for the old man?"

Lifting one shoulder in a negligent shrug, Cash still wouldn't look directly at him. "Naw. Why bother?"

"But you just happened to wander up here." Yeah, right. Cord eyed his brother and didn't bother to hide his skep-ticism.

Cash stared at him. "The stairwell door was open." He stepped into the room and looked around. "Can't believe all this stuff is still here." He nudged one of the equipment bags with his foot.

"Miz Beth doesn't throw anything away, especially if it's even remotely sentimental." A lump formed in Cord's throat, and he swallowed around it to add, "Or had any-thing at all to do with one of us."

"Sentimental to who?" Cash delivered a savage kick to the bag.

"Her, I guess, since she pretty much raised us. She and Big John never missed any activity one of us was into. Clay's debates and speech tournaments. Chance's and my rodeos. All of our games from Mighty Mites Football and Little League until we were out of high school. I bet if we dig deep enough, the score books John kept are up here somewhere."

Cash's upper lip curled into a snarl. "Some of the kids thought they were our parents."

Cord stared at his brother, his gaze thoughtful as he con-sidered where Cash's sudden vehemence came from. "At least they were there, bud. Our old man never made time for us in any way, shape or form." As Cord watched, an unidentified emotion flickered across Cash's face. It took a few moments for him to figure it out. "He wasn't there for us, either. None of us. He couldn't be bothered. Unless he was telling one of us what to do."

"Yeah, whatever." Cash kicked the bag again and then stared at him. "So what are you going to do about it?"

"About the old man?"

"No. About your own son."

Cord reached down and snagged a Tonka truck. CJ would like it. Tucking it under his arm, he brushed past Cash but paused at the door.

"I'm going to take care of him. Whatever it takes."

# Seventeen

Jolie ignored the restaurant's bustle as she pushed the food on her plate around with her fork. She wasn't hungry—hadn't been since her blowup with Cord after Halloween. She'd somehow managed to get through Thanksgiving, but since then there'd been another fight about CJ's birthday. She'd refused to let him go with Cord, though she'd allowed Cord to talk to her son, and had given CJ the presents Cord dropped by. Despite her insistence she didn't want to talk to him, Cord called. Often. And like an idiot, she answered. He pushed to spend more and more time with CJ. And with her.

Christmas was two weeks away and her life was careening out of control. She didn't know how to avoid the train wreck. Glancing up, she found her father staring at her.

"He's not good enough for you."

She just barely resisted the urge to sigh. "Dad, please."

"You deserve better, Jolene. You deserve a man who will put you and CJ first. A man who will fight for you. Cordell Barron is not that man."

"People change."

"Not that much."

"You don't know him, Dad."

"I know him better than you do, baby girl."

She stared at her father, doing her best to decipher the expression on his face. There was more to all of this—

especially his bragging about knowing Cord well—than he was letting on. "What's that supposed to mean?"

He just looked enigmatic, cutting and eating his steak as though she hadn't asked the question. She seethed in silence, following his example. She'd watched him play this game all her life and she'd learned to play with the big boys. Using her father's tactics got her through college, and then through the admissions process for nursing school. Her clinicals. Her boards. And she'd used them when she insisted she was moving to Houston to have her baby.

"Why are you defending him?"

Opening her mouth to refute, she snapped her jaw shut before speaking. Her dad was right. She'd just defended Cord. The man she was mad at. The man who wanted to twist her world into Gordian knots. She'd had it up to her chinny-chin-chin with alpha men, including her father. But there was only one man who captured her thoughts, held them and made her do and say things totally against the grain. Cord Barron. Damn him.

A tense détente continued until Rand finished his dinner. She'd still barely touched hers. Her stomach roiled with tension. Their waitress cleared their plates, brought dessert Jolie hadn't ordered and filled her coffee cup. She added two creamers and an overflowing teaspoon of real sugar. Ignoring the crème brûlée, she sipped her coffee, watching her dad over the rim of the cup.

"Eat your dessert, Jolene. It's your favorite."

Huh. He'd broken the silence first. Interesting. She was even more curious about his motivation for this tête-à-tête dinner as a result. Indulging him, she spooned a bit of the creamy concoction.

"I'm not a little girl anymore, Dad. You can't divert my attention with treats." She laughed and almost choked. "Or ponies."

Rand chuckled at the memory. "Pony. Singular. And I'm not the one who decided to braid his tail with ribbons."

She smiled fondly, savored another creamy bite and then plastered a serious look on her face. "You should try being honest with me, Dad."

"I am, sugarplum."

"Ugh. First 'baby girl.' Now 'sugarplum.' 'Princess' can't be far behind. Good grief, Dad. When are you going to treat me like an adult?" She wagged her finger. "Do *not* tell me—" She inhaled, and in a reasonable facsimile of her father's voice said, "When you act like an adult."

"Jolene, you don't even know why he broke up with you."

"Want to bet?" She gloated a little over her father's expression. She'd certainly caught him off guard.

"Why don't you tell me the Barron version?"

So she did. She spoke of wanting Cord all through high school. She told him how she'd tried to seduce him at that ill-fated frat party and how Cord had been a perfect gentleman. She admitted to sneaking around behind everyone's backs.

"You were devastated when he broke up with you."

"Yeah, Dad, I was. I loved him. With my whole heart. I was nineteen and I'd given him my virginity." She didn't laugh when her dad blushed, and then stewed a little. "Jeez, Dad. I was, like, the only virgin in my graduating class. And that wasn't for a lack of trying on the boys' part. It's because none of those high school boys held a candle to Cordell Barron."

She finished off the custard and pushed the dish away. "He didn't tell me anything that night. He walked into my room, said, 'It's over' and walked right back out. When he found out about CJ, we talked. Cyrus Barron, that old bastard. Cord left me because his father didn't give him any choice."

"That's bull."

"No, Dad. It's not. You know that evil old man. He laid things out to Cord. Showed him what he could have right before jerking the rug out from under him. He was young. So was I."

Rand attempted to interrupt, but she held up a warning finger to stay him. "Let me finish. You asked what I know and believe. I'm telling you." She sipped her coffee and regrouped her thoughts, even though coffee wasn't what she wanted at the moment. What she really wanted was a good stiff drink. But she'd met her dad at the restaurant and was driving, so coffee would have to suffice.

"St. Paddy's Day. I was out with the girls celebrating passing our boards. And there he was at Hannigan's, with Cooper and some of the guys. I planned to seduce him, Dad. And then get up and walk away, leaving him like he left me. Only we were both so drunk birth control was the last thing on my mind."

She didn't get the rise she intended. Instead, he studied her for a long moment before speaking. "Interesting. That's pretty much the same story he told me when I asked him. Unusual for a man like him to admit a weakness."

Jolie didn't breathe for a moment and then sputtered, "You've talked to him?"

"I had a talk with him one day when I picked up CJ at the ranch." His gaze arrowed in on her. "What was his excuse for leaving you pregnant with my grandson?"

"That's all on me, Daddy." She scrubbed at her forehead with the heels of her hands, but the action did little to alleviate the headache blooming there. She couldn't meet his gaze for a long moment. "You know he didn't walk away when I was pregnant. I never told him."

Rand's expression never changed. Jolie caught no flicker of his thoughts revealed on his face or in his eyes. He simply stared, mouth grim, eyes half-hooded by his lids. When he finally spoke, his words tore at her nerves like a cheese grater.

"I raised you better than that. I didn't agree with you at the time, and look what's happened by keeping that secret."

He leaned back and folded his arms across his chest. "The boy might have surprised us both. I know the man has."

Before she could retort, her cell rang. She would have ignored it, but it was her home number. Jolie answered and Mrs. Corcoran's voice spilled out before she could even say hello.

"You have to come home. You have to come right now." The nanny's words ran together.

"Mrs. C? What's wrong?" Jumping to her feet, Jolie snatched her purse and jacket and headed for the exit. Rand tossed money on the table and followed at her heels. He didn't question her, but steered her to his car and handed her into the passenger seat. Jolie stayed on the phone, listening to Mrs. Corcoran. Fear prickled across her skin, with anger hot on its heels. Her voice tight with emotion, she kept up a running commentary so her father could catch up.

"It's CJ. Some men came to the door. They have papers. Mrs. C is too upset to make sense of them. They're taking CJ. One took him upstairs to get some clothes and his backpack. Mrs. C says he's terrified and crying." Then she put the call on speaker.

She shivered as her father reached across the console and patted her knee. "We'll get to the bottom of this."

Jolie knew he meant to reassure her, but it wasn't helping. What was going on? "Mrs. C? Mrs. C! I want to talk to whoever's in charge."

A man's voice cut through the nanny's hysteria. "This is Harris."

"This is Jolene Davis. Why are you at my house?"

"We have an emergency pickup order for the minor child, Cordell Joseph Davis, pending a hearing on termination of parental rights."

Her heart seized, and she couldn't force words past the pain in her chest. Her father took over.

"This is J. Rand Davis. You touch my grandson and I'll see your ass in jail."

"I have a court order, sir. We are removing the child per that order."

A wail tore from Jolie's very core, but she clapped hands over her mouth to cut it off as her dad squeezed her leg. "My daughter and I are en route. I'm also notifying my attorney. You will do nothing until we arrive."

"That's not the way it works." The line went dead.

Tears overflowed, and Jolie could barely breathe between the sobs, her fear and a boiling anger so strong she could melt the polar caps. By the time they arrived at her house, the men had gone, taking CJ with them. Mrs. Corcoran sat at the kitchen table, sobbing. A Nichols Hills police officer stood there looking uncertain. When Rand pressed for an explanation, the local cop explained that Mrs. Corcoran had hit the panic button on the security system's alarm panel and he'd responded, but not in time to stop the men.

"Yes, sir," he told Rand. "The papers are on the table. They were signed by a district judge. I'm sure sorry 'bout all this. Your nanny told me you were on your way, so I figured it best to stay here with her until you arrived."

"I appreciate that, Officer." Rand's voice left icicles in its wake.

Fifteen minutes later, Mrs. Corcoran had calmed enough to make coffee. Rand and Jolie had both read the papers the men left behind, but none of it made sense to her. When one of Rand's attorneys arrived, he quickly leafed through the papers and explained while Jolie paced the length of the family room, pivoted and paced back.

"CJ won't go into the foster care system. Judge Braxton signed the order, which appears to be civil, not criminal. The order was filed on behalf of the alleged father, and I'm guessing that's where they took your son."

"Have some coffee, honey." Mrs. Corcoran held out a mug as Jolie stalked past her.

Jolie didn't want coffee. She didn't want a drink. She wanted blood. If Cord Barron had been there, she would have sliced him into little pieces and fried him up with hash browns for breakfast. "That means Cord took him. He's probably at Cord's house right this minute. How do I get CJ back?"

The attorney continued perusing the paperwork and it was her father who answered. "I'll call Judge Wilson." Rand patted the seat next to him. "Sit down, Jolene, before you wear out the carpet. The judge owes me a favor. He'll sign a temporary order returning CJ to you."

She didn't want to sit, either. Anger surged through her veins, leaving her hot and cold in waves. "CJ must be scared to death, Daddy. I want him home." Jolie made another pass across the room. "I can't believe Cord would do this, the sorry son of a bitch."

Rand folded his arms across his chest. "I suspect he's gotten desperate, Jolene. You haven't exactly been trying to work through the custody issue with him."

"Whose side are you on, Dad?"

Mrs. Corcoran cleared her throat. "Miss Jolie? Wasn't CJ's daddy who came with those men."

Jolie stopped dead, fingers and toes tingling from the surge of adrenaline. "What do you mean, Mrs. C?"

"The man looked like Mr. Cord, but it wasn't him. When CJ saw him, the little tyke stopped cryin' and ran to him. Called him Uncle Cash."

"That's it." She grabbed her purse and coat. "Give me your keys, Daddy."

"What are you doing, Jolie?"

"I want my son back. I'm going to go get him."

When Rand didn't react fast enough, she rooted in the pockets of his overcoat, found the keys and dashed for the door. She didn't wait for the men as she jumped into her dad's SUV and headed off in a reckless charge to reclaim her little boy.

That twenty-minute drive was one of the longest in her life. As she parked in front of Cord's condo, she let her anger surge. By the time her dad and the attorney arrived, she was standing at the door, tight-lipped, hands fisted at her sides, her heart thudding. She was going to kill Cordell Barron for this.

She pounded on the door. "Cord, open up!" She pounded again and yelled even louder.

Lights blazed on inside and a voice yelled, "What the hell? I'm comin'. Give me a sec."

The locks on the door clicked and the door swung open to show a sleepy-eyed Cord with bed-tousled hair, wearing nothing but gray cotton gym shorts. He absently rubbed fingers through the hair on his chest as he blinked at her, and then registered the presence of her father and the attorney.

Jolie had a moment when anger and fear toppled over into arousal. Damn, but Cord was sexy. How could this man dissolve her into a puddle of wanton desire just by opening the door? Especially now, since, according to those papers, he'd taken her son. What was wrong with her?

Cord stared at Jolie, his eyes narrowing as he recognized J. Rand. The other man standing outside his door looked vaguely familiar, but he couldn't place him. "What the he—?"

His question was choked off as Jolie slapped him. "Where's CJ?"

Cord really regretted the beers he'd drunk with the pizza he'd ordered for dinner. Nothing was making sense—not the rude awakening, being slapped by Jolie or her question. Jolie looked frantic. And pissed. Very, very pissed. He wondered just how many beers he'd had to drink because he sure couldn't figure out what was happening. Before he could ask what she meant, she hit his chest with a balled-up fist. "Where is he? What have you done with him?"

Cord stared at her, wondering how a crazy woman could make his shorts tent. He backed up a step so she couldn't slug him again. He looked at the clock in the foyer. It was after midnight. He'd fallen asleep during the ten o'clock news. "What's going on, Jolie? Why are you asking about CJ?"

"You filed those papers you threatened me with. You're trying to take CJ away from me."

"I did what? Whoa, baby. Slow down, back up and re-wind. What papers?"

"You sent men to my house to get CJ. They had a...a..."

"A temporary custody order," the man who'd come in with Jolie and J. Rand finished. He stepped forward and gave Cord the evil eye. "Michael Weller. I'm representing Ms. Davis in this matter."

"What matter?" Cord figured he looked as confused as he felt. "Jolie, I have no idea what you're talking about. I haven't filed any papers. I don't know anything about a custody order, and I damn sure didn't send anyone to your house to get CJ. Are you saying some men took him? Where is he?"

"He's supposed to be here."

"Supposed to be *here*? Why? I'm telling you, he's not!" Panic threatened to close his trachea so he couldn't breathe, but he didn't have time for that. He had to find out what had happened to his son. "I didn't take him, Jolie." He half turned to Rand, but stopped as tears welled in Jolie's eyes. She looked so lost all he wanted to do was wrap her in his arms and make it all better. He reached for her, but she jerked up her shoulder in self-defense. "Baby, talk to me. What's going on? Where's CJ?" He reached for her again, and this time she fell into his arms, tears staining her cheeks.

"He's gone."

# Eighteen

Heat drained from Cord's body, leaving only ice behind. "Who took him?"

"Your brother."

"Dammit, I have four brothers. Which one?" Cord attempted to focus, but his brain wasn't firing on all cylinders yet. Jolie's announcement had his heart racing like a hamster on a wheel. Who would take CJ? Chance? No way, not after what he and Cassie had gone through to be together. Chase wouldn't be bothered to leave Vegas. Or Nashville. Or wherever he currently happened to be. Clay was in Washington. He answered his own question when he ran out of brothers. "Cash."

She nodded mutely, trying to control her tears.

"I didn't have anything to do with this, Jolie. I promise we'll get him back." He breathed a little easier when her arms tightened around his waist. He brushed a kiss across the top of her head and reluctantly loosened his hold. "I need to get dressed and go get my—our son."

Jolie pushed away from him and flicked tangled hair back from her face. "I'm coming with you."

He didn't want Jolie there when he confronted Cash. Didn't want her to see how badly he'd been betrayed by his family, but he couldn't stop her, either. "I'll be ready in five minutes."

Four minutes later, he was locking the door and headed to his truck. Rand and Weller stood next to a Lexus, arguing with Jolie. She wheeled and marched toward him. "Where are we going?"

"The ranch."

She turned back to her father. "Do what you do best, Dad. I'll keep you posted." She climbed into his truck without help. Once they hit the interstate headed north, Cord barely spared her a glance as he focused on the lines on the highway, knuckles white where they gripped the steering wheel.

"Cord? Can we talk?"

"Not now, Jolie."

He'd never been so damn angry in his entire life. His old man had done some spectacularly stupid crap in his time. But this? Cord had no words—and any he might have wouldn't be coherent. The icy rage swirling in his gut left little room to think. Cord punched the Bluetooth button on the steering wheel and barked, "Call Chance."

Chance answered, sounding neither awake nor alert, which pissed Cord off for some reason. He yelled into the Bluetooth microphone, "Did you have anything to do with this?"

The sound of a jaw-snapping yawn echoed in the truck. "Do you know what time it is? What are you talking about, Cord?"

"Cash and some men showed up at Jolie's. They took CJ."

"Oh, hell, bud. What's our old man done now?"

"He filed some goddamned legal paper. Did you have anything to do with it, Chance?"

Stunned silence hummed in the truck, followed by bitter cussing streaming through the speaker. Cord had been thinking the same curse words. He swallowed and added, "I'm going to kill them, Chance. Both of them." He hit the end button and refused to answer when the screen lit up with an incoming call from Chance.

"You don't really mean that, Cord." Jolie sat twisted in

her seat so she could face him. She looked pale in the dim glow of dashboard lights.

"The hell I don't. That's my son, Jolie. *Our* son. You're his mother. They *took* him from you." He had to breathe around the burning knot in his chest before he could continue speaking, but then realized there was nothing else to say. He clamped his jaw shut and pressed the accelerator a little harder. The truck sped up and the white lines on the highway blurred beneath the big vehicle's tires.

At the ranch, Cord skidded to a stop in front of the main house, barreled out of the truck and sprinted for the front door. He didn't wait to see if Jolie was behind him. He hit the door with his booted foot and it crashed open. Miz Beth and Big John stood in the foyer. She was wringing her hands and John looked as if he was going to be sick.

"Where is he?"

"He's fine, Cord. He's asleep in his room." John's soft rumble attempted to convey a sense of calm, but he was as agitated as his wife.

Jolie's sobbing gasp kept Cord from storming up the stairs. He turned and pulled her to his chest, circling his arms around her shoulders. "Shh, baby. It's okay. We'll get him and go home."

"No. You won't." Cyrus stood in the arched doorway separating the entry from the great room. He glared at Jolie before flicking his gaze to Cord. "She's not welcome here."

"Fine. We'll get CJ and go."

The sound of screeching brakes outside sounded like nails on a blackboard. Cord didn't care. He just wanted to get CJ and go home with Jolie.

Cash stepped up to join his father and Cord saw red— literally. Before anyone could react, he strode to his brother and coldcocked him with a right hook to the jaw. Cash went down as if he'd been poleaxed. Cord turned to his father. "You're nothing but a dried-up piece of cow turd, old man.

I'm going upstairs to get my son, and then his mother and I are taking him home. I'm done with you."

"Cord—"

Chance was suddenly at his side. "Think, Cord. Just shut up and think."

Cyrus puffed up and opened his mouth but didn't get the chance to speak as both Cord and Chance rounded on him and said in tandem, "Shut up."

Cash began to stir. Chance offered him a hand up, which Cash ignored. He remained sitting, butt on the floor, knees bent, his forearms resting across them. He stared at Cord, surprise showing in his expression.

"When the hell did you learn to punch like that?"

"Shut up, Cash. I'm about two seconds from kicking the crap out of you." Cord looked around to apologize to Miz Beth, but realized she and Big John had disappeared. Jolie stood just inside the front door looking shell-shocked.

He faced his father. "What the hell were you thinkin', old man? Oh, wait. You weren't."

Cyrus bristled and jutted his chin, his expression as aggressive as the clenched fist he shook at Cord. "I'll tell you what I was thinkin', Cordell. And I'll tell you what I did. What you should have done months ago when that trash blew back into town with your bastard. I'm making sure my grandson grows up to be a Barron. A legitimate Barron. You should have given him your name—*our* name as soon as you found out. You should have made that boy yours."

The color red edged his vision again. If he didn't stroke out, he was going to beat his father to a bloody pulp. "You're wrong, Cyrus. He's not just my son. He's Jolie's, too. CJ will be a Barron. But he's also a Davis. CJ is our son. Jolie's and mine. I'm not taking him away from his mother. I want to share him with her."

Jolie stepped to his side and slipped her hand into his as Cyrus glared, his face a study in disappointment.

"I'm done with the lot of you. The boy stays here. He's

a Barron and he'll be raised as one. I'll make sure neither of you see him again. Take your whor—" Cyrus didn't get to finish the word as Cord's fist slammed into his jaw. He staggered back a half step before he straightened.

"You'll pay for this, Cordell. I will take away everything I ever gave you." His gaze brushed across Cash. "Clean this up, Cashion." With a final grunt meant to dismiss them all, he walked out the front door, his face a mask of disgust.

Cord shared a glance with Chance before staring down at his youngest brother. "You know, I thought it was pretty crappy when you had those foreclosure papers served on Cassie, but this? Damn, Cash. You are really rolling around the bottom of the outhouse now."

Cash wisely stayed on his butt. "Better me than a stranger, Cord. If the old man sent one of his thugs, we wouldn't know where CJ was. That's why *I* went to get him. And why I brought him here where—"

"What the—?" Cord forced his feet to take two steps back to put space between him and his brothers. "It would have been better not to do this at all. You could have stopped our old man. How could you do this to me? We're family."

Rather than kick—quite literally—his brother while he was down, Cord grabbed a decorative wooden box filled with doodads from a shelf and sent it crashing into the mirror hanging above a pine-and-deer-antler console table near the front door. The mirror shattered. "You're my goddamned brother, Cash, and you betrayed me."

Cash rolled to his feet in a lithe move. Without a glance at Cord or Chance, he strode to the door. He paused and stared back over his shoulder. "No, Cord. I'm not your goddamned brother. You and Chance and Clay are brothers. Chase and me? We never counted. We were always seconds." He walked out, slamming the door behind him, leaving Cord and Chance staring at each other.

Stunned, Cord found his voice first. "What was that

all about?" As he asked the mostly rhetorical question, he remembered his conversation with Cash in their old playroom. Yeah, the twins were technically half brothers to him, Chance and Clay, but he'd never considered them anything but family.

Chance frowned. "I don't know where that came from. We're brothers. All of us."

"Exactly. I always thought it was us against the old man. *All* of us, Chance. After the old man married Helen, she was our mom, the twins our brothers."

Tunneling his fingers through his hair, Cord felt rocked to his very foundation and completely out of control. He didn't like either feeling. At all. He wanted to grab the world with both hands and twist it, shape it, stuff it back into the mold he'd created so that everything was nice and neat and running the way he wanted it.

Chance stared at the closed door. "He's sure got a chip on his shoulder about something, though. I'll call Chase in the morning, see if he knows what's going on with Cash." Chance stepped closer and lowered his voice. "Look, we need to talk."

Cord sneered, but also replied in a quieter voice. "About Cash?"

"No. About—" Chance raised his hand in a vague wave "—all of this."

"Cash and a couple of his goons scared the nanny and took CJ. On the old man's orders. Without my knowledge or permission. What's there to talk about, Chance?" He held out his hand for Jolie. "Let's get CJ and go home."

Chance's next words pulled his attention back to his brother. "I want to see the order, check to see which judge signed it. This whole deal smells like an overflowing porta-potty on a hot July day."

"You got that right."

Chance exhaled and rubbed his eyes before addressing Jolie. "You may or may not believe me, Jolie, but here's the truth. Yes, I had a paternity test done to confirm that CJ is Cord's. And yes, I drew up some orders petitioning for a name change and amended birth certificate. Cord asked me to hold off filing. I did. I wish now I hadn't. If we'd fixed things in the beginning, it never would have come to this. I'm also positive that Cyrus used one of his pet legal sharks to draft whatever the hell was filed. I'm sorry. If you'll let me, I'd like to look at the paperwork you were given. And I'd like the opportunity to fix the mess my—" He choked off the expletive. "The mess our father made." He offered her a bitter smile. "Sadly, I've been there, done that and my wife occasionally sleeps in the T-shirt."

Jolie lifted a shoulder in a small shrug and flashed a tired smile. She leaned against Cord's arm as he gave her hand a gentle squeeze. "I'll go get CJ, 'kay?"

He nodded and reluctantly released her hand. Chance stepped up beside him as they watched Jolie climb the stairs. "We'll make this right, Cord. One way or another. And don't worry about the old man's threats. He can't do a thing. I've made sure he can't touch any of us."

Overcome with emotion, Cord grabbed his brother in a bear hug. "You've always had my back. You know I'll always have yours, right?"

Big John appeared with a broom and dustpan and cleared his throat. "Better get this mess swept up before the young 'un comes down."

Miz Beth arrived a moment later, dragging a large trash can behind her. Chance hurried to relieve her of it and bent to help John. The older woman touched Cord's arm. "Your father is a mean ole son of a gun, Cordell. Thank goodness you boys didn't fall close to that tree. I was ready to box Cash's ears when he walked in with CJ."

A quick laugh burst from Cord at the thought of tiny Miz Beth giving Cash what for. "At least he brought CJ here, Miz Beth, where you and Big John could look after him." And wasn't that what Cash had been trying to tell him? He'd been too pissed to listen.

Miz Beth used a corner of her apron to dash away the moisture gathered in her eyes. She was rising on her toes to plant a kiss on his cheek when Jolie screamed Cord's name. Miz Beth scrambled out of his way as he raced to the staircase and took the steps two at a time, Chance and Big John hard on his heels. He careened into CJ's room expecting to find blood-splattered walls or worse.

"Jolie? Jolie, baby. What's wrong?" Cord hauled her against his chest, checking out the room over her head. The bedclothes were rumpled but there was no sign of CJ. John checked the bathroom while Chance checked the closet and under the bed. CJ was nowhere to be found. John checked the window. It was closed and locked.

"Where is he, Cord?" Jolie seemed to clamp down on her panic. She gazed around the room. "Where's Ducky? Where's his backpack? Mrs. Corcoran said he'd had both with him when Cash took him."

"We'll search the house, Jolie. He can't be far."

"Do you… Would they…?" She was unable to finish her thought, but Cord knew what she was thinking.

"No. There's no way Cyrus or Cash could have taken him. He's here somewhere. Maybe he woke up and heard the yelling, got scared. He's probably hiding in the house."

They split up and searched the house from top to bottom, which took far longer than Cord wished. As they gathered downstairs in the kitchen, Big John appeared, a hangdog expression on his face. "Back door in the utility room isn't closed all the way. I'm sorry, Cord, but it looks as though he got out of the house." The older man glanced over his shoulder. "And it's starting to snow."

# Nineteen

The weak winter sun poked at the clouds riding low on the eastern horizon and touched the light dusting of snow with a handful of sparkles. The serene scene did nothing to alleviate the tension in the kitchen. Dark shadows bruised the skin around Jolie's red-rimmed eyes. Her face was drawn and pale, and she looked as exhausted as Cord felt. Cassie sat next to her, attempting to get her to eat some of the eggs and bacon Miz Beth had cooked.

With Kaden's help, they'd searched the barn, all the farm equipment and the stables. They'd awakened the ranch hands and checked each of the cottages. There'd been no trace of CJ, nor had he answered their desperate shouts. They did discover that Dusty was missing, too. Cord tried to take some comfort in that. The dog was big and furry and hopefully keeping CJ warm overnight.

A local newscast droned in the background, and when the morning weather forecast came on, Big John turned up the volume. The prediction wasn't good. A big storm was due by noon, with plummeting temperatures and ice. They had to find CJ and find him now. Cord regretted calling off the search in the dark hours before dawn, but Chance, Kaden and Big John had all convinced him that stumbling around in the dark wasn't smart. With daylight, they could find tracks, follow them. And search teams would arrive.

The back door opened and heads swiveled, hope plastered on every face, only to be let down when Cash walked in. He held his hands at shoulder level, palms forward as if he was surrendering. "You may not want it, but I'm here to help, Cord." His gaze snapped to Jolie and he squared his shoulders. "I'm sorry, Jolie. This is my fault. I saw CJ at the top of the stairs last night, watching what was going on. I didn't say anything."

Cord made a fist, ready to take another swing at his younger brother when Chance's hand clamped on his shoulder. "Breathe, Cord. Last night is done. We need all the help we can get to find CJ before the storm hits."

Cord inhaled sharply, his gaze never leaving Cash's face until he heard Jolie move. He glanced at her and her eyes met his. She tucked her chin a bare inch, her expressive face filled with a rush of emotions. She broke their connection with a flick of her eyes toward Cash but returned to capture his gaze once more.

"Yes," she said, her eyes still boring into his, but her words meant for his brother. "It is your fault." Cash winced and stepped back. "You should have said something. You should have not taken him to begin with. I..." She balled up her fist and pounded the granite top of the breakfast bar.

Cord grabbed her hand, wrapped her up in a hug. He knew her frustration. He wanted to put his fist through a wall. Or his brother's face. Again. But Cash was here. Apologetic. Wanting to help.

"Jolie?" Rand called to her softly from the doorway. Cord was glad Jolie's father had finally arrived. He let her go and she ran to the other man. Rand patted her back and he murmured soft endearments to her, but his gaze remained first on Cord and then on Cash.

"I have a team with me, Cord, and two more on the way. If the weather clears, I can get at least two helicopters in the air. Hell, I'll put them up even if the weather doesn't." Cash still didn't step farther into the room. "Just tell me what you want, what you need."

Jolie pushed away from Rand and faced Cash. "You're

still a royal jerk, Cash, but thank you. We can use your help." She stepped toward Cord, and he closed the distance between them, sweeping her into his arms. "Bring him home, Cord. Bring our baby home."

Controlled chaos followed her plea. Cash opened the back door to usher in some of his security team. Cooper Tate and his brother, Bridger, tromped in carrying boxes of electronic gear. Cash waved them into the dining room. Deputies from the Logan County Sheriff's Office arrived, along with members of the volunteer fire department. The table that had been the scene of a family Thanksgiving just weeks ago now became their "war room."

Cassie watched the weather on TV while she helped Miz Beth make coffee and food. Jolie stood at the wide window overlooking the backyard. Cord appeared behind her and circled his arms around her middle. "We'll find him, Jolie."

"I'm scared, Cord. He's just a little boy."

"I know, baby. But us Barrons are stubborn cusses."

The strangled noise she made was either choked laughter or a sob. He stood with her, letting the babble from the dining room wash over him. When he heard doors opening, he hugged her, kissed the top of her head and disengaged. It was time to find CJ and bring him home. "I'll be back, sunshine. With our son."

He left her standing there. She looked frail, but looks were deceiving. She was one of the strongest women he knew. Words formed on the tip of his tongue, but he couldn't spit them out. Not yet. Not until CJ was safe. Then he'd tell her. He'd be able to say the words then.

The search teams had their assignments and spread out, going to work. Cord joined the team leaders on the front drive. He wanted to go, but Chance and Cash both overruled him.

"Stay with Jolie, Cord. She needs you. We'll find him." Chance's breath fogged the air until the brutal north wind shredded it. The temperature kept dropping, the sun a pallid circle behind thick clouds. His brothers pivoted and marched off to join their assigned teams.

Growls from ATVs drowned out shouts and excited barks from the search dogs. Close to fifty people milled around, getting sorted out, ready to do their jobs. Rand appeared at his shoulder and Cord spared him a glance. The older man looked as exhausted as Cord felt.

"I'm sorry, Rand."

"For what, son? You didn't make your daddy a jackass. And I probably should apologize to you. I knew about CJ. Knew he was yours. But Jolie—"

A wry chuckle escaped before Cord could cut it off. "Yeah. Jolie is a lot like her father. She wants to do things her way."

Rand slapped him on the back. "That she does, Cordell. That she does. Gonna take a special man to win and keep her."

"I'm workin' on that, sir. I surely am."

"Good."

The other man flipped up the collar of his coat and tilted his head toward the house. "It's colder than a two-dollar whore's heart out here. Let's get inside."

After the team leaders cleared out, Jolie returned to the kitchen and went through the motions of helping Miz Beth and Cassie. She needed to do something—*had* to do something to keep from going crazy. She mindlessly shoved cups and plates into the dishwasher, all the while listening to the radio traffic in the next room. The news wasn't good. The snow had come too late to show any tracks CJ might have left and the wind was playing havoc with the tracking dogs.

Where would CJ have gone? He'd only been out here to the ranch a few times—to swim in the heated pool, to ride horses in the corral, to play in the barn. He'd have told her if he had a special place out here. Wouldn't he? She dropped the coffee mug in her hand and ran into the other room. Cord wasn't there. Her father looked up, a question in his eyes.

"Where's Cord?"

He stepped into the room. "I'm here, Jolie. What's wrong?"

"CJ. Did he have a special place here?"

Cord's forehead furrowed in thought. "Like what? A hidey-hole? I mean, he has his room. He liked to play in the hayloft of the barn. The pool."

Her breath—and her enthusiasm—whooshed out in a sigh of disappointment. "Oh." She wrapped her arms across her chest to hide her shivers. "I just… I don't know. I thought maybe…"

"Maybe what?" Cord walked up to her, his expression grave.

"I thought there might be someplace he liked to go." She swiped her hair off her forehead and muttered, "Never mind," before retreating back to the kitchen. The babble in the dining room overwhelmed her. She couldn't understand all the radio messages, and trying to decipher them gave her a headache. Coffee. She'd get some coffee. Or maybe hot tea. She was numb, but cold leached into her very bones. As though it would rob her little boy of his heat, and maybe his life. A hard shiver stomped down her spine, kicking each one of her vertebrae until she just wanted to curl up in the fetal position.

"Hang on, baby. Hang on for Mommy."

Cord wanted to follow her, but the need to listen to the radio, to know exactly what was happening, held him frozen. He twisted around to look out the window, pressing his forehead against the cold glass. The gentle swells of the nearest pasture undulated like frozen waves. A dark line of trees loomed beyond the red barn. He stared but didn't see the snow-dusted landscape. Was Jolie on to something? She knew their little boy better than he did—at least for now. His mind replayed everything he and CJ had ever done here at the ranch.

They'd taken ATV rides. Fished in the lake. He quit breathing for a minute. Surely CJ wouldn't have gone to the lake, not when it was so cold outside. Whipping his head around, he yelled over to Bridger, who was working the radio communications. "The lake! Has anyone checked the lake?"

"First thing, Cord. There's no sign of him there. No tracks. And the mud wouldn't have frozen until this morning. The search party would see any prints if he'd gotten close to the water."

He breathed through the momentary panic. This wasn't helping. He felt sick inside. Looking up, he saw her in the doorway to the kitchen. She looked wrung out but he figured he didn't look much better.

"Miz Beth made tea. Do you want some?"

He walked over to her and gathered her into his arms. "Not thirsty, sunshine."

"I hate your father." Her words were muffled against his chest.

"Makes two of us."

"I'm sorry, Cord. For keeping CJ a secret. For fighting you. I've been so…scared. Of losing CJ because he might love you more than me."

"No, baby. That wouldn't happen. I want to be his dad. I want us to be a family. I don't want to take him away. Shh. S'okay. No more secrets, sunshine. Never again. Not between us." Her sob was also muffled in his shirt, but he felt the shudders racking through her. He held her, absorbed her fear and sorrow as she cried, and he shed a few tears of his own. He hadn't cried since his mother died. Or Helen, when she was killed by that drunk driver. The old man yelled when they cried. Called them weak. He had a place he'd run away to…

"Ah, crap!"

Jolie startled in his arms and he turned her loose. "Cord?"

"The caves. Why didn't I think of that?" If he'd been sitting at a desk he would have banged his head on it.

"Caves?"

"There are some caves in the hills down by the river. I used to go there. CJ and I rode out there one time. I told him about exploring them when I was a kid."

"Tell Bridger. Call one of the teams."

"The teams can't get to him. The terrain is too rugged for the ATVs. I'll have to ride."

"Ride?"

"Horseback. It's the quickest way to get there."

"I'm coming with you." She jutted her chin and her eyes flashed.

Cord dropped a soft kiss on her mouth. Seemed the Davis family was just as stubborn as the Barrons. "Put on warm clothes. Miz Beth will find some for you. I'll go saddle the horses."

They rode for twenty minutes, the north wind nipping and biting every inch of exposed flesh. Sleet pinged off their heavy coats and clung to the manes and hides of the horses. Even the animals seemed to be shivering despite their thick winter coats. They were ranch stock, bred to work. They weren't the hothouse purebloods Kaden used in the breeding program. They crossed terrain marked with steep arroyos with crumbling red dirt sides. They skirted rocky outcroppings and pushed through scrub brush thick enough that an ATV would have no chance. As they rode toward the river and the rocky hills where Cord's cave was located, he and Jolie took turns calling CJ's name.

He glanced over at her but couldn't see much of her face besides her eyes. He lowered his muffler. "Can I ask you something?"

Jolie turned her head to watch him. "I guess so?"

"Do you trust me?"

"What? Where'd that come from?"

"I need to know, Jolie. Do you trust me? With taking care of CJ? With taking care of…you?" She didn't answer and the wind kicked up again but he didn't pull the muffler up. "I need to know, baby. I need to know if there's any hope for us, and if you don't trust me, if you believe that I could do to our son—to you—what my father did…" He swallowed hard, choking back his anger. "Do you believe I'm like the old man?"

"Oh, God, no, Cord! You aren't like him."

"But…" He stared at her when she wouldn't look at him.

"Deep down, no, I didn't believe you would take CJ— not that way. But last night, when I got that call, I was scared. Terrified."

"So you don't trust me."

"That's not what I said." Real heat singed her voice. "Why are you asking me this stuff?"

"I need to know if we have a chance."

A bark echoed before she could reply. Cord stood up in his stirrups and let loose with a shrill whistle. Excited barking answered him. "Dusty!" He reined his horse around and headed toward a rocky hill at a canter. Jolie quickly caught up. Cord whistled again, and the barks sounded closer. A flash of black-and-white caught his eye. He pointed toward the dog racing their direction. "There! It *is* Dusty." He kicked his horse into a full gallop, Jolie's horse following.

They met the dog at the base of the hill, sliding their horses to a stop with a sharp pull on the reins. Cord swung out of the saddle with a grace born of practice and called Dusty to him. He ruffled the dog's ears and fur. "Where's CJ? Is he with you?" He studied the hillside, then cupped his hands and yelled, "CJ? Are you here?"

Jolie's voice joined in. "CJ? Mommy and Daddy are here! Where are you?"

"Mommy?" A thin, wavering voice floated down. "Daddy?"

Dusty barked and charged up the hill, Cord fast on his heels. "Stay there, Jolie. I'll bring him down. I promise."

Cord found CJ tucked back into a shallow cave, wrapped in a thin blanket. "C'mon, bubba. Time to go home." CJ leaped into his arms, and Cord simply held his son for a long moment.

CJ wrapped his arms around Cord's neck, his legs around his waist. With careful haste, aware of the terrain and prancing dog both waiting to trip him, Cord clamored down the hill. Jolie had dismounted, and she grabbed CJ from him, kissing and hugging the boy. Cord pulled the two-way radio from his saddle pack.

"Bridger, this is Cord. Can you read me?"

"Loud and clear, Cord."

"We have him." Cheers erupted on Bridger's end. "He's cold and hungry. We'll be back in about thirty."

"There will be an ambulance standing by. Safe trip, Cord. And good news, cuz!"

The doctors at Children's Hospital gave CJ a clean bill of health but wanted to keep him overnight for observation. Almost the entire family had trooped through, leaving stuffed animals, balloons and candy behind. When things finally calmed down, and Cord and Jolie were left alone in the hospital room, he asked the question Jolie had avoided thinking about since they'd found CJ.

"Why did you run away, CJ?"

"The yelling. It scared me."

Jolie clutched him to her and Cord wrapped his arms around them both. "I'm sorry, CJ. Sorry for everything."

"I didn't mean to be bad."

"Ah, CJ. Don't. You weren't bad. It wasn't your fault, bubba. Sometimes, grown-ups are just...dumb."

Jolie squeezed the little boy's hand, but her smile was

for Cord. "Yeah. Sometimes grown-ups are just dumb."
She inhaled and blew the breath out hard enough to ruffle
her bangs. "Yes."

Cord looked confused. "Yes?"

"Yes. I trust you. To take care of CJ. To take care of me.
I trust you with my heart."

"Oh." A big goofy smile spread across his face. "Oh!"
He scrambled off the bed and grabbed his coat. He dug in
all the pockets, his expression growing more panicked.
Searching in one last place, the inside left chest pocket that
rode right over his heart, he found what he was looking for.

His big hand held something, but Jolie couldn't tell what.
Her heart rate ratcheted up, and she tried to breathe around
its pounding. He dropped to one knee beside the bed and
she was vaguely aware that CJ clapped his hands and giggled. When Cord opened his hand, a black velvet box sat
on his palm. Blood roared in her ears, and she gulped in a
breath, reaching for a calm she didn't feel.

"Jolie, I love you. I think I fell in love the moment I first
saw you. I've pretty much messed up from the very beginning, but if you'll give me a chance, I promise to love
you and our son every day until there are no more days."
He opened the box. A diamond-and-emerald ring glinted
under the fluorescent hospital lights. "Jolene Renee Davis,
will you do me the honor of being my wife? Of being the
mother of my children? Of loving me even half as much
as I love you?"

CJ poked her in the back. "Say yes, Mommy."

She blinked back tears, her cheeks aching from the smile
that stretched them to the max. "Oh, yes, Cordell Thomas
Barron. I will marry you." She fell into his arms. "I do love
you. I love you with my whole heart."

# Epilogue

Cord rolled over and gathered the woman sleeping at his side into his arms so they were spooned together. Jolie stirred and muttered something about sleep. He kissed her bare shoulder and rubbed his cheek against her sleep-tousled hair. Her lips looked plumped and she bore a slight rash from his beard stubble along her jawline. Considering this was their wedding day, he should feel bad about that, but didn't. That was what all the gunk littering the counter in the bathroom attached to the guest bedroom at Chance and Cassie's house was for. He cupped her breast, tracing his thumb over her nipple. It perked right up from his attention, but it was Jolie's grumbling that put a big grin on his face.

"I love you, sunshine."

She sighed, and he leaned over to capture the end of her breath with a gentle kiss. She shifted beneath him and he covered her with his body. If he were a gentleman, he'd go shower and shave before making love to her. But he wasn't. He was a man wildly in love with his woman, and he wanted to brand her as his for all time. Breaking their kiss, he trailed his lips down her chin and throat until he found her other breast. Flicking his tongue over that nipple, it caught up to its partner on the perky meter. She gasped as he scraped his teeth over the sensitive tip and his erection swelled.

Cord suckled her breast while his fingers continued to tease her other nipple. She arched beneath him, rubbing her thigh against him. He groaned and glanced at her. Eyes open, she watched him, her mouth quirked and her eyes narrowed. That was a dare if he'd ever seen one. With slow, sure certainty, he kissed his way across her rib cage. He paused at her belly button to lay a circle of kisses around its perimeter before dipping the tip of his tongue inside it. She giggled, as he knew she would. His Jolie was ticklish despite her protestations to the contrary.

Murmuring around the hitches in her breathing, she rolled her hips, tempting him to dip lower. He rubbed his chin through the soft curls at the juncture of her thighs. She opened farther for him. Well aware of the roughness of his morning stubble, he kissed her most secret of places—places he knew so well. He teased with his tongue and lips. And then he tasted her. Deeply. She was wet and ready for him.

"Please," she sighed.

"Please what, sunshine?"

"Please love me, Cord."

He rose above her and slid his aching erection into her softest depths. "Always, Jolie. I'll always love you."

He made slow, sweet love to her, their connection so deep he felt as if he was part of her—just as it should be. When he could stand it no longer, he shifted and angled her hips a little higher. Jolie's sharp inhalation told him he'd found the spot. Increasing the tempo, he drove them higher and higher until she clenched him and shuddered. His mouth crushed hers as his body followed her lead, and he swallowed his name on her lips.

Sometime later, Jolie cupped his cheeks and studied him. "Sweetheart?"

Cord crushed her to his chest. "I love you so damn much, Jolie. You're my life. You and CJ."

"You realize this is all kind of wrong, right? Making love on our wedding day, before the ceremony?" Her eyes twinkled and her mouth quirked in a mischievous smile.

"I'm going to start every day making love to the woman who branded my heart."

They had about thirty seconds' warning before a tiny whirlwind hit the door and blew through it. Cord managed to roll over and tuck Jolie into his side before CJ lunged onto the bed and started bouncing. "Mommy! Daddy! We're gettin' married today."

Laughing, he grabbed his son and pulled him down, careful to keep the blankets pulled over Jolie. Cord really needed to remember to lock their bedroom door. "We most definitely are, bubba. Go get Aunt Cassie to fix you breakfast. Mom and I will be down in a little bit."

"Okay!" Their son bestowed sloppy little-boy kisses on their cheeks, jumped off the bed and remembered to shut the door behind him.

Three hours later, the Crazy M ranch was filled with guests. Chance and Cassie had moved into the new house they'd built on her family property. Part luxurious log house and part historic Oklahoma giraffe rock, their home was a place of warmth and love—and the perfect place for Cord to marry Jolie. A large swath of early-spring grass carpeted an area between the house and a new barn. White chairs formed rows with a broad aisle down the middle—space wide enough for two horses to walk side by side.

Cord waited in the barn with his brothers. As they had for Chance the previous summer, they'd gathered in a show of solidarity. Chase had even turned off his cell phone. Cash was there as well, though he held himself apart from the rest. Cord would push Cash about his issues, but not today. Today was all about Jolie. And CJ. About becoming family. Horses snorted and pawed in their stalls, bridles jingling. CJ bounced between his uncles. The horses had been his idea. And the Western theme. Instead of tuxes, they wore knife-edge pressed jeans. Cord's shirt was white, the others' Oklahoma blue, and they all wore bolo ties cinched with turquoise—his groomsmen gift to each of them.

When the time arrived, Cord helped CJ mount his horse. The gray filly had been his Christmas gift to his son. He mounted his chestnut quarter horse and his brothers followed suit. They rode out of the barn, single file. Kaden waited at the back of the crowd to hold CJ's horse until it was time for the boy to ride down the aisle. First, the men would ride to the flower-entwined bentwood arbor where the minister waited. The bridesmaids, also mounted, would follow, then CJ, right before J. Rand escorted Jolie down the aisle. In a rare show of humor, Kaden promised he wouldn't let the bride bolt.

A local country band played a popular love song as his brothers led the way. When Cord arrived, he dismounted and turned to watch the procession. There were three bridesmaids—friends of Jolie. Cassie, the matron of honor. CJ. And then he saw Jolie. Soft sunshine painted the day with pastel colors and cast a glow only surpassed by the bride. He'd waited so long for this moment, hoped for it with every fiber of his being, and there she was.

She reined her mare to a stop. Cord vaguely heard the minister ask about who gave this woman. Then he was moving to her, lifting her down from the horse, holding her cradled in his arms before placing her on her feet. Words. Music. More words. And then he had a ring in his hand, a ring he slid on her finger as he said, "With this ring, I give you my heart. On this day, I give my promise to walk with you, hand in hand, wherever life takes us. I offer you my heart, my soul. You and me. Together. Forever."

Jolie said the words back, slipping a ring on his finger. Her eyes looked like emeralds sprinkled with diamonds, just like the engagement ring he'd given her kneeling there in CJ's hospital room back in December. He felt back in control now, and all was right in his world as the minister pronounced them husband and wife and said he could kiss his bride. He did, whispering across her lips, "You are my sunshine."

\* \* \* \* \*

# This was the closest she'd been to him.

Close enough to feel the warmth of his body radiating in the space between them. Close enough to see the deep golden flecks in his brown eyes. "I haven't done anything yet," she said.

"You're here. Right now, that's everything."

Even though Jane was waking up and starting to fuss at still being swaddled in the blanket, Trish couldn't pull away from the way Nate's eyes held hers.

"You don't have to buy me a phone." It came out as a whisper.

The corner of his mouth curved up and he suddenly looked very much like a man who would seduce his temporary nanny just because he could. "And yet, I'm going to anyway."

Trish swallowed down the tingling sensation in the back of her throat. This was Nate after a nap? What would he be like after a solid night's sleep?

And how the hell was she going to resist him?

\* \* \*

**The Nanny Plan**
is part of the No.1 bestselling series from
Mills & Boon® Desire™: Billionaires and Babies—
Powerful men…wrapped around their
babies' little fingers.

# THE NANNY PLAN

BY
SARAH M. ANDERSON

Published in Great Britain 2015
by Mills & Boon, an imprint of Harlequin (UK) Limited,
Eton House, 18-24 Paradise Road, Richmond, Surrey, TW9 1SR

© 2015 Sarah M. Anderson

ISBN: 978-0-263-25258-3

51-0415

Harlequin (UK) Limited's policy is to use papers that are natural, renewable and recyclable products and made from wood grown in sustainable forests. The logging and manufacturing processes conform to the legal environmental regulations of the country of origin.

Printed and bound in Spain
by CPI, Barcelona

Award-winning author **Sarah M. Anderson** may live east of the Mississippi River, but her heart lies out West on the Great Plains. With a lifelong love of horses and two history teachers for parents, she had plenty of encouragement to learn everything she could about the tribes of the Great Plains.

When she started writing, it wasn't long before her characters found themselves out in South Dakota among the Lakota Sioux. She loves to put people from two different worlds into new situations and to see how their backgrounds and cultures take them someplace they never thought they'd go.

Sarah's book *A Man of Privilege* won the 2012 RT Reviewers' Choice Award for Best Mills & Boon® Desire™. Her book *Straddling the Line* was named Best Mills & Boon Desire of 2013 by *CataRomance*, and *Mystic Cowboy* was a 2014 Booksellers' Best Award finalist in the Single Title category as well as a finalist for the Gayle Wilson Award for Excellence.

When not helping out at her son's school or walking her rescue dogs, Sarah spends her days having conversations with imaginary cowboys and American Indians, all of which is surprisingly well tolerated by her wonderful husband. Readers can find out more about Sarah's love of cowboys and Indians at www.sarahmanderson.com.

To Maggie Dunne, the founder of
Lakota Children's Enrichment.
You had a very large check and a whole lot of
gumption! While I changed many things,
I hope I kept your spirit of charitable action going!

To Maisey Yates and Jules Bennett, who came up with
the baby for this book. You guys are the baby experts!

And to Laurel Levy for making sure I got the details
of San Francisco right. I'll get back out there
to visit you someday!

# One

The auditorium was filling up, which was exactly what Trish wanted. Maybe four hundred people had crowded into the lower level and, in addition to the journalists from the college paper, some reporters from the San Francisco television stations were in attendance. Excellent. A good crowd would leverage some social pressure on her target. No billionaire would risk looking heartless by saying no to a charity in front of a big crowd.

Trish had been sitting in her spot—end of the third row, to the left of the podium on the stage—for over an hour. She'd gotten here early enough that no one had seen her smuggle in the check. She wished she could afford a cell phone—then she could at least play with that until the talk started instead of being the only person in the room who wasn't connected.

She was as ready as she was ever going to be. She just had to wait for her moment. Timing an ambush of one of the wealthiest men on the planet required precision.

Trish had planned everything down to her shirt—a great find at Goodwill. It was a distressed blue T-shirt with a vintage-looking Wonder Woman logo emblazoned over her breasts. It was a half size too small, but she had on her black velvet suit jacket, so it looked fine. Polished, with a geeky air.

Exactly like her target, Nate Longmire.

People continued to filter in for another thirty minutes. Everyone was here to see Longmire, the newest billionaire to come out of Silicon Valley's wealth generators. Trish had done her homework. Longmire was twenty-eight, which didn't exactly make him the "Boy Billionaire" that the press made him out to be. As far as Trish could tell, there wasn't anything particularly boyish about him.

He was six foot two, broadly built and according to her internet searches, single. But the plan wasn't to hit on him. The plan was to make him feel like she was a kindred soul in all things nerd—and all things compassionate. The plan was to box him into a corner he could only donate himself out of.

Finally, the lights in the auditorium dimmed and the president of the Student Activities Board came out in a remarkably tight skirt. Trish snorted.

"Welcome to the Speaker Symposium at San Francisco State University. I am your host, Jennifer McElwain…"

Trish tuned the woman out as Jennifer went on about SFSU's "long and proud" history of social programming, other "distinguished guests," blah-blah. Instead of listening, Trish scanned the crowd. Over half of the mostly female crowd looked like they were hoping for a wild ride in a limo to happen within an hour.

The sight of so many young, beautiful women made Trish feel uneasy. This was not her world, this college full of young, beautiful people who could casually hook up and hang out without worrying about an unexpected pregnancy, much less how to feed that baby. Trish's world was one of abject poverty, of never-ending babies that no one planned for and, therefore, no one cared for. No one except her.

Not for the first time, she felt like an interloper. Even though she was in her final year of getting a master's degree in social work—even though she'd been on this campus for five years—she still knew this wasn't her world.

*Suck it up*, she thought to herself as she counted the number of television cameras rolling. Five. The event was getting great press.

She was a woman with a large check and a secondhand Wonder Woman T-shirt waiting to ambush one of the richest men on the planet. That was her, Trish Hunter, in a nutshell.

"…And so," Jennifer went on, "we are thrilled to have the creator of SnAppShot, Mr. Nate Longmire, here with us tonight to discuss social responsibility and the Giving Pledge!"

The crowd erupted into something that wasn't quite a cheer but came damn close to a catcall as the Boy Billionaire himself walked on stage.

The audience surged to their feet and Trish surged with them. Longmire walked right past her. She had an excellent view of him.

*Oh.* Oh, *wow.* It's not like she didn't know what Nate Longmire looked like. She'd read up on his public persona—including that ridiculous article naming him one of the Top Ten Bachelors of Silicon Valley, complete with a photo spread.

But none of the pictures—not a single one of them—did the man justice. Attraction spiked through her as she studied him. In person, the tall frame and the broad shoulders weren't just eye-catching, they moved with a rippled grace that left her feeling flushed. He had on hipster jeans and Fluevog boots, but he'd paired them with a white tailored shirt with French cuffs and a purple sweater. A striped purple tie was expertly tied around his neck. He wore a scruffy beard and thick horn-rimmed glasses. They were the nerdiest things about him.

Longmire turned his face to the crowd and Trish swore

she saw him blush as the thunderous noise continued. He did not preen. If anything, he looked almost uncomfortable. Like he didn't quite fit in up there.

"Thank you," he said when the noise did not let up. "Please," he asked, a note of desperation in his voice, motioning for everyone to sit down. That, at least, worked. "There we go. Good evening, San Francisco State University!"

More applause. Trish swore he winced. He sat on a stool in the middle of the stage, gestured and the lights went down. A single spotlight fell on him. Behind him, a screen lowered to the ground and a slideshow began.

"Technology," he started as the screen flashed images of attractive people on tablets and smartphones, "has an enormous transformative power. Instant communication has the power to topple governments and reshape societies at a rate of speed that our forefathers—Steve Jobs and Bill Gates—only dreamed of." The audience laughed at this joke. Longmire gave them a tight smile.

Trish studied him as he spoke. He'd obviously memorized his remarks—not surprising, given that the press had reported his IQ at 145—just above the threshold for a true genius. But when the audience responded in any way, he seemed to draw back, as if he didn't know what to do when he went off script. Excellent. That was exactly the sort of speaker who wouldn't know how to tap-dance out of a blatant donation request.

"And you are on the cusp of this technological revolution. You have that power at your fingertips, twenty-four hours a day, seven days a week." Longmire paused to take a drink from a water bottle and clear his throat. Trish had the distinct impression that he was forcing himself through this. *Interesting*, she thought.

"The problem then becomes one of inequality," Longmire went on. "How can you communicate with the rest of humanity if they don't have those things?" Images of tribal Africans, destitute southern Asians, aboriginals from Australia and—holy crap, had he actually found a picture of…Trish studied the photo hard before it clicked past. No, that hadn't been her reservation out in South Dakota, but it might have been the Rosebud lands.

Well. Yay for him acknowledging the state of the Native American reservations in a five-second picture, even if the montage did irritate her. All the people of color had been relegated to the poor section of the talk.

"We have a responsibility to use that power—that wealth," he went on, "for the betterment of our fellow humans on this planet…"

Longmire talked for another forty-five minutes, calling for the audience members to look beyond their own screens and be conscious consumers of technology. "Be engaged," he told them. "A rising tide lifts all boats. Solar-powered laptops can lift children out of poverty. Make sure the next Big Thing won't be lost to poverty and disease. It all starts with *you*." This time, when he smiled at the crowd, it was far more confident—and far more practiced. "Don't let me down."

The screen behind him shifted to the official Longmire Foundation photo with the Twitter handle and website. The crowd erupted into applause, giving him a six-minute standing ovation while Longmire half sat on his stool, drinking his water and looking like he'd rather be anywhere but here.

The emcee came back out on stage and thanked Longmire for his "absolutely brilliant" talk before she motioned to where the microphones had been set up in the aisles. "Mr. Longmire has agreed to take questions," Jennifer gushed.

Timing was everything. Trish didn't want to go first, but she didn't want to wait until the reporters started to pack up. She needed a lull that was just long enough for her to haul out her check and get to the microphone before anyone could stop her.

About ten students lined up in either aisle. Some questions were about how Longmire had started his company in his dorm room and how a regular student could come up with a billion-dollar idea.

"What's something that people need?" Longmire replied. "I wanted a way to take my digital photos with me. Adapting a simple idea that would make it easier to share photos with my parents—and make it easy for my parents to share those photos with other people—led me to adapting the SnAppShot app to every device, every platform available. It was ten years of hard work. Don't believe what the press says. There are no overnight successes in this business. See a need and fill it."

When he was replying, Trish noted, he had a different style. Maybe it was because he was really only talking to one person? But his words flowed more easily and he spoke with more conviction. The power in his words filled the auditorium. She could listen to that voice all night— he was *mesmerizing*.

This was a problem. Trish rubbed her hands on her jeans, trying to steady her nerves. Okay, so he spoke quite well off the cuff—which he demonstrated when a few people asked antagonistic questions.

Instead of acting trapped, Longmire's face would break into a sly smile—one completely different from the cautious movement of lips he'd used during his prepared remarks. Then he would dissect the question at an astonishing rate and completely undercut the argument, all without getting off the stool.

Ah, yes. This was his other reputation, the businessman who, much like his technological forefathers, would occasionally sue people for fun and profit. Nate Longmire had amassed the reputation of a man who never gave up and never surrendered in the courtroom. He'd completely bankrupted his former college friend, the one he'd started SnAppShot with.

Trish caught herself fidgeting with her earrings. Okay, yes—there was always the chance that her little stunt wouldn't go over well. But she was determined to give it a shot. The only people who lost were the ones who never tried.

Finally, there was only one person in line on her side and Longmire was listening intently to a question from the other aisle. Trish looked back and didn't see anyone else coming forward. This was it. She edged her check out from behind her seat and then stood in line, less than two feet away from the check. She could grab it and hoist it up in seconds. This would work. It had to.

The person in front of her asked some frivolous question about how Longmire felt about his status as a sex symbol. Even as Trish rolled her eyes, Longmire shot beet red. The question had unsettled him. Perfect.

"We have time for one more question," Jennifer announced after the nervous laughter had settled. "Yes? Step forward and say your name, please."

Trish bent over and grabbed her check. It was comically huge—a four-feet long by two-feet tall piece of cardboard. "Mr. Longmire," she said, holding the check in front of her like a shield. "My name is Trish Hunter and I'm the founder of One Child, One World, a charity that gets school supplies in the hands of underprivileged children on American Indian reservations."

Longmire leaned forward, his dark eyes fastened on hers. The world seemed to—well, it didn't fall away, not like it did in stories. But the hum of the audience and the bright lights seemed to fade into the background as Longmire focused all of his attention on her and said, "An admirable cause. Go on, Ms. Hunter. What is your question?"

Trish swallowed nervously. "I recently had the privilege of being named one of *Glamour*'s Top Ten College Women in honor of the work I'm doing." She paused to heft her check over her head. "The recognition came with a ten-thousand dollar reward, which I have pledged to One Child, One World in its entirety. You've spoken eloquently about how technology can change lives. Will you match this award and donate ten thousand dollars to help children get school supplies?"

The silence that crashed over the auditorium was deafening. All Trish could hear was the pounding of blood in her ears. She'd done it. She'd done *exactly* what she'd set out to do—cause a scene and hopefully trap one of the richest men in the world into parting with just a little of his hard-earned money.

"Thank you, Ms. Hunter," the emcee said sharply. "But Mr. Longmire has a process by which people can apply for—"

"Wait," Longmire cut her off. "It's true, the Longmire Foundation does have an application process. However," he said, his gaze never leaving Trish's face. Heat flushed her body. "One must admire a direct approach. Ms. Hunter, perhaps we can discuss your charity's needs after this event is over?"

Trish almost didn't hear the *Ooh*s that came from the rest of the crowd over the rush of blood in her ears. That wasn't a *no*. It wasn't a *yes*, either—it was a very good side step around giving a hard answer one way or the other. But it wasn't a *no* and that was all that mattered. She could still press her case and maybe, just maybe, get enough funding to buy every single kid on her reservation a backpack full of school supplies before school started in five months.

Plus, she'd get to see if Nate was as good-looking up

close as he was at a distance. Not that it mattered. Of course it didn't. "I would be honored," she said into the microphone and even she didn't miss the way her voice shook, just a little.

"Bring your check," he said with a grin that came real close to being wicked. "I'm not sure I've ever seen one that large before."

Laughter rolled through the auditorium as Longmire grinned at her. Behind his glasses, one eyebrow lifted in challenge and then he pointedly looked offstage. The message was clear. Would she meet him backstage?

The emcee was thanking Longmire for his time and everyone was applauding and the rest of the evening was clearly over. Trish managed to snag her small purse—a Coach knockoff—and fight against the rising tide of college kids who had not been invited backstage for a private meeting with the Boy Billionaire. With her small purse and her large check, Trish managed to get up the steps at the side of the stage and duck behind the curtains.

The emcee stood there, glaring at her. "That was some stunt you pulled," she said in a vicious whisper.

"Thanks!" Trish responded brightly. No doubt, Jennifer had had grand plans for her own post-interview "meeting" with Longmire and Trish had usurped that quite nicely.

"Ah, Ms. Hunter. Hello." Suddenly, Nate Longmire was standing before her. Trish was a good five-nine—taller in her boots—but she still had to lean her head up to meet his gaze. "Excellent," he went on, looking down at her as if he was thrilled to see her. "You have the large check. Jennifer, would you take our picture?"

His phone chimed. He looked at it, scowled briefly, and then called up his SnAppShot app. He handed his phone to the emcee, who forced a polite smile. "Hand it up here," Longmire said, taking half of the check in his hand. Then he put his arm around Trish's shoulders and whispered, "Smile."

Trish wasn't sure she pulled off that smile. His arm around her was warm and heavy and she swore to God that she felt his touch in places he wasn't touching.

She would not be attracted to him. She couldn't *afford* to be attracted to him. All she could do was forge ahead with her plan. Phase One—trap the Boy Billionaire—was complete. Now she had to move onto Phase Two—getting a donation out of him.

Forging ahead had absolutely nothing to do with the way his physical touch was sending shimmering waves of awareness through her body. *Nothing*.

Jennifer took two shots and then handed back the phone. Longmire's arm left her and Trish couldn't help it—she shivered at the loss of his warmth.

"Mr. Longmire," Jennifer began in a silky tone. "If you recall, I'd invited you out for a dinner after the program. We should get going."

There was a pause that could only be called awkward. Longmire didn't even move for three blinks of the eye— as if this statement had taken him quite by surprise and, despite his ferocious business skills and dizzying intellect, he had no possible answer for Jennifer.

Jennifer touched his arm. "Ready?" she said, batting her eyes.

Trish rolled hers—just as Longmire looked at her. *Oops*. Busted.

But instead of glaring at her, Longmire looked as if Trish was the answer to all his questions. That look should not do things to her. So, she forcibly decided, it didn't.

"Gosh—I do remember that, but I think I need to address Ms. Hunter's question first." He stepped away from Jennifer much like a crab avoiding a hungry seagull. Jennifer's hand hung in empty space for a moment before she lowered it back to her side. "Call my office," Longmire said, turning on his heel. "We'll try to set something up. Ms. Hunter? Are you coming?"

Trish clutched her check to her chest and hurried after Longmire, trying to match his long strides.

That definitely wasn't a *no*.

Now she just needed to get to a *yes*.

Nate settled into the Apollo Coffee shop. He liked coffee shops. They were usually busy enough that he didn't garner too much attention but quiet enough that he could think. He liked to think. It was a profitable, satisfying experience for him, thinking.

Right now he was thinking about the young woman who'd trucked a comically large check into the hired car and carried it into the coffee shop as if it were the most normal thing ever.

Trish Hunter. She was drinking a small black coffee—easily the cheapest thing on the extensive menu. She'd insisted on buying her own coffee, too. Had absolutely refused to let him plunk down the two dollars and change for hers.

That was something...different. He was intrigued, he had to admit.

The large check was wedged behind her chair, looking slightly worse for wear. "That's not the real check, is it?" he asked over the lip of his grande mocha.

"No. I got a regulation-sized check that went straight into the bank. But this makes for better photos, don't you think?" she replied easily, without that coy tone women had started using around him about the time he made his first million.

"Not a lot of people would have had the guts to try and trap me like that," he noted, watching her face closely. She was lovely—long dark hair that hung most of the way down her back, brown skin that graced high cheekbones. With her strong features and strong body—because there was no missing *that*—she looked like she could *be* Wonder Woman.

She didn't act like the kind of women who tried to trap him with their feminine wiles. Instead, she sat across from him, drinking cheap coffee and no doubt waiting to tell him why he should cut her another check.

For a second—the amount of time it took for her to look up at him through thick lashes—Nate almost panicked. He wasn't particularly good with women, as evidenced by that nagging feeling that he hadn't handled Jennifer's dinner invitation well and the fact that he had flat-out ignored that message from Diana—the third one this month.

Ever since things with Diana had fallen apart—and then really gone to hell—he'd kept things simple by simply not getting involved. Which meant that he was horribly out of practice. But there was no way he would let another woman take advantage of him. And that included Diana. Hence why he would just keep right on ignoring her messages.

Trish Hunter wasn't doing the things that normally made him nervous—treating him like he was a sex god she'd been secretly worshipping for years.

She grinned, a small curve of her lips over the edge of her cup. That grin did something to him—made him feel more sure of himself. Which sounded ridiculous but there it was. "Did it work? The trap, that is."

Nate smiled back. He was terrible about negotiations with members of the opposite sex. Money, however, was something he'd learned to negotiate. And the fact that this lovely young woman wasn't playing coy—wasn't acting like he'd gotten used to women acting around him—only made him more comfortable. Everything was out in the open. He could handle this kind of interaction. "That depends."

Her eyes widened slightly and a flash of surprise crossed her face. It made her look…innocent. Sweet, even. "Upon?"

"Tell me about your charity."

She exhaled in relief. It wasn't a big gesture, but he saw it nonetheless. He wondered what she'd thought he would ask. "Of course. One Child, One World is a registered 501(c) charity. We keep our overhead as low as possible." Nate sighed. He hated the boring part of charity work. It was, for lack of a better word, *boring.* "Approximately $0.93 of every dollar donated goes to school supplies…" her voice trailed off. "Not the right answer?"

He sat up a little straighter. She was paying attention to him. He'd be lying if he said it wasn't flattering. "Those statistics are all required as part of the grant application process," he replied, waving his hand. "The lawyers insisted. But that's not what I wanted to know."

She raised a strong eyebrow and leaned toward him. Yes, he had her full attention—and she had his. "You asked about my charity."

Oh, yeah—her words were nothing but challenge. This was not a woman telling him whatever he wanted to hear. This was a woman who would push back. Even though he had the money and she had a very cheap coffee, she'd still push back.

That made her even more interesting.

And as long as he kept thinking of it in terms of power and money—instead of noting how pretty she was and how she was looking at him and especially how he was no doubt looking at her—he'd be just fine.

"Tell me about why a young woman would start an organization to get school supplies into kids' hands. Tell me about…" *You.* But he didn't say that because that would cross the line of business and go into the personal. The moment he did that, he'd probably start flailing and knock the coffee into her lap. "Tell me about it."

"Ah." She took her time sipping her coffee. "Where did you grow up? Kansas City, right?"

"You've done your homework."

"Any good trap is a well-planned trap," she easily replied, a note of satisfaction in her voice.

He nodded his head in acknowledgment. "Yes, I grew up in Kansas City. Middle-class household. Father was an accountant, mother taught second grade." He left out the part about his brothers. "It was a very comfortable life." He hadn't realized how comfortable until he'd made his money—and started looking at how other people lived.

Trish smiled encouragingly. "And every August, you got a new backpack, new shoes, new school clothes and everything on that list teachers said you had to have, right?"

"Yes." He took a calculated risk. Just because she had black hair and skin the color of copper and was running a charity that helped American Indians on reservations didn't necessarily mean she was a Native American herself. But there was no such thing as coincidence. "I take it you didn't?"

Something in her face changed—her eyes seemed to harden. "My sixth-grade teacher gave me two pencils once. It was all she could afford." She dropped her gaze and began to fiddle with one of her earrings. "It was the best present I ever got."

Nate, being Nate, didn't have a smooth comeback to that. In fact, he didn't know what to say at all. His mom, Susan, had worked as a teacher, and she'd occasionally talked about a student who needed "a little extra help," as she put it. Then she'd fill a backpack with food and some basics and that was that. But that was before she'd had to stay home with Nate's brother Joe full-time.

"I'm sorry to hear that," he said quietly. Once, he hadn't

believed there was a world where a couple of #2 pencils were an amazing gift. But now he knew better.

Her gaze still on her coffee, she gave him a quick, tight smile. He needed to move the conversation forward. "So you're working to change that?"

"Yes. A new backpack full of everything a kid needs in a classroom." She shrugged and looked back at him. The hardness fell away. "I mean, that's the first goal. But it's an important first step."

He nodded thoughtfully. "You have bigger plans?"

Her eyes lit up. "Oh, of course! It's just the beginning."

"Tell me what you'd do."

"For so many kids, school is…it's an oasis in the middle of a desert. The schools need to open earlier, stay open later. They need to serve a bigger breakfast, a bigger lunch and everyone needs an afternoon snack. Too many kids aren't getting regular meals at home and it's so hard to study on an empty stomach." As she said this last point, she dropped her gaze again.

She was speaking from experience, he realized. Two pencils and nothing to eat at home.

"Indians on the rez love basketball and skateboarding," she went on. "Having better courts and parks on the school grounds could keep kids from joining gangs."

"You have gang problems?" He always associated gangs with inner-city drug wars or something.

She gave him a look that walked a fine line between "amused" and "condescending." "Some people have perverted our warrior culture into a gang mentality. We lose kids that way and we rarely get them back."

He thought over her wish list, such as it was. "I haven't heard anything about computers."

She paused, then gave him that tight smile again. "It's the ultimate goal, one that will require far more than ten or even twenty thousand dollars of funding. Most schools don't have the infrastructure to support an internet connection, much less cloud storage. I want kids to have basic supplies and full bellies before I get to that. You understand, don't you?"

He nodded. He'd toured some bad schools—mold growing on the walls, windows taped shut to keep the glass from falling out, ancient textbooks that smelled like rot. But what she was describing...

"What is it you want from me, then? Just ten grand?"

The moment he said it, he realized that maybe he shouldn't have phrased it quite like that. Especially not when Trish leaned back in her chair, one arm on the armrest, the other curled up under her chin—except for her index finger, which she'd extended over her lips as if they were in a library and she was shushing him. She met his gaze full-on, a hint of challenge lurking in her eyes. The air grew tight with tension.

God, she was beautiful and there was something else behind that gaze—an interest in more than just his bank account. He should ask her out. She wasn't intimidated by him and she wasn't throwing herself at him. She was here for the money and all her cards were up front, no hiding funding requests behind manipulative sexual desire. Hell. He didn't meet too many women who could just sit and have a conversation with him.

Except...dating was not his strong suit and he was pretty sure that asking a woman out right after she'd requested a donation would probably cross some ethical line.

Damn.

"Of course, One Child, One World would be delighted with any funding the Longmire Foundation saw fit to disperse," she said, sounding very much like someone who'd written a few grants in her time.

"How'd you get to be a Woman of the Year?"

"One of my professors nominated me," she told him. "I

didn't know she was doing it. One day, I'm trying to organize a bake sale to raise a hundred dollars to cover postage back to the rez and the next, I'm being flown to New York and given a *lot* of money." She blushed. "I mean, a lot of money for me. I'm sure ten grand isn't very much to you."

"I can remember when that much was a lot of money," he admitted. He winced. That was a totally jerky thing to say and he knew it.

He was about to apologize when she said, "Tell me about your charity," turning his question back on him.

He regarded her for a second. "Is that another way of asking why I'm giving money away for free?"

"You *did* go to all that trouble of earning it in the first place," she pointed out.

He shrugged. "Like I said, I had a comfortable childhood. We didn't always get everything we wanted—I didn't get a car for my sixteenth birthday or anything—but we were fine."

How he'd wanted a car. Brad, his older brother, had a half-rusted Jeep he'd bought with lawn-mowing money that he swore made it a breeze to get a date.

Back then, Nate had absolutely no prospect of a date. He was tall and gangly, with dorky glasses and awful skin. They were still trying to integrate Joe into a mainstream classroom at that point and Nate was mercilessly mocked by his peers. The only possible way he could have gotten a girl was if he'd had a sweet ride to pick her up in.

Alas. No car. No date.

"Anyway," he went on, shaking his head, "I made that first million and I felt like I'd made it. But a weird thing happened—that million spawned a second million, then a third. And then the buyout happened and now..." He gave her an apologetic smile. "Honestly, what the hell am I going to do with a billion dollars? Buy a country and rule as a despot?"

It wasn't as if this background was entirely new information—he'd given interviews explaining the rationale for his foundation—but those were formal things with scripted answers, preapproved by his assistant, Stanley.

Right now, sitting here in a coffee shop with Ms. Trish Hunter, it didn't feel like an interview. It felt like a conversation. An honest one.

Nate nodded toward her shirt. "I bought Superman #1—you know?"

A smile quirked at her lips. "I do know. Didn't you pay the highest recorded price for it?"

"I did. It was *wild*—I felt like I was jumping off a cliff, to pay five million for a comic book."

"Did you at least read it? Or did you lock it up?" The way she asked the question made it clear—she would have read it.

"I read it. Carefully." He waggled his eyebrows at her, as if he were saying something salacious. She laughed. It was as close to flirting as he got. "With tongs. In a temperature-controlled room."

Her eyes lit up. "Were you wearing one of those hazmat suits, too?"

"No. Just gloves." She giggled at the image and he laughed with her. It had been totally ridiculous. "But what else am I going to do with this much money besides buy comic books?"

"You donated a lot to mental-health research," she said. She was leaning forward slightly, her body language indicating that she was really listening.

"I have a…personal connection to that." When she waited for more, he added, "I keep my family private. It's the only way to stay sane in this industry."

Yes, he had set up an endowment into schizophrenia, depression and bipolar research. That was the public action. The private one had been setting up a trust fund for the care of Joe. Mom was able to stay home full-time with Joe now, and they had reliable home health aides to assist. Nate had tried to give his parents a million dollars or an all-expenses paid trip around the world, but it turned out that peace of mind about their youngest son was all they really wanted.

And after what had happened with Diana…

Nate's private life stayed private. Period.

"Ah, understood." She tilted her head. "That explains why there's no press on it. I wondered."

He stared at her. Yeah, he expected that she'd done her homework, but it was unusual to have someone admit to digging into his past—and then agree not to discuss it. As the shock of her blunt attitude wore off, he felt himself grinning at her even more. "Thanks. So, you know—I'm rich, I no longer run my own company—what am I going to do with the rest of my life? I set up a fund for my niece, bought my brother a house, took care of—well, I took care of the rest of my family, fended off a few lawsuits. That only left me with about a billion. Giving away the money seemed like something to do. The Longmire Foundation has given away fourteen million dollars and I haven't even made a dent yet."

That was the truth. He was making more in interest than he could give away. The simple truth was that her request for a matching grant of ten thousand dollars was the product of about five minutes for him, if that. He could add two or three zeroes to the end of the check and never even notice the money was gone.

"Is that what makes you happy?"

He looked at her funny. Happy? He was rich. He wasn't the same gangly nerd he'd been in high school. He was a ruthless businessman, a hugely successful one. He owned his own jet, for crying out loud.

But there was something in the way she asked it…

"I'm doing good. That's what counts."

"Of course." She opened her mouth, paused—and then angled her body toward his. Her gaze dropped again, but only for a second. She looked up at him through her lashes. Energy—attraction—seemed to arc between them as he stared at her.

Her eyes were a deep brown, like dark chocolate. Sweet, yes—but much more than that. There was innocence, but now it had an edge to it—an edge that held a hell of a lot of promise.

He leaned forward, eager to hear what she would say—and whether or not it would sound like legal boilerplate or if it would sound like something else.

He leaned right into his coffee and promptly spilled what was left of his grande mocha into her lap.

"Whoa!" she shouted, hopping to her feet. The dark stain spread down her leg.

"Oh, damn—I'm so sorry," he mumbled. What had he been thinking? Of course she wasn't going to say something along the lines of "Maybe we should discuss this over dinner." He grabbed some napkins and thrust them at her. "Here."

This was terrible. He'd been doing just fine when it'd been a business negotiation, but the moment he hoped it'd go past that—it blew up in his face.

"I'm so sorry," he repeated. "I'll pay for the cleaning bill."

She laughed. And after she'd checked her seat for coffee, she sat down, spread a napkin over her lap, and grinned at him. "Don't worry about it."

"But your clothes…" Even now, he could see the droplets of coffee on her shirt.

"I'm used to spills and stains. Don't worry about it."

He wasn't sure if he believed her, but then he met her gaze. It was full of humor, yes—but he didn't get the sense that she was laughing at him. Just the situation. Clumsy billionaire knocks coffee into her lap.

He had to get out of here before he did even worse damage to her clothes or his pride. "Listen, why don't you come by my office in two weeks? I'll have my assistant start the paperwork and we can settle the terms then." He fished out his card, which just said, "Longmire Foundation," with the address and email. "And please—bring the dry-cleaning bill. It hurts me to think that I might have ruined your shirt."

A second too late, he realized he was staring at her chest. The jacket had fallen open a little more. It was a very nice chest.

God, what was he doing? Trying to make this worse? He shook some sense—he hoped—back into his head and handed over the card. "Say, Friday at two?"

"I have to work." She took the card and studied it. "This is in the Filmore area."

"Yes. I keep an office close to where I live." She was still looking at the card. "Is that a problem?"

"No, it's fine. I just thought you'd be down in the Mission or in SOMA. Close to where all the other tech billionaires hang out."

He waved his hand. "I like to walk to the office when it's nice out." She gaped at him, as if she couldn't believe a billionaire would stoop to walking on his own two feet instead of being carried on a gold-plated litter by trained elephants. "Truth be told, we're not some sort of secret billionaire club. And I don't really have much interest in the constant one-upmanship that happens when you get us all together. I like peace and quiet and a nice view. I like to be a little bit not what people expect."

That got her attention. She looked up at him, her dark eyes wide and…encouraging?

If she could still look at him after he dumped his drink all over her, then maybe...

She went back to studying the card. "I won't be able to get there until five. Is that too late?"

"Yeah, that's fine. I'll make sure Stanley knows you're coming."

"Stanley?"

"My assistant." Actually, Stanley was more than that—he picked out Nate's clothes and made sure Nate projected the right amount of geek-cred cool. If only Stanley had been here tonight, no one would have gotten a damp lap.

He'd have Stanley start the due diligence on her charity to make sure her numbers were correct.

She grinned up at him again, as if she wasn't sure how to process an assistant named Stanley. "I look forward to our meeting." She stood, crumpling up the napkins and stuffing them into her empty cup. Then she extended her hand. "Mr. Longmire, it has been an honor. Thank you so much for considering my proposal."

"It's a worthy cause." He took her hand in his and tried to shake it, but the feeling of her slender fingers warming his momentarily froze his brain. He wanted to say something suave and sophisticated that let her know he was interested in more than her charity.

He had nothing.

Maybe their next meeting would go more smoothly—in his office, Stanley would be ready to swoop in and save Nate from himself as needed. "And again—sorry about the coffee."

She waved him off and retrieved her large check from behind the chair. Thankfully, it didn't seem to be too splattered. "I'll see you on Friday in two weeks."

"I'm looking forward to it." That got him a nice smile, warm and friendly and comforting—like she realized ex-

actly how socially awkward he really was and was reward-
ing him for doing a decent job.

Nate watched her figure retreat from the coffee shop
and disappear into the foggy darkness, the check glowing
white. Trish Hunter. Yes, Stanley would have to do some
due diligence on her charity. And on the woman herself.
Nate wanted to know more about her—a lot more.

He sent for a car to take him home and was picking
up the coffee cups—his mother had always taught him
to pick up after himself and being a self-made billionaire
hadn't changed that—when his phone rang. Not the chime
that went with a message, but the ring of someone actually calling him.

His mother. She was pretty much the only person who
called him, anyway. She was too old to learn to text, she
said. That was her story and she was sticking to it.

"Hey, Mom," he said, heading out to the sidewalk.

"Nate? Oh, honey." She was crying. Nate froze halfway out the door. Instantly, all thoughts of Trish Hunter
and large checks and coffee were pushed from his mind.

"Mom? What's wrong?"

"Nate—oh, God. There's been an accident."

"Dad?" Panic clawed at him. His parents were only
in their fifties. He didn't want to lose either one just yet.

"He's fine. Oh, Nate…we need you to come home. It's
Brad and Elena…"

"Are they okay?" But even as he said it, he knew the
answer was no. His mother was crying. Something horrible had happened to his older brother and his sister-in-
law. "What about Jane?" When his mom didn't answer
right away, Nate nearly threw up. "Mom—is Jane okay?"

"The baby is fine. We were watching her so they could
go out… Come home, Nate. Come home *now*."

Dear God in heaven. "I'm on my way, Mom. I'll be there
as soon as I can." He hung up and called Stanley. This was

one of the benefits of being a billionaire. He didn't have to deal with emergency flights. He had an assistant—and a private jet.

"Stanley, get the plane ready. I need to go to Kansas City. Right now."

# Two

Trish had spent a good deal of time on this outfit. Wearing the Wonder Woman shirt again would be too obvious, even though it had washed clean. Trish had decided to go a little more formal for this meeting. She had on a coral skirt that came to midcalf. She'd paired it with a white shirt that was as crisp as she could get it in a public Laundromat and a denim jacket from Diesel—another major score from the thrift stores. Her only pair of cowboy boots were on her feet. Once they'd been black, but now they were a faded gray. Which was trendy enough, so she figured she was okay.

She was wearing the one good piece of turquoise she had, a teardrop-shaped pendant that hung on a thin silver chain. She'd twisted her hair up into a professional looking knot and had put in a pair of silver hoops that looked more expensive than they really were.

This was her being a business-professional Lakota woman. This was not her dressing to impress a certain billionaire. Not much, anyway.

She didn't have a cleaning bill to give him and she had the distinctive feeling that he wasn't going to be happy about that. What could she do? Tell him she needed $1.25 in quarters for the Laundromat?

The skirt had necessitated the bus, however. She hadn't wanted it to get tangled up in her bike spokes. So, at 5:08—

after almost an hour and a half—she finally arrived at his address in the Filmore district.

The Longmire Foundation was on the fourth floor of an austere-looking office building. On the ride up, Trish swallowed nervously. Yes, the conversation with Nate at the coffee shop had been pleasant and encouraging—but who knew what might have changed in the past two weeks? Because of how the event had played out in the press, she was worried that he might have changed his mind. The news reports had caught the look he'd given her when he'd asked her to meet him backstage and rumors about something else happening backstage had already started.

Trish had fielded a few phone calls, which was good. Sort of. Yes, any attention she could draw to One Child was good attention—but the quotes reporters had been looking for were much more along the lines of whether or not a romance had sparked.

Which it hadn't. Really.

So Nate Longmire was tall, built and twice as handsome in person as he was in photographs. So there'd been something between them—something that she hadn't been able to stop thinking about since the moment she'd walked out of that coffee shop. It'd almost been like…like she'd belonged there, with him. For just a little bit, he hadn't been some unreachable Boy Billionaire and she hadn't been a dirt-poor American Indian. He'd just been a man and she'd just been a woman and that was—well, it was good. With the potential to be even better.

And that potential? That's what she'd been dreaming about almost every single night for the past two weeks.

Well. They were just dreams. And she needed to stick with reality.

And the reality of the situation was that Nate was not her type. She didn't have a type, but whatever it might be, a Boy Billionaire clearly wasn't it. She would probably never have a total of five million dollars in her entire life—and he was the kind of guy who spent that on a comic book.

At least the Wonder Woman shirt had done its job, she figured. Now, in her fancy clothes, it was time to do hers.

She'd done her best to avoid answering any questions about her supposed involvement with Nate Longmire by throwing out every single stat she could about poverty on Indian reservations and how even a five-dollar donation could make a difference. In the end, unable to get a juicy quote out of her, the press had left her alone.

She'd noticed that, in any report, whether online or on television, Nate Longmire had always been "unavailable for comment." She didn't know if that was a good thing or not.

Trish found the right door—suite 412, *The Longmire Foundation* written in black letters on the glass—and tried the doorknob, but it was locked. A growing sense of dread filled her as she knocked.

A minute passed. Trish didn't know if she should knock again or…what? She had no other options. Nate said he'd be here—that Stanley would be here. He hadn't forgotten, had he?

She knocked again.

This time, a man shouted, "Jeez, I'm coming. I'm coming."

The door was unlocked and thrown open. Instead of Nate Longmire's well-dressed form, a man in a white tank top, oversize corduroy pants held up by bright red suspenders and more tattoos than God glared down at her. "What?"

"Um, hello," Trish said, trying not to be nervous. This guy had spacers in his ears. She could see right through them. She swallowed. "I have an appointment with Mr. Longmire—"

"What are you doing here?" the man all but growled at her.

"I'm sorry?"

The man looked put out. "You're supposed to be at his house for the interview. Didn't they tell you that?"

They? They *who*? "No?"

Mr. Tattoos rolled his eyes to the sky and sighed. "You're in the wrong place. You need to be at 2601 Pacific Street." He looked at her dubiously. "2601 Pacific Street," he repeated in a slower, louder voice, as if she'd suddenly gone deaf. When Trish just stared at him, he pointed again and said, "That way. Okay?"

"Yes, all right." She stood there for a minute, too shocked to do much but not look through the holes in his ears. "Thank you."

"Yeah, good luck—you're gonna need it," he called after her, then she heard the door shut and lock behind her.

Great. Trish was going to be way late. Panic fluttered through her stomach. Was this a sign—Nate had reviewed her case and decided that her charity didn't meet his requirements? Why on earth was she supposed to go to his house—especially if he was going to turn her down? This wasn't about to get weird, was it?

She did the only thing she could do—she started to walk. She loved walking through San Francisco, looking at all the Victorian houses and wondering what it would be like to live in one. To have a view of the bay or the Golden Gate Bridge. To not have to worry about making rent and having enough left over.

Her mother, Pat, had loved the music from the Summer of Love. When she was with a real jerk of a boyfriend—which was often enough—Pat would sometimes get nostalgic and talk about one day coming out to San Francisco to find Trish's father. That was how Trish found out that her father had come to this city when he'd abandoned his family.

Trish did what she always did when she walked the

streets—she looked in the faces of each person she passed by, hoping to recognize a little part of herself. Maybe her father had gotten remarried and had more kids. Maybe Trish would find a half sister walking around. Or maybe the woman her father had settled down with would recognize her husband's face in Trish's and ask if they were related.

Trish had lived here for five years. This on-the-street recognition hadn't happened, not once. But she kept looking.

She walked to Pacific Street and turned. This was such a beautiful place, right across from the park. Nothing like the tiny garret apartment in Ingleside she rented for the subsidized sum of $350 a month.

She found the right house—she hoped. It was a sweeping three-story Victorian home, the exterior painted a soft shade of blue with bright white paint outlining the scrollwork and columns. The curtains on the ground-level windows were closed and a painted garage door was shut. Next to that was a wide, sweeping set of steps that led up to the perfect porch for a summer afternoon, complete with swing.

It was simply lovely. The small part of her brain that wasn't nervous about this whole "interview at his house" thing was doing a little happy dance—she would finally get to see the inside of one of these homes.

But that excitement was buried pretty danged deep. To get inside the home, she had to get through the gate at the bottom of the stairs—and it didn't budge. How was she supposed to be *at* the house if she couldn't even get to the door? Then she saw a buzzer off to the right. She pressed it and waited.

Even standing here felt like she was interloping again. This wasn't right. Nate had been very clear—she was to meet him at the office. Trish had no idea which "they" should have told her about the change, but what could she do? She needed the donation, desperately.

So she rang the bell, again, and waited. Again. She caught herself twisting her earring and forced her hands back by her sides. This was not about to go sideways on her. This was fine. She was a professional. She could handle whatever was on the other side of that door with grace and charm.

Up on the porch, the door opened and a short, stocky woman in a gray dress and a white apron stood before her. "Hello?"

"Hi," Trish said, trying her best to smile warmly. "I have an appointment with Mr. Longmire and—"

"*Ay mia*—you're late," the woman said—but unlike Mr. Tattoo, she looked happy to see Trish. "Come in, come in." A buzzer sounded and the gate swung free. Trish climbed the stairs, schooling her features into a professional smile—warm, welcoming, not at all worried about the lack of communication about any changes to the plan.

"Hello," she said when she was face-to-face with the woman. "I'm Trish Hunter and—"

The woman latched onto Trish's arm and all but hauled her inside. The door shut with a resounding thud behind her.

"Who is it, Rosita?" Trish recognized Nate's voice as the one calling down the stairs.

"The girl," Rosita called back.

"Send her up."

It was only then, with Rosita the maid shooing her up the stairs so fast that she could barely take in the beautiful details of the entry room, that Trish heard it—the plaintive wail of a deeply unhappy baby.

It was pretty safe to say that Trish had absolutely no idea what was going on. But up the stairs she went, bracing herself for what baby-related carnage awaited her.

She was not wrong about that.

Nate Longmire—the same Boy Billionaire who had given an impassioned talk on social responsibility, the same Nate Longmire who had insisted on paying her dry-cleaning bill, the very same Nate Longmire that had looked positively sinful in his hipster glasses and purple tie—stood in front of one of those portable playpens that Trish had coveted for years. Nate was in a pair of jeans and a white T-shirt. That part wasn't surprising.

What was surprising was that Nate was trying to hold a screaming baby. The child was in nothing but a diaper and, unless Trish missed her guess, the diaper was on backwards.

"What on earth?" Trish demanded.

Nate spun at the sound of the exclamation from behind him just as Jane squirmed in his arms. Oh, hell—why were babies so damned hard to hold onto?

"Uh…" he managed to get out as he got his other arm under Jane's bottom and kept her from tumbling. The little girl screamed even louder. Nate would have thought that it was physically impossible for her to find more volume from her tiny little body, but she had.

"Oh, for Pete's sake," the woman said. The next thing he knew, Jane had been lifted out of his arms by a beautiful woman with striking dark eyes and—

Oh, God. "Trish!"

"Yes, hello," she said, slinging the baby onto her hip with a practiced air. "Where are the diapers?"

"Why—what—I mean—you're here?"

Trish paused in her search for diapers and gave him a look. It was a look that he deserved. Never in his entire life had he felt more like an idiot. "Yes. We had an appointment."

He started. "Your appointment?"

"Yes," she said, as she turned a small circle, surveying the complete and total destruction of the room that, until seven days ago, had been a sitting room and now was supposed to be a nursery. Even Nate knew that it wasn't a nursery, not yet. It was a hellhole. He couldn't tell if she was finding what she was looking for or not.

His mind tried to work, but that was like trying to open a bank vault where all the tumblers had rusted shut. He was *so* tired but Trish was here. He'd never been so happy to see a woman in his entire life. "You're here about the nanny position?"

That got him another look—but there was more pity in her eyes this time. "Mr. Longmire," she said in an utterly calm voice. She snagged a blanket and, with the screaming baby still on her hip, managed to smoothly lay the cloth out on the floor. "We had an appointment in your office at five today to discuss a matching grant to my charity, One Child, One World."

Oh, hell. "You're...not here about the nanny position?"

Trish located a diaper and then fell to her knees in an entirely graceful way. She carefully laid Jane out on the blanket. "Oh, dear, yes," she soothed in a soft voice that Nate had to strain to hear over the screaming. "You're so cold, sweetie! And wet, too? Oh, yes, it's so hard to be a baby, isn't it?" Trish changed the diaper and then looked up at him. "Does she have any clothes?"

"Why are you so calm?" he demanded.

"This is not difficult, Mr. Longmire. Does she have any clothes?"

Nate turned and dug into one of the suitcases Stanley had loaded onto his private plane. "Like a dress or something?"

"Like jammies, Mr. Longmire. Oh, I know," she said in that soothing voice again. "I know. I think he's trying his best, but he doesn't know how to speak baby, does he?"

For a blissful second, Jane stopped screaming and instead only made a little burbling noise, as if she really were talking to Trish.

Then the screaming started right back up with renewed vigor.

Nate grabbed something that looked like it could be jammies. Orange terry cloth with pink butterflies and green flowers, it had long sleeves and footies attached to the legs. "This?"

"That's perfect," Trish said in that soothing tone again. Nate handed over the clothes and watched, stunned, as Trish got the wriggling arms and kicking legs into the fabric.

"How do you do that? I couldn't get her into anything. And I couldn't get her to stop screaming."

"I noticed." Trish looked up at him and smiled. "How are you feeding her?"

"Um, my mom sent some formula. Down in the kitchen."

Trish rubbed Jane's little tummy. Then, like it was just that easy, she folded the blanket around Jane and tucked in the ends and suddenly, Nate was looking at a baby burrito.

"One second, baby." Then, to Nate, she said, "Don't pick her up—but watch her while I wash my hands, okay?"

"Okay?" What choice did he have? The baby was still crying but, miraculously, her volume had pitched down for the first time since Nate had seen her.

"Bathroom?" Trish asked.

"Through that door." As he stared at Jane, he tried to think. For a man who had done plenty of thinking while pulling all-nighters, he was stunned at how much his brain felt like the sludge at the bottom of a grease trap.

Trish Hunter. How could he forget her? Not even a funeral or a solid two weeks of sleep deprivation could erase the memory of her talking with him in a coffee shop. She'd been smart and beautiful and he'd—he'd liked her. He'd gotten the distinctive feeling that she'd been interested in him—not just his money.

Crap. He must have forgotten about their appointment entirely when his world fell apart. Which—yes, now he remembered—had occurred moments after his conversation with Trish in the coffee shop.

The woman he'd felt a connection with was the same woman who had just walked into his house and changed his niece's diaper.

Wait.

A woman he'd felt a connection with had just changed his niece's diaper. And gotten her dressed. And wrapped her into a burrito. And, if the indications were to be believed, was about to go down and fix a bottle of formula.

He'd been expecting a candidate for the position of nanny.

Maybe she had arrived.

Trish came out, looking just as elegant as she had before. "There now," she said in that soft voice as she scooped Jane up and cuddled the baby against her chest. "I bet you're hungry and I bet you're sleepy. Let's get some milk, okay?" Jane made a little mewing sound that came close to an agreement.

Trish looked at Nate, who was staring. "Kitchen?"

"This way."

Nate felt like he needed to be doing something better here—but he was at a loss. All he could do was lead the way down stairs and into the back of the house, where Rosita was looking like the last rat on the ship. When his maid saw Trish cuddling the slightly quieter baby, her face lit up. "Oh, miss—we're so glad you've come."

Trish managed a smile, but Nate saw it wasn't a natural thing. "Any clean bottles and nipples?"

Rosita produced the supplies, babbling on in her faint accent the whole time. "I tried, miss, but I never much cared for children." She got out the tub of formula and a gallon of milk and started to mix it.

"Wait—stop." Trish's voice was one of horror. Then she looked at Nate and then around the room again, just like she had in the nursery. When she settled upon the breakfast bar with the stools, she said, "Mr. Longmire—sit."

He sat.

"Hold out your arms like this." She slid Jane down into a cradled position. Nate did as she asked. "Good. Now. Don't drop the baby." Trish set Jane into his arms and then ran her hands over him, pushing his arms tighter here, looser there. Even in his exhausted state, he didn't miss the way her touch lingered on his skin.

He looked up at her. Her face was only inches away from his. If possible, she was even prettier today than she'd been in the coffee shop.

"I'm so glad you're here," he said. It came out quiet and serious.

She paused and met his gaze, her hands still on his bare skin. Heat flashed between them, that attraction he'd felt before.

She didn't say anything, though. She just kept arranging his body until—for the first time—Nate felt like he had a good grasp on his niece.

Although he still didn't have a good grasp on the situation. Well, one thing at a time. Baby first. Attraction second.

"All right," Trish said, sounding very much like a general about to engage in battle. "Dump that out, please. Do you have any other clean bottles?"

"Miss?" Rosita said, hesitantly.

"No milk, not yet. The formula's supposed to be mixed with water."

"Oh," Rosita and Nate said at the same time. Nate went on, "My mom just said she needed her milk every three hours and I thought…damn. I mean dang," he corrected, looking down at Jane.

"I am so sorry, Señor Nate," Rosita said in a low voice. "I…"

"Don't worry about it, Rosita. We both missed it. No harm done." He glanced back at Trish. "Right?"

"Probably not," Trish replied as she fixed a fresh bottle. "Is there somewhere we can go sit? I have a few questions."

"Yeah." She took the baby out of his arms and waited for him to lead the way.

Nate couldn't go back up to the disaster zone that was supposed to be the nursery. That was no image to present to anyone, but especially a lovely young woman who had a way with a baby and hadn't run screaming at the sight of Nate at his worst.

"Rosita, if you could try and make some sense of the nursery while Ms. Hunter and I talk?"

"Yes," Rosita said, sounding relieved to be off the hook. She scurried out of the kitchen faster than Nate had ever seen her move in the three years she'd worked for him.

Nate led Trish to his front parlor. He liked this old house, these old rooms. He kept his technology in a separate room so that this room, where he received visitors, had a timeless feel to it. The front parlor was an excellent room within which to think. No blinking lights or chiming tones to distract him—or disturb an upset infant. "Where do you want to sit?"

"This will be fine." She settled herself in his favorite chair, the plush leather wingback with a matching footstool. She propped her arm on the armrest and got Jane to take the bottle on the second try. Nate watched in surprise. He had hardly been able to get Jane to drink anything.

Of course, if they'd been making it wrong…

"So," she said when he perched on the nearby sofa. "Tell me about it."

Nate didn't like to talk about his family. He liked to keep that part of himself—his past, their present—private. It was better that way for everyone. But he was desperate here. "This doesn't leave this room."

She lifted her eyebrows, but that was the only sign that his statement surprised her. "Agreed."

"I didn't mean to forget our appointment."

"It's pretty obvious that something came up. Didn't it, sweetie?" she cooed at Jane, who was making happy little slurping noises. Nate was thrilled to see her little eyelids already drifting shut.

"I haven't slept more than two hours at a shot in the last two weeks. I don't…I told my parents I couldn't do this. I don't know anything about babies."

"Agreed," Trish repeated with a smile. Nate became aware of a light humming that sounded like…a lullaby?

He took a deep breath. He'd only told two other people about what had happened—Stanley and Rosita. "My brother, my perfect older brother, and his wife left Jane— that's the baby—with my parents to go out to dinner."

The humming stopped and Trish got very still. "And?"

He knew how bad it was to look weak—he'd almost lost his company back at the beginning because he'd been trying to be a nice guy and Diana didn't play by those rules. He'd learned never to show weakness, especially not in the business world.

But the horror of the past two weeks was almost too much for him. He dropped his head into his hands. "And they didn't make it back. A semi lost control, flipped over. They…" The words clogged up in his throat. "They didn't suffer."

"Oh my God, Nate—I'm so sorry." He looked at her and was surprised to see tears gathering in her eyes. "That's— oh, that's just horrible."

"I mean, Brad—that was my brother—you know, it

was hard to grow up in his shadow. He was good-looking and he was the quarterback and he got all the girls. He took—" Nate bit down on the words. He'd made his peace with Brad. Mostly. He'd done his best to put aside the betrayal for the sake of their mother. "We'd…we'd started to become friends, you know? It wasn't a competition anymore because he could never beat me in money and I could never beat him in looks and we were finally even. *Finally.*"

In the end, Brad had done him a favor, really. At least, that's how Nate *had* to look at, for his sanity's sake.

There was a somewhat stunned silence as Trish stared at him, punctuated only by the noises of Jane eating. "For what it's worth," she said in a quiet voice, deeper than the one she used on the baby, "you are an incredibly attractive man."

There it was again—that challenge, that something else that seemed to draw the air between them tighter than a bowstring. For a second, he was too stunned to say anything. He didn't feel attractive right now—just as he hadn't felt attractive when he'd been named one of Silicon Valley's Top Ten Bachelors.

But Trish—beautiful and intelligent and obviously much more knowledgeable about babies than he'd ever be—thought he was attractive. *Incredibly* attractive.

He realized he was probably blushing. "Sorry," he said, trying to keep control of himself. "I don't know why I told you that about my brother. I…"

"You've had a long couple of weeks. When did the accident happen?"

"I got the call as I was leaving the coffee shop. I guess that's why I didn't remember you were coming. I'm sorry about that, too."

"Nate," she said in a kind voice and Nate's mind went back to the way she'd touched him in the kitchen. If only he could think straight… "It's all right. I understand. Life happens."

"Yeah, okay." He could do with a little less life happening right now, frankly.

"So your brother and sister had a baby girl?"

"Jane. Yes."

"Jane," Trish said, the name coming off her tongue like a sigh. "Hello, Jane." But then she looked back at Nate. "If you don't mind me asking, why do *you* have Jane? What about your parents?"

Nate dropped his head back into his hands. It was still so hard to talk about. There wasn't the same stigma now, but back when he'd been a kid… "They couldn't take her."

"Not even for a week or so? No offense, but you don't have a baby's room up there. You have a death trap."

"I—" He swallowed. "I have another brother."

There was that stillness again. She was 100 percent focused on him.

"He's severely mentally ill."

"You say that like it's a bad thing."

"It's not. Not anymore. But there were…problems. He was institutionalized for a while until we could get the meds straightened out." He shrugged. "He's my brother and I love him. He loved Brad, too. Brad was his buddy. They'd go out and throw the football around…" His throat seemed to close up on him and he had to swallow a couple of times to get things to work again.

Trish looked at him like she wanted to comfort him. But she said, "No one knows about your brother?"

"In the past, other people have tried to use that against me. Against my family. And I will not stand for it." The last part came out meaner than he meant it to. She wasn't a threat. She wasn't Diana.

"You give to mental illness research."

"Because of Joe, yeah." He sighed. "He needs his routine. My mom takes care of him and I pay for home health workers. But the last few weeks, my parents have been so upset about Brad and Elena… Besides," he added, feeling the weight of the words, "I'm her legal guardian."

"I see," she replied. "Oh, that's a good girl, Jane. Here." She handed Nate the bottle and then casually moved the baby to her shoulder and began patting Jane's back. "So you're trying to hire a nanny?"

"Yeah. You want the job?"

Trish paused in midpat, and then laughed a little too forcefully. "That's not why I'm here."

He wasn't about to take *no* as an answer. So he didn't always know what to do around members of the opposite sex. He knew how to negotiate a business deal. He needed a nanny. She needed money.

"What do you mean? You obviously know what you're doing." The more he thought about it, the better he liked this idea. He'd already sort of interviewed her, after all. He liked her. Okay, maybe that wasn't a good enough reason to offer her a job changing diapers and burping a baby, but he was comfortable with her and she knew what she was doing and *that* counted for something.

She sighed. "Of course I do. My mom had nine kids with…four different men. Then she married my current stepfather, who had four kids of his own with two other women. I'm the oldest."

Nate tried to process that information. "Your mom had ten kids?"

"Not that she took care of them," Trish replied and for the first time, he heard a distinctive note of bitterness in her voice.

"You?"

Her smile was tight. "Me."

"Perfect."

"Excuse me?"

"Look, I need a nanny. More than that, I need *you*. I've had three people come to the door and no one's made it past five minutes, whereas you've gotten Jane to calm down and stop screaming. I swear this is the first time in two weeks I've been able to hear myself think."

And all of that had nothing to do with the way Trish had touched him, so he was still acting aboveboard here.

"Mr. Longmire," she said in a deeply regretful tone, "I can't. I'm due to graduate with my master's degree in a month and a half. I need to finish my studies and—"

"You can study here. When she sleeps."

Trish's eyes flashed in defiance, which made him smile. "I work two jobs," she went on, in a stronger voice. "I do research for the professor who nominated me for the *Glamour* award and I answer phones in the department."

This was much better. She was negotiating. And God knew that, despite the fact that he was so tired he was on the verge of seeing two Trishes cuddling two babies, he could negotiate a business deal. "For, what? Ten dollars an hour?"

Her back stiffened. "Twelve-fifty, if you must know, but that's not the point."

He felt himself grinning. This was what he'd liked in the coffee shop. She wasn't afraid to push back. She wasn't afraid to challenge him. "What is the point?"

"I have a plan. I have school obligations and employment obligations and charitable obligations that I *will* meet. I have to start organizing the back-to-school drive now. I can't drop everything just to nanny your niece. You'll find a perfectly qualified nanny, I'm sure."

"I already have."

"*No*, Mr. Longmire."

He did some quick calculations in his head. He had to keep her here with him. He needed her in a way he'd never needed any other woman. Everyone had a breaking point. Where was hers?

"I will personally call your professor and explain that you've been selected for a unique opportunity."

Her eyes flew wide in disbelief. "You wouldn't."

"Obviously you'll finish your degree, but you'll need to stay here during the month. Sleep here."

*"Excuse me?"* She looked indignant. The baby, who had actually stopped crying and was possibly asleep, startled and began to make mewing noises.

"I'll pay you five thousand dollars for one month."

Whatever biting rejection she'd been about to say died in a gurgling noise in the back of her throat. "What?"

"One month. I can probably find another nanny in that amount of time, but I need you now."

"Mr. Longmire—"

"Nate."

*"Mister* Longmire," she went on with whispered emphasis. The baby mewed again. Without appearing to think about it, Trish stood and began rocking from side to side.

Yeah, he was looking at his nanny. "One month. A temporary nanny position."

"I'll lose my lease. I'm—I can't afford much. My landlord wants me out so she can triple the rent."

"Ten thousand."

All the blood drained out of her face, but she didn't answer.

"Come on, Ms. Hunter. Ten grand could get you set up in a nice apartment. For one month of teaching me how to care for my niece and helping me find a more permanent nanny. I'd hazard a guess that you'd be moving out of that apartment after graduation, anyway. This can be the nanny plan. Just a slight change to your original plan."

Her mouth opened. "A *slight* change?"

Which was not a *no,* but also wasn't an agreement to

his terms. Where was her breaking point? Then it hit him. The charity.

"Twenty thousand," he said, impulsively doubling the salary. *Let's see her say no to that*, he thought. "In addition to that salary, I'm prepared to make a donation to the One Child, One…whatever it was. One hundred thousand dollars."

Trish collapsed back into the seat, which jostled the baby. She quickly stood again, but instead of rocking from side to side, she turned and walked to the window. "You wouldn't do that."

"I can and I will." She didn't reply. He realized she wasn't necessarily playing hardball with him, but what the hell did a couple hundred grand mean to him? Nothing. He'd never even miss it, but he might change her life. "Fine. Two-fifty. My final offer."

"Two…fifty?" She sounded like she was being strangled.

"Two hundred and fifty thousand dollars to your very worthy charity, to be paid half now, half at the end of the month, provided you stay here, handle the night feedings and whatever else has Jane up every two hours, and teach me how to do some of the basics."

"And…hire a permanent replacement?"

He had her then. She couldn't say no to that kind of cash and they both knew it. "That's the plan, yes."

She didn't reply and he let the silence stretch. Final offers and all that.

He watched her as she thought it over. She was gently rocking from side to side and he could see the top of Jane's fuzzy little head over Trish's shoulder. It looked…something in his chest clenched. It was probably just the sleep deprivation but, Trish standing at the window, soothing the baby—it looked *right*, somehow.

Was he really doing this—convincing this beautiful

woman to stay here, with him? To sleep under the same roof with him? What the hell? He'd wanted to ask her out, not move her in. Still, if she were living in his house...

*Stay*, he thought. *Stay here. With me.*

"This..." She took an exceptionally deep breath. "This *generous* donation—it's not contingent upon anything else?"

"Such as?"

"I can't sleep with you."

He let out a bark of a laugh, which caused her to half turn and *shush* him. "Do I look that bad?"

"I didn't mean to offend." Her gaze flicked over him again and he simultaneously remembered the sad state of his shirt and that earlier she'd decreed he was attractive. *Incredibly* attractive. He sat up a little straighter. "It's just that...I don't sleep with anyone."

*That seems a crying shame.*

The words waltzed right up to the tip of his tongue, but even in his sleep-deprived state, he knew better than to say them out loud.

She looked down at Jane's head. "I've raised *so* many babies already. Whatever money doesn't go to the charity directly goes to support my siblings. My youngest sister is nine. And I..." She sighed and looked out the window. The fog was starting to roll in. "I want her to have more than two pencils."

She turned back to him, determination blazing in her eyes. "It's not that I don't appreciate your generous offer, but there's more that I can do than change diapers and make bottles. I know exactly what sacrifices it takes to raise a child and I..." She glanced down at the baby in her arms and sighed heavily. "I'm not ready to make those sacrifices again. Not just yet."

"One month. That's all I need, Trish. And it's not contingent upon you sleeping with me." She raised her eyebrow at him, as if she doubted his resolve. "I give you my word of honor. Sex is not a part of the plan." He wasn't terribly good at seduction, anyway.

However, there was nothing in their bargain that ruled out him asking for a date after the month was up.

She got a weird look on her face, like she was trying not to smile and not quite making it.

"I just—look," he stammered, trying to recover. "I just need…you. You're perfect."

From this angle—the warming light coming through the window, her face half-turned to him—he couldn't tell if she was blushing or not. But she dropped her gaze and said, "One month. No sex."

"Twenty grand payment for you and two hundred fifty thousand dollars to your charity. Agreed."

She exhaled. "I want it in writing."

"Done. By tomorrow. But…"

"But what?"

"Will you stay tonight?" The words felt foreign on his tongue. He didn't ask women to stay over, not since the thing with Diana had wound up in court.

Her mouth—her deep pink lips—opened and shut before they opened again. "I have to get my things."

A spike of panic hammered into Nate's head. "What if she wakes up? While you're gone?"

"I won't be long. Here. Sit in the chair." She motioned toward the seat she'd just left. "I'll put her on your chest and she'll probably sleep for a few hours. Maybe you can get some sleep, too." She gave him a sly grin. "You look like you need it."

Was that flirting? Sex might not be part of the plan, but flirting was still on the table?

The power had shifted between them again. He held the money, but she had all the know-how. He did as she said, kicking his feet up onto the footstool and settling back into the chair.

She carefully placed Jane on his chest and again guided his arms around the baby until he was holding Jane tightly. Trish's touch—her fingers moving over his muscles—was warm, strong, *soft*.

He was *not* going to sleep with her. But it would be helpful in accomplishing that noble goal if she didn't touch him. "What if I drop her?" he whispered as Trish's fingers trailed off his forearms, searing him with her warmth.

"You won't." She was close to him then, almost close enough to kiss. But he'd just promised—no funny business. She patted the baby's head. "I'll be back. If she wakes up, just sing to her, okay?"

"Hurry," he told her, trying to sound as if this were all no big deal. "Take a cab. I'll pay for it."

There was a moment when their gazes met—a moment when something shifted between them. She looked down at him with a mixture of confusion and...tenderness?

Then she was gone, walking out the door and hurrying away.

He prayed she'd come back.

He couldn't do this without her.

# Three

"What the *hell* am I doing?"

"Sorry?" the cabbie asked in a heavily accented voice.

"Oh—nothing," Trish mumbled, turning her attention back out the window. She had only been in cabs a few times, when going to a symposium with a professor or something. Single travelers probably didn't randomly mutter to themselves.

But, seriously—what the hell was she doing? Moving in with a hot, sweet, *rich* man to take care of his niece? During the last month of her collegiate career? While she was supposed to be organizing the back-to-school drive?

For how much money?

Trish realized she was looking at her fingers, which were slowly counting off the twenty thousand dollars she was going to earn. She ran out of fingers and started over. That was five thousand dollars a week. A week! She didn't earn that much in five months with two jobs.

Twenty grand. That was more than she made in a year, if she didn't count the scholarships—which she tended not to do, since the scholarships didn't buy food or keep the lights on.

And Longmire—Nate—had just thrown that number out.

Along with that *other* number. Two hundred fifty thousand dollars.

Trish stared at her fingers, trying to process the magnitude of that number. Good lord, what her charity could do with that kind of money! New backpacks, shoes and winter coats for every kid on the rez and possibly a few other rezs as well. She could get new sports equipment and fund the afternoon snack in the schools and maybe even get some computers.

It was like a dream come true. Even the part where the hot, rich man was asking her to basically live with him. That was definitely the stuff of dreams. Her dreams, to be specific.

She pinched herself, just to be sure.

The cab pulled up in front of her apartment. "Wait, please," she requested as she got out. The landlady was sitting on her porch, making her disgust for Trish obvious. "Hello, Mrs. Chan," Trish said.

"You leaving?" Mrs. Chan demanded. It was her usual greeting. "You not leaving, you pay more rent. I get $1,900 a month for such nice place, but you only pay me $350."

"Yes, that was the lease we signed," Trish replied. "You get another $450 from the government." Mrs. Chan's "nice place" was a five-hundred-square-foot "garden apartment," which was another way of saying "one step above a root cellar"—only mustier. It'd been furnished, which was helpful when a girl couldn't afford even thrift-store furniture and had no way to get it home, anyway, but it was a combo living-bedroom and bathroom-kitchen. Two rooms in a hole in the ground. Not exactly the lap of luxury and nothing like Nate's elegant Victorian.

But, thanks to the subsidies, it'd been a place Trish could afford and it'd been her own. For the first time in her life, she hadn't had to wait for a bathroom and hadn't had at least two other kids in her bed with her. It hadn't been freezing in the winter and the water always worked. For the past five glorious years, she'd been able to breathe.

"You should pay more," Mrs. Chan sniffed. "My daughter—a *lawyer*—says so." This conversation happened on autopilot.

"Mrs. Chan, you get your wish today."

"What?" The older lady sat up straight and suddenly a bright smile graced her face. "You leaving?"

"I'm leaving. I have a…" She didn't know how to describe the situation. "I have a new place."

"You leave now?"

Trish turned back to where the cab was waiting. It felt too decadent, letting the meter run. "Yup. Right now. I just came back for my things."

"Oh, my." Honest to God, Mrs. Chan batted her eyelashes at Trish. "You such a sweet girl. I always like you."

Trish managed not to roll her eyes, but it took a lot of effort. "Can I get my deposit?"

Some of the sweetness bled out of Mrs. Chan's face. It wasn't like Trish needed the money right now—how weird was it to think *that*?—but she couldn't not get it. It was her $350. Getting the deposit money scraped together had practically taken an act of God—and a favor from her stepfather. She could pay him back now.

"I mail to you," Mrs. Chan finally said.

"Fine. I'll leave my address. I have to go pack."

She unlocked her door as Mrs. Chan rhapsodized about how Trish was "such a sweet girl." This wouldn't take long. She had no furniture to move—even the coffeepot that was possibly as old as she was had come with the apartment.

She started shoving clothes into laundry bags. The books took several trips and then the only thing left was her one true luxury—a laptop. True, it was an old laptop. She didn't particularly like to pull it out when there were people around because the last thing she needed were more funny looks.

But it was a computer and she owned it free and clear and that was what counted.

Forty minutes was all it took to erase the signs of her five years in this dank little apartment. The cabbie helped her load the last bag into his trunk and then they were off, back to the historical Victorian that contained a billionaire and a baby.

There was no going back. Mrs. Chan wouldn't let her come back, not without another grand in rent money every month. Trish was committed now.

The enormity of what she was doing hit her again. Oh, God. She was moving in. With Nate Longmire. Who was out of her league and yet also adorably clueless about small children.

Instead of panicking, she forced herself to make a list. She had so much to do. Explain what had happened to her bosses. Call home and make sure her mom had her new address. Finish her degree.

Live under the same roof as Nate Longmire. He who promised not to sleep with her.

Which was just fine. She did not want to be seduced. Not in the least. Seduction always came with the risk of pregnancy and that was a risk she was not willing to take.

Except...

She had the feeling that if she'd had her wits about her, she could have gotten a million dollars out of him, he was so desperate. But that felt wrong, too.

She'd gone in there for the money, but she didn't want to take advantage of him. Not after watching him struggle to keep his composure as he talked about his family.

Damn her helpful nature. As bad an idea as this was, she couldn't say no and leave him and that poor girl in such obvious distress. Mixing milk in with the formula? Good lord. That baby had probably only been a day or two away from a visit to the emergency room.

Rosita was waiting for the cab. She hurried down the wide stairs and rushed through the gate as Trish unloaded all of her worldly possessions. "Oh, good—you've come back," she said as she handed over a credit card to the cabbie.

"I promised I would."

"They're still sleeping," Rosita went on. "*Ay mia*, this is the most quiet we've had in weeks."

"Will you help me unload? I don't even know where I'm going to be sleeping."

"I made you up a bed. This way, please."

Hefting one of her duffels over her shoulder, Trish followed the maid inside. She paused to peek into the parlor. The man and the baby hadn't moved. Nate still had a firm hold of Jane. The little girl was curled against him, breathing regularly. And Nate?

God, it wasn't fair that he should look so good, so sweet, sleeping like that. It almost made Trish's heart hurt. She'd helped raise nine other babies—and she couldn't remember seeing any father in her house holding his child. She liked to think that, once upon a time, her father had held her before he pulled up stakes and came to San Francisco.

She knew that many men cared for their children. But Jane wasn't even Nate's child—and he was still trying his hardest.

No. She was not going to crush on him. This was not about her attraction to Nate Longmire, no matter how wealthy and good-looking and easy to talk to he was. This was about funding her charity for the foreseeable future and making sure that little girl was well cared for. Trish had too much to do to allow an infatuation to creep into her life and that was final. They'd both agreed to the plan and she would stick by that plan come hell or high water.

She followed Rosita up the stairs. This time, she was able to actually look around. The staircase was a magnificent creation that, at the landing, broke into two sets of stairs, one on each side of the wall. The whole place was so clean it almost glowed in the early evening light. Expensive-looking art—some of it old-looking oil paintings, some of it framed movie posters from schlocky old movies she'd never heard of—decorated the walls in coordinating frames. The walls were a pale green, cool and refreshing, with coordinating chairs in the landing.

Oh, yeah, this was much fancier than anything she'd ever lived in before. This was even fancier than the hotel she'd stayed in for the *Glamour* award in New York. That'd been a very nice hotel—a Marriott—but this? This was officially the lap of luxury. And it was Nate's.

Rosita took the staircase to the right and Trish followed. She wondered if she might go up to the attic—she'd be out of the way there—but Rosita led her down the hall on the second floor.

"That is Señor Nate's room," Rosita said, pointing to the other side of the hallway. "It runs the length of the house. The nursery and the guest room are on this side. Here we are." Rosita opened the first door on her right.

Wait—what? She was going to be right across the hall from him? That felt…close. Too close. He would be too accessible.

But that flash of panic was quickly overridden by the room Rosita led her into. "Oh, my," Trish breathed. A huge, beautiful room awaited her. She'd never had a beautiful room before. The wallpaper was a deep blue-and-cream floral pattern. An actual chandelier hung in the middle. The room had a small bay window that held two sitting chairs and a small table. To one side was a fireplace with deep blue glazed tiles. A flat-screen television hung over the mantel, which was decorated with small vases and figurines. And on the other… "That's an amazing bed."

"Yes. Señor Nate's mother prefers this room when she is able to visit."

The bed was huge. At least a queen-size with four posts that reached up almost to the level of the chandelier, the whole thing was draped with gauzy fabric. The bed was made up with color-coordinating pillows and a down comforter that looked so light and fluffy Trish couldn't wait until she could sleep in it.

Alone. She would be sleeping in that bed *alone*. That was the plan.

Except all the dreams she'd been having for the past two weeks came crashing back down on her head. Nate would be right across the hall, no longer a fantasy, but a flesh-and-blood man who had, in no uncertain terms, said he needed her.

Oh, this was going to be a long, hard month.

"The bathroom, miss," Rosita said. "It connects with the nursery."

"Okay, good." That way, she wouldn't have to walk into the hall in the middle of the night in her T-shirt and boxer shorts and run the risk of stumbling into Nate Long-mire. Because that would be terrible. Awful. She was just sure of it.

Her head began to spin. This was too much. Too much money. Not her life. She didn't get paid this kind of cash to watch a billionaire's baby while sleeping in a guest room that was far bigger and cleaner than any other place she'd ever lived.

Her knees wobbled and she sat heavily on the bed. Of course it was soft and comfortable. And it was hers. Hers for the month.

"Tell me about him," she said to Rosita. The maid's eyebrows jumped. "I just agreed to move into his house and I really don't know...anything." She'd done her homework a few weeks ago and yes, he'd shared that little moment down in the parlor. But suddenly that wasn't enough.

Because there'd been huge holes in his biography online. The lawsuits he'd filed—and won. He'd sued a woman named Diana Carter because she'd claimed that half of SnAppShot was hers and had tried to sell it. They'd been old college friends, according to the filings. There were rumors that they'd been more, but that was it—just rumors. And Nate had run her into the ground.

But those were dry legal texts. Anything else that might have provided context about what went on between "old college friends" was simply not there. The information was conspicuous in its absence.

"Señor Nate? He is a good man. Quiet, not messy. Does not make me uncomfortable. Very polite."

"Okay, good." That was mostly how he'd come across during their meeting at the coffee shop. Well, maybe except the messy part.

"He likes to sleep late and he drinks maybe too much coffee," Rosita added in an entirely motherly sounding voice. "But I do not mind. He pays me very well and the work is not too hard. Mostly cooking, cleaning and laundry. It is a very good job."

"Does he…I mean to say, will there be other guests? Who spend the night?" She didn't know why she'd asked that question, but it was out there and there was nothing she could do about it now. She felt her cheeks flush.

It was a matter of self-preservation, that was all. If other people were going to be in and out of this house, that was something she needed to know for Jane's sake. She'd have to lock both her and Jane's doors to make sure no "guests" accidentally wandered into the wrong room. It had nothing to do with not wanting to see Nate going into his bedroom with someone else and closing the door behind them.

"Ay, no! Señor Nate keeps to himself. His helper—

Stanley," she said, drawing the name out in an unflattering way, "he will sleep on the couch sometimes, down in the media room. That is only when they are working on a project. But no. No other guests."

"Stanley—does he have a lot of tattoos, a horrible sense of fashion and big holes in his ears?"

Rosita nodded. "I do not like him. He is loud and messy and rude. But Señor Nate says he is a good man, so I cook for him when he comes over."

Yeah, that pretty much summed up the man Trish had talked to at the office. Loud, messy and rude. "Anything else you think I should know?"

Rosita stepped back and gave Trish the once-over. "No, miss. Just that I'm glad you've taken the position. I..." her voice dropped to a whisper. "I do not care for children. Never had one of my own. They make me nervous," she admitted with an awkward laugh. "That is why this was such a good job. Other people, they want you to look after the children and I...I am no good at it. And it is far too late for me to suddenly become good at it. You understand? It would be hard to find another position as good as this one and I am getting too old to start over."

Trish patted Rosita's arm. Being a woman who currently had no desire to have children, she understood. Some people just didn't like babies. Oftentimes, Trish had to wonder if that included her own mother. Why else would she have left her oldest to care for each new infant?

"No worries. I'm going to unpack a little and then check on them." She looked at the clock beside the bed. Even the clock was fancy—a built-in dock for smartphones and more plugs than she recognized. If only she had a smartphone to dock there. "They've probably got another forty minutes or so before they wake up."

Rosita started to leave but paused at the door. "Miss? I do all the cooking. Anything special you like?"

Trish blinked at her. She was not a gourmet cook. She existed on the cheapest groceries she could afford, and those usually came from corner markets and little shops that carried ethnic foods. Her big splurge was, once a week, buying a nice cup of coffee. If she got really wild, she might eat two whole packets of ramen noodles for dinner. She did not dine at nice restaurants. She didn't even dine at bad ones.

The prospect of this nice woman cooking her food was beyond Trish's comprehension. "I'll eat anything."

Rosita nodded and closed the door behind her.

Trish flopped back onto the bed and stared up at the gauzy canopy. This was, hands down, the craziest thing she'd ever done. Moving in with a billionaire. What the hell?

But already it was hard to think of Nate as just the Boy Billionaire, not when she'd seen him so upset over his family and napping with his niece. She hadn't just moved in with a billionaire. She'd moved in with *Nate*.

She forced herself to stop thinking about the way his very nice arm muscles had tightened under her touch and the way certain parts of her own body had tightened in response. *If* she allowed herself to dwell on those moments— and that was a pretty darned big *if*—well, those thoughts were best kept for after everyone had gone to bed in their separate bedrooms, with all doors safely shut.

Right now, she had things to do. Moving quickly, she unpacked her meager wardrobe. The room had a closet that was almost as big as her kitchen/bathroom in the basement of Mrs. Chan's house, and all the hangers were those fancy padded ones wrapped in satin. Her second-hand clothes looked jarringly out of place on them.

She put her laptop on the table in the window—the little nook would be a wonderful place to do her work—and lined up her books on a built-in bookshelf on the far side of the canopy bed. Finally, she was unpacked.

Time to get down to business. She pulled off her boots and considered her options. Baby duty required wash-and-wear clothes and her professional outfit wasn't it.

As she stripped down to her underwear, she thought about what Rosita had said. Nate was quiet, kept to himself.

He didn't bring women home with him. And, aside from Stanley, who slept on the couch, he didn't bring men home with him, either.

Trish threw on the Wonder Woman T-shirt and a pair of jeans, and then removed her earrings and braided her hair back so that it couldn't be yanked by small hands. She was not going to think about Nate and whom he did or did not bring home with him. It was none of her business whom he slept with, as long as he didn't—what had Rosita said? As long as Nate didn't make Trish "uncomfortable."

He'd promised. No sex.

During the month.

Which left what might happen after the month as something of an open question.

Trish shook her head and forced herself to think about the real reason she was here—Jane, the baby. The poor girl.

God, Trish didn't want to be a mother again so soon, not to someone else's child, but…Jane needed her and Nate needed her. And Trish—she needed a well-funded charity that could make a huge difference in her people's lives.

Just a month. She was a temporary nanny. That was the plan.

She opened her door and, barefoot, peeked into the nursery. Rosita had done an admirable job in the hour and a half since Trish had last seen the nursery, but the place was still a mess. Boxes and suitcases were stacked against the walls, baby things spilling out of them. The playpen was almost in the middle of the room and—wait. She stepped around it. A pair of formal sitting chairs—much like the ones in her room, only in a deep rose color—sat in the bay window. That, in itself, wasn't that remarkable.

But one of the chairs had a suitcase that had clearly been used as a footstool. A used coffee cup sat on the little table and a phone—she assumed it was Nate's—was next to it. The whole area looked rumpled, much like Nate had when she'd showed up.

Oh, dear God—no wonder that man was so tired. He'd been sleeping in the chair to be closer to Jane.

She shook her head. He had *no* idea what he was doing, but he was doing his best. She'd work on the nursery tomorrow. There wasn't even a changing table. She'd have to ask if Nate could afford to get a crib, a table and another dresser...

She caught herself. Of course Nate could afford that. Hello, Boy Billionaire who'd just thrown close to three hundred thousand dollars at her. A couple of thousand on some furniture wasn't anything to him.

She left the mess behind and went downstairs to the parlor. She studied the room. For being a tech billionaire, there was very little actual tech in this room. Instead, old toys were artfully arranged on the built-in bookcases around a fireplace with an elegant floral pattern done in bright blue tiles. The mantel that went over it was hand-carved and polished to a high shine. And there, in a place of honor, was Superman #1 in a glass case.

Earlier, when she'd seen the distress Jane was in, Trish had acted without thinking. Her instincts were to get the baby changed and clothed and fed and napping in quick succession.

There was a distinctive possibility that she *might* have been bossing a billionaire around.

But now the situation was not as dire. The baby was resting. Nate was asleep. She didn't know if she could walk in there and pluck Jane off his chest or if that would be crossing a line she shouldn't cross. She really shouldn't touch him. Not like she'd already touched him. No more touching. Touching was not part of the plan.

As she was debating doing that or going back and showing Rosita how to make the formula properly, Nate's eyes fluttered open. He saw her standing there and blinked a few times.

"Hey, Wonder Woman," he mumbled as his long legs stretched out.

"I'm not really a superhero," she felt obligated to remind him.

That got her a sleepy grin. Oh, my. Yes, Nate Longmire could be quite attractive. "You came back."

"I keep my word." She paused. "Listen, about the money…"

His eyes widened. "What about it? Not enough?"

"No—no—it's just—that's an insane amount of money. You don't have to pay me that much. Really. I hadn't even considered the room and board as part of the agreement. And the room—it's really nice. I mean, that alone is worth—"

"Don't worry about it," he sighed as his eyelids drifted shut again. "We agreed. I keep my word, too."

He couldn't be serious. She hadn't been negotiating, not really. She'd just been too stunned to tell him no earlier. "But—"

"The deal is done." His voice was harder now—the same voice he'd used when he had refused to take *no* for an answer. "Not open to renegotiation, Trish."

She tried very hard not to glare at him. "Fine. I have a favor to ask."

One eyelid opened back up. She could almost see him thinking, *another favor?* "Yes?"

"I need to borrow a phone so I can call my family and

tell them where I'm at and I haven't seen a landline in here."

"I don't have a landline," he said as if she'd observed that he didn't have any woolly mammoths in the closets. Both lids swung up in a look of total confusion. "You don't have a phone?"

"Nope." Shame burned her cheeks. She lived in the most technologically advanced city in quite possibly the entire world—and didn't even own a cell phone. "I have a laptop," she said, desperate not to sound pathetic. "I assume you have Wi-Fi or something I can log into, to finish my classwork?"

He regarded her for a minute. She got the feeling he was fully awake now.

"You need a phone."

"I'm fine, it's just that—"

"No, you need a phone," he said with more force. "In case of an emergency. I'll have Stanley get you one. I've cleared most of my schedule, but I have a few events I need to attend and you need to be able to get ahold of me."

"Nate…"

She was going to tell him he absolutely could not buy her a phone. She had existed for twenty-five years without a mobile device just fine. He was already giving her too much.

But when she said his name, something in his eyes changed—deepened. And all those things she was going to tell him floated away like the fog.

"You are too generous," she said, unable to make her voice sound like a normal version of herself. She could never pay him back, not in a million years. "You're giving me too much. I'm not…" *worth it.*

She almost said it out loud but managed not to.

His eyebrows lifted and he opened his mouth and she was suddenly very interested in what he was about to say, but Jane awoke with a start and a cry. Her head lifted up and crashed back into Nate's shoulder. "Ow," he said. "You've got a hard head, Janie girl."

"Here." Trish strode into the room and lifted Jane out of his arms. "I told you that you wouldn't drop her."

"I bow to your superior knowledge," he said working his head from side to side.

She caught a whiff of stale milk. *Old* stale milk. Nate Longmire was on the verge of curdling before her very eyes. "I don't want to tell you what to do…"

He looked up at her, a curious grin on his face. "Don't let that stop you. What?"

"You might consider a shower."

An adorable blush turned his cheeks pink, then red. "That bad?"

She wrinkled her nose at him. "Go. I've got Jane."

He got to his feet and leaned in. For a blistering second, she thought he was going to kiss her. He was going to kiss her and she was going to let him and that was the stupidest thing she'd ever thought because she did not let people kiss her. She just didn't.

He pressed his lips to the top of Jane's head, nestled against Trish's shoulder. Then he straightened up. "Thank you."

This was the closest she'd been to him. Close enough to feel the warmth of his body radiating in the space between them. Close enough to see the deep golden flecks in his brown eyes, no longer hidden behind the hipster glasses. "I haven't done anything yet."

"You're here. Right now, that's everything."

Even though Jane was waking up and starting to fuss at still being swaddled in the blanket, Trish couldn't pull away from the way his eyes held hers.

"You don't have to buy me a phone." It came out as a whisper.

The very corner of his mouth curved up and he suddenly looked very much like a man who would seduce his temporary nanny just because he could. "And yet, I'm going to, anyway."

Trish swallowed down the tingling sensation in the back of her throat. This was Nate after a nap? What would he be like after a solid night's sleep?

And how the hell was she going to resist him?

The baby saved her. Jane made an awful noise and Nate reeled back in horror. "Um…yeah. I'll just go shower now." He stepped around her and all but ran toward the door.

"Coward," she called out after him. "You're going to have to learn sometime!"

"Can't talk, in the shower!" he called back. It sounded like he was laughing.

Trish sighed. "Come on, sweetie," she said to the baby. "It's you and me for the month."

She needed this baby—needed the constant reminder of why she didn't sleep with anyone and especially not with the man who was paying her a salary. She was not going to get caught up in Nate Longmire being an atypical billionaire who looked at her like she was the answer to his prayers, even if she was—in a strictly nanny-based sort of way, of course.

Thank God for dirty diapers.

# Four

Nate stood under the waterfall showerhead with his forehead slowly banging against the tiled wall.

When had an easy plan, such as to not sleep with a nanny, suddenly become something that seemed so insurmountably difficult? He didn't seduce people. And when people tried to seduce him—like that woman at the last talk he'd given, the one where he'd met Trish—he managed to sidestep around it.

What was it about Trish Hunter that had him struggling to keep his control in his own home?

It's not like he was a prude. Okay, he sort of was, but it wasn't because he didn't like sex. He did. A lot. But sex was…it was opening yourself up to another person. And that he didn't like. Not anymore.

He didn't pick up women and he didn't get picked up. It was a holdover from a long, painful adolescence, where he'd learned to take care of himself because he sure as hell wasn't going to get much help from anyone else. And yes, it was the fallout from Diana. He wasn't going to put himself in that kind of position again if he could help it. Better to stick it out alone than open himself to that kind of inside attack again.

He turned the cold knob up another three notches.

It didn't help.

He wasn't innocent. College had been good for him on

a couple of different levels. He'd started this company. Started dating. He'd gone to MIT, where no one knew about Brad Longmire or his football championships. Nate had no longer been Brad's little brother. He'd been Nate.

And what was more, he wasn't the biggest geek on campus, not at MIT. He'd blended. For the first time in his life, he'd belonged. He'd filled out, started growing facial hair and gotten lucky a few times. He'd met Diana...

No. He wasn't going to think about that mess. All the paperwork was signed, sealed and approved by the judge. He didn't care if she was trying to get ahold of him again. He was *done* with her.

But Trish...

His hand closed around his dick as Trish's face appeared behind his closed eyes, smiling down at him from where she'd stood in the doorway. She'd looked like an angel as he'd blinked the nap out of his eyes. He'd swear there was a glow around her. And then? She'd tried to give the money back. She could ask him for a million dollars and he'd happily sign the check tomorrow, as long as she stayed and kept Jane happy and healthy.

She hadn't. She'd tried to give some back.

As he stroked himself, he thought of the way she'd been looking at him when he woke up—one arm leaned against the doorjamb, her Wonder Woman–clad breasts no longer hidden behind a respectable jacket. She'd looked soft and happy and glad to see him.

He. Would. Not. Sleep. With. Her. He'd given his word.

Not for the month, anyway. After that...

After that, he'd ask her out. Ask her to stay—not for the baby, but for him. They'd talk and he'd kiss her and then he'd lead her up to his room and they'd fall into bed together, hands everywhere. Lips everywhere. He wouldn't be able to keep his hands off her.

She'd be on top of him, stripping that superhero shirt off, her thighs gripping him as he thrust up—

Groaning, he reached a shuddering conclusion. *Hell.* It was going to be a long month.

He let the water run on cold for a few more minutes until he was sure he had the situation under control. He'd been in control for years now. He could handle a beautiful young woman living under his roof, no problem.

He was drying off when he heard something—a high, trilling sound that seemed different from all the screaming that Jane had been doing in the past week but was just as loud.

Oh, no. The baby—he shouldn't have taken a shower, not while she was awake. What had he been thinking? Nate wrapped the towel around his waist and shot out of his bathroom, running across the hall toward the sound.

He slipped around the corner to find Trish sitting on the floor with Jane—bouncing the baby on her knee?

"What's wrong?" he demanded.

"What?" Trish looked up and her eyes went wide. "Oh! Um…"

Jane made that noise again and a sick dread filled him. He'd told his mom he couldn't do this. But what choice did he have, really? "What's wrong with her?"

"She's fine," Trish said in a reassuring voice. "We're playing. That's a happy noise." Her gaze cut to his chest—then to the towel—and then back up.

"It…is?" He was wearing a *towel*. And nothing else. He grabbed at it so fast that he almost knocked it loose and suddenly he was very aware that flashing his new nanny probably invalidated any promise, written or spoken, not to have sex with her.

He did the only thing he could do—he stepped to the side, so that his body was on the other side of the doorway.

"It is," Trish replied. "She's had a good nap and a clean

diaper and I bet this is the best she's felt in a little while. Isn't it, sweetie?" she said to the baby. Then she leaned forward and blew a raspberry on Jane's tummy.

The baby squealed in delight and Trish laughed. It was a warm, confident noise.

Then she looked up at him, her full lips still curved up with happiness. "We're fine, if you want to—you know—put on clothes."

"Right, right." Feeling like a first-class idiot, he ran back to his room and threw on some shorts. What the hell was wrong with him? Seriously. That had bordered on totally disastrous—much worse than knocking a coffee into her lap. He absolutely could not afford to do anything to drive her away.

He dug out some clean clothes. In any other situation, he might have called Stanley for advice on what to wear—but what the hell. She'd already seen him at his worst.

Oh, Lord—what had he done? He should have held out. He should have hired a grandmother who was as wide as a bus and had whiskers or something. Not a beautiful young woman who was going to drive him mad with lust. Who was going to challenge him.

He forced himself to run a few lines of code through his mind as he gathered up his very dirty clothes and dumped them in the hamper. The original code to SnAppShot. He knew it by heart. That code was like a security blanket. Whenever he couldn't sleep—which was often—he'd mentally scroll through that code.

Then he got a clean pair of jeans and, after a moment's consideration, his Superman T-shirt. Superman and Wonder Woman, saving the universe one baby at a time. Stanley wouldn't approve, but what the hell.

This time, Nate walked with a purpose back to the nursery. Trish now had the baby on the floor and appeared to be tickling her feet. Whatever she was doing, Jane was kicking and wriggling and making that loud, not-crying noise again.

This was okay, this noise. If Trish said it was okay, it was okay. Loud and unsettling, but okay.

She looked up at him from the floor, where she was lying on her side and had her head propped up on one hand. "You look…good. Nice shirt."

He felt his cheeks get hot. "Couldn't have been much worse, I suppose?"

"It can always be worse," Trish replied. Her eyes darted back down to his chest. Almost unconsciously, he stood up straighter. It'd been one thing for her to stare while he'd been wet and basically naked. But was she checking him out?

She dropped her gaze and he swore the color of her cheeks deepened. "So…"

He leaned forward. "Yes?"

"Jane's going to need a few more things," Trish said in a rush.

"Like what?"

Trish stood and lifted Jane onto her hip with that practiced air. "Everything. This room is a disaster, you know. Were you sleeping in the chair?"

Nate looked over the nursery. The place was still a wreck—and that got his mind firmly back into the here and now and far away from whether or not Trish might have liked what she'd seen a few minutes ago. "Well, yeah. Rosita doesn't live here. She goes home at six most days and comes in at ten because I sleep late. And I was just afraid…"

"That you wouldn't hear her?"

"Or SIDS or something," he agreed. "Elena—Jane's mother—was worried about SIDS, I remember that." God, it was almost too much to bear. He'd liked Elena. She kept Brad grounded and had told Nate to keep the beard because it made him look a little like Ben Affleck and that couldn't be a bad thing, Nate had figured.

But Elena and Brad were gone and Nate was suddenly the guardian of their daughter.

He leaned against the playpen for support.

"You okay?" Trish asked.

"I just…I can't believe they're not coming back, you know? To just have them up and disappear out of my life like *that*?" He snapped his fingers.

"I know." Trish stepped into him and put her free hand on his shoulder. The same fingers that just a few hours ago had skimmed over his skin, making sure he could hold his niece, were now a reassuring hold on him. Without thinking about it, he reached up and covered her hand with his.

"Do you?" He had no business asking—and even less business asking while she was touching him—while he was touching her back. Even if that touch was a reassuring touch, full of comfort and concern and almost no lust at all.

"I do." Then, mercifully, she released her hold on him. She switched Jane to her other hip—the one closer to him—and leaned so the little girl's head was touching him.

Weirdly, that was what he needed. He didn't have his brother or sister-in-law anymore, but he had Jane. And it was his duty to take care of this little girl. He wasn't married and he hadn't foreseen having children anytime soon, but…she was his flesh and blood.

He was a father now. He had to stand tall for her. For them both.

He tilted his head to the side and looked at Trish out of the corner of his eye. She was watching him with concern. Jane made a squealing noise and Nate jumped. "Yeah, that's why I was sleeping in here," he said, getting himself back together. "She makes all these weird noises that don't seem normal…"

"They are," Trish said calmly. "How old is she?"

"Almost six months."

Trish stepped back from him and twirled around. Her mouth open wide, Jane let out a squeal of delight. Trish stopped spinning and looked in her mouth. "Hmm. No teeth yet. But if she's having trouble sleeping, that might be part of it."

"Oh. Okay." Teething. Yet another thing he didn't have a clue about. "That's normal, right?"

Trish grinned at him, then unexpectedly spun again, making Jane giggle. Yes—definitely a giggle. "Right. We've got to get this room whipped into shape."

"One moment." He pulled out his phone and video-messaged Stanley.

Stanley's face appeared. "What? It's after seven."

"And hello to you, too. I need you to go shopping. Start a list," Nate said. "Company phone for Ms. Trish Hunter."

Off to his side, Trish sighed heavily, but she didn't protest.

"And?" Stanley said.

Nate looked at Trish. "And?"

"A crib, changing table, dresser drawers, a rocker-glider chair, stroller, car seat, high chair, size two diapers, more formula."

"Did you get all that?" Nate asked.

"Is that the girl? She came here first. I had to send her your way," Stanley said in that absent-minded way of his that meant he was taking notes.

"Yes," Nate said. "She took the position. Also, I need you to do the due diligence on One Child, One..." he could not remember the last part of her charity's name. It just wasn't there.

"World. One Child, One World," Trish helpfully supplied. Her eyes had gotten big and round again.

"One Child, One World," Nate told Stanley. "I'm going

to be making a donation for two hundred fifty thousand dollars. Also, please put Ms. Hunter on the payroll."

"Salary?" Stanley said.

"Twenty thousand for one month."

There was a moment's pause in which Stanley's eyebrows jumped up. "Can I have a raise?"

This time, Nate did snort. For as much as he paid Stanley, the man was constantly haranguing him for more. "No."

"She must be *highly* qualified," he said in that distracted way again. "Good body, too."

Nate cringed. "She's also listening."

After a frozen pause—his eyes wide in horror—Stanley cleared his throat. When he spoke again, he did so in his most professional voice. "When do you need this by?"

Nate looked at Trish and was surprised to see that she was trying not to laugh. "As soon as possible," she managed to get out.

"Right. Got it." Stanley ended the call.

Nate stood there, staring down at his screen. He really didn't know what to do next. Trish did have a good body. And an excellent sense of humor about it, too.

"Well. That wasn't awkward at all."

He grinned. "The least awkward conversation ever, possibly."

They stood there. There was tension in the room, but it wasn't the kind that normally had him tripping over his words or his feet. He was comfortable with her. And, despite all the not-awkwardness, she seemed pretty okay with him. Enough to send him to the shower because he reeked.

"Señor Nate?" Rosita called up from downstairs. "Dinner is on the table. Do you need me for anything else? It is after seven o'clock…"

Nate glanced at Trish, who shook her head. The past few nights, when Rosita had fled from the house at exactly six—leaving Nate all alone with Jane—he'd been filled with a sense of dread that was far heavier than anything else he'd ever had to overcome.

But not tonight. A sense of calm brushed away the nagging conviction that he couldn't do this. And that calm was named Trish.

"I think we're going to make it," he called back. "See you on Monday?"

"Yes," Rosita called back, sounding relieved.

The sound of the front door shutting echoed through the house. "She's a very good cook," he felt like he had to explain, "but she doesn't really like kids."

"So she said. And Stanley?"

"Don't feel too sorry for him. He gets fifty bucks an hour." Her face paled a bit—no doubt, she was thinking about the twelve fifty an hour she'd earned as of this morning. "I know he's a little rough around the edges, but he's the height of discretion. They both are."

"You value your privacy."

"Doesn't everyone?" Which was a true enough statement, but he knew that wasn't what she was asking.

She'd as much as admitted that she'd dug into his history. But he didn't want to go down that path right now. Just because she was someone he'd like to get to know better and who was technically living under his roof at this very moment didn't mean he had to just open up and share his deepest secrets with her.

So he did the only thing he could do. He changed the subject. "Shall we have dinner? Then I can show you the rest of the house and you can teach me how to make the formula." Because he was going to have to learn it sometime and that was a concrete task that probably wouldn't involve lingering touches or long looks. Hopefully.

Like the long look she gave him right then, punctuated only when she shifted Jane to her other hip. There was something in her eyes, as if she didn't believe what he'd just suggested. "Yes," she said after that measured gaze, "We shall."

# Five

Trish lay in bed, not sleeping. This house sounded different. She was used to the shuffling of Mrs. Chan over her head and the blaring of the evening news. But Nate's house?

This place was quiet. Nearly silent. In the distance, a foghorn sounded.

She'd never had so much quiet. Funny how it felt loud. Was this why Nate lived here—he could hear himself think?

They'd gone up to the dining room, where the best danged chicken enchilada dinner she'd ever eaten had been waiting for them in a dining room that was not rated for kids. The table had ten chairs and was set upon a thick white shag rug. Trish had suggested that Nate remove the carpeting before Jane started eating solid foods.

And then there'd been the view. Not that she'd been able to see much in the fog, but Nate had said that the floor-to-ceiling glass windows that separated the dining room from the patio had an excellent view of the Golden Gate Bridge. Trish hadn't had a view of anything but the sidewalk in five years. There was even a fenced-in yard with trees and grass. Nate had asked her if he should get a swing set or something for Jane. After that, Nate had showed her the media room and the home gym in the basement.

Trish didn't belong here. This house, the food, everything about Nate was out of her league. Had she really felt like an interloper at San Francisco State University? Good lord. That was nothing compared to finding herself suddenly living in the absolute lap of luxury with a man who took such a vital interest in his niece's welfare.

Trish's current stepfather was a pretty good guy. He supported Pat and the kids still living at home and that counted for a hell of a lot. He'd even loaned Trish the $350 for her security deposit five years ago—and that had only been two years after he'd hooked up with Pat.

But there'd been so many men who'd passed through Pat's and Trish's lives and not one of them had ever taken an interest in the kids. Not someone else's kids, not their own kids. Trish's own father had abandoned them, for crying out loud.

To watch Nate try so hard—care so much—well, it spun her head around. One of the reasons she'd gone out of her way to avoid a relationship, and men in general, was because she didn't want to be saddled raising a child on her own. She knew exactly what kind of sacrifices a baby would require and she was done making them for other people.

But Nate… He'd stood shoulder-to-shoulder with her in the kitchen and made up three bottles of formula until he'd gotten it right and he hadn't complained at all. In fact, they'd wound up laughing together after his first attempt had resulted in something closer to a pancake batter than formula. He'd taken another crack at changing a diaper, too. Willingly.

Not like the man who'd come into her life when Trish had been nine. That year had made her tougher than she knew she could be. She'd decided then that she would protect her little brothers and sisters. She would get her education even if it took her two years longer to graduate and then she would get the hell off that rez. And when she'd made it, she'd do everything she could to make sure that no other kid went hungry.

She would never again be at the mercy of a man.

Which did not explain why she was living in Nate Longmire's home, caring for his niece, completely dependent on him for her meals and money. Taking this position was something so impulsive, so not thought-out, that even her mother, Pat, would be surprised.

She was completely at Nate's mercy right now and all she had to go on was that his maid said he was a good man and he'd promised sex wasn't part of the plan. That was it. She tried to reason that at least Nate had a reference—her mother had hooked up on far less—but it didn't change the fact that, for the first time in her life, Trish had followed in her mother's footsteps. When a good-looking man had said jump, she'd asked how high and tossed everything to the side to take care of another baby.

Trish didn't know what to think anymore. The certainty with which she'd lived her life for the past ten, fifteen years—suddenly, she wasn't so certain that she was absolutely doing the right thing.

Trish went around and around with herself. Then she heard a soft *whump* and she sat up, her ears straining. The clock said one-thirty. She must have drifted off at some point.

Then she heard it, the building whine of a baby who was not quite awake yet. She threw off her covers and hurried through the adjoining bathroom door. She turned on the bathroom light and let the door open enough that she could see her way to the playpen.

Jane had gotten herself loose from her swaddling and was flailing about. "Shh, shh, it's okay, sweetie," Trish said as she picked up the baby. "I'm here. Let's go get a bottle, okay? Let's let Nate sleep."

The moment the words left her mouth, the overhead lights flipped on. Jane flinched and began to cry in earnest.

Blinking hard, Trish spun to see Nate standing in the doorway in a T-shirt and a pair of boxers—not all that different from what she was wearing.

"Everything okay?" he asked in a bleary voice.

"The light—turn it off."

"What?"

"Nate," she hissed in a whisper. "Turn the light off. Please. You're upsetting Jane."

"Oh." He flipped the light off and Jane quieted back down to a pleading whimper. "Was that bad?"

"We should keep it as quiet and as dark as possible during the night." She could see what had happened now. Every time the baby had made a noise, Nate had hopped up and turned on the overhead lights, which had woken Jane up even more. No wonder he hadn't slept.

She realized she was aware of Nate standing there in his boxers—and she didn't like being that aware of him, all sleepy and rumpled and still very attractive. Like a man who'd feel just right curled up against her in bed. Her nipples tightened under her tank top.

No, no—bad. Bad thoughts. She could only hope that, in the dim light, he hadn't noticed. She shifted Jane so the baby covered her breasts and headed toward the door. She kept her voice low. "I've got this. You go back to bed."

He yawned. "Anything I can do to help?"

"Nope. Just going to get her a bottle, get her changed and lay her back down."

Nate scratched the back of his head. "You want me to get the bottle for you?"

She stopped then, not three feet from him. "You're paying me to do night duty, you know." Besides, the odds of him doing something not conducive to getting a baby back to sleep were pretty high.

He looked as if he was going to argue with her, but then he yawned again. "Okay. But you'll let me know if you need me, right?"

"Right." She started walking again, but Nate didn't get out of her way. She was forced to squeeze her body past his in the door frame.

Unexpectedly, he leaned forward and kissed the top of Jane's head. "Be a good girl," he murmured. Then he looked up. He was close enough to touch, except for the infant between them. "You're sure you don't need me?"

An unfamiliar sensation fluttered across Trish's lower back, like static electricity right at the base of her spine. It tightened muscles in unfamiliar areas, sending a dull ache through her body.

"No," she whispered so softly that he was forced to lean forward a bit just to hear her. For some insane reason, she wanted to run her fingers over his beard. She clutched the baby tighter. "I'm…I'm fine. We're fine."

"Good night, Trish." He pushed off and walked back to his room.

It was only when his door was safely shut that Trish sagged against the door frame. "Good night, Nate."

Oh, heavens. One night down.

Twenty-nine nights to go.

Through the fog of the first decent night's sleep in two weeks, Nate heard Jane fuss twice more during the night. Both times, he woke up with a start, his heart pounding in terror. The baby—

But then, both times, he heard the soft footsteps moving around his house and he remembered—Trish. The woman who was taking care of Jane. The beautiful woman who made him think about things he had long ago learned not to think about. Like sex.

And he lay there both times, fighting the urge to get up

and check on Jane—and Trish—because, after all, he *was* paying her to get up in the middle of the night.

He shouldn't have gotten up the first time, but he was still a tad jumpy about the whole situation. And then Trish had been there, her body silhouetted against the dim light from the bathroom like an angel of mercy, come to save him from himself. Her bare shoulders had been haloed with the light and her curves—

He'd almost kissed her. He'd promised he wouldn't and he almost had, anyway. It'd been the sleep deprivation, that was all. He must be too tired to think straight because he knew he could control himself better than that.

So, in a monumental effort of self-control, he stayed in bed, drifting between true sleep and awareness. The first time, the house eventually became quiet again and he slept. But the second time—even though Trish was not being loud—he still heard her moving around downstairs.

He rolled over and looked at the clock. Six-fifty in the morning. Ugh. He normally slept much later than this, until nine or ten. He tried to bury his head in a pillow, but it didn't work.

He pictured Trish moving through his house, Jane on her hip, looking like she belonged here. He remembered the way she'd looked at him when he'd tried to make the bottle of formula—a smile she was trying to hide and a warmth in her eyes that couldn't be hidden.

That warmth—that had to be why he'd not-so-subtly hit on her last night. He was out of practice. He wanted to think that she looked at him like that because there was some interest on her end—the same interest he thought he'd seen in the coffee shop.

Of course, if she knew about what had happened with Diana…maybe she wouldn't look at him like that anymore. It's not like he had to worry about Brad swooping in and charming the pants off Trish, though.

The moment he had that thought, enormous guilt swamped him.

God, he was a mess and because he was such a mess, he'd almost broken his promise to Trish. That wasn't like him.

What if, after last night, she'd changed her mind about staying? What if he'd crossed a line he couldn't uncross? Then he'd be little better than Brad had been, unable to keep it zipped around a woman who should be hands-off. And he'd be on his own with a baby again, trying not to screw things up and probably screwing up, anyway.

Panicked, he dragged his tired butt out of bed and threw on a clean pair of jeans. He'd apologize, that was all. He'd do a much better job of keeping a mental wall between Trish Hunter, his nanny, and Trish Hunter, woman of his fantasies. He was not ruled by his baser urges. He was better than that. He was better than Brad, God rest his soul.

Nate hurried downstairs, trying to come up with a mature, responsible way to apologize for his behavior and failing pretty badly.

He looked in the parlor, but they weren't there. The kitchen was also empty, but there were more used bottles in the sink. It wasn't until he got to the dining room and saw the open doors that he found them.

The fog from the night before had mostly burned off, leaving the world with a hazy glow similar to the most-used filter on SnAppShot. And in the middle of the patio sat Trish. Her hair was long and loose, spilling down over the back of the padded patio chair she occupied. Her feet were bare and kicked up against the railing. She had on a long-sleeved flannel top to ward off the morning chill, so her shoulders were covered, thank God. She'd also added a pair of jeans. Jane was on her lap, a small blanket tucked around her and both were facing out to bay, where the outline of the Golden Gate Bridge was just emerging from the mist. The scene was one of complete and total peace. Trish was rubbing Jane's little tummy and humming again—a tune Nate didn't recognize.

He hesitated. The scene was almost too perfect—there was no way he wanted to kill the moment by stumbling out and opening his mouth. He just wanted to feel the serenity in this moment a little longer. All his anxiety seemed to ease.

"Good morning," she said in that sweet voice of hers.

Nate stepped out onto the patio. Jane rolled in Trish's arm and, grinning a particularly drooly grin, stretched out a hand for him.

This was something new. The baby was actually glad to see him. "Good morning. Long night?"

Trish twisted to look at him over her shoulder, her long hair rippling like silk in water. Her face lit up as she looked at him, as if not only was she not going to hold his midnight madness against him, but she might just welcome a little bit more madness. "I've had longer. God, this is an amazing view."

No more madness. That was the deal. Nate offered his finger to Jane, whose smile got even wider. "She's happy," he said. "I mean—well, you know what I mean. I hadn't seen her happy until you came."

Trish dropped her gaze to the baby's head and smoothed the fine hairs. "A decent night's sleep and a full tummy will do that."

He *had* to make sure Trish stayed. He needed her in a very concrete way that had nothing to do with his attraction to her. "Look, about last night…"

"There's coffee, if you want some. It's not good coffee," she interrupted, turning her gaze back to the bay. "But it *is* coffee. You'll have to show me how to use that machine."

Jane made a cooing noise and turned back to the view, too. But she didn't let go of Nate's finger.

Well. This was awkward. He decided the manly thing to do was to set the record straight. Time to suck up his pride. "I'm sorry that I crossed a line last night. I wasn't all the way awake and—"

She looked up at him again and this time, there was confusion in her eyes. "What line did you cross?"

"I…" he swallowed and dropped his gaze. "I…"

"You wanted to kiss me?"

So. After all these years of being a geek and a klutz and failing at a majority of social interactions involving the opposite sex, he was *finally* going to die of embarrassment. Fitting. "Well, yeah."

She tilted her head, as if she were pondering this admission. "But you didn't."

"Because that was the plan. I don't want to break our deal. You're making Jane happy. I want you to stay the whole month." The words fell out of his mouth in a rush.

"You didn't kiss me. You didn't come into my room in the middle of the night. You aren't trying to force me to do anything I don't choose to do of my own free will."

The way she said it hit him like a slow-swung sledgehammer because no matter how clueless he could sometimes be, even he heard the truth behind those words.

He hadn't done any of those things.

But someone else had.

"I would *never*," he got out, his voice shaking. White hot fury poured through his body at the thought of someone doing any of that to her.

She nodded. "Then I'll stay. A deal's a deal. There's nothing wrong with attraction if we don't act on it."

"Okay. Good." Then what she'd said sunk in. Did she mean his attraction? Or did she mean she was attracted to him, too?

It didn't matter. Because even if she was attracted, she

wasn't going to act on it. Because that was the deal. For the month.

After the month was up…

He looked down and saw a mostly empty coffee cup on the patio table. "I'll get you some more coffee."

"Thanks."

Nate was gone so long that Trish was on the verge of going to look for him. But the early-morning sun had burned off the rest of the fog and the view was simply amazing and this chair was very comfortable and…

And he'd wanted to kiss her. But hadn't.

So she stayed in her chair and played with Jane. The little girl's personality had done a complete 180 in twenty-four hours. Jane was a happy, smiley baby who was definitely teething. "You're a sweetheart, you know that?" Trish cooed to her as the baby bit down on one of her fingers. "I bet you were the apple of your mommy's eye."

A pang of sadness hit her. Jane would never know her mother—and would never remember Trish, either. Trish would be long gone before that could happen. All she could do was make sure that Nate was set up to care for the girl.

And then…

No. She wasn't going to get ahead of herself. Just because Nate was attracted to her didn't mean a damn thing in the long term. The short term was why she was here. She needed to start Jane on solid foods and get some teething rings. But first, Trish was going to make sure the baby stayed up until after the lunch feeding. What this girl needed was a regular sleep schedule, the faster the better.

Finally, Nate re-emerged, a tray in his hands. "Breakfast?" he said, setting the tray down on the small table.

Trish leaned over and saw that he'd assembled bacon, scrambled eggs and toast, in addition to a carafe of coffee—and a fresh bottle of formula. "Oh," she breathed at the sight of all that glorious food. "I wondered what was taking so long."

"It turns out that you make really bad coffee," he said, settling into the other chair. "So while it was brewing, I decided to make breakfast. And I didn't know if Janie needed another bottle or not, so I brought one just the same."

"You cook? I thought that was why you had Rosita." She selected a piece of toast and took a bite. He'd buttered it and everything.

"She's only been with me since I bought the house. Before I sold the company, I couldn't bring myself to spend the money on a cook. It's that frugal Midwestern upbringing. And a man's got to eat. Her cooking is better, but I can get by." He speared a couple of pieces of bacon and said, "Eggs?"

"Yes, please." Trish had another moment of the surreal. Was one of the most eligible bachelors in all of Silicon Valley really making her *breakfast*? How was she supposed to stand strong against this? "This is really good. Thank you."

He nodded in acknowldgment, because his mouth was full of food. They ate in comfortable silence as sunlight bathed the Golden Gate. The neighborhood was waking up. Trish could hear more traffic on the street, and the muffled sounds of voices from the surrounding houses. But the noise still felt distant. "It's so quiet here."

"I worked with a landscape architect to dampen outside noise." He pointed to the trees and shrubs and then at the trailing vines that surrounded the patio. "There are fences on the other side that you can't see—that keep prying eyes out, too. You can't be too careful. You never know what people will try to turn up."

There it was again—another allusion to something that he wanted to keep buried. "Where did you live before you moved here?"

"I had an apartment in the Mission District," he admitted. "Predictable, huh?"

"Very," she agreed. Even the eggs were good. Jane tried to grab a piece of toast, but Trish handed her the bottle instead. She wanted to have a better understanding of the girl before she started feeding Jane things like bread.

"What about you?"

"A 'garden' apartment in Ingleside. I lived there for almost five years—the whole time I've been in the city."

He chewed that over. "So you came here from where, again?"

"Standing Rock reservation. It straddles the line between North and South Dakota. We lived on the South Dakota side." She tried to call up the mental picture of the never-ending grass, but it didn't mesh with the view of the San Francisco Bay she was looking at. "It's a whole bunch of nothing and a few Indians. Our school was one of those portable trailers that someone parked there about twenty years ago." She sighed.

"Wait. You said you were twenty-five."

"I am."

"You didn't go to college until you were twenty?" She must have given him a sharp look because he added, "I mean, I'm just surprised. You're obviously intelligent. I would be less surprised if you'd graduated a year early or something."

She set her plate aside. Her appetite was gone and Jane was getting squirmy. She pulled the baby back into her arms and held the bottle for her. "I suppose if I'd gone to a normal school or had a normal family, I might have. But I didn't."

"No?"

She debated telling him about this part of her life. He was going to be funding her charity for the foreseeable future, after all. Maybe if she could make him understand how bad it really was, he'd be interested in more than just cutting her a check. He might take an active advisory role in One Child, One World. It could be a smart strategic move.

Except...except then he'd know. He'd know everything and when people knew everything, they had a hard time looking at her as Trish Hunter, regular woman. Instead, they looked at her with pity in their eyes or worse—horror. She didn't want his pity. She didn't want anyone's pity. She wanted respect and nothing less.

She considered lying. She could tell him that she'd gotten two years into a mathematics program and decided she just didn't like sines and cosines that much.

But she didn't want to lie to him. He'd been nothing but honest and upfront with his situation. So she decided to gloss over the harsh realities of her life, just a little. Not a lie, but not the painful truth.

"Life's not always fair. For various reasons, I had to miss a couple of years to help out at home." That was the understatement of the century, she thought with a mental snort. Raising her siblings—and burying one—wasn't "helping." It was taking care of *everything*.

He appeared to weigh that statement. "No, life's not always fair. If it were...we wouldn't be here."

"Exactly." She'd still be back in her underground cavern of an apartment, listening to Mrs. Chan berate her for paying such a low rent and counting down the days until she got her master's degree. "Although having a billionaire serve me breakfast on his private patio isn't really all that bad, is it?" She managed a grin. At least her mouth had managed not to add "hot" to "billionaire." Score one for really bad coffee.

"Just making the best of a lousy situation," he agreed. "Better than it was yesterday, I'll say that much."

"Agreed." Yesterday, she'd eaten dry cereal out of the

box—but not too much, because that box had to last her another week.

"What about tomorrow?"

"It's Sunday?"

"Okay," he said, rolling his eyes in a very dramatic way. "Next week, then. We should probably get a schedule set out. You need to finish your degree and I can probably handle Janie on my own for a while…right?"

"You will be fine. You're a quick study."

She swore he blushed at the compliment and danged if it didn't make him look even better. "If you say so. When do you have classes?"

"I managed to get them all on Tuesdays and Thursdays. I worked the other three days, but I guess I'm not doing that anymore right now?"

He shot her a look that could only be described as commandeering and she remembered that, even if he had made her breakfast, he was still a billionaire who had a reputation as being ruthless in business—and that he basically controlled her time. "Right."

"Well, SFSU isn't exactly within walking distance. It'll take me an hour or so to get there by bus, but if I follow the schedule right, I won't—"

"You're not taking the bus," he informed her.

She physically flinched at his harsh tone. "Excuse me?"

"I mean," he said, "it's not a good use of your time to take the bus. Losing you for a couple of extra hours each day just so you can take the bus is unacceptable. I do own a car. You're free to use it."

A car she could use. There was only one problem. "I couldn't do that."

He waved her hands. "You are, at this exact moment, working for me. Your time is valuable to me. I'm not going to let you waste that time because you don't want to borrow my car."

She glared at him. She couldn't help it. "I don't have a license." His eyebrows jumped up, as if that was the last thing he'd expected her to say. "I mean. I've driven, of course. But I…"

He leaned forward, all of his attention focused on her. "Yes?"

"I couldn't afford to take the driving test and there was no hope of being able to afford a car, so what was the point?"

"Then we'll call for a car," he decided. "That's how I travel a lot, anyway."

*"No."*

"Because it's too expensive?"

"Well, yes," she said her cheeks shooting red. "I can afford the bus." Even with the overwhelmingly generous salary he was paying her, she couldn't start spending money like she had it. She had to make that twenty grand last for as long as possible.

"And I can afford a car service."

She glared at him openly then. "You're not going to make this easy, are you?"

"Are you kidding? This *is* the easy part. I'm paying the tab. I'm the boss. You'll take a car. I'll drive you myself if I have to." She raised an eyebrow. "Once you install the car seat, that is."

"This is ridiculous," she muttered, turning her attention to the meal.

"No, ridiculous is a five million–dollar comic book. This is a wise use of your time."

"You're already paying me too much—housing me, feeding me," she said quietly. "And the phone." She was going deeper into his debt and that feeling left her… unsettled.

He scoffed. "It's not like I'm going to have my private jet fly you the five miles." Then he turned on the most stunning smile she'd ever seen. "The jet is only for trips over ten miles."

She laughed at him, but that smile did some mighty funny things to her—things that spread a warmth through her body that warded off the last of the early-morning chill.

He'd almost kissed her. And she'd almost let him.

"What about you? What's your schedule?"

"I can be home this week, but I have a gala charity function I really should attend next Saturday night. I think the next two Saturdays are also booked. If that works with your schedule."

"That's fine." That'd be three less nights that she had to be around him, because it was becoming very clear that being around Nate Longmire was a dangerous place for her to be.

Because, after less than twenty-four hours, she was already becoming too attached. She'd lived in that hole in the ground for five years and had walked away without a second thought because it was nothing more than a hellhole with a bed in it. But this place? With the feather beds and beautiful decorating and amazing views and every comfort she'd ever dreamed of growing up?

This place where Nate lived, where Nate slept with a baby on his chest, where Nate made her breakfast and insisted on taking care of her?

It'd be hard to walk away from this, to go back to living in cheap and crappy apartments. To being alone all the time.

To having no one care if she was an hour later on the bus or not.

Trish was in *so* much trouble.

# Six

Nate found himself on the phone with the Chair of the School of Social Work at San Francisco State University first thing Monday morning, explaining how he'd poached the chairwoman's best student worker for a nanny position. And then pledging some money to the Social Work program to ease the strain he'd put on the chairwoman's department.

A complete baby's room showed up Monday morning, along with Trish's phone and a passable legal contract codifying their agreement. They both signed with Stanley serving as witness.

Then Nate and Stanley put the furniture together under Trish's increasingly amused direction. Nate let her arrange the room as she saw fit and Stanley followed his lead.

It was only when Trish took Jane downstairs to get her a bottle and try to nap in the quiet of the parlor that Stanley dared open his big mouth. "Dude, she is *hot*."

"It's not like that."

Stanley snorted. "It never is with you. Man, when was the last time you got laid?"

Against his will, Nate felt himself blush. "That's not relevant to the discussion."

"Like hell it's not. And don't try to tell me it's not because you're not into her." Stanley punched him in the arm, which made Nate almost drop the side of the crib he was holding. "I've seen you stick your foot into your mouth around every species of female known to mankind and I've yet to see you actually talk to a woman like you talk to *her*. It's almost like aliens have taken over your body and made you *not* lame or something. And what's even more unbelievable is that she totally seems to be digging you." Stanley shook his head in true shock.

Nate glared at him. He didn't want to particularly own up to the conversation he'd had with Trish at breakfast the other morning, where she'd easily identified how interested he was and conveniently sidestepped whether or not she felt anywhere near the same. "I've stuck my foot in my mouth enough already."

"Yeah?" Stanley looked impressed as they tried to get the crib to lock together like it did in the instructions. "What went wrong? Tell me you didn't stick your tongue down her throat on the first kiss."

"I didn't kiss her," Nate got out. His brain oh-so-helpfully added, *yet*. Yeah, right. "She made her position very clear. No sex."

Stanley whistled. *"Dude."*

"And may I just take this moment to remind you—again—that if I ever hear a word of this conversation even whispered by the press that I'll—"

"Personally turn my ass into grass, yeah, yeah, I got it. You know I can keep my mouth shut." But he looked at Nate expectantly.

If it were anyone other than Stanley...but the man was the closest thing to a confidant that Nate had. "Look, she's an amazing woman. You have no idea."

Stanley chuckled. "No, but I'm getting one."

"But," Nate went on, "we had a deal and you know I won't break a deal."

"Yeah," Stanley said in a pitiable voice, as if this was

the saddest thing he'd ever heard, "I know. You're very reliable like that."

"What about her charity? Did you finish the due diligence?"

"Gosh, gee, I was a little busy freaking out the workers at Babies 'R' Us," he said in an innocent voice. "Apparently, single men who look like I do rarely go shopping for baby things by themselves. So no, not yet. I'll get started after we get this damn crib together. You still going to the event on Saturday?"

"Yeah."

"Remember, I have a family thing. If I set your tux out now, can you get your tie on by yourself?"

Nate debated the odds of that. He didn't think so, but Stanley rarely asked for time off. "Probably."

Stanley nodded, but Nate didn't miss the look of doubt. "You going to take *her*? You know that Finklestein's going to try and set you up with his granddaughter again."

"Oh, God," Nate moaned. He'd forgotten about Martin Finklestein, a pillar of San Francisco's high society who'd become convinced, upon Nate's entry into the billionaires' club, that he and Lola Finklestein were perfect for each other. "I had forgotten. Is it too late to cancel?" He debated telling Stanley about the most recent message he'd gotten from Diana, but decided against it. He was just ignoring her at this point. He didn't need help to pull that off.

Stanley snorted. "Just take Trish."

"And do *what* with the baby? We haven't even gotten to the point where I'm ready to start interviewing other nannies yet and there's no way in *hell* we're going to use that service again."

"Mental note made," Stanley said. "There!" He slid the panel in and the crib stood on its own. "Man, babies are a hassle."

That made Nate laugh. "Dude, you have no idea."

\* \* \*

Trish was trying to get Jane on a sleep schedule, which meant that the baby was supposed to stay awake from whenever she got up until at least one, so, for a couple of hours around lunchtime, Jane was a tad fussy.

And by "a tad fussy," Nate really meant that Jane reverted back to her pre-Trish state of near-constant screaming. He found the noise to be almost unbearable, but Trish would just smile and power through as if baby wailing was music to her ears.

Nate was forced to admit that the payoff was pretty nice. Jane started sleeping from one to three in the afternoon within a matter of days and went from getting Trish up three times a night to two, which meant that everyone— even Nate—was sleeping better.

He even did okay when Trish went to school on Tuesday and Thursday—in a hired car. She only left after she was confident that both Nate and Rosita could fix the formula and Nate could change the diapers. "Call me if you have a problem," she said. "But you can do this."

That she'd said it when Nate was so clearly about to panic was nice enough. But what was even nicer was the way she'd laid her hand on his biceps and given his arm a light squeeze. Then, after kissing Jane's little head, she'd gathered up her bag and headed out to the hired car.

"What do you think?" Nate had asked the little girl.

Jane made a gurgling noise.

"Yeah," Nate had agreed. "I feel the same way."

The day was long. The screaming wasn't too bad and he'd gotten Jane to go down for her nap. That was something he hadn't even gotten close to in the week before Trish showed up.

Still, Nate was waiting for her when the hired car pulled up in front of the house at five-fifteen and Trish got out.

Jane had woken up at two-fifteen and had not been exactly a happy camper without Trish.

"I'm so glad you're back," he said when she walked into the house.

"Rough day? Come here, sweetie." She took Jane from him. "It looks like you're doing okay. She's dressed and everything this time."

Nate blushed. "She's just fussy. I don't know if she's teething or if she just wanted you?"

"Oh, sweetie," Trish said in that soothing voice as she rubbed Jane's back.

Jane buried her tear-streaked face into Trish's neck. Nate was once again struck by the feeling of how *right* the two of them looked together. Trish would never be Elena and God knew that Nate would never be Brad, but life wasn't fair and they were doing the best they could.

Suddenly, he wanted to ask her to go to the gala with him. She'd look amazing in a gown, her arm linked through his as they strode up the steps of the Opera House. That would get Finklestein to back off about Nate settling down with his granddaughter.

Except…Nate was reasonably confident that Trish didn't own a ball gown and that she wouldn't let him buy her one without one hell of a fight.

And there was the problem of Jane. Rosita was back to her happy self now that she was not responsible for Jane's well-being. There was no way Nate could ask his maid to babysit and who else did he trust? Stanley? That wasn't going to happen, either.

So he resigned himself to fending off Finklestein's advances—again.

Once Trish had Jane, Nate called his parents. He knew Joe would be down for a nap, thanks to the meds he was on. Nate resisted the urge to put them on video chat—some things were just beyond his parents. His mom answered.

"Hey, Mom. How are you?"

His mother sniffed. "We're getting by. How are you? How is Jane?"

"Good. Really good. She's teething, but I think she's doing as well as could be expected. I hired the perfect nanny and she's just done wonderfully with Jane. She got the nursery all set up and Jane's even started sleeping better."

"Oh, thank God," Mom said, the relief obvious in her voice. "We've been just worried sick about you two together. Honey, we're so sorry we had to ask you to take Jane, but you know Joe hasn't been dealing with any of this very well and—"

"I know, Mom. But it's going to be okay. Trish is here—that's the nanny. Trish Hunter. She knows what she's doing. I'll send you a couple of pictures later, okay?"

"That would be wonderful, dear."

They talked a bit more about how Joe was doing and how the town was reacting to the loss of one of its golden boys. Then Mom said, "Oh, Joe's up. Honey, we'll talk later and maybe after things calm down here a bit, I'll see about coming out, okay?"

"That'd be good, Mom. I know Jane will be happy to see you again."

"We're so proud of you, Nate," Mom said. It was her usual closing statement, but it hit Nate differently this time.

"I love you, too. Tell Joe I said howdy." He ended the call.

If only he knew what was going to happen next. Obviously, he was going to be a father. But was he going to find love and get married? Would he settle down with Lola Finklestein? Okay, he knew the answer to that one—no.

But…Stanley had been right. Nate didn't talk to a lot of women. Would he just have nannies who helped raise

Jane until she was old enough that he could handle her by himself?

The thought of Lola and other nannies bothered him. Then he thought of how Trish looked in the morning, watching the sunrise with Jane tucked on her lap.

She was only here for a month—less than a month, now. That was the plan.

But after the month was up?

He didn't know.

It wasn't until Thursday afternoon, from the cushy backseat of a hired car on her way back to Nate's house after her classes that Trish used her brand new smartphone to call home. Even with the hired car, it was going to take about forty minutes to navigate all the rush-hour traffic. Trish had time to call.

"Hello?" Patsy's thin voice answered on the fourth ring.

"Hey, baby girl," Trish said. She'd always wondered why her mother had named two of her daughters after her—Trish and Patsy. They were all Patricia.

"Trisha!" Patsy squealed. "I miss you. When are you going to come back? Are you going to send me any more presents? I really liked the cool notebooks you sent me last time."

"Whoa, whoa—slow down, girl." Trish couldn't help but grin at her youngest sibling. The Hello Kitty notebooks had been on super clearance here because no one wanted them, but out on the rez? They were a prized possession. "Are you still going to school? I expect to see a good third-grade report card before any more presents show up."

Patsy sighed heavily and Trish was sure she could hear the accompanying eye roll. "Yes. I'm going every single day. Mrs. Iron Horse says I'm her best reader."

"Good."

"When are you coming back?"

"Not for another couple of months," Trish replied gently.

"What? Why not?" Patsy pouted. "I thought you were going to come back after you finished your school."

"Something came up. I got a new job and I have to stay here for a while."

Patsy was silent as she thought this over. "Do you like it? The new job?"

"Yes," Trish said without hesitating. The good food, the nice house, the amazing view—even without the huge paycheck, this was something of a dream job. That didn't even count Nate Longmire. And Nate? He counted for quite a lot. "I'll be home after the job is over. Is Mom home?"

"No, she got a new job, too. But Dad's here—you want to talk to him?"

"Sure. Put Tim on." As far as Patsy was concerned, Tim was her father. He'd come into their lives when Patsy had been only two. But Trish couldn't think of Tim as her father. He was a good guy, but she just couldn't do it.

*"Daddy!"* Patsy yelled in Trish's ear. She jerked the phone away from her head and winced. For such a little girl, Patsy had a heck of a set of lungs. "It's Trish!" Then she said in a normal voice, "I hope you can come home this summer. Then I can show you the award I got for writing an essay in Lakota!"

Homesickness hit Trish hard. She'd been there for all the other kids' awards and honors. She'd spent her entire adolescence making sure that the other kids got to basketball practice or assemblies or awards ceremonies. But she'd missed the past five years of that. "That's *so* awesome, baby girl. I can't wait to see it."

"Here's Daddy. Bye, Trish!"

"Bye, Patsy."

"Hey, Trish," Tim said in his gruff voice.

"Hi, Tim. How's it going?"

"Not bad. Your mom got a new job. Your sister Millie

got her a job at the state trooper's office. She's typing up the police reports at night."

"Really? Does she like it?" Because the Pat that Trish remembered couldn't hold down anything—a man, a job, a house. Nothing. It'd all been on Trish.

"Eh," Tim said. "You know how she is. But she gets to find out a lot of gossip as it's happening and she likes that, so I think she'll stay with this for a while."

"Yeah," Trish said. "I know how she is. Hey, the reason I'm calling is that I got a new job and I wanted to give you the address I'll be at for the next month."

"Gimme a sec," Tim said. She heard him rustling through papers and pens. "Okay, shoot."

Trish recited the address and then the new phone number. "I got a huge signing bonus," she went on. "I can pay you back that $350 you loaned me for my security deposit."

There was a moment of silence on the line that Trish wasn't sure how to interpret. "Trish, that was a gift."

"Well, I can pay you back. This is a really good job and—"

*"Trish."* It was as sharp as she'd ever heard Tim speak. "It was a gift. I've tried to help out all your brothers and sisters here, but you were so independent. The best I could do for you was to front you a little traveling money and give you a chance."

"You really don't have to do that," Trish said. Her throat was in danger of closing up and she wasn't sure why. "I mean, if you hadn't come along, I wouldn't have been able to leave. I'd have had to stay home and…" and continue being a mother to Pat's babies.

Trish never would have made it to San Francisco, never would have gotten one degree and almost completed a second one—never would have started her charity. She'd be stuck on that rez, no prospects and no hope. Nothing but doing her best to make sure that all of her siblings had the best chance *she* could give *them*.

"You don't have to give me anything more than what you've already given me," she finished in a low whisper, her voice shaking. "At least use it to get the kids something."

Tim had the nerve to laugh. "You always were the hardest of hard-headed kids. Toughest girl I ever did meet. I guess you had to be, what with Pat being Pat."

Then, before she quite realized it, she asked, "Why do you stay with her?"

She'd always wanted to know. She got why men would hook up with Pat—she was beautiful and liked to have a good time. Despite the ten kids, she still had a good figure. But looks weren't everything and no one else had lasted anywhere near as long as Tim. Sooner or later, Pat's drama would cancel out whatever good grace her face bought her and men would walk. Sometimes that was a good thing and sometimes it wasn't.

Tim kind of chuckled. "Love does funny things to a man, I guess." He sounded wistful. "I know she's not perfect and I'm not, either. I got the failed marriages to prove it. But there's something about being with her that makes me feel right with the world. And when you've seen as much of the world as I have, you know that's no small thing."

"Yeah, I guess…"

Tim laughed. "You're an old soul, Trish. You had to grow up early and quick. But take it from an old man—you're still young. You'll know what I mean one of these days. Keep the $350 and do something nice for yourself or run it through your charity or whatever. It's your money. I don't want it back."

"Thank you, Tim. I…" She swallowed, trying to get her voice under control. "It means a lot to me."

"Don't mention it. You want me to tell your mom you called?"

"That'd be great. Tell her I'm glad she's liking her new job, too."

"Will do. Take care, Trish."

The call ended. Trish sat in the back of a very nice car being driven by a very nice man, taking her back to a very nice house with a home-cooked meal and an attractive, interesting billionaire who liked *her*.

There was nothing about this that made her feel right with the world.

# Seven

He couldn't tie the tie. This was why he paid Stanley money—to tie his damn ties for him.

Every time Nate tried to loop the ends around and under, just like the how-to video on YouTube, it came out… not tie-like. More like a four-year-old's attempt to tie his shoes than a polished, James Bond–like piece of neckwear.

"Hell," he mumbled as he undid the mess again. Maybe he wouldn't wear the bow tie. Maybe he'd go tieless and proclaim it was the latest fashion trend. It might even be a fun sociological experiment—how many people would follow suit because the richest man in the room said so?

Or he could still just cancel. That was an option, too. Sure, it was a gala sponsored in part by the Longmire Foundation and yes, people were probably starting to wonder if he'd died, since he hadn't been seen in public in three weeks. But he was Nate Longmire. He could do whatever he wanted.

"Knock, knock," Trish said from the doorway. "We came to say good-night."

Nate turned and saw Trish silhouetted from the light in the hallway. Jane was in her arms, her little head tucked against Trish's neck.

Mental correction—he could do *almost* whatever he wanted.

"Ready for bed?" he asked.

Jane turned her head away from him, which Trish had explained meant not that she didn't like him, but that the little girl was too tired to process.

Still, it stung in an entirely childish way. Nate crossed the room and kissed the back of Jane's head. "Good night, Janie. Sleep well."

He straightened up. Trish was looking at him, her large brown eyes taking in everything.

They stood like this a lot—so close together he could see the way her eyes shifted from a lighter brown to a deeper chocolate color. Close enough to kiss, except for the baby in between them. And, of course, there was no kissing.

In theory, he was getting better at not thinking about it. It was a nice theory, too. But right now...

She blinked, which pulled him out of his thoughts and back into reality. "You need some help with your tie?"

"You know how to tie a tie?"

The corners of her mouth quirked up. "I can't do much worse, I suppose. Can you wait until Jane's down?"

"Sure." He watched as she turned and walked across the hall. She settled into the glider chair and told Jane a story about Goldilocks and the Three Bears while the baby had her bedtime bottle.

Nate knew he should stay in his room, finish getting ready, maybe try the tie one more time. That was the safe thing to do—the legally advisable thing to do. But he was drawn across the hall, watching Trish rock Jane to sleep.

There it was again—that feeling of absolute peace as he watched Trish nurture the baby. She looked up at him, her eyebrows raised as if she were expecting him to ask a question or something, but he just shrugged a shoulder and watched.

Yeah, it could be that the serenity was simply because he was so damned relieved that Jane was being well cared for—that he wasn't solely responsible for her tiny person. But there was something more to this, something he didn't quite recognize.

Something Stanley had said came back to him—"I've yet to see you actually talk to a woman like you talk to *her*."

Comfort? Familiarity? No, that wasn't quite it, either. They'd only been coexisting for the past week, really. They'd had some good chemistry at a coffee shop and then he'd hired her in a moment of true desperation.

Jane finished her bottle and Trish gently patted her back before laying her out in the crib. She touched her fingertips to her lips and then brushed them over Jane's head as she murmured, "Good night, sweetie."

Then she turned and, slowly, walked toward him. He knew he needed to move—at the very least, he needed to get out of the way so they could shut the door and let Jane sleep.

But as she approached him, a knowing smile tugging on the corners of her mouth, he couldn't move. She was beautiful, yes, but there was so much more to her than that. She was kind and thoughtful and, perhaps most importantly, she didn't make him feel like an idiot.

She didn't hesitate. She walked right up to him and took hold of the ends of his tie. "Here," she said in a breathy whisper, gently pushing him back and out of the doorway. His hands lifted themselves up and settled around her waist—for balance, he justified after the fact. "Let me."

Without releasing her grip on his tie, she turned and pulled Jane's door shut. Then they were moving again as she backed him toward his bedroom.

He let her. He'd let her do whatever the hell she wanted right now. If she wanted to tie his tie, that'd be fine. If she wanted to rip his shirt off his chest, well, that'd be fine, too. He had other tuxedo shirts.

"Ah," she breathed, stopping well short of the bed. *Damn.* "I think I can do this."

"I'm sure it'll be better than what I was coming up with."

She grinned as she started looping the tie. "You look good in a tux. Very…"

He stood a little straighter. Her body underneath his hands was so hot he was practically sweating. "Yes?"

"Very grown-up. Not like a Boy Billionaire at all." He felt the tie tightening around his neck.

"I suppose that's a good thing?" Was that the same as "incredibly attractive"? That's what she'd told him once, when he was having a very bad day.

"It is. Damn." The tie loosened. "Let me try again."

He grinned down at her. "I think that's the first cuss word I've heard you say."

"Is it? I guess I've trained myself not to say bad words around kids." The necktie tightened again. "Where are you going tonight?"

"The Opera House for the gala charity function for ARTification, a big fund-raiser. The Longmire Foundation is a sponsoring partner." Her eyebrows jumped. "Well, that just means I gave them money and didn't do any of the planning."

She grinned, but it faltered. "Okay, I think I know what to do this time." One of her fingers touched the underside of his chin and lifted. "Look up, please."

Her touch took his theoretical mastery of his desire for her and pretty much reset it at zero. It took all of his concentration not to dig the pads of his fingertips into her glorious hips.

"I wanted to take you to this," he said before he knew what he was doing.

Her hands stilled for a moment. "You did?"

"Yes."

"You didn't ask me."

"I didn't think you'd say yes." He was careful to keep his chin up. "I don't know if you know who Martin Finklestein is, but he's pretty much decided that I should marry his granddaughter."

"And that's a problem?"

"Lola Finklestein makes me nervous." He forced a small smile. "Don't tell anyone I said that."

She didn't respond as she adjusted the tie. He felt her hands smoothing the bow. The tips of her fingers fluttered over his neck, right above his collar. Blood began to pound in his ear. "Is that why you wanted me to go with you? To run interference with Lola?"

He should say yes. He should back away. He should do *anything* but look down at her, so close. So damn close and not a single baby in between them.

But then her hands were smoothing over the shoulders of his tuxedo shirt, running down the front of the shirt. *She* was touching *him*.

"No." His hands moved without his explicit permission, tightening around her waist and then sliding toward her back. Pulling her in. He wanted to fill his hands with her skin, to know how she'd feel under him. Or over him. He wasn't picky. "I wanted…"

He swallowed and looked down. She was staring up at him, her lips parted and her cheeks flushed. She looked… like a woman who wanted to be kissed. He didn't know if she stepped into him or if he stepped into her, but suddenly what space had existed between them was gone and her arms were around his neck and he was lifting her toward his lips.

"You," he whispered. And then her lips were against his and he was kissing her back and it was good. *So* good. His hands kept right on moving of their own accord, sliding down until he'd cupped her bottom, the pads of his fingertips digging in as he pushed her higher. Her mouth opened for him and he tasted her, dipping his tongue into her honeyed sweetness. He went hard in an instant, pressing against the soft warmth of her stomach. Her nipples seemed to respond, growing hard and hot against his chest—so hot he could feel them through his shirt.

God, her mouth—this kiss—it was right. She was *right*, tucked in his arms where he could taste her and feel her body pressed against his and—and—

She pulled away. Not very far, but far enough that he had to stop kissing her, which was harder to do than he expected.

Her arms unlinked from around his neck and then, as coolly as if the kiss had never happened, she was smoothing the shirt over his shoulders. "You're going to be late."

"Um…yeah." That was not exactly the kind of thing a man liked to hear after the kind of kiss that left said man practically unable to walk. "I should—I should go."

She stepped away from him and it was only then that he saw how the kiss had affected her. Her eyes were glazed and her chest was heaving with what he hoped was desire. As he watched, the tip of her tongue darted out and ran over her top lip as if she were tasting his kiss and he almost lost it. Almost fell to his knees to beg her forgiveness but he was *going* to sleep with her, contractual language be damned. All that mattered was him and her and absolutely no bow ties.

She took another step back. "Don't—" She took a deep breath, which did some interesting things to her chest. "Don't let Lola steamroll you, okay?"

He managed a perfectly serviceable grin, as if her body in his arms was not a big deal at all. "Don't worry. I won't."

Nate didn't want to do this. He did not want to walk into one of the premiere high-society events of the social season. He did not want women to look at him like he was a lamb being led to sacrifice on the altar of Eligible Billionaire Bachelors. He didn't want to sit through a dinner on a dais in front of the room and know that people were watching him to see if he would do something of note.

"Mr. Longmire," an older gentleman who looked vaguely familiar said as he hurried forth and shook Nate's hand vigorously. "We weren't sure if you were actually going to make it."

"Yes," Nate said, feeling the wall go up between him and his surroundings. He hated social events in general and formal ones in particular. The only way to get through this was to pretend that he was somehow above the proceedings. That's how he'd gotten through the lawsuits and it probably had contributed to his reputation as being ruthless.

He'd be much happier back home—even if Trish had locked herself in her room and he spent the night in the media room, staring at code.

He'd kissed her.

At the very least, he'd kissed her back.

But hot on the heels of that delicious memory of her tasting him and him tasting her, a terrible thought occurred to him.

He'd broken the deal.

Oh, *no*. How could he have done that? A deal was a deal and he *always* kept a deal.

Except for this. Except for Trish.

Worst-case scenarios—each more terrible than the last—flipped through his mind. They all ended in basically the same way—Trish packing up her things and being gone by morning, all because he couldn't resist her.

The older gentleman's welcoming smile faltered. "Yes, well, this way, please. Mr. Martin Finklestein has been asking after you."

"I bet he has." The older man's smile faltered so much that he lost his grip on it entirely, which made Nate feel bad. He was sure the rumor mill was working overtime as it was. "Lead on, please."

The older man—Nate could *not* remember his name—turned and all but scurried off toward the bar. Alcohol was already flowing, all the better to get people to crack open their wallets.

Nate followed. He was aware of people pausing in their conversations and watching him as he passed, but he was too worried about what Trish might be doing at this very moment to give a damn.

"Ah, Nate." The bright—some might say grating—voice of Lola Finklestein snaked through the hushed conversations and assaulted his ears. "There you are!"

He turned toward the voice. It was a shame, really. Her voice notwithstanding, Lola was a beautiful woman. She had a mass of thick black curls that were always artfully arranged. She had a swan's graceful neck and a slim figure. She was a beloved patron of the arts and of course she was heiress to the Finklestein fortune. By all objective measures, she was one hell of a catch.

Despite it all, Nate couldn't stand her. Her voice rubbed his nerve endings raw and she always had an odd scent, like…peaches and onions. He couldn't imagine spending the rest of his life stuffing cotton balls in his ears and lighting scented candles to cover the smell of her perfume.

Especially not after that kiss. Not after having Trish in his arms.

"Here I am," he agreed, feeling like a condemned man standing before the gallows.

"We've been worried sick about you. Where on earth have you been keeping yourself for the last three weeks? You know that the Celebration of the Zoo last week was just no fun without you."

"Couldn't be helped," Nate said. Which was a lame excuse—but still much better than being subjected to all kinds of condolences from this crowd. That was one of the reasons he kept Brad and Elena's deaths out of the press. He simply couldn't bear the thought of Lola hugging him and crying for his family.

He kept his back straight and what he hoped was a polite smile on his face. Of course, he'd seen photos of his "polite smile." It barely broke the threshold of "impolite snarl," but it was the best he could do.

He just wanted to be back at home. With Trish.

Was there a chance, however small, that the kiss had been the start of something else? Something more?

"Well, you're here now," Lola said, leaning in to brush kisses across both of his cheeks. "Oh, I have someone I want you to meet." She turned. "Diana?"

The name barely had a moment to register before a blonde woman in a blue dress separated from the others. Nate's brain crashed so fast, it felt like someone had tripped the surge protector in his mind.

She looked different now. Her face was tighter, her breasts larger—and was her nose slimmer, too?

Diana *Carter*.

The woman who'd nearly ruined him.

"Oh," she said in the breathy voice that he'd only heard on a few occasions—like when he'd told her about the first big round of investing he'd managed to secure for SnAppShot. And when he'd introduced her to Brad. "Nate and I do know each other. We go way back."

"Diana. You're looking…lovely." He realized he'd forgotten his polite smile, but this was possibly the worst thing that could have happened tonight.

Well, not the worst. Trish could have slapped him after that kiss. She could still leave.

But this was a close second.

Diana batted her eyes at him.

Damn it all. A *very* close second.

"I need to talk to you. Privately," he added as Lola stepped forward. Lola frowned.

Diana's demure face froze before she purred, "Of course."

"This way." Nate stalked off to a corner, chasing a lingering waiter away with a glare. "What are you doing here?" he demanded when they could speak without being overheard.

She gave him a reproachful look, as if he'd wounded her pride. "Is that any way to greet your fiancée?"

His teeth ground together. "*Former* fiancée. And yes, it is."

"About that." She sighed, her new and improved chest rising dramatically. "I was actually hoping to talk to you."

Nate's mouth opened to tell her where she could go but he slammed the brakes on and got his mouth shut just in time. If he looked hard enough, he could see the woman he'd once thought he'd loved. The Diana he'd known had been pretty enough, but with glasses and a habit of smiling nervously. She'd been shy and a little geeky and intelligent—exactly the kind of woman he'd thought he'd needed.

Until he'd taken her home to meet his family. And then she'd revealed that she was something more than all that.

"Why?"

Diana dropped her gaze and then looked up at him through her thick lashes. It felt entirely calculated. "I thought…we could let bygones be bygones." She exhaled through slightly parted lips. "I thought we might start over."

His mental circuitry overloaded and suddenly he was back at a single blinking cursor on an otherwise blank screen. The woman who'd broken his heart *and* tried to claim half of his company as her own because they'd just started dating when Nate thought it up— "You want to *start over*?"

She had the nerve to look hopeful. "Yes."

No. *No.*

"Brad's dead."

This time, Diana's reaction wasn't schooled or calculated. The blood drained out of her face and she took a shocked step backwards. "What?"

"You remember Brad? My older brother, the one you slept with because—and stop me if I'm not remembering this part correctly—you told me it was because he was 'like me' but better? He's dead."

Diana fell back another step. Her hand dropped to her side and what was left of her champagne spilled onto the floor. "What—when?"

"After we settled in court, he married an old girlfriend and they had a baby. They were very happy." He didn't know why he was telling her this. Only that, on some level, he felt like she deserved to know. "Until three weeks ago. A car accident. And now they're both dead."

Diana covered her mouth with her hands, her eyes painfully wide. "I didn't—I hadn't heard. I didn't know."

"No, of course not. After you cheated on me—after you tried to cheat me out of my company—I learned to keep things close to the vest. I learned how to avoid giving people anything they might use against me. I learned how to keep things out of the media."

Diana shook her head from side to side, as if she could deny that she'd changed him. That he'd let her change him. She took another step back and Nate matched it with a step forward. "I have you to thank for that. So, to answer your question, no. We can't start over. We can't go back. I can't trust you. Not now, not ever. You said it yourself, didn't you? 'I can do better.' That's the justification you had for falling into Brad's bed. He was better than me in everything but brains. That's the justification you used to try and take half of SnAppShot. And now that I'm the richest damn man in the room, you realize you can't do better, can you?"

"No—that's—I'm—"

He couldn't stop. He couldn't lock it down and bury all of this behind his wall of distance. In a moment of panic, he even tried to recall the original code to give him some measure of control over himself, but all he had was a flash of white-hot anger. Because she'd changed him. She'd made him afraid to be himself because being Nate Longmire hadn't been good enough. And he was tired of only being good enough because he was a billionaire.

That's not how Trish saw him. He was not a bank account to be conquered. He was a man who hadn't figured out all the mechanics of changing a diaper, who wasn't afraid to ask for help. He was not a meal ticket to be exploited until there was nothing left.

"It is. And I'm not the same naive nerd anymore, grateful for a pretty girl who didn't think I was a total loser."

"I never said that about you." She seemed to be regaining her balance. "I *cared* for you."

"But you didn't care enough." All of his anger bled out of him.

She had changed him. She'd made him tougher, smarter. He knew how to play the game now. It wasn't all bad. Just a broken heart. Everyone had one, once. He couldn't hold a grudge. "I wish you luck, Diana. I hope you find the man who's good enough for you. But it's not me. It never was me and we both know it. Now, if you'll excuse me."

He turned and walked off, pushing through the crowd like they were just so many sheep in Armani tuxedos. He couldn't bear to be here for another moment. He needed to breathe again and he couldn't do that with this stupid tie around his neck.

"Nate? Wait!"

He didn't know why he slowed. He'd said what he needed to say. But he slowed, anyway.

Diana Carter—the woman who had held so much sway over his life—caught up to him. "Nate," she said, her perfectly made-up eyes wet with unshed tears. "I'm sorry. I'm sorry for what I did. I'm sorry about your brother and his wife. Please—" Her chest hiccupped a little. She reached over and touched his shoulder. "Please accept my condolences on your loss."

"Thank you." He patted her hand where she was touching him and then, on impulse, lifted her hand to his lips.

She nodded in acceptance. "She's a lucky woman."

"Who?"

Diana gave him a watery smile, then she leaned up on her toes and brushed a kiss on his cheek. "Whoever she is. Goodbye, Nate."

"Goodbye, Diana." Their hands touched for another moment and then, by unspoken agreement, they separated. Nate had to bail. He couldn't do this, he couldn't sit in the front of this crowded room and pretend he was above the dinner and the speeches and all the people trying to figure out how to get closer to him. He couldn't put up his walls. Hell, he couldn't find his walls. Even his original code, which always kept him calm, failed him.

"Nate?" The voice was unmistakable. *Lola.* "Nate! Where are you going? You just got here!" Honestly, it was like fingernails down a chalkboard.

Nate kept going. He'd had things to say to Diana. He'd been close to marrying her, after all. But Lola? No, he didn't have things to say to her.

He dug out his phone and called for a hired car as he stalked out of the Opera House.

He had things he wanted to say to Trish.

He hoped like hell she'd listen.

# Eight

Trish had her laptop on her lap, her thesis document open.

She wasn't looking at it.

She wasn't looking at anything, really. Her eyes were focused out the big curved picture window in Nate's front parlor, but the darkness was not what she was seeing.

No, what she was seeing was the way Nate's pulse had jumped in his throat when she'd grabbed the ends of his tie. She was feeling the way his hands had settled around her waist.

She was tasting the kiss on her lips. *His* kiss.

This was a fine how-do-you-do, wasn't it? She'd kissed him. She didn't kiss people. She didn't sleep with people. She kept anyone who might even be remotely interested in her at twenty paces. Technically, that made her a twenty-five-year-old virgin, although she'd never thought about it in those terms. Not often, anyway. Sure, sex was probably a lot of fun—why else did her mother keep having it?—but she wasn't going to pay for twenty minutes of pleasure with the rest of her life.

She was not her mother's daughter, damn it all. At least, she hadn't been until one week ago. She was only four months from being twenty-six. By the time Pat Hunter was twenty-six, she had three kids, was pregnant with her fourth and had six more yet to come. She couldn't hold a job or a man. She was barely getting by.

That's not what Trish was. Trish was educated. She had a plan. She had things to do, things that would be derailed by something so grand as falling in love and so base as getting laid. She kept her eyes on the prize and her pants firmly zipped.

Until Nate. Until the very moment when he'd walked out on stage, if she was going to be honest about it. She hadn't had a single intention of doing anything remotely sexual with, about, or to Nate Longmire when she'd researched him. She'd noted he was attractive in the same way she might admire a well-carved statue, but there'd been no attraction. No desire.

There sure as hell was now. Because she'd kissed him. Prim, proper—some would say prudish—Patricia Hunter had kissed Nate Longmire.

What was she doing?

Wondering what sex with Nate would be like, that's what. Wondering if she'd actually go through with it, or if her healthy respect for the consequences would slam her legs shut again.

She could do it, after all. She was smart enough to use protection. She could enjoy safe sex with a man she was attracted to without losing herself in him, like Pat always had.

Couldn't she?

Dimly, she was aware of traffic outside, but it wasn't until the front door slammed shut that she became aware of her surroundings.

Then he was there. Nate Longmire filled the parlor doorway, each hand on the door frame as if he was physically holding himself back.

"Nate! Is everything all right?" She glanced at the clock. It was only 8:45. "I wasn't expecting you home for hours."

"I want you to know something," he said, his voice low and from somewhere deep in the back of his throat.

A shiver raced down her back at his commanding tone. "I want you to understand—I do *not* break a deal."

He bit the words out as if he were furious with them—or with her. She sat there for moment in a state of shock. This was, by far and away, the most enraged she'd ever seen him. "Oh?"

"I keep my word. My word is my bond. That's how my father raised me." She saw his fingers flex around the door-jamb. Would he rip the wood right off the wall? "When I say I'm going to do something—or not do something—then that's how it is. Canceling those two events because of Brad and Elena—it drove me nuts. But it couldn't be helped."

She closed her laptop and set it aside. She couldn't tell if he was going to fire her for kissing him or rip her clothes off. And worse—she didn't know what she wanted to happen. "I see."

"It's when people break their word to me, that's when the trouble starts. People make promises to me and then they break them and I won't stand for it."

He spoke with such conviction. Surely he wasn't trying to sound erotic, but heat spiked through her. He was barely holding himself back. She should probably be afraid of this display of anger—of power.

She was *totally* turned on. "You can be ruthless. That's your reputation."

"I have to be." It came out anguished, as if it wounded him to sue people back to the Stone Age. "Kill or be killed." Even from twenty feet away, she could see the white-knuckled grip he had on the frame. But he didn't take another step into the room. "I was engaged. To be married."

"You were?"

"To Diana Carter." The admission seemed to hollow him out a bit.

The name rang a bell. Nate Longmire v. Diana Carter. The court case. The rumors that maybe there'd been something else between them, rumors that could be neither confirmed nor denied because the court records were sealed. "Wait. Isn't that the woman you sued over the right to the SnAppShot code?"

He nodded, a short crisp movement of his head that did nothing to dislodge his grip on the door frame. "She was there tonight. I try not to think about her, but I realized tonight that because of what she did, she's affected *everything* that I do."

This time, Trish stood. When she did—when she took a step toward him—his head jerked up and he got that ferocious look on his face again. "What did she do?"

"We were engaged. I took her home to meet my family and she slept with my brother."

Her mouth dropped open in surprise. Not what she was expecting to hear. "She broke her promise."

"And then claimed half the company was hers, since we'd been together when I started it."

"And tonight?" She took another step toward him. And another.

"She wanted to start over. But I can't trust her." He swallowed, his Adam's apple bobbing above his bow tie. "Not like I trust you."

She considered this. "Do you? I mean, we haven't known each other very long."

"I trust you with my niece's life. That's far more important than a stupid piece of code."

She took a few more steps toward him, closing the distance between them. His head snapped up. "Don't come any closer."

"Why not?"

"Because I keep my promises. And I promised you that I would not have sex with you. That I would not take advantage of you just because you're beautiful and intelligent and I'm as comfortable with you as I've ever been with any woman, including Diana. Just because I trust you." She took another step forward and he actually backed up. He didn't let go of the door frame, but his feet were now in the hall. "And if you come any closer, I'm not going to keep my promise."

The words ripped out of his chest and seemed to hit her in the dead center of hers. She put her hand over her heart to make sure it was still beating.

"All those women tonight, trying to catch my eye," he went on. "Lola and Diana and the rest of them, looking at me and seeing a prize they could win. And all I could see—all I could think about—was *you*. I wanted to take you because I wanted you there with me. And since that couldn't happen—since Jane is upstairs—I came home."

"Will you keep your promise to me?"

He swallowed again, looking haunted. "I *have* to. Three more weeks, right? I'll hire a new nanny and you'll move out and then…then I'll ask you to dinner. That's how it has to be. I can't kiss you. Not like I did earlier. Not like I wanted to since I met you. I gave you my word." He sounded like he was ripping his heart out with that last bit.

A promise. A promise he intended to keep, no matter how much it hurt him. She didn't know too many men who kept their promises like that. Hell, she didn't know too many women. People lied and cheated and did all sorts of horrible things to each other in the name of love all the time with very little thought to how it might affect others. Just like her mother had.

Just like her father had.

But not Nate. He'd given her his word and he'd keep it, even if it killed him.

*That* made all the difference in the world.

She didn't give him the chance to back away any farther. She closed the remaining distance between them so fast that he didn't have time to react. She stepped into him and put her arms around his neck and refused to let him go.

He tensed at her touch. "Don't." It was half order, half plea.

"Because you'll break your promise?"

He closed his eyes. He was back to his white-knuckle grip on the door frame, doing everything in his power to not touch her. "Yes."

She loosened her arms from around his neck and trailed her fingertips until she had the ends of her best bow tie in her hands. "I made no such promise, did I?"

Nate jolted against her—hard. She swore she heard the crack of wood giving way. "You don't sleep with people. You said so yourself."

She pulled on the ends of the tie, slowly loosening it until it hung down against his tuxedo shirt. "People in general, no." She slipped the top button free. He had a nice neck. The next button came loose.

"Trish," he groaned. His eyes were still closed but his head had started to tilt forward—toward her. "What are you doing?"

She undid another button. "Making sure you keep your promise."

His eyes flew open and he stared down at her in true shock. *"How?"*

"By seducing you." As the third button gave, she leaned up on her tiptoes and placed a kiss against the exposed skin of his neck, right under his Adam's apple. She could hear his pulse pounding through his veins. "If you want me to."

Then—and only then—did he relinquish his hold on the poor door frame. His arms swung down and surrounded her with his strength. She wanted to melt against him, but she didn't. Not yet. There'd be time for that later.

She toyed with the pointed tips of his collar. "Do you want me to?"

"This doesn't have anything to do with money or charities or anything, right?"

She leaned forward and kissed his neck again as she worked another button free. His pulse jumped under her lips, a wild beating that matched her own heart's rhythm. She was doing this, seducing Nate Longmire, the Boy Billionaire.

Except, she wasn't, not really. She wasn't seducing one of the most eligible Billionaire Bachelors. She was just seducing Nate. Beautiful, geeky Nate, who *always* kept his promises.

"No." Then she skimmed her teeth over his skin and felt him shudder. His body's response did things to her. Sweet, glorious heat flushed her breasts and spread farther. She was doing this to him. And he was letting her. "This is between you and me. That's all I want. Me and you."

"Trish," he groaned.

"I take that as a yes, then." She pushed him back, but only so far that she could slide his tuxedo jacket off his shoulders. It hit the ground with a whoosh and then she was working at his buttons again.

He didn't touch her, didn't try to lift her T-shirt over her head. He just stood there as she undid the rest of his buttons, his chest heaving with the effort of *not* touching her.

He had on a white undershirt, which was irritating. Formal clothing had so many layers. She slid her hands under his tuxedo shirt and stepped in again. This time, she kissed him proper.

And this time? He kissed her back. His arms folded around her again and she was pressed against his massive chest.

Oh, *yes*. Trish didn't actually know much about the art of seduction, but even she knew that was a good thing.

The heat focused in that spot between her legs and the only way she could think to ease the pressure was to lift one leg and wrap it around Nate.

But it didn't ease the pulsing heat. Instead, when Nate grabbed her under her thigh and lifted her higher, it brought her core in contact with something else—something long and thick and—

"Upstairs," she demanded, her back arching into that thick length.

She wasn't sure what she'd expected him to do. Turn and race up the stairs, maybe. That's what she would have done.

But she wasn't Nate. He hefted her up and leaned her back against the poor, misused door frame and kissed the hell out of her. She really had no choice but to put her legs around his waist, did she? And when she did, his erection ground against her. "Oh. *Oh!*"

"Mmm," he hummed against her mouth as he devoured her lips. Then he shifted his hips and heat exploded between them. Her body shimmied under his.

She could have stayed like that forever, except the door frame was exacting its revenge on her back. "Take me to bed, Nate. *Now.*"

"Yes, ma'am," he said.

And then Trish was floating through the air as Nate carried her up the stairs as if she weighed nothing, as if each step weren't driving his erection against her, as if she weren't on the verge of climaxing when he bit down on her shoulder.

*Oh, yes.*

Then they were in his room and he was kicking his door shut—quietly—and he'd laid her out on the bed. He started to strip off his shirt, but she sat up and said, "No, stop. That's my job."

His hand froze on his cuff links. "It is?"

"I'm doing the seducing around here," she replied,

pushing his hand away and undoing the offending cuff link herself. "That was the deal, right?"

"Absolutely," he agreed.

So Trish got to her knees on the bed and undid his other cuff so that she could push the very nice shirt off his shoulders and then strip the undershirt off him and then *finally* she could see the massive chest.

"You are built," she whispered as she ran her fingers over his muscles.

She skimmed her fingertips over his nipples and was rewarded with another low groan. His only other reaction was to clench his hands into fists, but he held them by his side. He didn't say anything. The last of his self-control, hanging by a thread.

He had a smattering of dark brown hairs in the space between two nicely defined pecs and a treasure trail that ended in the waistband of his pants. She followed it with her fingertips, then hooked her fingers into his waistband and pulled him into her so she could kiss him.

"Trish," he moaned into her mouth. "You're going to kill me."

She responded by running her hands over the huge bulge in his trousers. The heat pouring off him was electric. *He* was electric, setting her nerves on fire and threatening to overwhelm her. He shuddered under her touch.

"Oh, my, Nate," she whispered as she stroked his length through the fine wool of his trousers. He was built in *so* many ways. "Oh, *my*."

"Please," he begged.

"You have condoms?"

"Yeah. Somewhere."

"Go get them. Right now." Because once those pants got unbuttoned, there'd be no stopping, no turning back.

She might be doing the wild and crazy thing of seducing Nate Longmire, but that didn't mean she wanted to get carried away. She wanted to enjoy this night, this time, with him without having to deal with the consequences.

He pulled away from her so fast she almost toppled off the bed. She caught herself and sat back on her heels, watching him. She hadn't spent much time in his room. She'd seen it only when she'd tied his now-crumpled tie. It was the whole side of the house, with the bathroom in the back. The room was done in cool grays and blues, with a more modern touch than her room.

And the bed itself? She had no idea how they'd gotten a California King into this house but they had. And she was going to make good use of such a large bed.

He checked a drawer in the bedside table, then went around to the other side. "Got them," he muttered.

He came back to where she was waiting and stood there, an unopened box of condoms in his hand, like he wasn't sure what should happen next.

"Okay?" she asked. She had him shirtless and he was definitely interested, but now that he'd had a moment to think, a hint of doubt had crept into his eyes.

"Yeah. Yes," he repeated with more force. He closed his eyes and took a deep breath. "It's just…been a while." Then he opened his eyes and cupped her face and kissed her, soft and sweet and full of promise. "You?"

"You could say that." He lifted an eyebrow, but she didn't elaborate. She had no room in her life for antiquated notions of virginity, anyway. She'd already raised nine kids—ten, if she counted Jane. Her virginity was completely irrelevant to the situation.

But she could tell he was trying to figure out the best way to ask that question, so she went back on the offensive. She pulled him down into another kiss as she let her hands move over all those muscles.

"Shoes," she murmured. "Take them off."

He kicked off his shoes and peeled off his socks, but

when he went for his waistband, she grabbed his hands. "Wait," she told him. "Watch."

Then, because it seemed like the thing to do, she stood on the bed. Slowly, she peeled her T-shirt over her head. Nate made a noise in the back of his throat that was part groan, part animalistic growl as he stared at her simple beige bra.

Then she undid the button and slid down the zipper on her jeans. As the jeans slipped past her hips, she wished she had a pretty matching set of underwear instead of ones of cheap cotton. She wanted to be sexier for him.

Not that he seemed to mind her mismatched set. As the jeans slid free of her legs and she kicked them off, his mouth fell open. "Trish," he groaned again, his arms held tight at his side, his hands fisted. "Look at you. You're *stunning.*" His voice shook with raw desire.

And just like that, she felt desirable in spite of her under things. She walked over to where he stood. The added height of the bed meant that, instead of having to crane her neck up to look at him, she was a few inches taller than he was. She draped her arms around his neck again.

*Stunning.* She hadn't often felt beautiful. She'd had some people try to compliment her, but the best she usually got was "striking."

"And you, as I believe I noted before, are incredibly attractive."

He grinned up at her, the doubt gone from his eyes. "Can I touch you now or are you still seducing me?"

"I didn't say you couldn't touch me, did I?"

In response, his hands skimmed up the back of her thighs, over her bottom. He moved deliberately, trailing his fingertips along the waistband of her serviceable panties, over her hips, and along the elastic of her leg bands.

She couldn't help it. She closed her eyes and let her skin take in his every movement. She tingled under his touch, little shocks of pleasure wherever his fingertips caressed her.

"You are so beautiful, Trish," he whispered against her chest. Then he pressed his lips against the inner curve of her breast, right above the bra cup. "Let me show you how beautiful you are."

He turned his head and kissed the other breast as he began to unhook her bra. A moment of panic flashed over her—what was she doing? Having sex with Nate? Was she *crazy*?—but then the bra gave and he pulled it off her shoulders and she moved her arms to let it fall helplessly between them and he—and he—

He licked her left nipple like he was licking an ice cream cone. As his tongue worked her into a hard, stiff peak, he glanced up at her. "Watch me," he ordered and then he closed his lips around her nipple and sucked.

"Nate!" she exclaimed in a whisper at the sudden pressure. She wanted to cry out and scream his name, but she didn't want to wake the baby. She laced her hands through his hair. "Oh…"

"Good?" he asked, his voice muffled against her skin.

"Yes," she said. In response, he sucked again, harder. *"Oh…"* she managed to say again. Her legs started to shake.

One of his hands slid down her back again, tracing her bottom before coming between her legs from behind. The position locked her body to his. Softly—so softly—his fingertips rubbed over the thin fabric of her panties. The sensation of someone that wasn't her touching her there was so overwhelming that she couldn't even make a noise.

"Open your legs for me," he whispered. "Let me show you how beautiful you are."

Despite the way he had her legs pinned with his arm, she managed to scoot her knees a little farther apart without losing her balance.

"Mmm," Nate hummed as he licked her other nipple. His fingers rubbed in longer strokes, so close to hitting that hot, heavy weight in the front.

So close—but not quite. He was going to drive her mad with lust. Her! Trish Hunter, who had always been above such base things. With Nate's mouth on her, his fingers against her—

She ground against his fingers as she held his head to her breast. "Nate," she moaned when his teeth scraped over her nipple. "Oh, *Nate*…"

"Like that. Just like that, Trish." His voice was low and deep and sent a shiver up her back. "Oh, babe."

She wasn't doing the seducing anymore. He'd taken the reins from her and she was only too happy to hand them over. She really didn't know what she was doing, after all. But Nate?

He knew. He knew *exactly* what he was doing to her.

Then his mouth left her nipples and he kissed his way down her stomach. He hooked his thumbs into the waistband of her panties and slid them down. And then she was nude before him, nothing between them but a pair of tuxedo pants.

She had a moment of panic—she hadn't exactly prepped for this encounter. As Nate drifted south and she lost her grip on his hair, she fought the urge to cover herself.

"Let me see you—all of you," Nate said, catching her hands and lifting them away. "You're so beautiful, Trish."

"Nate…" Now that he wasn't holding her up, her knees were practically knocking.

But that was as far as she got before he pressed a kiss against the top of her thigh, then the other. And then?

Then he gripped her by the hips, tilting her back ever-so-gently, and ran his tongue over the little button that he hadn't quite managed to hit earlier.

Her body seized up with pleasure. She'd touched herself, of course. But this? This was something else. Something entirely different.

"I—I can't stand," she gasped as his tongue stroked her again and again. Light heat shimmered along her limbs, making her muscles tighten and weaken at the same time. *So different*, she thought. "I can't take it, Nate."

He looked up at her and for the first time, she saw something wicked in his eyes. "Babe, we're only just getting started."

# Nine

This was really happening. Nate wondered if he might be dreaming, but then he'd tasted her sweetness on his tongue. None of his dreams had been this good.

Trish, in the bare flesh, was so much better than any fantasy he'd had.

Her eyes went wide at his words. "What?"

If he were a suave kind of guy, he'd figure out how to sweep her off her feet and lay her out on the bed without causing bodily harm to either of them, but he wasn't going to risk that right now. So he took her by the hands and guided her down to her knees on the bed, which meant that they were almost eye-to-eye.

"When I'm done with you, you *won't* be able to stand," he promised, tilting her back in the bed. The look of shock on her face told him pretty much everything he needed to know.

She didn't have a whole lot of experience. Maybe none. And yet, she'd still worked him into a lather.

It was time to return the favor.

He hooked his elbows under her knees and pulled her to him. She made a little squeaking sound, so he said, "Let me love on you, Trish." Then he lowered his mouth to her again.

She really did have a honeyed sweetness to her and he couldn't get enough of it—of her.

Years of sexual frustration—of avoiding hookups and dodging would-be brides, all because he didn't want anyone to break a promise they never intended to keep—seemed to surge up within his chest and he poured all of that energy into every action of his mouth, his tongue, his teeth. Trish's hips shifted from side to side as he worked on her and her hands found their way back to his hair again.

"That's it, babe. Show me how you want it."

"We can't wake the baby," she panted in a forced whisper.

"I'll be quiet, I promise." Then he slipped a finger inside of her.

Her tight muscles clamped around him with such force that he almost lost it right then. He licked her again and was rewarded with a noise that went past a groan into almost a howl.

"Come for me, Trish. Show me what you can do." He flicked his tongue back and forth over her, so hard and hot for his touch.

"Nate," she gasped out. "Nate—oh, Nate!"

His name on her lips, his body inside of hers—this was worth it. Years of self-denial—all worth the way they fit together.

He reached up to grasp her dark pink nipple between his thumb and forefinger and pulled. Not hard, but enough that she gasped again and came up off the bed a couple of inches.

Then he felt it—her inner muscles clamped down on him and her head thrashed from side to side and her mouth opened, but nothing came out. She came silently, her gaze locked onto his.

He couldn't remember being this excited. He was probably going to lose it the moment he plunged into her wet heat, but it didn't matter. He'd done this for her, given her this climax.

But he couldn't waste time patting himself on the back. Trish propped herself up on her elbows, her eyes glazed with satisfaction. "Boy," she said weakly. "I'm sure glad I did the seducing here."

"Me, too." He forced himself to pull away from her. He needed to be rid of his pants right now. He was so hard he was going to break the damned zipper. That's what she did to him.

But she sat up and swatted his hands away from his trousers. "Mine," she said as she jerked the button free and ripped the zipper down. "I can return the favor." The pants fell down and there he was, straining his boxer-briefs to the point of failure. She ran her hands over his length again. "If you want."

There it was again—that hint of innocence. "I consider myself well and truly seduced." As he said it, she rubbed her thumb over his tip.

He jerked under her hands, so close already. He couldn't withstand the pressure of her mouth on him and he didn't want to disappoint her.

"Condoms," he got out through gritted teeth.

She snagged the box and haphazardly tore it open. He took a condom from her and held as still as he could while she yanked his underwear down.

He ripped open the foil packet but before he could sheath himself, she'd taken him back in hand. *"Built,"* she murmured, encircling his width with her hand and stroking up, then back down.

"Trish," he hissed. "I need to be inside you. *Right now.*"

She looked up at him with big eyes. She was panting now, the haze of desire edging back. "I love it when you're all ruthless like that."

He paused halfway through rolling on the condom, then finished the task at hand. "You do?"

"Very powerful." Her gaze darted down to where he was sheathed. "That'll...that'll work, right?"

"Right." He climbed onto the bed, scooting her back so that she was against the pillows as he went. "Tell me if it's not working, okay?"

"Okay," she said as she looped her legs around his waist.

He kissed her as he fit himself against her. "Beautiful," he murmured as he tried a preliminary thrust.

Her body took him in, but she still sucked in air.

"Okay?"

"I think—just a second—"

"Take your time. I've got all night." Which was not, in the strict sense of the word, true. He could feel her hips shifting beneath his as she adjusted to his width and it about killed him.

Then she shifted again, her hips rising toward him and, without being conscious of the motion, he pushed in deeper. "Oh!" she said, but he didn't hear any pain in her voice. Just surprise.

"Okay?"

"Yes. I think so..." Her hips flexed and her tightness eased back just enough that he was able to go deeper. And deeper. Until finally he was fully joined to her.

"Oh, babe," he groaned as he pushed back against the climax that already threatened to swamp him. "You feel so *good*."

"Um...okay."

He kissed her eyelids. Yeah, she'd never done this before. He had to make this count. "Ready?"

She looked worried, as if she were expecting a marching band to show up. "For?"

"This, babe." He withdrew and thrust back in, focusing on keeping his breath even and his climax firmly under control. *"This."*

"Oh. *Oh!*" As he pulled out and thrust in again, everything about her changed. Her hips rose up to meet him and her eyelids drifted shut as she felt him move inside of her. "Oh, *Nate*."

"Yeah, babe." They fell into a good rhythm, the give-and-take between his body and hers something different than he remembered. He wasn't as experienced as some, but he'd learned a lot during the two years he and Diana had been together.

He put that experience to good use now. He and Trish—they fit. Her warmth, wet and tight, took everything he had and then some, until she was arching her back and thrashing her head around and opening her mouth but not making a single noise as everything about her tightened down on him.

"So beautiful," he managed to get out again as her shockwaves pushed him faster and harder until he gave up the fight with himself and surrendered to her.

Then they lay still. He remembered to pull out so he didn't compromise the condom. But after that, he just lay on her chest.

"Oh, my," she finally breathed as she stroked his head.

"Is that a good 'oh, my' or a bad one?"

"Good. Very good." She sighed dreamily. "I didn't…" the words trailed off and she looked worried again.

He hefted himself up onto his forearms so he could look at her. "Thank you."

A wary look clouded her eyes. "For?"

He grinned down at her. "For not making me break my promise. Not at first, anyway."

"Oh." She exhaled. "I thought you were going to say something foolish, like thanking me for my virginity or something archaic like that."

He started to laugh in spite of himself. *Must be the euphoric high*, he thought, because he did not remember being this happy after sex. "Archaic?" He slid off to her side, but he didn't let go of her. One hand around her waist, pinning him to her chest. "You really hadn't done that before?"

After a moment where her body tensed up, she relaxed in his arms. "I didn't want to. I mean, I did, but…"

"You weren't ready to be a mother." That's what she'd said. He just hadn't realized how deeply that commitment went.

"No." She laced her fingers with his. "I didn't know it was going to be like that."

As the words trailed off, the keening wail of Jane crying cut across the hallway. "Oh," Trish said, visibly shaking off the last of her desire. She sat up and looked around as if coming out of a dream. "I've got to go."

He sat up and reached for her. "Trish—"

But she was out of bed, gathering up her clothes and all but sprinting out of his room. "I've got her," she called back over her shoulder, right before she pulled the door shut.

What had just happened here? One moment, she was sated and happy in his arms and the next?

Basically running away from him.

A sinking pit of worry began to form in his stomach. He tried to push it aside—she'd seduced him, not the other way around—but it didn't work. They might have followed the letter of their agreement, but not the real spirit of it.

He'd slept with her.

What had he done?

Trish used the bathroom and dressed quickly, making soothing noises to Jane the whole time.

She'd slept with Nate. Her first.

She needed to get Jane quieted back down so that Nate would go to sleep because she couldn't bear to talk to him right now, couldn't bear to lay in his arms and feel his body pressed against hers.

"Shh, shh, I'm here, sweetie," she hummed to Jane as she picked up the baby. She glanced at the clock. The little girl was up two hours before she should be. "Is it your teeth? Poor baby." For once in her life, she hoped it really was Jane's teeth—and not that Trish and Nate had been too loud.

She carried the baby downstairs and got one of the wet washcloths she'd stashed in the freezer. "Let's try this and see if we can go back to sleep, okay?" She headed back up to the nursery and sat in the glider, rocking Jane and humming softly as the little girl soothed her sore gums.

Trish wished she could soothe herself, but alas that didn't look like it was going to happen anytime soon. She kept a close eye on the door to the nursery, wanting Nate's shirtless form to appear and hoping like hell it didn't.

She'd slept with him. There was nothing wrong with that, per se. But…

She'd liked it. His mouth on her body, his body inside of hers? The way he'd made her feel?

God, how she'd liked it.

In the moment when he'd pulled free of her, she'd almost cried out to lose that connection with him. And when he'd tucked her against his chest, his arms tight around her waist?

She'd been on the verge of taking him in her hand—on the verge of seducing him a second time, just because she wanted that connection back. Because she wanted that feeling of clarity when his body pushed hers over the edge.

And she knew that, if he appeared in the doorway and said, "Come back to bed, Trish," she'd be helpless to say no, helpless to do anything but march right back into his bedroom and strip off her clothing again and explore his body over and over until they were both spent and dazed and the only thing in the world was Nate and Trish and a very big bed.

She would be his. Body, mind and soul. There'd be no turning back.

She'd be just like her mother.

This realization made her start, which jolted poor Jane. The baby started to fuss again. "Shh, shh," Trish whispered, finding a still-cold corner of the washcloth for Jane to chew on.

Of course Trish knew that sex had to be fun. That's why people did it so much, right? That's why her mother couldn't stay single—why she'd pick up a man at a bar and screw him in the parking lot and then, when he turned out to be an asshole, she couldn't kick him out of her life.

Trish had asked her once why she kept going with men who didn't even seem to like her. And Pat had replied with tears in her eyes, "Oh, Trish, honey, I know that the bad times can seem pretty bad. But when it's good…" and she'd gotten this far-away look in her eyes, a satisfied smile curling her lip up. "When it's good, it's *so* good."

Which hadn't made any sense to Trish at the ripe old age of ten because, as far as she could tell, there was nothing good about the men her mother picked.

As she'd grown up and come to understand the mechanics of sex—and as she'd explored her own body—she still hadn't understood what the big deal was. She could bring herself to a quick, quiet little orgasm, but that wasn't enough to make her want to throw away everything she'd worked for.

Except now she knew. She knew how a man could make her feel, make her body do things that Trish couldn't do to herself. Oh, Nate…with his big hands and bigger muscles and his damned principles about keeping his promises.

Jane had fallen asleep at some point in the past twenty minutes, but Trish was in no hurry to put the baby back in her crib. She needed this small child—needed the physical barrier Jane provided. Hadn't that been the problem tonight? Trish had tied Nate's tie without a baby between them and she'd kissed him because a man had no business looking as handsome as he did in that tux.

And then he'd come home early just because he wanted to see her. Her! She was nothing—a poor Indian woman who didn't even know who her father was. Tonight, Nate had walked away from heiresses and self-made women— women who matched his social standing and his love of modern technology—for her. There was no way she could keep up with him.

What a mess. Easily the biggest mess she'd ever gotten herself into, all because she liked him. Because she *let* herself like him instead of holding him at an arm's length.

What could she do? Quit? She looked down at the baby sleeping in her arms. She'd gotten Jane calmed down and mostly on a schedule. It'd be easier for Nate to hire a nanny now because he knew what to expect from a nanny and he knew what Jane needed.

But. Of course there was a "but."

If she quit, would he withhold the funding he'd promised? He'd signed a contract; so had she. She didn't think he would. He was a decent man—possibly the best man she'd ever met. But rejection did nasty things to people. She'd watched her mother curse and cry and throw their few dishes against the wall when she'd found out her current man was seeing someone on the side and Trish had huddled in her room with her siblings when the breakups happened.

But if Trish stayed…she'd want Nate again. And again. She'd want to spend the night trying different positions, different ways to make him cry out her name in that hoarse voice. She'd want to sleep in his bed, his strong arms firmly around her waist, his chest warming her back. She'd want to wake up with him and have breakfast with him out on the patio of this house and count the hours until

Jane went down for her nap so that Trish could pull Nate into his room and do it all over again.

She could stay here with him, raise his niece for him. She could do whatever he wanted, as long as he kept making love to her.

The intensity of this need scared her. For once in her life, she understood her mother, how she could overlook the health and safety of her children in favor of a man who might make her feel like Nate had made Trish feel.

Because if she stayed here with Nate and raised Jane— became a permanent nanny during the day and his lover at night—well, then what would happen to One Child, One World?

How was Trish supposed to look her baby sister in the eyes and say, "Yes, I know I said you should put your education and career ahead of any man, but he's a *really* great guy!"

Because that's what her mother would say. That's what her mother would do.

Trish was *not* her mother.

And that was final.

# Ten

Nate drifted in and out of consciousness as he waited for Trish to come back. He heard her go downstairs and then, sometime later, he heard her go down again, which didn't make any sense. When had she come back up?

His head was heavy with sleep. He'd sort of forgotten how much really awesome sex took out of him. But when he heard her come back upstairs again and yet she still didn't come back into his room, he forced himself to roll over and check the time on his phone.

Three-thirty.

He blinked at the red numbers again, but they didn't change. That wasn't right, was it? She'd left the first time around eleven and he knew she hadn't come back to him.

He sat up and rubbed his eyes. Where was she? He hadn't heard Jane crying.

He slipped his briefs back on and silently opened his door. Both Jane's door and Trish's were shut.

Maybe she'd fallen asleep in the glider, he reasoned. Both she and the baby had passed out and that's why she hadn't come back.

He tiptoed across the hall and opened Jane's door. The glider was empty and the little girl was in her crib, making those noises that Trish had promised him were perfectly normal for babies to make.

Which meant only one thing. Trish had gone to bed. Alone.

He backed out of the nursery and closed the door. Then he looked at Trish's door. He could knock but the hint was not-so-subtle. She'd gone back to her own room instead of his.

He ran through the evening's events. He hadn't cornered her, hadn't pressured her. She'd come to him of her own accord. She'd started it—he'd finished it, though.

Foreplay? *Check*. Orgasms? *Double check*. Cuddling? A little, right until the baby cried. All good things—unless…

Unless she'd changed her mind—about him, about sex, about sex with him.

Well, he wasn't going to figure out this puzzle standing in the hallway in nothing but a pair of shorts in the middle of the night.

But tomorrow, he and Trish were going to talk.

Trish heard Nate's door open, heard Jane's door open. Oh, God—he was looking for her. Would he come to her door, begging her to come back to his bed?

She curled herself around her pillow, willing him not to. She had to be stronger than this. She had to hold herself back from him and that was going to be damnably hard at—she checked the clock—three thirty-seven in the morning.

*Go back to bed*, she mentally screamed into the night. *Don't come in here*.

Jane's door whispered shut. Trish heard Nate take a footstep toward her room, then another. She tensed with fear—or need. Her brain was shouting, *no!* while her body, her traitorous body, was already clamoring for his touch. Trish was this close to throwing the covers off and flinging open her door and rushing into his arms.

She had to be stronger. She *was* stronger, by God.

The footsteps stopped. The house was silent. She pictured Nate standing on the other side of her bedroom door—so close, yet so very far away.

Then, just when she couldn't stand it another second—she *had* to go to him—she heard him walking again. His footsteps grew more distant, and then his door shut.

She should have been relieved.

Why did she feel like crying?

Trish felt like hell. She supposed that was to be expected. Her body was punishing her for her late-night activities in ways that made regular old sleep deprivation look like a cakewalk.

Somehow, Trish got the bottle made and the coffee started. She didn't even bother to attempt breakfast. Her stomach was so nervous at the thought of Nate coming downstairs and—well, even looking at her would be bad enough. Talking would be sheer torture. Yeah, there was no way she could handle breakfast at this point.

The morning was hazy with fog, but Trish decided to sit out on the patio with Jane, anyway. Fresh air and all that.

Plus, it put a little more space between her and Nate. And maybe she could come up with a way to *not* throw everything she'd ever worked for away because of him.

Jane was fussy, which helped. Trish focused on the girl with everything she had. Jane was why Trish was here. Jane was why she needed to stay. Not because of Nate.

She really did need to finish the month, she thought as she held Jane's bottle for her. For one thing, the poor girl had been through a lot and was just getting settled into her routine. It would be another setback for her if Trish just up and left.

And for another, there was the money. The other reason she was doing this. Nate was going to fund One Child,

One World for the foreseeable future. She could not tuck tail and run just because she could fall in love with him.

She could *not* fall in love with him.

The idea was so crazy that she started laughing. Would it be possible to *not* fall for him? That was where her mother always screwed up. If she'd just wanted the sex, that would have been one thing. The trouble came when she fell in love with whatever man she had and refused to let him go, no matter what common sense dictated.

Maybe Trish could take the sex and leave the love. After all, she'd spent the past few decades not allowing herself to get close to anyone. And, up until the moment she met Nate, she'd been very good at it.

She could enjoy Nate, safely, and not love him. She could refuse to give into the madness that had ruled her mother. It would be—well, it'd be physical. Short-term and very physical. But nothing more.

Could she *do* that?

Behind her, she heard him in the kitchen. Unconsciously, she tensed, which made Jane pop off her bottle and start to whimper. "Oh, now," she soothed, getting Jane to take her bottle again. "None of that. That's my good girl."

Pots and pans rattled. He was making breakfast. He was just too damn nice, that was the problem. Too damn perfect. This would be so much easier if he'd been a royal ass, or a really lousy lover or just a horrible person all the way around. Was that too much to ask, for him to be awful? Because that was the kind of man who didn't interest her at all. That was the kind of man she'd never tumble into bed with.

How was she supposed to even *look* at him this morning? After what she'd done to him? And especially after what he'd done to her?

*This* was the awkward part of being a twenty-five-year-old virgin. Everyone else in the world had figured out how to handle the post-hookup interactions back in college. They either left afterward or slipped out of bed in the morning or…or she didn't know what. They probably never had to sit around, playing with a baby while their lovers made them breakfast.

Life was so much easier without sex in it.

But what could she do? Nothing. It's not like she could wander off into the fog with a baby in her arms to avoid talking to him. She had to sit here and deal with this like a grown-up, because that's what she was.

Finally, after what felt like a small eternity, she heard the patio door slide open and felt Nate walk out. "Good morning," he said as he set his coffee cup on the table. No tray—no breakfast.

"Hi," she got out. It sounded weaker than she wanted it to, damn it all.

He leaned over and kissed Jane's head, then turned and made eye contact with her. He held it for just a beat too long and panic flared up in her stomach. Was he going to kiss her? Yell at her? What was happening here?

Then he turned back and shut the patio door. "Not much of a view this morning," he said in a casual voice.

"The fresh air feels good." Were they going to pretend it hadn't happened? "Um, thank you for making breakfast."

"Rosita left homemade pecan rolls in the fridge. They're still baking. And you made the coffee. It was the least I could do." He settled into his chair and, thankfully, turned his gaze toward the wall of fog, his mug clutched between his hands as if it were a shield. "You didn't come back to bed last night," he said in a quiet voice.

Trish swallowed. She didn't know why this was so hard. She'd been a practicing grown-up since she'd been—what, five? She'd stared down hard men and defended her siblings and done everything in her power to escape the life her mother had. She could do this. She could have a completely rational conversation with a man she really, really liked who'd seen her naked. No sweat.

"Jane's teething. I got up several times. I didn't want to wake you up. One of us should sleep," she added weakly. Then she mentally kicked herself. Stop sounding weak! She was not weak!

"Ah," he said, in that same quiet voice. "I thought…I thought it might have been something to do with me. With something I did. Or didn't do."

She blinked at him. "No, it's not that. It's just…"

Words would be great. If only she had some.

"If I did something that you didn't like," he went on, "you can tell me. I promise, my ego can handle it."

*But I don't know if I can handle it*, she thought.

He sipped his coffee, patiently waiting for a reply from her. But then Jane pushed her bottle away and stretched her plump little arms over her head and began to whine and Trish was thankful for the distraction.

"Here," Nate said as Trish started to maneuver Jane onto her shoulder. "I've got her."

He got up and lifted Jane into his arms and began to rhythmically pat her on the back. He didn't sit back down, though. He went and stood at the edge of the patio, a few feet farther away from Trish.

He was over there thinking he'd been a lousy lover when the truth was, he'd been amazing. Trish stared into the fog, trying to pretend she wasn't about to say this out loud. "Actually, it was amazing. I didn't think it'd be that good."

Out of the corner of her eye, she saw him pause before he continued patting and rocking Jane. "Oh? Well. Good to know." He was trying to sound casual, but she could tell he was smiling, just by the tone of his voice.

Last weekend, she'd sat on this porch and decided not to tell him why she was so good with kids and why she wouldn't sleep with him. He hadn't needed to know, she'd rationalized then.

But now? After what they'd shared? "You want to hear the whole story?"

"I want to understand you."

Heat flooded her body and that tingling sensation tightened across her lower back again. This man seriously needed some flaws and fast.

"My father—or the man I think of as my father—left when I was four. My brothers Johnny and Danny were two and one, so I suppose that he might not have been my real father. But he's who I remember." She did manage to look at him. "They both joined the army the moment they were eligible. Johnny's down at Fort Hood and Danny's done a tour of Afghanistan."

"Then what happened?"

Trish closed her eyes. She could still feel the weight of Jane's small body against hers. Just like all the other small bodies that had lain in her arms. "There was a gap of about three years. I think my mom was trying, I really do. I remember being home alone a lot with Johnny and Danny. I got pretty good at opening cans and heating them up so we'd all have something to eat. Then, when I was seven, Clint happened."

"I take it that was not a good thing."

"Nope. Mom got pregnant again and…" she sighed, pushing back on the memory. "Mom had Millie but then Mom was never home so I got used to taking care of the baby. The boys started sleeping on the floor and Millie and I took the bed. Then Mom had Jeremiah. And there just wasn't enough food. Not for five of us."

"How old were you?"

"I was nine. Then Mom got pregnant again. And Hailey was not a healthy baby. I wound up skipping most of my sixth-grade year to take care of her."

"Your mom wouldn't take care of a sick baby? My mom quit her job teaching elementary school when we couldn't get Joe into a stable routine at school. My grandmother thought it'd be better for all of us if we put him in an institution, but Mom wouldn't hear of it. He was her son. It was her job to take care of him. It was all of our jobs."

She studied him. He really did seem pissed off at her mother. "Well, she did have a job. That helped. For a while, anyway. But no, she couldn't take care of Hailey. She couldn't really take care of any of us. But I could." She looked at Jane, who was falling into a milk coma on her uncle's shoulder. "I graduated with honors when I was twenty because of Hailey and Keith, who was born when I was fourteen. Keith..."

"Was he okay?"

"There was something wrong with him, with his heart. He died. When he was fourteen months old. I couldn't save him. And I always thought, you know—if we'd been able to get to a doctor, maybe..."

That *maybe* had haunted her for years. Just because, every single time her mother got knocked up by yet another man, Trish wanted to scream and cry and ask her what the hell she thought she was doing—it didn't mean she didn't do everything in her power to save that baby when he'd gotten here. But she'd only been fifteen. She had very little power to do anything. Including saving her little brother.

"I'm so sorry," Nate said. He'd grown quiet. "That must have been so hard on you."

Trish sniffed. "And that doesn't count Lenny, Ricky or Patsy. I left home when Patsy was five. It was the hardest thing I've ever done because I knew..." her words trailed off as her throat closed off. "Because I knew she'd be on her own. That I wouldn't be there to make sure she went to school or did her homework or had a real dinner every night."

"And your mom?"

"Oh, she's fine. She got her tubes tied after Patsy because the doctors said she couldn't have any more kids. She's…it's like she's my older sister, you know? Not my mom. My flighty older sister that's always screwing up. But the guy she's with now, Tim, he's a good guy. Good job, not rough. Helps take care of the kids. I hope he sticks around."

"Why did she do it? Why did she have so many kids when she couldn't take care of them? Because it wasn't fair of her to assume that you'd do it. It wasn't fair to you."

"Life is not fair. It never has been and it never will be. If it was, your mom wouldn't have had to quit to take care of your brother and Jane's parents would be on their way to pick her up right now and…" She almost said, "Diana wouldn't have cheated on you." But she didn't.

Nate sat down in his chair, Jane cuddled against his chest. "You don't—didn't—sleep with people because of your mom?"

"Yeah. She'd fall head over heels in love with some guy, have a couple of his babies, and then it'd all fall apart. I guess she thought the kids would help her hold onto a man, but it never worked that way. The funny thing is, she can't have kids with Tim and he's the one that's stuck around the longest. Seven years and counting."

The silence settled over them. She wondered how long his folks had been together. If he'd had an older brother… maybe thirty years? Maybe more?

"I don't want to be like her," Trish admitted, letting her words drift into the fog. "I don't want to be so in love with a man, so in love with sex with a man, that it becomes my whole world. I don't want to forget who I am. I don't want to have to be someone else to keep a man. I can do *so* much good in this world, more than just changing diapers."

"And to do that, you didn't get involved?"

"No." She swallowed, feeling unsure of herself. "It was easier that way. No distractions. I got off the rez, I got to college, I started the charity. And I…I can't give that up." *Not even for you*, she thought.

He turned Jane around so that the little girl was sitting on his lap, facing out into the fog. Trish saw that Jane was only half-awake, her eyelids fluttering with heaviness.

"So why didn't you come back to bed last night?" he asked softly.

"Because."

He snorted and finally turned to look at her. "That's not much of an answer."

She took a deep breath, but she didn't break his gaze. "Because I'm just the temporary nanny. I can't stay here with you forever. I can't give up my goals, my whole life, to play house with you. I can't turn into my mother and—I can't fall in love with you, Nate. I just *can't*."

"Ah," he exhaled, his eyebrows jumping up. "And you think that by sharing my bed you…might?"

She thought back to the way their bodies had fit together, how he'd made her feel alive and vibrant and perfect. How she'd wanted him again and again, how she'd felt like she was standing on the edge of a very tall cliff and all he'd have to do to get her to jump was ask.

"I might," she admitted.

*If I haven't already.*

# Eleven

"So," Nate said in a voice that sounded remarkably calm, all things considered. "How would you like to proceed?"

"What do you mean?" Trish had turned her beautiful eyes back to the fog.

"With your remaining time here, assuming you'd like to finish out the three weeks."

She dropped her chin. "I don't want to break our deal," she said in a quiet voice. "I gave you my word just as much as you gave me yours."

Yeah, and part of his word had been *not* sleeping with her. That had lasted all of a week. Barely eight whole days.

He tried to think rationally, but that wasn't working. Because, rationally, not only should he have been able to stay away from her, but he should have been able to *keep* staying away from her.

He had to smile. How many other women in the world would take him to their beds and then tell him they couldn't come back because they couldn't risk falling for him and his billions in the bank? How many would keep their word to him?

Not that many. Maybe not any, except for Trish.

He ran his code as his tired brain tried to come up with a solution that didn't involve her leaving before the rolls were done in the oven.

"I can't leave," she said. "It'd be bad for Jane to go

through so many caretakers so fast. She's teething and we're just getting into a rhythm and you don't have anyone else lined up."

*Can't* wasn't the same as *won't*. *Can't* made it sound like he was forcing her and that was the last thing he wanted. "This is all true, but I don't want that to be the only reason you stay."

"You're paying me," she reminded him.

That was better, he thought. She sounded a little more like herself—more confident, more willing to push back. Trish sounding vulnerable only made him want to fold her into his arms and tell her he'd take care of everything, just so long as she stayed with him.

"Insane amounts of money," she added. "Both in salary and in donations. That was the deal. I won't take your money and run."

"The deal was we didn't sleep together. And now we have. The deal is open for renegotiation."

A wary look crossed her face. "How do you mean?"

"Look, I'm going to be honest. I like you. A lot. And I really enjoyed last night. You were amazing and it's going to be hard to look at you every day and not want to take you to bed every night."

She didn't immediately respond, which made him pretty sure those weren't the right words. The fact that he was making even a little bit of sense was a minor miracle, when all he really wanted to do was deposit this sleepy baby back in her crib and curl his body around Trish's and sleep for another five or six hours.

He probably should tell her that hey, one-night stands were fine and she knew where he was if she wanted another fun night in the sack—he should keep himself walled off, above the situation, just like he always did when he was out of his league.

But instead, no—he was laying it all on the line because, damn it, he liked her, he trusted her and, by God, she was someone he could fall for, too. For the first time in five years, waking up alone had bothered him. He'd wanted to see her face when he opened his eyes, to kiss her mouth awake.

He didn't want a casual one-night stand or even a casual one-week stand. It wasn't like he wanted to marry her or anything. He wasn't that old-fashioned. But he wanted something...in between.

He wanted a relationship.

From behind them, a buzzer sounded. "That's the rolls." He stood up, jostling Jane back from her semistupor as he handed the baby to Trish. "I'll be right back."

The rolls were slightly underdone, but that was good enough. He didn't want to stand in this kitchen for five more minutes while she was out there, talking herself out of another night of passionate sex with him. So he plated up the food and loaded everything onto the tray and tried his damnedest not to run right back to her.

If it came down to it, could he not touch her for another three weeks? He'd made it five years without taking a lover. Surely he could keep his hands—and other parts—occupied for another measly twenty-one days?

Jane had perked up a bit and Trish was singing and using the baby's chubby little legs to act out the song. It was a perfect image of what a family—his family—could be. Was it wrong to want more mornings like this? Breakfast on the patio, just the three of them?

He set the tray down and ate his breakfast while he waited. He'd respect her decision. He had no choice, because she was right. It would be hard on the baby if she left. It'd be hard on him, too, but he was a grown-ass man. He'd deal. Jane just needed more stability at this point in her life.

So this was parenthood, he realized as he burned the

roof of his mouth on a roll. Putting the baby's needs ahead of his own.

Stupid maturity.

Finally, after what seemed like ninety-nine verses, the song ended. Nate watched the two of them together. Jane clearly adored Trish—he hoped that, wherever she was, Elena would approve of his choice for a nanny.

And Trish was smiling down into Jane's face as if she really did care for the girl. Was it wrong to be attracted to a woman who would care so much for a child that had no connection to her?

Trish lifted her head and caught him staring. Her warm smile faded beneath a look of pensiveness. "How are the rolls?"

"Hot."

She managed a smirk so small, he almost missed it. "Shocking, that."

He forced himself to grin. "Come to any decisions over there?"

Jane squealed and tried to grab a roll. "I think," Trish said, capturing Jane's little fingers before they could get burned, "that we should finish this conversation during naptime."

That was a perfectly reasonable thing to say—after all, there was something a little weird about discussing sex with a baby around—but it still left him disappointed.

Jane trilled again.

"Right. Naptime. Looking forward to it."

Trish hesitated in the doorway of the parlor long enough that Nate looked up from the book he was reading. "She go to sleep okay?"

"Yes."

Nate was sitting on one end of the couch, close to the

leather chair. She could either sit in the leather chair or next to him.

He closed his book and waited for her to make her choice.

So she stood. "I feel like I owe you an apology," she said. "I've never had an affair before. I don't feel like I'm handling myself very well."

"An affair. Is that what this is?"

"Isn't it?"

"Right now it's closer to a one-night stand. Without the standing," he added as her cheeks heated. "An affair implies more than one night together."

"Oh, okay." Right. She couldn't even get her terminology right. Yeah, she was pretty bad at this. "About that." She forced herself to take another step into the room.

"Yes?" He sat up and, putting the book aside, leaned forward. But he didn't come toward her, he didn't sweep her into his arms and say the kinds of things that might weaken her resolve. He just waited for her to choose.

"I'd like—I mean, I think I'd like to, you know, maybe have an affair." Calling it an affair made it sound sophisticated and glamorous—nothing like the wild, indiscriminate coupling her mother engaged in. Trish was a responsible woman who could have an affair with a handsome, wealthy, powerful man *without* losing her head—or her heart.

She hoped.

The corner of his mouth crooked up. "You don't sound certain."

"I just want to make sure things don't get complicated. Messy," she explained.

"You don't want to fall," he clarified for her. The way he said it made her feel like she'd rejected him, which didn't make a lot of sense.

Wasn't she agreeing to the affair? How was that rejecting him? He didn't expect her to fawn over him, did he? "I don't want to fall," she said firmly. She could do this—indulge in a little passion without losing herself. She would *not* fall.

Falling in love with Nate Longmire was not a part of the plan.

"I've been thinking about that."

"You have?"

He nodded and stood. "Just you and me and a casual affair."

*Casual.* That was both the right word and not at all. "How would we do that?"

"We could have some…rules. Guidelines, if you will. No spending the night, no funny business when Jane is awake—"

"Right. Guidelines." She liked the sound of that. Boundaries. Like the three weeks they had left. That was a boundary that would keep her from falling in a very real way. Nate would hire another nanny and Trish would move out and that space—*that* would keep her from falling. It had to. "Nothing in front of Rosita or Stanley or anyone. And no seeing other people while we're being casual, right?"

"Sure." He grinned at her. "I doubt either of us would have, anyway."

"I suppose not." She felt herself exhale a little. She knew she wasn't doing a bang-up job at this, but it didn't appear she was botching it beyond all hope. "What else?"

"Just this." Suddenly, Nate was moving, his long legs closing the distance between them and his hands cupping her cheeks. He was kissing her so hard that her knees didn't entirely hold her up. "Just that I'm glad you said yes," he whispered against her mouth.

"Oh, Nate," she breathed as his lips trailed down her neck. This desire she felt—this need—surely this wasn't a bad thing, right? This wasn't the kind of thing that was going to push everything she'd ever worked for aside. Right?

They had guidelines to help keep everything from spiraling out of control. She could have an affair with Nate, enjoy being with him and sleeping with him.

And she would do it without falling.

They settled into a routine after that. Trish couldn't bring herself to sleep with Nate when Jane was down for a nap, but that didn't stop her from kissing him. She'd never even made out before, so just tangling up with Nate on the couch or against the counter in the kitchen, or when they caught each other on the stairs—anywhere, really, where Rosita wouldn't walk in on them—was a gift. A gift that left her in a near-constant state of arousal.

So by the time she closed Jane's door for the night, Trish could hardly wait to get her hands on him.

And he was ready for her. Instead of the leisurely kissing and touching that happened during the day, they would rip off each other's clothes and fall into bed as fast as they could.

Nate did not disappoint. The more they made love, the better it got. After the first week, when he'd introduced her to most of the basics, he started asking her what she wanted—what she'd always wanted to try, what she was curious about. For so long, Trish hadn't even acknowledged that she *had* sexual desires—if she didn't cop to them, then she didn't really have them. So suddenly to have a man who not only was interested in her, but also interested in making sure her fantasies were fulfilled was sometimes more than she could handle. It took her three days to admit that she wanted to go down on him—in the shower. Which he was more than happy to help her try out.

Nate didn't push her, though. And he didn't complain

when, after they were panting and sated, she gathered up her clothes and went back to her own bedroom.

Which got harder every night. The more time they spent in each other's arms, the more she wanted to wake up in his arms.

And the more she wanted to do that, the more she *had* to go back to her side of the hallway. Because she knew what was happening.

Despite the guidelines, despite the routine—despite it all—she was falling for him. And that scared the hell out of her.

Because there was only a week to go until her time was up.

She had no idea how she was going to leave.

# Twelve

Trish turned to him as the door shut behind the third and final nanny candidate, a squat Polish grandmother with impeccable references. The first candidate was a middle-aged former receptionist who'd been laid off in the Great Recession and the second was a young woman about Trish's age who just "loved kids!"—as she so enthusiastically phrased it.

"Well?" Trish said, leaning against the closed door with her hands behind her back. "What did you think?"

"I think I should hire you to do all my interviews," Nate said, moving in on her and pinning her to the door with a kiss. She'd grilled each woman on schedules, sleeping philosophies and life-saving qualifications. All Nate had had to do was watch. "You're ruthless."

"I just want the best for Jane." She pushed him back, but she was smiling as she did it. "Rosita will see us," she scolded quietly.

"I don't care." And he didn't. It was Friday. He only had Trish here for another three days. Monday morning, the new nanny would start. Trish would move out. She'd come back to help settle the new nanny into the routine on Wednesday, if needed, but that was it.

He kissed her again, feeling her body respond to his. Three more days of feeling her tongue tracing his lips, her body molding itself to his. And then…

She pushed him back again. "Nate," she said in her most disapproving voice, even as her fingers fluttered over his shoulders. "Focus. You need to pick a new nanny from the three candidates."

"Do I have to?"

She gave him a look. He knew he sounded childish, but picking a new nanny put him that much closer to not having Trish around anymore. If there were any way to stall hiring her replacement, she'd have to stay, right?

Because he wanted her to stay.

He and Trish had not spent a great deal of time talking about what happened next. He wanted to keep seeing her, obviously. The past month had been something he hadn't even allowed himself to dream of. The sex was amazing, sure, but what he felt for her went beyond the physical. He connected with her in a way that he hadn't connected with another woman—another person—since he'd fallen for Diana almost ten years ago. This time, he was older, smarter—more ready for it. This wasn't a casual affair, not anymore. This was a relationship—the one he wanted.

Yes, they'd had these guidelines that were supposed to keep her from falling for him. Unfortunately, nothing had prevented *him* from falling for *her*.

Because he'd fallen, hard. Unlike when he'd met Diana, Nate knew he wasn't with Trish just because she was the best he thought he could do. He wasn't the same insecure geek he'd been back in college. He could have his pick of women, if he really wanted to. They'd line up for him, starting with Lola Finklestein.

That wasn't what he wanted. He just wanted Trish. He missed her like hell when she was in class every Tuesday and Thursday and it no longer had to do with his panic over Jane. He could take care of Jane now. He'd learned her different noises and her likes and dislikes and he was doing a passable job at changing diapers—all because

Trish had patiently walked him through the ins and outs of basic fatherhood.

He wanted to be a better man for her. Every night he tried to show her how much he cared for her, how much he wanted her to stay with him. And every night, she slipped away from him again.

When he tried to bring up the prospect of dating, she kept shutting down on him. He knew that she had made arrangements to crash with a friend for the remaining week and a half until she graduated, and then she planned to go home and see her family for a while. But beyond that...

"You pick," he told her as he traced his fingertips down her cheek. "I trust your opinion."

"Nate. You *have* to pick. I'm—"

"Señor Nate?" Rosita called from the kitchen. "I am going to do the shopping." Nate stepped clear of Trish just as Rosita walked out of the kitchen, her purse on her arm. "Is there anything that..." Her eyes darted between Trish and Nate. "Ah, anything you want?" she finished in a suspicious voice.

"No. You?" he asked Trish.

"Maybe another box of those teething biscuits Jane likes?" Trish suggested. She managed to sound perfectly normal, but she couldn't stop the blush.

*"Sí,"* Rosita said, a look Nate couldn't quite make out on her face.

Trish stepped away from the door so Rosita could pass. Nate caught the small smile Rosita threw to Trish, and then the housekeeper was out the door. "What was that about?"

"I think we've been busted." Trish frowned at the closed door.

"Does that mean we don't have to sneak around anymore?" As he said it, he moved back to her, wrapping his arms around her waist and resting his chin on the top of her head. They stood like that for a while, just enjoying each other's warmth. They had time. Jane was still down for her nap. And later, they'd load her into the stroller and go for a walk. Then, tonight, she'd come to his bed again.

It was a damn good life. One he didn't want to end. Not in three days, not in three months. Maybe not in forever.

He had to find a way to make her stay. The sooner, the better.

"Nate." She looked up at him and rested the tips of her fingers just above the line of his stubble. "You have to decide. Not me, not Stanley and not Rosita. *You.* It's your choice."

Suddenly, he didn't know if they were talking about the three nanny candidates or if she was talking about them.

"I already found the perfect woman," he told her, tightening his arms around her. "You." He took a deep breath. This was the moment. He wasn't going to let her slip away from him. He *needed* her. "You should stay."

She tensed in his arms. "That's not what I mean."

"Why not?" She started to slip out of his grasp, but this time, he didn't let her go. He put his hands on her shoulders and turned her to face him. "Trish. Look at me."

Almost as if she was doing so against her will, she raised her gaze to meet his. He was surprised to see that she looked…afraid?

He was all in. "I want you to stay."

"I can't," she said in such a quiet whisper that he barely heard her. "Oh, Nate—don't ask me this. I can't."

"Why not?" he demanded. "Jane loves you," She sucked in a hard breath and her eyes began to shine with wetness. "I'm falling in love with you," he went on. "You fit here."

"No, I don't. Can't you see?" She laughed, a sharp thing that cut him. "I grew up in a three-room house with mold growing up the walls and electricity that only worked some of the time. I slept in a bed with two or three little kids my entire life. We didn't have food. We didn't have things."

She waved her hands around her, at all the nice things he had. "And now? I'm still so poor that I buy all my clothes from a thrift store and before I moved in here, I lived on ramen noodles and generic cereal—that I ate dry because I couldn't afford milk. I do *not* fit here." Her voice dropped. "I don't fit *you*, Nate. Not really. This was…an affair. A casual affair between two people living in forced proximity. That's—" Her voice caught. "That's all this was."

"No, it wasn't. You fit me," he said, beginning to feel desperate. "You fit *me*, Trish. We can change everything else. Anything you want. Name it. I won't let you go back to living on the edge like that. Not when I can take care of you. Not when I need you." He cupped her face in his hands. "I need you, Trish."

"You need—" She gulped. "You need a nanny."

"Stop it, Trish. You know that's not true. I need *you*. You're not some interchangeable woman. I can't just swap you out and carry on as if nothing has changed. I'm different when I'm with you. I'm not nervous or geeky or nothing but a bank account. You make me *me*. You make me feel like everything's finally right in the world."

She closed her eyes and shook her head. "Oh, Nate. Don't make this harder than it has to be. We had a deal, you and I. A temporary nanny. A casual affair. That was the plan. No falling."

The desperation turned and suddenly he was mad. Why was she being so stubborn? She had feelings for him, he knew she did. He gripped her by the arms. "I want a new deal. I want a different plan."

"Don't do this," she whispered again, trying to back away from him, but he held tight. "*Don't*. I can't fall."

"What's it going to take, Trish? To get you to stay. Twenty thousand a month? Two hundred and fifty thousand for your charity? That was our deal, right? I want an extension on our contract."

*"Nate."*

She was trying to cut him off, trying to stop him, but what did billions in the bank mean if he couldn't take care of her? If he couldn't make sure that she never felt poor ever again?

If he couldn't get her to stay?

She was worth more than that to him. She was worth more than all of it. All that cash was pointless if it couldn't get him what he really wanted—her. "Anything you want, name it. Just…stay with me, Trish."

Too late, he realized he'd gone too far.

"Oh, Nate." She shook free of his grasp and looked up at him. Tears streamed out of the corners of her eyes. "I—I can't. I can't give up everything I've ever been, everything I've ever wanted to accomplish, to raise another baby that's not mine. There's so much more I need to do in this world right now and I can't sacrifice all of that, not yet." Her eyes filled with tears. "I'm not ready to be a mother. Not even a mother. A nanny."

"You're more than that to me, babe. You know that."

She shook her head. Why couldn't he make her see reason? "I can't turn my back on my own family, my tribe, just to play house with you."

"This isn't playing house. I want you to live with me. I want you to sleep in my bed with me." Why was that a bad thing? He didn't understand. "I want more than casual. I want more than an affair. I want *you*."

"On your terms, Nate. We aren't equals. We can *never* be equals." Her voice broke.

Where had he gone wrong? Since when had telling a woman he loved her become such a mess? Panic bubbled just beneath his surface, threatening to break free. He'd never been that good with women, never known what to say to them. That'd been what he loved about Trish—he could talk to her. But not right now. His words were failing him.

"I would always be dependent on you," she went on, her face pale. "I would always need you more than you needed me."

"That's not true."

She smiled at him, a weak and sad smile that hurt to see. "Just because you can't see that doesn't mean it's not true." She touched his face but pulled her hand away quickly, as if she'd been burned. "I…I can't need you as much as this."

"Why not?" He said louder than he meant to, but was she being serious? "I need you, too. That doesn't make me weak and it doesn't make you weak, for God's sake. It makes me want to take care of *you*. So let me."

She stood before him, her face creased with pain. Then, unexpectedly, she leaned up on her toes and kissed him. For a moment, he thought that was her giving in, her agreeing to stay. He tried to wrap his arms around her to hold her tight. *Thank God*, he thought.

Then she was away from him. "Of *course* I care for you," she said, skirting around him. "I could love you for the rest of my days."

*"Could?"* he asked incredulously as she started up the stairs.

"But I can't lose myself in you. I can't…" A sob broke free of her chest and she stopped, four steps up. "I can't forget who I am."

"I'm not asking you to do that. Damn it, Trish—I'm asking you to stay!"

She turned, looking down on him with a face full of pain. He started up the stairs to reach for her, but she backed away from him. "If I agree to your new terms—if I agree to stay—then what? Another month passes, we fall more in love, you extend the contract again, one month at a time."

"Don't you want to stay with us?" he demanded. "Isn't that what you want?"

"Oh, God, of course I do. But this isn't real, don't you see? All of this," she said as she swept her arms around, "and…you—God, Nate." Her voice caught in another sob. "People are depending on me. I have things I *have* to do."

"So do them from here!"

She shook her head. "I can't. I can't be your kept woman. I—I have to go."

Before he could do anything else, she spun and raced up the stairs, her shoulders shaking under the strain of her sobs.

What the hell? Okay, so he shouldn't have brought money into the conversation. That was a mistake, one he wouldn't make again. But…

A kept woman? That wasn't what was happening here! He was in love with her, for God's sake! And she might be in love with him, too—wasn't that what she'd said when she'd said she could love him the rest of her life?

So what was the problem here?

Overhead, he heard her door shut—and the lock click. He could go after her, go in through Jane's room. He could make her see reason—

And what? Argue with her until she agreed just to keep the peace? Force her to stay?

He sat heavily on the steps, pulled down by a weight in the center of his chest. For some reason, his brain decided that this would be the perfect time to revisit Diana's betrayal. To remember walking into the house that was supposed to be empty and hearing the distinctive noises of sex. To remember reasoning that it was just Brad with his latest girl. To remember calling Diana's phone to see where she was—and hearing it ring from the coat stand right at his elbow.

To remember walking up the stairs in his parents' home,

each footstep heavier than the last. Opening the door to his brother's room and seeing Diana, naked and bouncing on top of Brad.

Realizing with crushing certainty that he'd screwed up somewhere along the line—that he hadn't been enough for her. He'd been good enough until someone better came along.

He'd closed himself off after that. He didn't let himself get close to people, to women, because he couldn't be sure they weren't after something else—his company, his money.

He'd let himself get close to Trish. He'd trusted her with a part of himself he'd held back from every other person. He'd let himself be more real with her than he'd been in… years. Maybe in forever. He'd let himself think that he was enough for her. Him, Nate Longmire. Not the Boy Billionaire, not the philanthropist who cut the checks. Just him.

And what had she done?

She'd decided he wasn't enough. He wasn't enough; Jane wasn't enough. The two of them could never be more important to Trish than a bunch of backpacks.

He wasn't more important than two new pencils. Not to her.

Damn, but that hurt.

Trish packed quickly. Anything to not think about what had just happened. What was still happening.

*Nate…*

The moment she felt herself waver, she pushed back. Her mother would do anything to keep a man happy. Her mother would quit her job, ignore her children—anything, as long as it kept her man coming back for more.

And Trish? She could do it. She could agree to what Nate wanted, when he wanted it, as long as he kept on loving her. Even that last kiss—it'd almost broken her resolve.

She couldn't do it. She couldn't give herself over to him and cast everything that she'd held dear to the wind.

So she packed as fast as she could. She couldn't stay, not a moment longer. Every second she was around Nate was another second of temptation. Another second she would break.

It didn't take that long. Since she'd completed her schoolwork, she'd sold most of her books back already. She only had a few that were worth keeping more than they were worth the few dollars she'd get at the bookstore.

Her clothes fit into the duffel. She packed up her laptop, her shoes and the phone.

No, the phone was his. She didn't need it, didn't need the constant reminder of how Nate wanted to take care of her. If she kept his phone… Besides, they didn't get a lot of cell-phone reception on the rez, anyway. Who would she call, except him? She put it back on the dock.

What was she doing? This whole thing was ridiculous. It'd been ridiculous since she'd first agreed to his contract. She had no business being in this nice house, surrounded by nice people and things and food. But more than the material comforts, she had no business being in Nate's bed, having a casual affair. She had absolutely no business being with a man who was going to break her heart.

She couldn't stay. She couldn't give herself over to him, mind, body and soul. She could not lose who she was to become the woman he loved. That was what her mother did.

That's not what Trish did. She shared a name and a physical resemblance with her mother, but that's where it ended. Trish was a strong woman with a plan.

A plan that had never included falling in love with Nate. Except she had. She *had*.

She buried her head in her hands, trying not to sob. She'd been wondering if maybe it wouldn't be such a bad thing to stay for another two weeks—finish out the school year living here, taking the comfort of Nate's bed—until she went home for a couple of months. She'd been sorely tempted. It was just another twelve, fourteen days at the most. Where was the harm in that? And then, after she'd spent some time away from Nate, she'd be in a better position to figure out how she wanted to proceed with him. Because she hadn't been done. She'd just…needed to get some perspective to make sure she didn't lose herself in him.

How had this happened? That was the problem. Somewhere, the attraction she'd felt at their first meeting had blossomed into something else, something infinitely more. Watching Nate cuddle Jane? Eating breakfasts out on his patio? Talking about comic books and charities?

Lying in his arms at night? All those stolen moments during the day?

A month ago, she hadn't loved him. A month ago, the little girl still sleeping in the next room had been in dire straits, only days from a trip to the emergency room.

A month ago, everything had been different.

Including Trish.

She was not her mother's daughter. No matter how much she wanted to open that door and run down to him and tell him that she was sorry and he was right and she'd do anything he wanted, just so long as he said he loved her and he kept on loving her. She wouldn't.

She had to walk away. Before she lost herself completely.

Her things packed up into two sad bags, Trish forced herself to go through the bathroom to Jane's room. The little girl was restless, although her eyes were still closed. She'd probably picked up on the sudden tension in the house, Trish thought.

"You're a good girl," she told the drowsy baby as she stroked the fine hairs on her little head for the last time.

"You take good care of your uncle Nate, okay? Make sure to smile at him and make him laugh like you do, okay?"

Jane shook her head from side to side, as if she was trying to tell Trish to stay, too.

"He's going to be a great daddy for you," Trish went on. "He loves you and he'll take good care of you." She thought back to all the times Nate had cuddled Jane or changed her or fed her—all the times he'd been a father.

All the times she'd been so surprised that he would be a father to someone else's child only because she didn't know men would do such things.

She leaned down and kissed Jane's head. "Goodbye, Jane. I love you. I won't forget you." The thought made her start to cry again because she knew that Jane would never remember her.

She hurried back to her room—no, it wasn't hers. It was merely the room she'd slept in for a month. Nothing here was hers, except for the sad duffels. She hefted them onto her shoulders and, with one last look, headed out.

As she trudged down the stairs, part of her brain was screaming at her that she was being stubborn—she didn't have to go! So Nate had been less than smooth. He wasn't always, she knew that. She was overreacting and she should let him take care of her.

But she was so much more than a temporary nanny with benefits. She ran a charity that hundreds, maybe thousands of children depended on for food and school supplies and the chance at a life better than the ones they'd been born into. She owed it to those kids—the ones who would never have a billionaire uncle to suddenly show up and make everything better—to do her best for them. For Patsy, her littlest sister. Trish was defined by her actions, not by the man she was sleeping with. She'd told him she would not fall for him and, at least on the surface, she had to hold that line.

She was a temporary nanny who'd had a casual affair and now it was time to go back to her real life. That's all there was to it.

Nate was waiting for her at the bottom of the stairs, hands on his hips. Just the sight of him nearly broke her resolve. *Be strong*, she told herself. Her mother would cave. She was not her mother.

But this was Nate. Her Nate. The man who'd said he was falling for her...

"I want you to stay, Trish," he said in a voice that was almost mean.

In that moment, she buckled. He was everything she wanted but... *Be strong*, she told herself. "You'll be all right? You and Jane? For the weekend?"

He stared at her as if she were speaking Lakota instead of English. "Don't we mean *anything* to you? How can you just walk away from her? From *me*?"

"I...I have to do this." Her own excuses rang hollow because he was right. Jane meant something to her. She wasn't just a baby that Trish had to take care of because no one else would.

And Nate? He wasn't just a man—any man, like her mother would have settled for. He was a man who stepped up when he had to. He took an active role in his niece's care. He didn't just take from Trish—he listened to her, he made her feel important.

"And that's it?" He made a sweeping gesture with his hands, as if he could clear everything away. "That's *that*?"

He was breaking her heart. For so long, she'd guarded herself against just this—the pain that went with the end. That's what her mother had taught her. It always ended and when it did, it always hurt. Every single time.

"I don't know," she admitted. "We just—I need some space. This has been a *great* month," she hurried to add, "but everything's happened so fast and I need to step back and make sure that I'm not losing myself. I've got to graduate and go home for a while. Maybe for the summer, I don't know. And after that…"

"Will you call me? At least let me know where you wind up tonight, so I won't worry about you."

Oh, God. Somehow, admitting this was almost as hard as leaving because it felt so *final*. No calls, no texts. A definitive break. "I left the phone upstairs."

All the blood drained out of his face. He knew it, too. "Oh. Okay. I see."

"Nate…"

"I, uh, I called for a car. It'll take you wherever you want to go."

"Thank you." She didn't know what else to say. She'd never broken up with anyone before. She'd only seen the screaming, crying fights her mother had had. He was being polite and respectful and, well, Nate.

Then, unexpectedly, he stepped up the few stairs separating them and cupped her face in his palms and touched his forehead to hers. She was powerless to stop him. "You probably don't want me to say this, but I don't care. I love you, Trish. Think about that when you go home. *I love you.* It doesn't make me less to love you. It makes me want to be someone *more* than who I was before I met you."

She gasped and closed her eyes against the tears. She couldn't do this, couldn't break his heart and hers—

Outside, a car horn honked.

Nate moved again, but instead of kissing her, he grabbed one of her bags and carried it down the rest of the way. He opened the door for her.

Struggling to breathe, Trish picked up the other bag and walked out into the weak afternoon sunshine.

It'd always been easy to stick to her principles, to keep herself safe from the messy entanglements that had ruled her childhood and all the children that they'd produced.

But putting her few belongings in the back of the trunk of some hired car? Silently standing there as Nate opened the backseat door for her? *Not* telling him she'd changed her mind when he leaned down and said, "I'll wait for you," right before he closed the door?

"Where to?" the driver said.

No, nothing about this was easy.

But she did it, anyway. She would not live month to month, at the mercy of this deal or that. She would *not* be ruled by love.

"San Francisco State University," she told the driver in a raw voice.

And that was that.

# Thirteen

The day of graduation dawned bright and hot. Trish was already sweating in her cap and gown. Underneath she had on a pair of cutoffs and her Wonder Woman shirt. It was foolish to hope that the shirt would imbue her with enough power to make it through all the speeches and waiting to finally cross that damn stage and get her master's degree without dying of heatstroke, but it was the best she had.

"Who's the speaker, again?" Trish asked her neighbor after she took her seat in Cox Stadium.

"I don't know," the woman replied. "It was supposed to be Nancy Pelosi, but they said she canceled at the last minute."

"Great." Trish pulled out the water bottle she'd hidden in the sleeves of her master's gown and took a long drink.

As the university president and student body president made remarks about everyone's dedication in achieving their chosen master's degrees—the undergraduates were graduating tomorrow—and how their true potential could now be unlocked and so on and so on and *so on*, Trish only paid the bare minimum of attention. She was running through her plans.

Somehow, Stanley had tracked her down in the library. He'd brought her three checks—one for twenty grand and another for two hundred and fifty thousand, made out to

One Child, One World. The last one had been her security deposit from Mrs. Chan. All he'd said when he found her was, "You doing okay?"

"Yes, I'm fine. Nate, is he okay?" she'd asked in a rush. "Is Jane okay?"

"She's fine." Stanley had given her a look that she couldn't interpret before saying, "And Nate, well, he's been better." Stanley handed her a padded envelope. Then the tattooed, pierced man was off again, leaving Trish alone with a vague sense of guilt as she looked at the hundreds of thousands of dollars in her hands.

She'd opened the padded envelope to find her phone and the charger. The phone was charged and she had a waiting text message.

Just in case. Nate.

She'd sat staring at the phone for a good twenty minutes. Just in case.

Just in case she wanted to call him. Just in case she changed her mind.

That was almost as unbelievable as the rest of it. All those men her mother had "loved"? All of them had had someone on the side. None of them had ever kept their promises, except for Tim.

Except for Nate.

Then she'd all but sprinted to her bank. Because she was now rich, comparatively, she was going to buy an actual plane ticket to Rapid City, South Dakota, instead of taking the bus. From there, she'd figure out a way to get home. It might take her a few days, but she'd make it there one way or another.

And after she'd been home for a few days…well, she

had to see how it went. She didn't plan on staying on the rez, but she had no apartment in San Francisco to come back to. After today, she had nothing to tie her to this city except Nate. If her father still lived here, she hadn't found him and he hadn't found her. She could make a fresh start somewhere new—somewhere with cheaper rents—or...or she could come back to Nate. If he'd still have her.

"I'll wait for you," he'd said when he'd closed her car door. She desperately wanted to believe him but at the same time, she was afraid to get her hopes up, afraid to think that there really was a future between them.

Because how would it work? She didn't even have a proper job lined up. If—and that was a big *if*—she went back to him, she wanted to walk up to that door on her own merits, not because she was crawling back.

But she had no idea how to level the playing field—the huge, gaping playing field—that existed between them.

She was getting ahead of herself. Before she could even think about that, she had to get through the next few days. The idea of getting on a plane was a terrifying one—so terrifying that, when the commencement speaker was announced, she didn't hear the name. But someone behind her whooped and then the crowd was cheering. Trish looked up to see...

Nate.

Nate Longmire, wearing a fancy cap and gown, strode out onto the stage and shook the university president's hands.

*Oh, God*, was all she could think before he stepped up to the microphone. What was he doing here? This couldn't be a coincidence—could it? No. This was intentional. This was because of her.

"Congratulations, graduates!" he said with one of those

tight smiles that she recognized as him being nervous. "I know you're all disappointed that Congresswoman Pelosi was unable to make it—" There were a variety of muffled groans from the audience. "But," Nate went on, ignoring the noise, "I had such a great time here about two months ago that I jumped at the chance to talk to you one more time."

Sporadic applause erupted. Someone wolf-whistled.

"Today I want to talk about the power each and every one of you possess," Nate continued. Even she could see him blushing at this distance. "You may be sitting there, asking yourselves, 'now what?' You may have student debt. You may not have a job. Maybe you've got someone, maybe you broke up."

"Oh, hell."

She didn't realize she'd spoken out loud until the woman sitting on her left said, "What?"

"Oh. Sorry. Nothing." Nothing except that her last— her only—lover was up on stage, slowly circling his way through a commencement speech that was all about her.

"You may not think you have any power to change things—to get a job in this economy, to find the 'right' person, to affect change in your surroundings. I'm here to tell you that's not true."

"You okay?" the woman on her left asked. "You don't look so good."

"I'm—fine. I'm fine." Trish forced herself to look away from Nate and smile at her neighbor. "I just can't believe Nate Longmire is up there, that's all."

The woman smiled. "He's even better-looking in person."

"Yes," Trish agreed weakly. "Better in person."

"I recently spent some time with a SFSU graduate by

the name of Trish Hunter," Nate was saying. As he talked, he searched the crowd until his gaze fell upon hers. The corner of his mouth moved and she knew he was glad to see her.

She wasn't sure if she was breathing or not—she was definitely light-headed. What was he *doing*?

"I was impressed with her education but more than that, I was impressed with her dedication. Despite a limited amount of funds, Ms. Hunter has single-handedly run a charity called One Child, One World, which provides school supplies and meals to Native American children living in poverty on reservations in South Dakota."

The audience settled back into their heat-induced stupor as he went on about her charity, her awards and, yes, her dedication. Trish couldn't do anything but gape at him. This wasn't happening, was it? Maybe she'd just had a heatstroke and was hallucinating this whole thing.

He was really here. He was—well, he was fighting for her. No one had ever fought for her before, not like this. She'd known he wasn't the same kind of man her mother had always chased—but this?

He wasn't going to run away. He wasn't going to hide behind lies.

Something Tim, her stepfather, had said to her the last time they'd talked floated back into her consciousness—"There's something about being with her that makes me feel right with the world. And when you've seen as much of the world as I have, you know that's no small thing."

The epiphany hit her so hard she jolted in her chair. Her mother—her flighty, careless mother who chased after any man she could catch—had been happily married for almost seven years to a decent guy who wouldn't even let Trish give him back a security deposit. She'd stayed married to him because they made each other feel right with the world.

Nate had said it himself. "You make me feel like everything's finally right in the world," he'd told her during the last few moments she'd stood before him and wavered.

And Tim was right—it was no small thing. It was something huge. It might be everything.

Would she really keep pushing herself away from Nate just because her mother had a long, scarred history of making bad choices? Or was Trish forcing herself to make a bad choice, just because it was the opposite of what her mother would have done?

Did Nate make everything right in her world, too?

"And so," Nate finally said, "I am happy to announce that the Longmire Foundation will be awarding two endowments. The first is to establish a scholarship for Native American students who enroll in San Francisco State University. The other is an endowment of ten million dollars to One Child, One World to help prepare those Native students for college and beyond."

Trish shot to her feet and tried to ask him what the *hell* he was doing, but all that came out of her mouth was a gurgling noise.

"Ah, yes, there she is, ladies and gentlemen. Please give Ms. Hunter a round of applause for all her hard work."

The crowd broke out into what could only be called a standing ovation as people cheered for her. She barely heard it. All she heard was Nate leaning forward and saying, "Ms. Hunter, if I could speak to you after you graduate?"

"That's you?" the woman on her left said. "Girl, you better move."

But Trish couldn't because she was trapped in the hell

of having a last name that started with an *H*. All she could do was go through the motions. The rest of the graduation passed in an absolute blur. Trish didn't remember hearing her name called, barely remembered walking across the stage to get her diploma. She did, however, have full recall of when some university higher-up pulled her out of the line that was moving back toward the seats and ushered her off the stage. "...Very exciting," he was saying as he led Trish to where Nate was waiting. "An endowment! This is excellent news..."

Nate was waiting for her in the shadows under the stands of the stadium, cap in hand and gown unzipped. He had on a button-up shirt and a tie and he looked *so* good.

Suddenly, Trish was very conscious of the fact that she was in cutoffs and a T-shirt. Just another way they didn't match up.

"What did you do?" she demanded the moment Nate was in earshot.

He grinned at her as if he'd expected her to say that, but then he turned to the official. "If I could have a moment with Ms. Hunter..."

"Oh, yes. Yes, of course!" The man hurried back into the sunlight, still muttering, "Excellent news!" as he departed.

And then she and Nate were alone. "What did you *do*, Nate?"

"I removed the money from the equation."

"By giving me ten freaking million dollars? Are you *insane*? That's not removing it—that's putting it front and center!"

"No, I didn't. I gave your charity the money, free and clear. No strings attached. You'll be able to draw a salary as the head of the charity and do all those things you wanted to do—basketball courts and after-school snacks and computer labs. All of it."

He hadn't forgotten her wish list. Why did that make her feel so good? "What do you mean, no strings? You just *gave* me ten million dollars!" Her voice echoed off the bottoms of the stands.

"No, I didn't," he repeated with more force. "I divested myself of some of my money to a worthy charity. I do that all the time."

"But—but—"

He touched her then, pulling her deeper into the shadows. "I gave *you* a choice."

*"What?"*

"I want you to come back to me," he said, dropping his voice down. "But I don't ever want you to feel that you're not my equal, that you're not good enough for me. And I sure as hell don't ever want you to feel that I hold all the cards. So, here we are. I give your charity money that I'll never miss and you'll do so much good with it—and you'll be able to pay yourself a salary." He grinned. "Knowing you, it won't be very much, but still."

"I don't see what this has to do with you giving me a *choice*, Nate. How is this not the same deal as before?"

In the safety of the shadows, he trailed his fingers down the side of her face. "This money is for your charity. It's not contingent on you moving back in with me. That's what no-strings-attached means. I won't take this money back—in fact, I believe certain government regulations would frown upon that. No matter what happens next, the charity gets the money. *That's* the deal."

"But—"

"If you want to come back to me—or if you want me to come to wherever you are—then you and I will both know that it's not because you couldn't say no to the money. You won't have to rely on me. You will be your own woman. That's what you want, isn't it?"

"I want…" She had to lean away from his touch. "But it won't change the fact that the money came from you."

"I doubt that any of those kids on the rez will give a damn where the money came from," he said in a matter-of-fact voice. "And you're missing the *if*. *If* you come back to me. It's your choice. It always has been."

"Nate…"

"I messed up the negotiations last time," he went on. "A good negotiator always knows what the other side wants and the first time, you wanted funding. It was easy to give it to you because all I needed was a nanny. But the second time, that's not what you wanted and I should have known it because I didn't want you as a nanny anymore. The situation had changed."

"You…didn't?"

"You wanted something else—you told me yourself. You didn't want to lose yourself in me. I didn't figure out what that meant at first." He grinned and despite the fact that she'd been yelling at him, he still looked thrilled to see her. "But I think I've got it now."

"What?" Her words failed her. She knew she was repeating herself, but she couldn't get a grasp on this situation.

"I think you wanted a promise," he said, going down on one knee in the shadows under the stadium bleachers. "A promise that I would honor your wishes—that I would honor *you*—with no strings attached. I didn't give that to you then. But I'd like to try again." He reached into his pocket and pulled out a small, bright blue box. The size that usually held a ring.

The air stopped moving in her lungs as he opened the box. "What are you doing, Nate?"

"Making you a promise," he said. A splendid pear-shaped diamond was nestled on a silver band. "Trish Hunter, will you marry me?"

Her mouth opened, but no sound came out as she looked from the ring—the promise—back to him.

"I want to marry you. I hope you want to marry me." He cracked a nervous little grin. "It usually works better that way."

"But I was going to go home!"

"I want you to go." He stood and, taking her hand in his, slipped the ring on her finger. "I want you to think about this, about us. I don't want you to come back to me because you're worried about Jane or you think you owe me. I don't want you to lose yourself. I want you as you've been. You push back when I do something dumb, you teach me how to do things. You make me a real person, Trish— not some caricature of a billionaire geek with too much money. You give me a purpose. You make everything feel right in my world and that's something I honestly wouldn't ever get back."

"You're not that—not to me," she told him, her words getting caught in the back of her throat. "You're just Nate and you're a wonderful man. I'm—I'm afraid, Nate. I'm *afraid*. I don't have any great role models for how to make a relationship work. I spent so long not being in one that to suddenly fall in love with you? You were my first. And when I was with you, I didn't feel like the same person I'd always defined myself as—the poor American In- dian woman, the responsible daughter of an irresponsible woman. You—you make me feel right, too. And I felt it *so* much it scared me. It still scares me because I could love you so much. *So* much."

He grinned down at her. "There's that word again—*could*."

"I…" she took a deep breath. "I do love you. You've shown me what a man can be—not someone cruel, not someone who comes and goes. A man who'll stay, who'll do the right thing even if it's hard. Even if…"

"Even if it scares me. Like taking a baby home with me." He took a step in and touched his forehead to hers. "I hired the Polish grandmother, by the way. She's very efficient. Just so we're clear—I'm not asking you to be a nanny. I'm asking you to be my wife." He grinned. "My *permanent* wife."

"Oh, Nate." She kissed him then, a light touching of the lips.

He wrapped his arms around her and held her tight. Suddenly, everything that had been wrong about the past few days was right again because Nate was here and she was here and they were together. "I missed you," she whispered. "I was already thinking about calling you after I made it home."

He squeezed her tighter. "I couldn't wait that long. I couldn't let you go without knowing exactly how much I need you. I want you to come back to us because you know that you belong with me."

"Yes," she whispered. "You're right. Loving you doesn't mean I lose myself. I feel like, for the first time, I've *found* myself."

He tilted her head back and stared into her eyes. "I'm already yours, Trish Hunter. Will you be mine?"

This was what she wanted. To know that love wouldn't destroy her like it always had her mother, to know that Nate would fight for her. For them. "I'm yours, too. You're the only man I ever want."

He kissed her then, full of passion and promises. "Come home," he said when the kiss ended. "Sleep in my bed with me. And tomorrow we'll work on getting you out to the rez, okay? That's the plan."

"Tomorrow," she agreed. "But tonight…"

He kissed her again. "Tonight is ours."

That was a promise she knew he'd keep.

\* \* \* \* \*

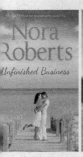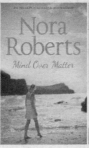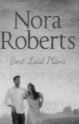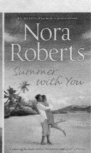

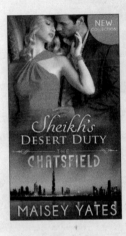

# MILLS & BOON®

**PASSIONATE AND DRAMATIC LOVE STORIES**

---

## A sneak peek at next month's titles...

**In stores from 17th April 2015:**

- **Minding Her Boss's Business** – Janice Maynard
  *and* **Triple the Fun** – Maureen Child

- **Kissed by a Rancher** – Sara Orwig *and*
  **The Sheikh's Pregnancy Proposal** – Fiona Brand

- **Secret Heiress, Secret Baby** – Emily McKay
  *and* **Sex, Lies and the CEO** – Barbara Dunlop

---

Available at WHSmith, Tesco, Asda, Eason, Amazon and Apple

*Just can't wait?*
Buy our books online a month before they hit the shops!
**visit www.millsandboon.co.uk**

**These books are also available in eBook format!**

# Join our *EXCLUSIVE* eBook club

## FROM JUST £1.99 A MONTH!

*Never miss a book again with our hassle-free eBook subscription.*

★ Pick how many titles you want from each series with our flexible subscription

★ Your titles are delivered to your device on the first of every month

★ Zero risk, zero obligation!

*There really is nothing standing in the way of you and your favourite books!*

## Start your eBook subscription today at www.millsandboon.co.uk/subscribe